ACT OF REVENGE

ACT OF REVENGE

A Novel

DICK COUCH

Act of Revenge

Published by SEAL Productions Press LTD

ISBN-13: 9781499175592

Dedication

This book is dedicated to the warriors who come home from war. All warriors who go off to war eventually come home and when they do, they must then deal with the issues they left behind when they went off to war.

OTHER BOOKS BY DICK COUCH

Fiction

SEAL Team One
(Avon, 1990)

Pressure Point
(Putnam Books, 1992)

Silent Descent
(Putnam Books, 1994)

Rising Wind
(Naval Institute Press, 1997)

The Mercenary Option
(Pocket, 2003)

Covert Action
(Pocket, 2005)

Act of Valor (Novelization)
(Berkley, 2012)

Op Center–Out of the Ashes
(St. Martins, May, 2014)

Nonfiction

The Warrior Elite (2nd Edition): *The Forging of SEAL Class 228*
(Crown Books, 2001/2013)

The US Armed Forces Nuclear, Chemical, Biological Survival Manual–Editor
(Basic Books, 2003)

The Finishing School: Earning the Navy SEAL Trident
(Crown Books, 2004)

Down Range: Navy SEAL Operations in the War on Terror
(Crown Books, 2005)

Chosen Soldier: The Making of a Special Forces Warrior
(Crown Books, 2007)

The Sheriff of Ramadi: Navy SEALS and the Winning of al-Anbar
(Naval Institute Press, 2008)

A Tactical Ethic: Moral Conditioning for Modern Warriors
(Naval Institute Press, 2010)

Sua Sponte: The Forging of a Modern American Ranger
(Berkley, 2012)

Always Faithful, Always Forward: The Forging of a Special Operations Marine
(Berkley, June 2014)

ACKNOWLEDGMENTS

I'd like to thank John Tortorici, Bruce Kaplan, Cliff Hollenbeck, Gerry O'Toole, and Clark Gerhardt. Your help with this book was invaluable. Any inaccuracies rest entirely with the author.

CONTENTS

AN INTRODUCTION

First of all, thank you for your purchase of *Act of Revenge.* I hope you enjoy the reading as much as I did the writing. My body of work to date has been a balance of fiction and nonfiction, yet this is my first original novel in close to a decade. As we have been a nation at war, my focus has been on nonfiction and the SEALs, Green Berets, Rangers, and Marine Special Operators–their training and deployment in support of the Global War on Terror. With the winding down of direct combat operations in the active theaters, I now have a chance to return to what was my first love when I began writing–novels.

I'm often asked how it is to go back and forth between fiction and nonfiction. They are indeed very different. As I've often said, in writing a novel I get to hang out with my imaginary friends for a few hours each day, while a work of nonfiction is a115,000-word term paper. Yet each is compelling in its own way. A novel is a much more free-flowing enterprise. The characters are of my own creation; I introduce them, see to their initial development, and set them in motion. They take on duties and responsibilities that have to do with pace and plot, and they drive the action. I'm not so much writing as I'm running along behind my characters, taking notes. They take charge of the story. They decide what happens next as they act out the scenario. I have an idea how the story will end, but sometimes my characters fool me, and then the ending is a surprise for both the reader and myself. That's what happened in *Act of Revenge*. Nonfiction is both less creative and a great deal more work. The individuals I write about–the military special operators, the training cadres, the enabling support cadres, and the command and control entities are real people–warriors all. It's their story, not my own, so I have to be accurate and true to what is taking place in *their* world. And there's the travel. Whether it's component training at a domestic training facility or an operational embed overseas, it's still time away from home. As my dear wife, Julia, has reminded me, I've been gone about a third of our married life–about the same as our military special operators since 9/11. Candidly, it's hard work and challenging work, but it has its rewards. The SEALs, Green Berets, Rangers, and Marines I write about are among the finest warriors ever to serve our great nation. That I have been allowed to share a part of their journey and to tell their story is indeed a high honor and a privilege. It has been well worth all the long days and nights on the training ranges at Coronado, Fort Bragg, Fort Benning, Camp Lejeune, and the overseas travel in the battle space. I can only hope that my efforts in print have been equal to their courage, professionalism, and sacrifice.

Act of Revenge. What happens when a talented special operator, in this case a senior SEAL petty officer, is called home from deployment to find his brother has been the victim of a vicious and unspeakable crime? When traditional law enforcement is unable or unwilling to pursue those responsible, what are his options and where does his duty now lie? Garrett Walker ably served this author in *The Mercenary Option* and *Covert Action*. His brother, Don Walker, helped me in *Silent Descent*. Now Garrett is home and must confront evil more pressing than anything the Taliban, al-Qaeda, or Saddam's Republican Guard ever threw at him. And it's personal–so personal that he must now take those skills he learned as a SEAL and honed in years of direct combat and use them in a way he never imagined. *Act of Revenge* is a medical thriller, it's a complex and deep-seated love triangle, and it's the return of a prodigal. But it's more than that. It's what happens when those who feel they are beyond the reach of the law are met by a Navy SEAL for whom the standard battlefield rules of engagement no longer apply.

Act of Revenge not only marks my return to the world of fiction but is the first work now available under my own SEAL Productions Press LTD imprint. Enjoy.

Dick Couch
Ketchum, Idaho

Part One:
AFTER ACTION

They were well inside the Pakistani border and into the upper elevations of the Samana Range. These cross-border incursions onto the sovereign territory of the only Muslim nuclear power had become decidedly less frequent given the strained relationship with the Paks, but no less dangerous. This operation, like all such missions, had been planned with careful attention to the risks and rewards. The rewards came from the target-rich environment. The Taliban and al-Qaeda leaders had come to feel secure in the mountainous border regions of the Hindu Kush where the Pashtun tribes gave them sanctuary. That security was now threatened by American special missions units whenever they crossed the border. The risks were that the presence of American military units operating in Pakistan had international repercussions, as well as a threat to the fragile, pro-Western government in Islamabad. But to the men on the ground, the real threat was falling into the hands of the enemy. There could be no worse death than the one awaiting an American captured by one of these mountain tribes that were loyal to al-Qaeda. They hated all outsiders, even Pakistani government officials, but they had a special, religious animus for the American infidels who dared to venture into their tribal lands. Fortunately, the warriors in the special missions units that made these border crossings were hard to capture and even harder to kill.

This element was a four-man hunter-killer team looking for a single al-Qaeda leader thought to be hiding in a small compound near the city of Dargai. They had been inserted by a special operations MH-47 Chinook helicopter in a small valley some twenty-five miles south and eight thousand feet below their current position. It had taken them two days to get to where they now waited. At least two of them were on watch during the day while the other two were tucked into a snow cave to rest and conserve body heat. At night they all went to ground as the November temperature plunged well below freezing. The shot they hoped to make could only be done during the daylight hours, and while the compound they were watching was heavily guarded, all outside activity ceased during the long, cold nights. It seemed to these special warriors that they were at the ends of the earth with no friendly presence for hundreds of miles. That was not entirely true. Seven miles above their heads, a Global Hawk drone aircraft ran a rack pattern that kept them under surveillance, visually during the day and thermally at night. In the unlikely event a roving band of Pashtun tribesmen should approach their location, the drone's controller, sitting in an air-conditioned operations center in Nevada, would alert them over a dedicated satellite communications link.

Stan Nakamura was camped behind a pair of stabilized binoculars watching the compound below. He had rounded features and thin wisps of facial hair. Nakamura was a small, compact man, probably no more than five-six with his muscular frame rounded off by layers of cold-weather dress. His outer shell was a light, mottled-gray pattern that blended with either rock or blown snow. He was wearing a light combat load and watch cap. Like the SEAL beside him, he was lying on his Thinsolite ground pad, the same pad he'd slept on the previous night in the snow cave. It was early afternoon with the sun full up but partially blocked by mountain peaks that cast shadows into the valley below. The temperature was still in the teens at the team's location, but they had purposely set their perch where it would always be in the shade. It was colder, but there was no chance of reflected sunlight to disclose their position.

"Think he'll show today, Senior Chief?" Nakamura asked.

"Today, tomorrow, who knows. Hopefully before our chow and batteries run low. It'll all depend on the weather." He looked at the long valley shadows to gauge the angle of the sun. "Today might be as good as any."

The senior chief petty officer lying next to Nakamura also watched the compound in the shallow valley below, but his view was through the 22X scope married to a very long and sinister-looking rifle. Senior Chief Garrett Walker had been a Navy SEAL for close to two decades. As a young petty officer, he'd cut his operational teeth when his platoon went into Afghanistan right after 9/11. He was then deployed to Iraq ahead of the conventional forces during the Iraqi invasion. He had personally been at war with his nation's enemies ever since—primarily in the Middle East and Southwest Asia. Someone had once asked him, someone who was *not* a Navy SEAL, just how many of these enemies he had killed. His answer had been, "Not nearly enough; there are still too many of them out there. But you can be sure that the ones I've put away had earned a bullet."

Unlike his shooting partner, Garrett Walker was a slim six-two. He had wide-set green eyes, and his nose and cheekbones were punctuated by sharp, angular features. A shock of wiry brown hair peeked from under his rolled-up balaclava. The thick beard and mustache wreathed a tight, controlled mouth. Except for an occasional glance at the sky or the surrounding peaks, his cheek remained welded to the stock of the weapon as he watched through the scope. A short while later he spoke in a low voice.

"Hey, Stanley. Get the other guys ready to move. I think we might have a play."

Nakamura was watching the compound, as was his team leader, but he had seen nothing. Still, he rolled from his mat and made his way to the snow cave's entrance. Soon the other two SEALs were making their way out, blinking in the bright daylight. They carried their weapons and dragged their rucksacks behind them. Without asking questions, they immediately began prepping their gear for travel. This didn't take long, as SEALs on a covert mission like this had to be ready to move at a moment's notice. They returned to the cave and brought out Nakamura's and Walker's rucks. With the gear staged and ready, the two SEALs moved to either flank and took up security positions with their M4 rifles. What Garrett Walker had seen, but Stan Nakamura missed, was the slight movement of a man in the compound's small minaret. It was the call to prayer. On cold days they prayed inside. When the sunlight touched the compound, as it did today, they often came into the courtyard to pray.

"They're coming out now," Walker said in the same low, measured voice. "Put the extraction bird on standby and let's get a solution."

Nakamura pulled a satellite phone from his vest and made a short call. At a small military outpost outside Jalalabad, seven special operations airmen filed from their tent and made their way across a dirt strip to the lone MH-47 Chinook. The huge rotors of the aircraft drooped sadly as it sat waiting patiently for its crew. Soon the two turbines began to spool up, and the rotors, moving slowly at first, gradually gathered speed. The crew made their preflight checks and waited as the big helo stood ready, idling on the ground. Back at the shooting perch in Pakistan, Stan Nakamura and Garrett Walker began their ritual. If there was a shot taken, Garrett would take it, only because it was his turn to be on the gun. Had it been Nakamura's, their duties would have been reversed.

Nakamura took up the small shooting computer that rested between them and checked the current settings. It was not much larger than a pack of cigarettes. He'd already preloaded the information for the range to the target, the type of ammunition, the barrel twist rate, the target altitude, their present altitude, the slant angle from rifle to target, and the Coriolis factor—the effect of the earth's rotation at this latitude. Taking data from a portable barometric suite, he entered the information for current air temperature and air pressure. From the Global Hawk, he received and entered a current estimated average wind speed over the course the bullet would travel. The computer took but a nanosecond to complete its work and flash the information on the LED readout.

"Up seven, left five."

"Up seven, left five," Garrett repeated and adjusted the scope—a Nightforce NXS 5.5-22X variable optic with a 56-mm objective. "What'd the eye in the sky say about the windage?"

"It amounted to a right three—seemed a little much to me."

"I agree," Garrett replied and backed the windage off an incremental click.

"What was the sonic reach?" Garrett asked.

"Twenty-seven hundred yards." According to the computer, the round they were shooting would travel at supersonic speed, under these conditions, for that distance. It was always preferable to have the bullet traveling at supersonic speed when it reached the target, both for accuracy and impact.

Nakamura checked the scope settings and squeezed Garrett's arm—the gun was properly doped and checked. Walker then took what looked like a pocket cigar humidor from his vest and laid it next to the breach of the rifle. He slipped the catch and opened the container to reveal four 4.5-inch shining brass cartridges. They looked like four small ballistic missiles—which, in fact, they were. Clipped to the inside of the container lid was a small, soft cloth, the kind often used for cleaning eyeglasses. Using the cloth, Garrett took one of the mini missiles and slipped it into the breach of the weapon. At the ranges they were shooting, the smudge or moisture from a fingerprint could affect the flight of the round. He then sent the rear-mounted handle home and locked the bolt in place. He closed the case and returned his cheek to the stock of the weapon.

After a minor shift of his body position, he reported, "All set."

"All set," Nakamura echoed.

The weapon that was now poised and in position was a CheyTac Intervention .408 long-range system, perhaps the most accurate sniper rifle in the world. The weapon had a seven-shot repeating capability, but for a shot like this, it would be one round/one kill, or nothing. At the valley compound, a file of men in Pashtun tribal dress filed into the courtyard and began to unroll their prayer rugs.

"See him?" Garrett asked.

"Not yet. No, wait—the third guy from the end in the second row?"

"Got him—even though they *do* all look alike." He adjusted the focus knob on the scope. "Yeah, that's him." It was their running joke—to Nakamura, all Caucasians looked alike, so Garrett said the same of all Asians. "Get that bird airborne."

Nakamura made another call, and a few minutes later, the big Chinook lifted into the air and headed east.

"Okay, I'm taking the shot."

"You want to give the bastard a few minutes to pray, Senior Chief?"

"What for? He's got seventy-two virgins waiting for him; he's got no time to waste."

Garrett went into a deep breathing cycle as he settled the crosshairs onto the kneeling form. He was to the side and rear of the east-facing man. In unison with the others at prayer, he sat upright on his heels for a moment, then bent forward to touch his forehead to the prayer rug. Garrett touched the trigger and took up the slack so that just a slight additional pressure would fire the weapon. He elected a torso shot and placed the reticle on the prostrated form just below his right shoulder. The man raised himself upright, away from the crosshairs. Garrett exhaled very slowly, then held his breath. As the target again lowered himself to the rug, Garrett began slowly increasing the trigger pressure. The big rifle seemingly jumped of its own accord, and the surprise of the impact immediately told Garrett he'd shot well. In silence, he and Nakamura watched as the bullet tore its way to the compound below.

Abu Ubaidah al-Masri, his eyes closed and mumbling the ancient text, had just begun to raise his head from the prayer rug. He was 2,273 yards from the muzzle of Garrett's rifle. The 419-grain copper-nickel-alloy bullet was still sonic, so it arrived ahead of the sound of the rifle. It took al-Masri in the rib cage, clipped his right lung, shredded his heart, and exited his torso after tearing through his left lung and opening a gaping wound in his left side. The round miraculously hit no bone, so it passed through him damaging only soft tissue, but that internal damage was massive. He exhaled audibly, involuntarily, and remained prostrate while the others had come to the upright prayer position. By the time the echoes of the shot began to rumble down into the valley, Abu Ubaidah al-Masri, a young Muslim extremist whom Osama bin Laden had personally groomed for future leadership in the cause, was now a martyr.

Garrett Walker knew al-Masri had been hit and assumed it had been a fatal shot. While he broke down the big rifle for travel, Stan Nakamura watched the confusion in the compound below. Men with beards and turbans scrambled from their prayer rugs and ran for their weapons. A few of them ran for their cell phones, and that's what the SEALs worried about. The men below could not get to them but those that they were calling, might. Once the SEALs were ready to move, they'd be heading away from the compound in the opposite direction. It was the security elements that al-Qaeda now had scattered across this and other mountain ranges who could move to intercept them as they traveled to their extraction point. Within a matter of seconds, the four SEALs were kitted up and ready to head out. Nakamura watched as two mujahideen fighters dragged the lifeless body of al-Masri inside, a broad swath of dark blood tracing the route over the stone courtyard.

"He's history, Senior Chief. It's a clean kill."

"Roger that. Let's move." Garrett Walker's concern, now that the shot was taken, was to get his team safely away and out of Pakistan.

It took them fifteen minutes to clear the mountain pass behind them on a trail that had been tramped into the snow by smugglers and refugees. Once they cleared the fourteen-thousand-foot crest, they moved rapidly down the western slopes toward their pickup point. As they did, a dozen Taliban fighters, alerted by those at the al-Qaeda compound, moved to intercept them. They were well positioned and watched as the four SEALs hurried toward them; they were in a perfect position for an ambush. The American intruders were still a half mile away, but in a headlong flight down the mountain. In Nevada, a young second lieutenant recently out of the Air Force Academy was monitoring the SEALs' journey on a satellite video feed. She was the Global Hawk's controller. A moment later, she saw the Taliban squad move into position below them. She quickly called for her supervisor and armed the Hellfires.

"What've you got, Sally?"

"Major, it looks like some bad guys are setting up on that special missions unit in Pakistan. My bird is in position and armed. I'm ready to drop on your authorization."

The major studied the video for a few seconds, then said, "You are cleared hot. Drop authorization granted; weapons free."

The lieutenant slewed the laser cursor onto the group of enemy fighters and quickly received a tone from the warheads of the specially modified Hellfires. The missiles were tracking the laser spot. A moment later, one Hellfire dropped from the left under-wing pylon of the Global Hawk and began its descent. Two seconds later, a second Hellfire left the right pylon, following its brother down. Each in turn fired its rocket motor. The 2.6-second burn time accelerated the missiles to 1.4 Mach. The young lieutenant kept the laser curser on the enemy mujahideen, but that was not essential. The guidance systems of both missiles were now diving on a set of GPS coordinates on the ground. If for some reason they lost laser lock, they would fly to these precise coordinates.

"Sailor Two-Five, this is Control, over."

Garrett Walker halted the file and keyed the transmit button in the stock of his M4 carbine. "This is Two-Five, Control. What do you have for me, over?"

"Hold your position. We have inbound ordnance on some bandits along your route, how copy?"

"Understand ordnance inbound; we are holding until further notice, Two-Five, out."

Garrett and the other SEALs immediately dropped to the ground and took a fetal position, hands over their ears and breathing through their mouths. They'd all had experience with close air support in the form of bombs and rockets, and they knew to take the shock wave seriously. It took close to twenty-two seconds for the Hellfires to travel the eight miles from the Global Hawk to men on the ground. The Taliban fighters had split their element so half of them were on one side of the trail and half on the other. But the Global Hawk controller had been skillful enough to slew her laser from one group to the other just after the first impact. The two missiles bracketed the trail, roughly in the middle of each group.

"Nicely done, Lieutenant," the major said. "Very nicely done." The controller sat back, took a deep breath, and keyed her mic. "Sailor Two-Five, you are cleared to proceed. Believe we got them all, but stay alert." As an afterthought, she added, "From where we sit, we're rather removed from the action. Any chance for a BDA, over?"

"Sailor Two-Five proceeding and thanks," Garrett replied. "We'll do our best with the BDA. Two-Five out."

The four SEALs moved off the trail to flank the site of the missile strikes and approached with caution, two moving and two in secure shooting positions. All they found were craters in the snow smeared with blood and dirt littered with clothing, boots, and weapons. Farther off the trail, they found two men still alive, one conscious and one not. They gave both a shot of morphine and left them for the cold to finish the work of the Hellfires.

On the way down the trail, Garrett checked in. "Control, this is Sailor Two-Five. Your battle-damage assessment to follow: two WIAs and ten plus KIAs—the former both terminal. Many thanks for your assistance. This group of swabbies owes you one, over."

"Roger Two-Five. Good luck, Control out."

It wasn't long before Garrett heard the *thump-thump-thump* of the inbound 47. Moments later, they were making their way through a world of blowing snow from the rotor wash and finally saw the smiling face of the .50 gunner on the Chinook's tail ramp. They had barely time to strap in before the big helo was straining for altitude as it headed back for the Afghan border and Jalalabad.

Back at the Air Force control center in Nevada, the major was reviewing the video of the operation. He carefully counted the mujahideen as they moved from the cover of the mountains to the ambush site. Then he turned to his second lieutenant.

"Sally, you just rang up thirteen confirmed kills. How do you feel about that?"

She gave it a moment's thought. "Okay, I guess. It's one for the good guys." Then she turned back to the console that controlled her drone, programming it for the next mission.

At the special operations base near Jalalabad, the command pilot had just cut power and the rotors began to coast to a stop. Garrett made his way forward to the helo's cockpit.

"Thanks for the ride, Captain," he called into the pilot's ear.

"Our pleasure, Chief. Understand you smoked the dude."

"That's affirm. And the drone pilot took out quite a few more. Good day all around."

The SEALs descended the rear ramp and made their way over to a small group of their teammates waiting with two extended-cab pickups. One man detached himself from the group and motioned for Walker to join him off to one side. Garrett saw a look of deep concern on his face.

"What's up, J.D.? Something wrong?"

Lieutenant Commander John Dawson was the special missions troop leader and the officer in charge of this detachment. Garrett and the other detachment SEALs had a great deal of respect for Dawson. He was a proven combat leader with more than ten years in the teams. Dawson paused a moment, hands on his hips, then met Walker's eyes.

"Senior, there's just no good way to do this, so here it is. Your brother Don was killed this morning. He died in a firefight just outside of Mazar-e Sharif. "He paused and put a hand on his senior chief's shoulder. "I don't have all the details, but it seems he and some of his Afghan commandos were clearing a building when he caught a stray round—went just under the lip of his helmet. There was nothing that could be done; he died instantly."

Another SEAL appeared behind him. "Let me take that for you, Senior," he said as he took the rucksack off Garrett's shoulder. Garrett made no move to stop him. He dropped to one knee, holding his M4 rifle to steady himself.

Don was with SEAL Team Five, working with the Afghan special forces. They were in frequent e-mail contact, and Don was very excited about the progress of his Afghans. He called them some of the best counterinsurgency fighters he'd ever worked with—true brothers-in-arms. The record of the Afghan Commandos and their SEAL advisors was impressive. Don was a first class petty officer on his sixth combat rotation—his third to Afghanistan. The last SEAL killed in action had been close to six months ago. *This was all wrong; things in this armpit of a nation were supposed to be getting better.* Garrett felt sick to his stomach. *Dear God, why Donnie? This can't be happening! Not Donnie!*

Dawson knew there was nothing to say to ease Garrett's pain, and he had the good sense not to try. It took time to absorb news like this; it was an all-too-familiar occurrence, but no less an easy one. "I've got you space on a flight from Jalalabad to Kabul where they are taking him. From there we'll get you both to Kuwait. You can take your brother home from there. Frank," he said to the SEAL holding Garrett's ruck, "stay with him." Then, to the man kneeling with his head down, he said, "When you're ready, Garrett, I'll take you to the air base at Jalalabad—get you on your way as soon as possible." He wanted to say something else, but what? He turned and walked away.

The journey of Don Walker from Kabul, Afghanistan, to Little Rock, Arkansas, was complicated but not difficult. The armed forces of the United States are bureaucratic and often inflexible, but when it comes to the repatriation of their combat dead, they are highly efficient—almost benevolent. Garrett had been detached on emergency leave to escort his brother back home. As it worked out, the C-130 carrying just the two of them landed at Ali Al Salem Air Base in Kuwait barely an hour ahead of the C-17 that was to take them partway home. It had come from Kandahar with three other American servicemen on their final trip home.

Garrett rode in the back of a pickup with Don's coffin to join the three other fallen warriors aboard the C-17 bound for Ramstein Air Base in Germany. Upon landing there, Don and Garrett left by military ambulance for the commercial terminal. Garrett watched as his brother's flag-draped casket was loaded into the belly of a Lufthansa Airbus A380 with considerably less ceremony than had been given him on the American bases. The Air Force ambulance dropped him at the departure gate, and he joined the familiar airport queues, first at the ticketing counter and then in the security screening lines. Late that afternoon, they were over the North Atlantic on a great circle route for New York's Kennedy Airport.

As Garrett and Don flew over Ireland, a casualty assistance officer and a Navy chaplain drove up the lane to the Walker farm. There is no easy way to tell parents that their son is coming home in a box. It is official policy, when possible, to notify the survivors, in this case Don's parents, at the same time. For the several minutes that it took to summon Russell Walker in from the fields, Polly Walker sat alone in her parlor, agonizing silently as she wondered which of her Navy sons was dead—Garrett or Don. When Russell Walker finally arrived, he slowly entered the room with hesitant steps. He took his wife's hand, and they bravely sat together on the divan by the Franklin stove while the chaplain spoke in a low, calm voice. He told them that the day before, a half a world away, their youngest son was killed in a firefight somewhere in northern Afghanistan. They were also told that their other SEAL son, Garrett, was accompanying Don on the trip home.

The day following the chaplain's visit, Garrett and Don arrived. Garrett delivered his brother into the care of the county funeral home director, a man they had known most of their lives, he then continued on to the family farm to see his parents. It was the first time in more than a decade that Garrett Walker had been home.

Carroll County lies in northwest Arkansas along the Missouri border. Nestled in the foothills of the Ozark Mountains, its rolling hills are a gentle blend of oak and hickory with a few cultivated stands of white pine. Where the land allows, there are small tracts of soybeans and sweet corn. Carroll County, with towns like Berryville, Green Forest, and Blue Eye, had not kept pace with the rest of the nation. It was one of those few, isolated pockets of small-town America where the people all know one another, and it was not unusual for a neighbor or local resident to discipline a child who was not his or her own. They also took a collective parental pride in the success of a local boy or girl. The news of Don Walker's death spread quickly, and the county mourned as one. There were four Walker boys, no girls, and they had been a spirited crop of corn-fed farm kids. They were Russell and Polly's boys, but over the years the community had also participated. The Walker boys were all gifted athletes. For most of the nineties, there was hardly a year when at least one of them had not been a standout on the Carroll County High School football and basketball teams. That's how they measure youth in Arkansas, though all of them had been exceptional students as well. The tragedy of Don Walker's death spread well beyond the small, weathered two-story home on the Walker farm.

For two days, Garrett, along with his two brothers, stood alongside his parents as they received a steady stream of extended family and friends. All had their favorite childhood or high-school story about Donnie Walker, the youngest and probably the most likable of the boys. The refrigerator, freezer, and pantry were overflowing with casseroles and covered dishes. The abundance of food was rotated around the drop-leaf table in the dining room, and any spoilage was later fed to the hogs. Rural folks bring food to a bereaved home like Sicilians bring envelopes with money to a wedding. It is a gesture of respect and condolence. Don's death aside, it had been an especially difficult two days for Garrett. When Garrett Walker left abruptly many years earlier, he had not remained close with the family as had the other boys, only visiting once in the past ten years. Brandon and Don returned home whenever they could, for Thanksgiving and Christmas, or for a few days during bird-hunting season. Jim Walker, now the youngest, remained in Carroll County near his folks after graduation. Garrett managed some time alone with Jim, but he and Brandon avoided each other.

The night before the burial service, Garrett managed to slip away to a tavern in the neighboring Boone County. He needed to be alone. So much family after so long an absence had made him uneasy and restless. He felt like a stranger in a not-entirely strange land.

"Scotch, neat, and make it a double," he said as he slid quietly onto one of the bar stools. It was half past ten, but there were a surprising number of late-night drinkers for a weekday. Work was sometimes scarce in northern Arkansas, and most bars cashed unemployment checks. The bartender gave him a second glance and moved down the bar. He knew most of the people who came into his roadside tavern, and most were locals and beer drinkers. Garrett looked around the bar. It was like a thousand others scattered around the South and Midwest.

At times during the last couple of days, he reflected, it was as if he had never left Arkansas. Other times, he felt like a total outsider. This part of the country, the people, even this bar—all were frozen in time. There were subtle changes; when he was growing up here, kids wore their baseball caps with bills forward and their jeans tight. Now it was just the opposite. Some styles might have changed, yet they were still country folk, mild-mannered and easy to be with, and he found this curiously reassuring. For the last sixteen years, his world had been one of constant change and violence. Over the years, Garrett had lost most of his soft drawl, but he felt it easing its way back into his speech, almost against his will. The bartender set the drink in front of him. It was a generous pour.

"You one of them Walker boys, aren't you?"

"That's right," Garrett said as he nodded his thanks. He'd forgotten just how confining it was to be known as one of the Walkers, but that was how he had grown up.

"Real sorry to hear about your brother. He was a heck of a ballplayer, but then I guess you all were." Garrett smiled patiently. "Now, which one are you? Yer the one that's in the Navy, too, right?" Garrett forced another smile and again nodded. The bartender lingered self-consciously for a moment, then said, "Well, it was just a damn shame to hear about it, that's for sure." Garrett laid a twenty on the bar, but the bartender pushed it back to him. "Yer money's no good here this evening."

He then moved down the bar to service two empties from the tap behind the counter. Garrett sipped his scotch in silence, sorting through old memories. His family, the farm, this rural backwater—they were a part of him, but a part of his life that he had sealed and stored away. Had it not been for Don's death, he might never have come back again. Don had been his link with the past. As Navy SEALs, they spent a great deal of time overseas, but their paths occasionally crossed in San Diego or Norfolk. "Mom sends her love," Don would say, or "Dad wants to know when you'll be coming home." Don was always after him to take some leave and visit the folks. *Well, little brother*, he reflected bitterly, *you finally got me to make that visit home.*

Garrett had already put Don's death behind him—quietly and reverently, as if his brother's life had been the treasured photograph of a childhood sweetheart who had been killed in an automobile crash. He'd thought a great deal about his brother these past few days. The grief that had nearly overwhelmed him when his troop leader told him Don had been killed had quickly given way to understanding and appreciation. Don died with his boots on; he had lived the life of a warrior and had died as one. Only those who routinely risk their lives and experience death around them truly understand this. They were in a dangerous business, but that was by choice. Garrett smiled to himself at the thought; Don had been just as addicted to the adventure, the danger, and the rush of combat as he was. Garrett had the opportunity to meet briefly with Don's platoon officer who had escorted Don from Mazar-e Sharif to Kabul. The officer summed up the best that could be said of a brother SEAL: He died in combat, and he died well. *Perhaps it's only of comfort to someone like myself, or someone like Don, but it is very important for a man to die well. It's the last thing we do.*

Garrett was on his second drink and was recalling a funny story that one of the Basic Underwater Demolition/SEAL, or BUD/S, instructors had told him of Don's exploits in SEAL training. Garrett remembered trying to talk Don out of joining the Navy or at least finishing college and becoming an officer. Yet he had been secretly pleased when Don came through training and joined the teams as an enlisted man like himself. There was good duty for an enlisted man in the Navy SEAL teams—good duty if you liked the challenge of special operations combat and being away from home a great deal. Or, if you were like Garrett Walker, the teams were your home. Don had excelled in the difficult SEAL basic training, and the instructors didn't pull their punches just because he had a brother in the teams. However, Don didn't sign up to be like his older brother; he had always loved the water and was an experienced diver long before he became a SEAL. SEALs lived with the ever-present prospect of death. While news of a fallen brother never came easy, most had, like Garrett Walker, conditioned themselves to hold on to the sweetness of the memory rather than to dwell on the loss. It's a warrior thing; when a warrior dies, the essence of his life lives on with his brother warriors. With Don, as with others who had gone before him, he was still with Garrett, and with his platoon mates still deployed in Afghanistan.

The spell was broken when a man at the other end of the bar escorted his mug of beer down to where Garrett was seated.

"Ah heard that it was yer brother who was kilt by them terrorists over in I-rack. Son, Ah was gawd-awful sorry to hear about that."

Garrett didn't bother to correct the man. He looked to be near his father's age, but it was hard to tell. There was a John Deere cap perched on a coarse thatch of gray hair, and he had the watery blue eyes and ruddy complexion of a steady drinker. He wore wrinkled cotton trousers and a flannel work shirt buttoned up to the collar. There was a small brass American flag pin clipped to the front of his cap.

"Thank you," Garrett replied.

"Y'know, I never knew my daddy 'cause he was a marine and got kilt at the Chosin Reservoir in Korea. By Gawd, it's maybe time we done something about them furriners that think they can fool aroun' with America. They attack our cities, and now there's all this bidness about their atomic bombs in Pak-ee-stan and I-ran. Yessir, maybe it's about time for us jes to bomb the livin' shit out of them. By the way, mah name's Dallas Hacker," he announced as he extended his hand.

Garrett looked hard at the man and was struck by the contrast between this American, who considered himself a patriot, and his dead brother. How did he tell this well-meaning redneck that Don had died fighting alongside some very capable and brave Afghan commandos, men both he and Don called brothers-in-arms? It always surprised him at just how quickly these prejudices could be fanned to life, especially after 9/11. For a moment, Garrett was tempted to try to explain that there were only good and bad men, not Iraqis or Afghans or Arabs or Russians—no them and us. But he had long since given this up, especially with civilians who could never quite grasp the bond one warrior could feel for another. Still, he was always fascinated that it was usually the warriors, men like Don and himself, who understood that it was the character of the man, not his nationality, skin color, or ethnicity, that mattered. *Perhaps,* he mused, *that's why Don and I chose to be in uniform; we could appreciate the worth of a man and the purity of a warrior, more than a Dallas Hacker could ever understand.*

"Dallas, I'm Garrett Walker," he said, taking the man's hand firmly, "and I want to thank you very much for your kind words." With that, he tossed down the remainder of his drink, pushed his twenty across the counter to the bartender, thanked him for the drinks and walked out.

A low-hanging sun was just starting to burn the frost from the tall brown grass, and there was still a bite in the air. The bare hardwood forests held a light mist close to the gently rolling hills, broken only by a few fallow bean fields in the low-lying areas. Rural Arkansas, especially here in the high valleys that swelled to meet the Ozarks, was a lush country of dramatic beauty, but December was not its best month. Don wouldn't have minded, Garrett thought. He'd have been able to fade into that dense thicket of oak just beyond the cemetery plot and come up with a rabbit or a fox, maybe even a deer. But as good as Donnie had been in the woods, he had been even better in the water. Garrett himself had his own reasons for becoming a Navy SEAL, but Donnie had had a real love affair with blue water. For some reason, landlocked young men flocked to the SEAL teams, more so than those who grew up on the coasts. Perhaps the restless action of the ocean surf had a special magic for those who had only known freshwater lakes and streams.

Garrett knew that if he had only Don's wishes to consider, he'd have buried his brother at sea. He was closer to the blue ocean than to Arkansas. Nonetheless, Garrett brought Donnie home to Carroll County because he knew what it would mean to his parents. The Walker home was a ninety-acre truck farm that barely kept food on the table. Russell and Polly Walker were good farmers, but their best crop had been their sons. *Perhaps this was as it should be—dust to dust.* As he looked across the small cemetery to an adjacent field, still raw and scarred from the fall disking, he decided, *I'm not sure just where home is for me, but it's sure not here. When my time comes, I'll want to sleep with the fishes.*

"You ready, Momma?"

She nodded without speaking and took her husband's arm. Polly Walker was a tall woman, rawboned but with a gentle cast to her features. Garrett marveled at her. She worked alongside her husband day in and day out on the farm, but she somehow retained the personal grace and composure of a banker's wife. Russell Walker, on the other hand, was as brown and wrinkled as a walnut and as hard as cured leather. Beneath the rough exterior, Garrett knew his father was not as strong as the sad woman who clutched his arm. Garrett knew his mother's heart was breaking, but she carried herself with tragic dignity. A large throng of people waited near the open grave to pay their last respects. This was not the overflowing crowd that had gathered at the church for the memorial service, but a large gathering nonetheless. Garrett followed his mother and father up a gentle rise from the church to the burial site.

The Reverend Jackson, or Father Jack as he was known to his parishioners, had baptized all the boys, admonished them for their youthful transgressions, and prayed for their souls on Sunday. Now he had to bury one of them. He was a stern, hardworking, compassionate country preacher. Father Jack was not one to carry on about the celebration of life or God's greater plan in which we all play a small part. One of his flock had been taken too soon, and he was not happy about it. In a short eulogy that was perilously close to blasphemy, he allowed that God in His infinite mercy had sure better known what the hell he was doing when he called home a fine young man like Donnie Walker. Father Jack's words were short, to the point, and reflected the pain and sense of loss that they all felt. As Don Walker was lowered into the rich Arkansas dirt, two sailors in dress-blue crackerjack bell-bottoms lifted the American flag that draped the casket and slowly began to fold it. It was a ritual as old as the republic itself.

They were a little clumsy in the performance of their duty. These two Navy men were not ceremonial sailors pressed into service from some nearby Naval Reserve unit. Both had several rows of combat decorations and wore gold SEAL devices on their breasts. They were tough men with a stern look to them; they were warriors from a sister SEAL team of Don Walker's. When they were finished, they handed the blue triangle with white stars to an officer, who grasped it in the prescribed manner—one hand flat on top and the other flat on the bottom. Then he pivoted and formally presented the flag to Polly Walker.

"On behalf of a grateful nation and a proud Navy," he said in a low, clear voice, "I present this flag to you in recognition of your son's honorable and faithful service to his country."

Polly Walker took the flag and clutched it to her breast, while her husband lowered his weathered face. Garrett put his arm around his mother while Jim Walker took his father's hand. Brandon and his wife sat just behind them with their heads bowed sharing in his parent's grief. The officer stepped back and saluted, the sun glinting from the SEAL pin on his chest. Across the gravesite, six more SEALs held their M4 rifles at the ready, pointed toward the heavens.

"Salute our fallen brother!" the officer called out. "Ready!"

"Aim, fire!" *Bang.*

"Aim, fire!" *Bang.*

"Aim, fire!" *Bang.*

Then a bugler sounded taps. He stood well away from the burial site, so the notes from the horn reached the gathered mourners just a fraction of a second ahead of the first echo from the nearest hill. The bugler knew his craft and held every phrase of this last call until each reverberated tone found its way into the hearts of those gathered at the open grave. When the last note perished in the cold air, the silence was deafening. "Taps," when delivered by an accomplished bugler, is cold and beautiful and final.

As the last mournful echoes dueled across the hills and died away, the officer snapped away his salute. He executed a smart right face and was about to withdraw. Then he turned back to the bereaved couple and dropped to one knee. He placed one hand on Russell Walker's knee and another on Polly's arm.

"I know there is little I can say at a time like this. Your son was a fine man. I was privileged to know and serve with him." He paused and bit his lip, trying to say what he felt in a manner these farm parents would understand. "He served well, and he died a hero. Several of the men with him on that last mission would not be alive today had he not fought so well. He ... he was a very brave man. Our commodore and Don's commanding officer both send their sincere condolences. We in the teams who knew and served with Don will miss him a great deal."

With that, the Lieutenant Commander Don LeMaster stood and again saluted the grieving couple. He then joined the two flag tenders behind the six other SEALs who stood with their M4s at the order arms. All were from SEAL Team Three in Coronado, California. LeMaster was the executive officer at Team Three but had served with Don Walker on a previous combat tour. He was one of his former platoon officers. Don's teammates with Team Five were all still on deployment. It was the duty of the non-deployed teams to see to the funeral needs of their fallen brothers.

Father Jack closed the ceremony, inviting those gathered to join the Walkers at the wake, which was to be held in the basement of the church. Wakes were traditionally held at the family home, but in anticipation of a large gathering, the church basement had been pressed into service. Friends and relatives had arrayed mounds of homemade dishes on cloth-covered card tables in preparation for the occasion. There was an ample supply of scalloped potatoes and creamed corn. Out back in the church maintenance shed, Ball jars containing a smooth, clear liquor waited on the shelf. Father Jack allowed no drinking in the church, but he had been known to join the menfolk for a quick taste in memory of a departed soul. By early afternoon, the mourners were making their way to their cars. The SEALs in their dress blues waited by two rental sedans. Finally, the remaining three Walker boys escorted their parents down the front steps of the church. Polly Walker saw the waiting men in uniform and looked to Garrett. He, too, was now in dress blues.

"You're not coming with us back to the house." It was not a question, nor was there censure in his mother's voice—only disappointment.

"No, Mom. We have a flight to catch this afternoon out of Fayetteville. There's nothing more I can do here, and I have to get back to my unit—back to my men."

After a long moment, she stepped forward and rose on her toes to kiss him on the cheek. As she did so, she whispered in his ear. "You need to get past this, son. You know … we are all still family."

Garrett understood, yet he could not meet her eyes. "I know, Mom, I know." He turned to his father, who looked small and very frail. "Good-bye, Dad," he said offering his hand. "Take care of yourself."

"I'll try, son." There was an unsure, distant look in his eyes. "Come back when you can. Maybe this summer, and we'll do some bird shooting."

"Thanks, Dad. Maybe I will."

His two brothers stood next to their father. Jim was dressed in an ill-fitting sport coat, plaid shirt, and knit tie. He needed a haircut, but that did little to degrade his strong features and soft brown eyes. Now that Don was gone, he was the baby of the family. Brandon was a little taller than Jim. He had a smooth, polished look. The expensive, conservative suit and wool topcoat would not have been conspicuous had he been attending a burial service in San Francisco or New York.

"Look after them," he said to his brothers, and turned and walked quickly toward the waiting SEALs. Brandon watched him go without a word. Garrett had almost reached the other SEALs when Jim caught him by the arm.

"That's it? You're going to leave it like that?" Garrett did not respond. "What the hell's the matter with you, anyway?" Jim continued.

"It's not your affair, Jim. Stay out of it."

"The hell it's not. He's your brother and so am I; you've only got two now, you know."

"God damn it, Jim, leave it be. It's got nothing to do with you." With that he turned away and joined the men in uniform who were waiting for him. He was absorbed into the group, which quickly began to swarm into the two sedans. As Garrett slid into the rear seat of the lead car, the officer behind the wheel turned to him.

"Senior Chief, if you need some more time here, I can authorize it."

"Thanks, XO, but it's time for me to get back to my men. We have another month on this deployment. I want to see them through the tour and get them safely home."

Lieutenant Commander LeMaster started to say something, but the grim expression on Garrett's face told him he would be wasting his time. As the two cars eased away from the church, Garrett could see his brother Jim with an arm around each of his parents, helping them along the access road to their car. Walking behind them was his brother Brandon. His wife was a tall, attractive woman wearing a long coat pulled up tight around her neck and holding on tightly to Brandon's arm. It was obvious that she'd been crying, yet there was a certain dignity and distinction to her features that emerged through the sadness. A gust of wind tugged at her rich, dark hair and she looked up. She and Garrett were able to exchange a brief glance before the car sped away.

Part Two:
THE TAKING

Brandon Walker threaded his way across the busy lobby of the Desert Flower Inn, dodging hotel guests and an occasional well-laden bellhop leading new arrivals to the reception desk. It was Friday, almost one o'clock, and the first wave of weekend gamblers was beginning its assault on the tables. On the weekends, Las Vegas called them in from California like lemmings to the sea—or, in this case, away from the sea. They came from all over the country and in many varieties. There were slick ones in linen slacks with their sport jackets worn over designer T-shirts. Many were elderly retirees with fanny packs belted under sagging paunches. All would snuggle alongside each other at the tables like piglets on adjacent teats. Brandon Walker, clearly not one of them, could have passed for a casino executive or a high-class pimp as he worked his way to the bank of elevators at the far end of the lobby. Once inside the ornate, mirrored car, he punched the button for the convention center on the top floor.

"Looks like the reception room of a goddamn cathouse," slurred the only other occupant, a jowly man in a checked sport coat and white slacks. Brandon gave him a quick glance and smiled politely. The guy looked like someone who just might know, Brandon thought. "Don't take any wooden nickels, pal," the man chuckled as he left the elevator. Brandon continued on in silence, watching the digital display tick off the floors as the car raced skyward.

Brandon Walker had strong features, yet there was a certain softness about him that suggested he was very approachable. At six-two, two hundred pounds, he was not a small man, yet he carried it well so he didn't appear that large. He wore a conservative Brooks Brothers suit, white shirt, and a silk floral tie. Brandon was comfortably in his late thirties, but his youthful appearance made him look much younger. He had good shoulders and moved with a practiced ease that suggested more than an occasional round of golf or game of tennis. His brown hair was thick and wavy with sun streaks. He kept it long and combed straight back, yet off his collar. The only feature that seemed out of place were his hands; they had the look of a laborer's, oversized with large knuckles. The elevator doors parted, and he walked into a busy, overly decorated foyer that served three conference rooms. Brandon skirted the crowd, making for the room on the far left, and he almost made it.

"Hey, Brandon, how you been, buddy?"

"Hello, Eric. How're things at ClinicSoft?"

"Pretty fair, my man, except for losing those accounts that you've managed to seduce away from us."

Brandon smiled, trying to stay on the move without seeming discourteous. "What can I say? We've got an aggressive bunch of resellers."

"And a damn good product," Eric whispered, "but we don't aim to go quietly." Then, in a louder voice, he said, "Hey, you take care, now."

"You, too, Eric."

Brandon slipped into the room and promptly stepped off to one side. He glanced quickly around, missing nothing. He noted the layout and the placement of the lectern. Earlier that morning, he had updated his briefing package and downloaded it into the projection system. The room was nearly full but for a few stragglers who roamed the aisles looking for vacant seats. An older man with an impatient manner spotted him and hurried over.

"Brandon, where have you been?" He made an exaggerated show of looking at his watch. "You should already be up there!" he moaned as he frantically gestured toward the front of the room. He was dressed like Brandon, but with a far more conservative tie.

"Relax, George, these things never begin exactly on time." George started to argue, but Brandon continued, "But it's probably as good a time as any to get started." He quickly surveyed the bar and a table laden with fruit and cheeses. "First-rate setup, George. Really, well done." He made his way over to the bar and ordered a tonic with a wedge of lime.

Brandon maneuvered up the center aisle, pausing several times to shake hands or to return a shouted greeting. As he turned to face the crowd from behind the lectern, the gentle buzz of conversation dissolved to scattered whispers. The audience numbered about eighty. Brandon surveyed the crowd and saw what he had expected: a talented and reasonably polite gathering of software salespeople who, for the most part, were excited about the industry and their work. Few made less than a six-figure income, most considerably more. He also knew they wanted him to get on with it so they could catch an early plane home—or get back to the blackjack tables. His notebook computer rested on the lectern. Brandon took a sip of his tonic while he tapped several digits on the keypad. Then he entered the data and eased the lectern to one side, careful not to spill his drink.

"Computer, begin presentation." The lights lowered by half, and the screen behind Brandon and to his right faded to a piece of starlit sky. A dull murmur lifted from the crowd as the stars coalesced into the MedaSystems logo—the gold-block MSI letters superimposed on a silver caduceus. There's always a few who have never experienced a voice-activated computer, Brandon mused, or not seen it used in a presentation. He then stepped away from the lectern to address them.

"Good afternoon. My name is Brandon Walker, marketing director for MedaSystems International. On behalf of MedaSystems and our licensees across the country, thank you all for joining us this afternoon. During this presentation, which will last no longer than thirty-seven minutes, we want to show you the most advanced line of health-care management software in the industry."

Brandon pulled a laser pointer from his inside pocket and called to the projector suspended from the ceiling. "Advance!" The logo exploded into stardust, then reassembled into a colored pictorial of the MedaSystems's hardware components.

Brandon worked through his presentation in a conversational, yet thoroughly professional manner, and with enough humor to keep the after-lunch crowd from drifting. "And as you can see," he concluded, "our systems have the ability to track any test or procedure from the clinic to the lab, to the specialist's office, to the hospital, and to the pharmacy, and throughout the continuum of care—anytime, real time. Our systems use the very latest in web-based technology. This also allows any authorized caregiver to easily monitor a patient's clinical status, test results, medication, and billing. The system architecture is designed for speed and reliability, and is very user-friendly. And, finally, it comes with the MedaSystems technical support package." A glance at his watch told him he had been talking for thirty-five minutes. "At this time, I'd like to thank you for your attendance and interest in MedaSystems. I've allowed a couple of minutes for a question or two before we open the bar."

The questions were brief, but a number of the attendees sought him out following the presentation after they had secured themselves a drink. Brandon worked the crowd for close to an hour, swapping business cards and talking shop. After the last person left, he retrieved his computer from the lectern.

The older man did not approach him until he was alone.

"Once again, you were superb." His smile appeared guarded, but not altogether insincere.

"That's why you pay me the big bucks, isn't it, George?"

George shrugged and shot Brandon a quick smile. George Grant was the founder, CEO, and major stockholder of MedaSystems. He paid Brandon Walker a handsome salary, and Brandon's contract with his company had strong performance incentives and generous stock options. "Yes, that's exactly right. Any hot prospects?"

"Several." Brandon pulled a compact personal digital assistant from his suit-coat pocket and scribbled a notation. "I've got five appointments scheduled for this afternoon and early evening, most of them from our clinic managers meeting this morning. With any luck, I'll close a couple of them."

Grant broke out in a full smile. "My guess is that you'll get lucky. Will you be needing me?"

"I really don't think so," Brandon said honestly. "They know our product and our pricing structure. I just have to get their names on the contract."

"Then I'll be heading back this afternoon. How about you?"

A frown crossed Brandon's face. "As much as I'd like to, I don't think I can get away. But you can bet I'll be on the first flight out tomorrow morning."

After Grant had left him, Brandon slipped over to the bar and ordered another tonic. He took up residence at a nearby table and began to sort through the business cards he had collected from his audience. He was annotating a list of prospects into his Ipad when a very attractive woman in her early thirties stopped at his table. She leaned on the back of the chair across from him and gave him a wide, friendly smile.

"That was an excellent presentation this afternoon, Mr. Walker."

"Thank you, and it's Brandon." He rose and extended his hand. "And you are … ?"

"Jordan … Linda Jordan. I'm with the Meade Group. We're a medical consulting firm out of San Diego."

Linda Jordan was dressed exquisitely in a tailored Dana Buchman business suit. She wore a simple strand of pearls and gold earrings. Her thick dark hair framed an attractive face—too attractive for the heavy makeup she wore. She was slender, almost painfully so, with the drawn, anemic features of a runway model. He had an instant feeling that something about her didn't quite match up. If she were in the audience during his presentation, Brandon was surprised that he hadn't noticed her. He tried to watch for audience reaction when he spoke, and he'd always had a knack for names and faces. It was his business, and he was good at it.

"Of course, I'm familiar with Meade, Linda. It's been a long week, and I've met an awful lot of new people." He recovered his seat.

"I'm sure you have. I hope it's been a successful week."

"Well, yes, actually it has been. But then we have a state-of-the-art system, and it pretty much sells itself."

"Oh, I don't know. I was at your presentation, Mr. Walker—I mean, Brandon—and you seem to do a very good job of selling your product. Mind if I join you for a moment?"

"I'm sorry. Please have a seat." Before he could rise, she slid into the seat across from him. "Ah, Linda, I wasn't aware that the Meade Group had an interest in our medical programs. Are you a software vendor?"

"Not really. We consult with HMOs and hospitals that are in the market for computer services, and to be honest, I'm new to the company. They sent me here to learn about new products on the market. Tell me, how long have you been with MedaSystems?"

Brandon gave her one of his patient smiles, not really wanting to get into a "Let's get acquainted" conversation. He decided to give her a few minutes, as she was new to the industry and seemed fidgety. "Since the company was founded, almost ten years now." Brandon fingered his glass. "Can I get you something from the bar?"

"Why, thanks. I'll have a scotch on the rocks."

As Brandon returned to the table, he tried to study her without appearing to stare. Made up or not, she was a stunning woman. There was a slight nervousness to her that was almost masked by her poise, and a forced, yet polished, charm. The software business was a cutthroat game. Good looks didn't hurt, but you made your living by your wits and your product knowledge. He still couldn't shake the feeling that she didn't seem right for the part.

"Is this your first time to Las Vegas?" Brandon asked.

"I wish. I dealt blackjack here for two years out of college, then moved on. How about you?"

"Once a year for the clinic software convention." Then, to make sure this wasn't going in the wrong direction, he added, "I usually try to bring the family, but with three kids in school, it can get complicated. Are you married?"

"I was for a while, but it didn't work out." A shadow passed across her face, but she quickly recovered. "I've got two girls, but they're spending the school year with their dad back east. Well, cheers," she said, and knocked back half the scotch with one gulp. *Christ*, Brandon thought, *I don't think that I was ever that nervous when I started.*

They made small talk for a while, swapping stories about incidents in Las Vegas. She clearly didn't want to talk about business, and, Brandon sensed, she didn't appear to want to seduce him, either. He knew from experience that he was the kind of man women often came on to, and he was relieved that this time that didn't seem to be the case.

He glanced at his watch and smiled apologetically. "I hope you won't think I'm being rude, but I gotta run. I have several meetings yet today and an early flight back tomorrow."

"I understand perfectly," she replied.

Brandon collected his Ipad and slid it into his briefcase. She rose and they shook hands. He left with the distinct feeling there was more to his visit with Ms. Jordan than met the eye. But he had just enough time to get to his next appointment, and he was able to catch an elevator as the door was closing. Immediately after Brandon's departure, Linda Jordan went to the bar for another scotch, which she finished off as quickly as the first.

Brandon Walker didn't get to the hotel restaurant until nine o'clock that evening, an hour later than he had planned. At his request, the maître d' showed him to a small, quiet table in the corner. He had indeed been lucky and had purchase orders for four MedaSystems software systems in his briefcase. At ten fifteen, he had just finished an average New York steak and was enjoying the last of an excellent Napa Valley merlot split. He was about to call for his check when the waiter set another glass in front of him.

"Excuse me, but I didn't order more wine."

"Compliments of the lady." He pointed to a table at the far side of the dining room. Linda Jordan smiled and raised a tumbler to him. She was dining opposite a large man with dark hair, his broad back toward Brandon. He didn't seem to notice or acknowledge her gesture to Brandon, remaining perfectly still and seemingly uninterested. Brandon returned the smile and lifted his own glass in a show of appreciation.

"Tell the lady I said thanks, and I'm also ready for my check, please."

The waiter nodded and hurried off. Brandon finished the wine as quickly as he dared without seeming to gulp it. Only professional salespeople know just how tired you can be from a long day of pushing your product. It could be punishing work. The high from the four closed deals was rapidly giving way to fatigue. He was now looking forward to stretching out in the expansive king bed upstairs and channel surfing with the remote until he fell asleep.

Brandon nodded politely toward Linda Jordan, who was still at her table and talking with her companion when he left the restaurant. He had all but brushed her from his mind when he found her standing next to him as he waited for the elevator.

"Oh, hello again. Uh, thanks for the drink," he managed to say. Once again, he had an odd feeling about her, but he was far too tired to concentrate on it. He could only focus on getting to his room, calling his wife, and settling in for the night.

"You're welcome," she replied cheerfully. "Did your meetings go well?"

"Yes, I had a pretty good day. How about yourself?"

"Okay, I guess. Made a few contacts, learned a lot." The elevator arrived, and he followed her in.

"What floor?" Brandon inquired.

"Six."

Brandon hesitated for a moment, mildly surprised as he punched the button. "Happens to work for me, too," he replied.

Their ride was interrupted halfway up as two very drunk conventioneers clambered onto the elevator. The next stop deposited Brandon and Linda Jordan on the sixth floor. They walked in an awkward silence for a short distance down the hall. Brandon paused at room 621. "This is where I live. Uh, it was nice to meet you, Linda. Good luck with the … with the new, ah . . ."

"Brandon, are you all right?"

"Fine. I just feel a little dizzy. I'll be just fine."

"You're not going to pretend to faint on me now, are you?" she said with a coy smile.

"Uh, no, of course not. But for a moment there, I wasn't too certain." He took out his keycard but had difficulty finding the slot.

"Brandon, you don't look too well. Here, let me help you with that." She opened his door, and, in spite of himself, he put a hand on her shoulder. "Let's get you inside." He hesitated, but she continued, "You really don't feel good, do you? Let's make sure you're okay." She helped him in, but he stopped her a few feet into the bedroom.

He seemed to recover a bit. "I'm fine, thanks. I think I just need a good night's sleep."

"I understand. Here." She handed him his keycard and turned to leave. "You sure you're all right?" He smiled weakly and nodded. "Well, then, have a safe trip home. Good night."

"Good night." He started to walk her back to the door, but she was gone before he had the chance. Again, a brief, sudden wave of nausea swept over him. He shook it off, glad to finally be alone.

He pulled off his jacket, started to hang it up, but draped it across the chair instead. He dropped heavily on the bed next to his briefcase, sliding it across the bedspread to the other side. With an effort, he swung his feet up and lay back on the pillows. Suddenly, he was very weary and felt a powerful headache coming on. Without undoing the laces, he pried his shoes off and let them hit the floor at the end of the bed.

"Christ, am I wiped," he said aloud.

At home, Brandon Walker watched very little TV; in hotel rooms, he was compulsive. He fumbled for the remote and began clicking through the channels. A battered Bruce Willis staggered across the screen—*Die Hard* number something—and he let the remote slide from his hand. *Got to call Cathy at the next commercial*, he promised himself, as he lay motionless, staring blankly at the TV screen.

Sometime later, his eyes fluttered open. He had been dozing but it now seemed very difficult to shake off the sleep and wake up. Bruce Willis had been replaced by a black-and-white Jimmy Stewart. *Cathy!* He attempted to reach for the telephone, but something was terribly wrong. His mouth was thick and unmanageable, as if his tongue had grown suddenly twice its normal size. His body felt dense, like a bag of sand, too heavy to move. It was as if someone had covered him with a dense blanket made of lead fiber. With all the effort he could summon, he struggled to heave his body toward the phone. He managed to roll half over, which put him near the edge of the bed, but his momentum carried him over the side, past the bed table and onto the floor. Brandon hit the carpet with a hard thud but he felt nothing. *Is this a nightmare? What the hell is wrong with me? I've got to call home; I have to talk to Cathy.* But he could do nothing but lie on his back, semiconscious, staring at the ceiling. He was a captive in his own body. He had no control or ability to move.

Shortly after three o'clock in the morning, Linda Jordan led two men quietly down the hall. They lagged back a short distance, cautiously glancing around, but the corridor was empty. Jordan stopped at Brandon Walker's door and quickly let herself in with the keycard that she had switched with him earlier. Ready to play the seductress on the prowl, she quickly saw there was no need. The glow of the table lamp revealed the form on the carpet by the bed. Brandon lay on his back, barely conscious, staring glassy-eyed at the ceiling.

The far-off sound of voices made him vaguely aware of people in the room, but he was powerless to respond. As if staring through a very narrow portion of a wide-angle lens, he saw the outline of a woman standing over him. She seemed vaguely familiar and foreign at the same time. She was roughly pushed aside, and Brandon Walker slid deeper into an impenetrable cotton fog.

"Is he now unconscious from the drink?" The speaker was a large man in a dark, ill-fitting suit. He had heavy features and coarse dark hair that was carefully barbered, but unkempt nonetheless. A black mole camped on the bridge of his nose and another attached itself to the side of his chin. When there was no response, his hand shot out like a snake's tongue and caught her across the side of her face.

"Is he? I asked you question."

She hesitated, then stammered, "I … why, yes, damn it … can't you see?" Linda Jordan's eyes flicked between Brandon and the big man standing over him.

The big man grunted. He then lifted his foot and put it down hard, grinding his heel into the back of Walker's hand, causing several loud popping sounds. Brandon's eyes narrowed, but there was no other movement. Grunting again, the big man turned to the second man, a sallow, older fellow in a shabby tan summer suit. He stood tentatively at the entrance to the room holding two large leather cases. He was covered with perspiration.

"Okay, let's get him onto the bed."

The second man lowered the cases to the floor. He took out a soiled handkerchief and began to wipe his face. Strands of thin, damp white hair arced in crescents down around his ears. The one in the dark suit gave him a cruel look, and the older man quickly stepped over and took Brandon's feet. Together, they hefted him onto the bed and rolled him facedown. Linda Jordan put her hand to her mouth and turned to leave.

The big man snarled, "Not to leave yet."

"But … but I've done what you asked. What more do you want from—"

He raised his arm in a backhanded gesture but did not strike her. She shrank from him.

"You go when I say."

She closed her eyes and leaned against the wall, then slid down to a squatting position. The big man shot a glance at his companion and motioned with his head toward the inert form on the bed. His older companion hefted his bags onto the dresser and began to unpack them. Linda Jordan turned her head to the wall and buried her face in her hands, unwilling to watch what they were about to do to Brandon Walker.

Master Chief Garrett Walker sat on a dirty swivel chair and looked at the flat plasma screen on the plywood wall above his head. The display, was a real-time feed from a Predator drone tracking an ongoing SEAL operation. The screen showed a grainy black-and-white scene of a compound some sixty miles northwest of the special operations base just outside Kandahar. Then two H-60 Blackhawk helicopters nosed into the presentation, and a half dozen SEALs trundled from the compound to the waiting helos. From either flank of the file, several more SEALs from the security element, folded back in and boarded the Blackhawks. The two helos, as evidenced by the blur created by dust clouds, rose in turn and rolled out of the picture. The compound remained in the center of the picture and continued to rotate in a clockwise direction, an illusion created by the counterclockwise orbit of the Predator.

"This is Youngblood Five-Oh." The crackling voice came over a wall-mounted speaker. "Off target with a good count. Target muj is in custody, I say again, target muj in custody."

There was a murmur of approval from the dozen or so other men in the small SEAL tactical operations center. Garrett picked up the handset on the table in front of him. As he did so, he glanced around and the room fell silent. "Roger, Youngblood, this is Tac Three. Hold you off target with a good count," he said into the handset, his voice amplified and filling the room from the speaker. "What is your ETA?"

The reply came after a short pause. "ETA two-five mikes at our home plate, over."

"Roger two-five. You will be met. Bravo Zulu, Youngblood. Tac Three out."

The call signs and pro-words were unnecessary as their state-of-the-art communications were hypersecure and reliable, but old procedures die hard. If nothing else, procedure made for clarity. Garrett returned the handset to the table and looked up to meet the eyes of their unit's intelligence officer.

"I'm on it, Master Chief," he said as he headed for the door. His voice was charged with excitement. He would collect one of the interrogators and two masters-at-arms for security, and meet the inbound helos. They would take charge of the muj, slang for mujahideen and a euphemism for an al-Qaeda operative, and escort him to the interrogation facility on the base. This night, they had scored big. This muj was an emir of one of the Mujahideen revolutionary councils, a senior al-Qaeda leader responsible for the surge in the al-Qaeda presence in southern Afghanistan. It was rare when they found one of these elusive leaders, and rarer still when they were able to take one alive. Just as rare, the operation had been a unilateral, US-only operation. Seldom did any American assault element go on a mission without a strong Afghan presence. Garrett Walker sat back in his chair, feeling the tension drain out of him. He'd been up for close to forty-eight hours.

The man seated next to him on a rusted folding chair was dressed like Walker—shorts, T-shirt, and running shoes. They looked as if they could be brothers, and in many ways, they were. Commander Jim Toohey was in charge of all SEAL and allied special operations in Kandahar and Helmand Provinces. He and Walker had been seaman recruits together and in the same SEAL training class. They had been assigned to the same team and SEAL platoon and had made their initial deployment together. Toohey, like many talented enlisted SEALs, had qualified for the Navy's Seaman to Admiral Program. This took him out of the teams for three years while he earned a college degree and became a commissioned officer. Now he was commanding officer of SEAL Team Five. Garrett Walker had been to college and had been offered the way to a commission, but he had elected to remain in the enlisted ranks. When Garrett had been promoted to master chief petty officer, the Navy's top enlisted rank, Toohey had sought him out to be Team Five's master chief petty officer—the command's command master chief and senior enlisted advisor. Now they were back together, and together they led SEAL Team Five in what both knew were the waning days in Afghanistan.

Toohey had two bottles of water and handed Garrett one of them. "Good operation, Tag. This was one dude that al-Qaeda did not want to see us bring in."

"The platoon did a nice job," Garrett replied as he brought the bottle from his lips, "and we can credit the intelligence section for this one. They've been tracking that muj for several months, and they finally nailed him."

Walker and Toohey sat in companionable silence in the nearly deserted operations center. Garrett Walker had joined the Navy after two years of college. He acquired the name Tag Walker during his short college football career at the University of Michigan. He was a defensive back and a vicious hitter. Midway through his freshman year, the strong safety who played ahead of him pulled a muscle, and Garrett started in his place for the Ohio State game. State had a gifted all-American receiver who immediately went to work on Garrett. During his first defensive series, the Ohio State wideout burned him twice, once deep and once short. He then began taunting Garrett across the line of scrimmage, calling him an Arkansas hayseed. On the following series, the State receiver leaped to catch a quick pass in the flat. As he smoothly turned to sprint upfield, Garrett met him running full speed and almost cut him in half. The sound of the collision echoed across the stadium. As the hundred-thousand-plus fans fell silent, the two men lay motionless on the field. After a moment, Garrett was up and back in the defensive huddle; the Ohio State receiver had to be carried from the field with a serious concussion and a broken femur. Garrett was then overheard to say, "I only tagged him," and the name stuck. Garrett sustained a partially separated shoulder from the encounter, but he continued to play the rest of the game.

"The intel section certainly did a helluva job finding this guy, but it was on your hunch that we went after him tonight," Toohey said, "and it was a good call." Garrett shrugged imperceptibly. "You could have gone with them tonight. Why didn't you?"

Garrett again shrugged. Both he and Toohey would occasionally go on missions with the operational platoons, but it was more to keep their hand in the game than assume a leadership role. Between the two of them, they had both led countless combat operations. When they did go into the field, they were almost religious about keeping themselves with the support element or a blocking force. They were seldom part of the assault element. The platoon officer in charge or the platoon chief led the SEAL platoons in combat. Neither Toohey nor Walker wanted to usurp this leadership, or be tempted to do so. Both knew and understood the opium-like attraction of leading men in combat, so when they did go on a mission, they made it a point to stay well in the background. And with the focus on training Afghans and away from unilateral direct-action missions, it was good for the younger leaders to get this experience.

"I thought about it," Garrett replied, "but Lieutenant Burke and Chief Kaplan were on top of this one. They have a handle on all of them, but this mission especially. This one's gonna really get noticed." The muj they were bringing in was the senior al-Qaeda leader in Kandahar Province; his capture will deal a serious blow to the enemy's attempts to reassert control in the region.

"True enough," Toohey admitted. With neither he nor his master chief on the operation, all the credit for capturing this insurgent leader would fall to the platoon and the platoon leadership. "So no hard feelings, then? About any of it?"

Garrett Walker glanced at his commanding officer and saw Toohey looking at him soberly. A senior SEAL operator like

Garrett Walker had some control over his operational destiny, especially with the war on terror still in full swing. If he had chosen, he could have remained in operational rotation, and his deployment activity would have been largely behind-the-gun work. He would still be out leading combat operations—killing bad guys. His reputation as a premier combat SEAL was well established. Any operational command would welcome him in this role, including the super-secret special-missions units. When he accepted the job as the SEAL Team Five command master chief, he became management. His job became that of preparing others for the fight—grooming other SEALs for combat leadership. It was challenging work, but not the same as putting your own gun in the fight. Garrett had not come to this easily, and probably would not have taken the job without his friend's urging. *And just maybe I wouldn't have taken it if Don hadn't been killed in action last year*. But in his heart, he knew it was time to give back, to help others put their guns in the fight. He was silent a long moment, then turned to Toohey.

"It's okay, Jim, really. I'm not going to say I don't miss being out there on patrol. God knows I miss the rush that comes from kicking in some dirtbag's door. And who knows, I may want to go back to that in the future. For now, this is good. The new guys are terrific. They're on their game, and they're getting better with each operation." He put a hand on Toohey's shoulder. "So it's okay. I'm fine with it." He rose and drained his water. "I think I'll go meet those inbound helos. The guys deserve a good 'attaboy' for this night's work."

Toohey was tempted to join him but refrained. The command master chief's presence would do; he represented the command as much as Toohey did, and it was the one small compensation of those who sent others into combat. Walker would make it a point to shake the hand of each platoon SEAL. And Commander Jim

Toohey knew that when Garrett Walker shook a brother SEAL's hand and said, "Well done," it was something special.

Toohey rose. "Thanks, Tag, for everything. I better get a message off to the general. He'll want to know who we got and all the details. RHIP." As Toohey knew and Garrett Walker was learning, RHIP did not mean "Rank hath its privilege;" it meant "Rank hath its paperwork."

"Roger that, sir. I'll get a quick debrief from Burke and Kaplan and be in to see if you need anything."

Toohey headed for his office and Walker for the helo pad.

By late morning, the Kandahar special operations base was quiet. There was a watch-keeping staff at the tactical operations center, but most of the SEALs and operations support staff were asleep. Since the majority of special operations missions were carried out at night, they slept days—vampire hours, as they call them. The SEAL billets at the camp were large military-style tents with wood flooring. The bunks were two-tiered and aligned along each wall of the tent. Between each bunk were footlockers stacked with operation gear. Most bunks had an M4 rifle close by. Muted red lighting above the curtained doorways at either end of each tent gave the rows of bunks, with their blanketed forms, the appearance of a Martian larvae chamber. An occasional snore rose over the hum of the external air-conditioning units that piped in cool air.

On the top rack near one of zippered tent flaps, a single dark form was noticeably more restless than the others. Garrett rolled from one side to the other within the confines of the thin single mattress, and finally onto his stomach. He remained perfectly still for some time. Suddenly, his whole body jerked, and he moaned softly as he rolled to one side to draw his knees up to his chest. For a time, he suffered in silence until the pain became too intense.

"Ugh! God … Almighty!"

He lay awake for several moments, trying to come to terms with the pain that came in mounting waves. When he sensed there was a remission coming, he readied himself, then swung down to the wooden deck. In spite of the pain and his size, he moved like a cat. Garrett stood erect for a moment, hands on hips, basking in the red shadows. Suddenly, he grasped the small of his back with both hands and dropped to one knee. The pain seared him as if an unseen hand were opening his side with a hot knife. Garrett Walker was in intense pain.

Garrett was lean but well built, clad in black undershorts and olive-drab T-shirt, with close-cropped hair. His wide shoulders melted to a surprisingly small waist. The shirt had dark splotches from his sweat. Through the thin cotton fabric, the muscles in his back rippled and contracted with the surges of pain.

"Jesus H. Christ!" he said through clenched teeth.

"You all right, Master Chief?" a voice called from one of the tiered cocoons.

"Yeah, I'm okay." He rose shakily and steadied himself with one hand on the bunk frame. But he was not okay; he hung his head as the pain carved furrows in his dark features. "Probably just some indigestion from the slop they serve us at the chow hall."

The voice grunted in reply and rolled over. With some difficulty, he took a folded pair of camouflage trousers from under his mattress. He pulled them on quickly while his feet found the shower thongs on the floor. All the while, he continued to curse the pain under his breath. He then quietly made his way to the exit and slipped out of the tent.

Garrett Walker stepped into the searing sunlight. The dry heat gathered around him like a blanket. He blinked for a moment, then made his way along the rocky pathway to the head—a modular shower and toilet facility identical to the hundreds of others found on American bases across Afghanistan. Inside, he found a sink and began to scoop handfuls of cool water onto his face and back of his neck. The pain was still with him, but now it was a heavy, throbbing ache. He pushed himself erect and stared at the lined face in the mirror. There was a hardness to the features that spawned a hawklike countenance. A light stubble coated the bottom half of the face, and the brown hair was cut short, military style, with a slight part on the left side. It was the *same face* as Brandon Walker's—his brother's face, an angular, chiseled face, yet with no hint of softness.

The pain began to subside but did not entirely dissipate. He reached behind him and tentatively massaged the area of his kidneys. It still hurt, but was not sensitive to his touch. Over the years, Garrett had suffered his share of injuries and broken bones, but nothing like this. *What the hell is happening to me?* He stumbled from the head and out into the midday heat and walked slowly across the compound toward the operations center. They always had a pot of coffee on.

"You're up early, Master Chief," the watch officer said conversationally as Garrett busied himself at the urn.

"Yeah, I know. Couldn't sleep."

"The guys did a great job last night. Looks like the muj they picked up may be a candidate for Club Cuba," he said, referring to the detention facility at Guantánamo Bay. Then, seeing Garrett's twisted features, he asked, "Are you all right?"

"I'm not sure. I woke up with this pain in my side, like someone shoved an ice pick between my ribs. Strangest damn thing, but it's almost gone now."

Garrett made his way to the office he shared with Commander Jim Toohey. The commander was at his desk hunched over his computer. He glanced up at his command master chief as Garrett slouched into the chair at his desk.

"You don't look so good, Tag. Something wrong?"

Garrett shivered as he shifted in his seat. For reasons he couldn't explain, he was experiencing waves of dull pain and coldness. He mentally shook them off. These were things he was trained to deal with. SEAL training was all about pain and cold water. SEAL operations were often painful and cold. For men like Garrett Walker, it was a way of life.

"Getting old, Jim. That and too much inactivity. Need any help with that after-action report?"

Slowly, his mind rose from the fog, a fog so thick and smooth it was like he had just surfaced in a cauldron of dry ice. Brandon Walker sensed that he was awake, yet he didn't seem to have the ability to move; he could see nothing, feel nothing. There was a sound—a ringing that seemed to go on forever, then it would stop and leave him alone. Since all he could do was listen, he concentrated very hard, straining for the slightest noise. For long periods of time, there was no sound at all. *Is this a dream?* he wondered. *Where is my body? Or am I insane?* For some reason, he was sure that his body was with him. *But if my body is here, why can't I feel it; why can't I move?* He was confused and frightened, almost to the point of panic. *What has happened to me? Was I in an accident?*

Then the ringing began again. *There has to be a way I can get to that ringing, find out what it is,* he thought, but again he could see nothing, feel nothing. *I have only my mind and my hearing. I have to try to remember ... where am I, what was I doing before this?* But before an answer came, he dipped back into the fog, and rational thought again eluded him. Suddenly, he was back in grade school, where he used to amaze his classmates with his ability to wiggle his ears. The image brought a smile to his face—and a realization. *I can smile; I can move the corners of my mouth!*

Slowly, Brandon Walker began to shed the sluggish, muddled world that held him prisoner. He methodically began to take charge of his mind, then his body. He felt his ears wiggle, which brought another smile. With some difficulty, he moved his eyebrows. Then he forced his tongue to move, and, finally, to pry apart his dry, encrusted lips. With the strength normally reserved for someone lifting a refrigerator, he managed to open one eye, then the other. They were heavy and matted, but he could see a faint strip of light above him. *If only I could move my hands, I could wipe my eyes and see better.* He almost drifted back into the fog, but then the ringing began again. Somehow he knew he had to get to that ringing. It was a shrill sound, too shrill for a telephone—or was it? With all his might, he tried to move, but nothing happened; he was numb. *I've got to get my bearings, see where I am.* His eyelids were so heavy that it took all his energy and concentration to keep them from closing. He had an overwhelming fear that if he let his eyelids close it would be over for him, that the fog would claim him forever.

Brandon wrestled with his rational mind and his overwhelming fear. The reality of his situation was beginning to take hold. This wasn't some kind of an awful dream, it was real, a living nightmare, and he was fighting for his life. He knew then that he must not give in to the comfortable white cloud that wanted him back. A sensation of intense cold seemed to close in and grasp him. Some unknown force from the fog called softly to him and began to reclaim his mind and weaken his spirit.

I can't give in to it, he thought. *I simply can't. I don't know how I got here, but I'm not going to go easily. I've got to fight!* He forced his eyes to move to the right, then the left. He could detect light to his left and willed his head to move toward it. Then he saw it! Through blurred slits, he could make out his arm lying outstretched on a bed. It was an unfamiliar bed, but he was thrilled to visually connect with his own body, if only to confirm that some physical part of him was really there. He was making progress, and this gave him a sudden, pleasing surge of hope.

Okay, he thought, *one thing at a time.* He focused on his hand; it seemed so far away. Again he discovered that it took time and all his concentration, but finally he moved a finger, then two. *I can move my hand, but I can't feel it.* A thousand questions crowded his mind, but he swept them aside, focusing only on moving his unfeeling hand. *Move the hand; make the arm move.* It took several minutes, which seemed like hours to Brandon Walker, to bring his hands to his face. He was able to make them clumsily brush about his eyes, but he still could feel neither fingers nor eyes. In frustration, he slid a finger to his mouth, biting down as hard as he could. Tears of relief squeezed from the corners of his eyes as he finally felt a twinge of pain. *That confirms it—I'm alive!* He allowed himself a moment to savor this triumph, after which he again wondered, *If I'm alive and this is not a dream, how did I get this way?*

The questions started again. *Was I in an accident? Am I paralyzed? Where's Cathy? Why isn't she here with me?* He was baffled and becoming very weary. Yet as he lay motionless, his mind wandering, he realized that the room had become lighter. A single shaft of daylight now knifed through a part in the drapes to weakly illuminate the room. *Is it morning?* He suddenly remembered that it should be night. He had been watching TV in his room. Yes, that's right, his room! He was at the Desert Flower, at a convention with MedaSystems—four new orders! *I'm still in Las Vegas!* He rolled his head to the left and made out the TV remote lying near him on the bed. It was easier this time to get his arm to move and reach for the controller. He began to fumble with it, searching for the right button until finally the TV was on, illuminating the room. Suddenly, he could make out more of his surroundings—desk, chair, mirror.

"Yeth!" he gulped in triumph, surprised that he had just spoken.

He turned his head toward the other side of the room and eyed the telephone. It sat perched on the edge of the bed. *Why the edge of the bed?* He didn't remember placing it there, but then he didn't remember a lot of things. It seemed so near, yet, in his current condition, it might well have been a continent away. He tried for it anyway. It was then that he saw that his right hand was mangled and that his little finger extended from his palm at a very odd angle. *That's strange; it should hurt but it doesn't.* He reached again for the phone, but his deformed hand functioned more like a club. On the third try, he watched in horror has the receiver disappeared over the side of the bed.

"Shit!" He dropped his arm back down onto the bed, utterly defeated. He needed several minutes to recover. As he considered his next move, the ringing began again, yet different. It was a shrill, insistent sound, almost a frantic purring. This time it was obvious that it didn't come from the telephone nearby. *Ringing, but not from the telephone?* The ringing had long stopped by the time he figured it out. Somewhere close by was his briefcase, which contained his cell phone. *Who's trying to reach me? Was it Cathy? Is she looking for me?* He was feeling desperate and terribly alone. *I've got to let someone know that I'm here, that I'm alive!*

The telephone ... it's my only link to the outside, my only chance. He attempted to roll over or throw his left arm over his chest but soon found out that he still didn't have control over his body. He was, however, becoming aware of a painful throb in what used to be his right hand. *It's now or never*, he thought, as he again forced his right arm across the bed. With his mangled hand, he cupped the base of the telephone and dragged it slowly to his side. The cord, stretching under the weight of the receiver, recoiled at the last moment, hoisting the receiver over the edge of the bed. Gaining confidence, he managed to maneuver the handset up to his ear. With his last bit of strength, he managed to reach his left hand across his body and felt his way around the keypad. Again his mind raced. *Who should I call? I'm feeling pain, so I know I'm hurt ... Call Cathy, but what if I can't reach her ... I need medical help! Hotel room—need to dial nine-one-one.* He found the 9 key, pushed it, and was rewarded with the outside dial tone. Then, with weak and shaky fingers, he carefully tapped 9-1-1.

"Nine-one-one. Please state your emergency." He was so overcome with relief that he almost dropped the receiver. "Is someone there? What is your emergency?"

"Yes … yes! I'm in trouble … I'm paralyzed. I need help!"

"Please speak up, sir. I can hardly hear you."

His mouth was thick, like he had just come from the dentist. "I need help. Please, help me!"

The voice on the other end was businesslike but skeptical. "All right, sir, but you'll have state your emergency before I can help you."

Brandon pressed his head tight against the receiver; tears flowed from his eyes, running down his cheeks and into his ears.

"I've … been in some sort of an accident. I can't move."

"All right, sir. Where are you right now?"

"In Las Vegas, in a hotel."

There was a patient sigh. "Sir, you'll have to be more specific. What hotel?"

"Ah, the Desert Flower, room six twenty-one."

"All right, room six twenty-one. Have you tried calling the hotel desk?"

"Look, I'm hurt—bad." He wanted to crawl down the phone line and strangle the woman. "The fucking ads say dial nine-one-one. I dialed nine-one-one!" Then, in a softer, more desperate voice, he added, "You have to believe me, I need help. I think I'm dying."

"All right, sir, just calm down." The operator was starting to believe something was wrong, but what? Stroke, heart attack, a mugging, a drug overdose, way too much to drink? "Can you tell me what's wrong?"

Brandon wanted to curse the patronizing voice, but he knew he had to make her understand. The rage and frustration enabled him for the first time to raise his head. What he saw frightened and puzzled him.

"I'm … uh, lying on my back on the bed, and I've been drugged or something. I can't move. My hand has been hurt—crushed. I seem to be lying on plastic bags … looks like bags of ice, everything seems to be wet . . ." His head dropped heavily back to the mattress, and he clutched the phone for his life. "I don't know what's happening, but the bedspread is soaked red. I must be bleeding."

"Did you say "ice"?" The contemptuous edge to her voice was now gone; she suddenly became deadly serious.

"It makes no sense," Brandon said almost to himself, then to the phone, "but it's the truth."

"All right, now, listen carefully. I want you to do something for me."

"I'll try."

"First, give me your name."

"Walker. Brandon Walker."

"Okay, Brandon, I want you to very carefully feel along your side and the small of your back. Are you able to do that for me?"

Why don't you ask me to fly? he thought. To the operator, he again said, "I'll try."

His left hand responded better than he expected, moving on command. He could now feel shafts of pain in his back, and he was aware of an incessant stomachache and nausea. And he was beginning to feel the cold. Cradling the phone in his mashed right hand and shoulder, he ran his left hand down along his side. His fingers passed over a wet, slimy flap that he couldn't immediately identify. Rolling slightly, he followed it carefully until he came to a small piece of metal, then another. That was enough; he now knew that the flap of skin was an entry wound. The nausea now almost overwhelmed him. He recovered from his shock and pressed the phone to his ear with both hands, almost losing it as his left hand was slick with blood.

"There's a long cut in my side, and it's bleeding." He paused to catch his breath, suddenly feeling very spent. "There are metal clips holding it together. You've got to believe me. I … I need help."

"Okay, Brandon, I believe you. Help is on the way." The voice had now gone from serious to sympathetic. "Now I want you to hang in there, Brandon, and keep talking to me."

Brandon started to speak but nothing came out. He thought he could hear the 911 operator talking frantically to someone else. The room was starting to spin, and his right hand continued to throb relentlessly. The pain that had been his ally was becoming unbearable. Suddenly, he was again aware that he was very, very cold and on the verge of slipping back into the white, foggy cauldron from which he had struggled so hard to escape. *Is it going to end like this? God, don't let this be happening. What did I do? Why is this happening to me?*

"Brandon, are you still there? Talk to me, Brandon."

Cathy … I should have called Cathy.

"Brandon, please talk to me … Brandon . . ." The voice trailed off as the phone slid from his hand.

Ten minutes later, an anxious hotel security man opened the door and a team of paramedics in blue overalls rushed into Brandon's room.

"Mother of God," said the team leader softly. She quickly checked that he was breathing, holding a stethoscope to his chest to listen to his heart. Then she snapped on a pair of latex gloves and moved to his side. Brandon was bare to the waist, his pants undone and loose around his hips. The dark, pleated suit trousers clung to him, soaked with blood and urine. His hair glistened with sweat and lay matted on the dirty sheets. There was an alabaster cast to his skin that was in sharp contrast to his blue lips and nipples. Gently, she rolled him partially onto his side and saw the long incisions. Her eyes widened as she inspected the metal clips holding the sections of skin together. She pulled the wet, half-empty bags of ice from under him and again eased him onto his back. The bed was a soggy shade of pink from the blood and water. Moving to his face, she pried back an eyelid and stabbed at it with her penlight. Quickly, she stepped back.

"Let's move. Get a large-bore IV with saline going, full flow, and let's get him on oxygen. Then we're gonna logroll him to his belly and move him very carefully. I want that gurney right here and lowered to the level of the bed. Let's move, people." She watched while the others worked, talking to the hospital on her cell phone. "All right, get that thermal blanket around him ... good, now let's move him! Easy now, be careful!"

Brandon only sensed the commotion around him. He thought he heard voices, and then there was a bright flash. Vaguely, he knew that he was being handled. More commotion, more noise, more movement. Then a prolonged wailing. *I'm sorry, Cathy. I'm so sorry. I should have called you.*

A man in a blue blazer stood at the elaborate portico of the Desert Flower and watched the ambulance speed away. He had a Motorola transceiver in his hand and a small earphone tucked in one ear. A throng of early morning gamblers and a few joggers stood around the door and on the steps to watch.

"Everything's under control, folks," he called to the onlookers. "Just a mild heart attack. He's going to be just fine. That's right, only a mild heart attack. Everything's okay." The small crowd dispersed quickly, anxious to get back to the gaming tables and slots. The man in the blazer spoke quietly into the Motorola.

The morning sun was just peeking over the Black Mountains when the small corporate twin, flying low across the desert, banked sharply to line up on the packed dirt strip. At the last moment, the gear snapped down, and the little aircraft dropped neatly to the ground. The seldom-used strip near the old mining town of Alunite, Nevada, occasionally saw duty as an emergency field or for a bush pilot practicing his back-country technique. This morning, it was deserted. The pilot applied the brakes carefully, but he still used the entire length of the strip. The plane did a tight pirouette and faced back the way it had come. One engine jerked to a stop while the other continued to idle smoothly. A young man in a fashionably shabby leather jacket opened the boarding hatch and peered out. He lowered the steps fully and dropped easily to the ground. After a moment, he walked along the trailing edge of the wing to the tip. There he paused, lit a cigarette, and waited.

Hidden in the sage and scrub, an old Cadillac DeVille stood by, the two men inside intently watching the man with the cigarette. It was an older-model car, and the paint was dulled by the desert sun. The driver let the man smoke for several moments, then flashed his lights very briefly. The man by the wingtip crushed his cigarette and immediately lit another. The door of the Caddy gave a metallic groan as the driver heaved it open. A large man emerged from the driver's seat and walked around to the trunk. He removed a bulky Coleman-like ice chest. It was not a light container, but he handled it easily.

"Wait here. Not to leave until we have taken off, understand?"

The second man nodded nervously and slid over behind the wheel. The big man set off for the aircraft.

The pilot met him, and they nodded without speaking. They walked to the open hatchway together. The pilot helped the big man crowd through the small opening, then handed up the cooler. He then scrambled aboard and secured the hatch as the larger man strapped the small ice chest to the metal deck. The pilot quickly regained his seat in the cockpit while his new passenger wedged himself into the copilot's space. Neither man acknowledged the other or said a word. A moment later, the still engine coughed to life. The pilot immediately ran both engines to full power, sending up a rooster tail of dust behind him. He released the brakes, and the aircraft lurched forward. About halfway down the strip, the little plane leaped into the air, crabbed into the slight crosswind, and took in its gear, gathering speed but not altitude.

The sun was now full up, but the shadows were still long. The man who remained in the Cadillac watched until the aircraft merged with the horizon. Only then did he take the envelope from his inside jacket pocket and quickly count the money. He was an older, seedy-looking man who looked no less miserable now than he had in Brandon Walker's hotel room. With a trembling hand, he pushed the envelope back into his jacket. With the other, he found a flask in his side pocket and hoisted it to his lips. He drank greedily as two rivulets escaped and circled his chin from either side. When he had drained it, he tossed the empty flask onto the passenger's seat. He then swung the big car around in a spray of dust and gravel and headed back up the dirt road that eventually led to Highway 93.

Las Vegas Memorial Hospital was only a short distance from Interstate 15 making traffic from the Strip easily accessible. It saw just about everything, from gunshot wounds to attempted suicides to cancer. The hospital also had an expansive wing dedicated to cardiac care, well endowed by the casino owners. Elderly, overweight Americans contributed a significant amount of revenue to the City of Las Vegas. While they gambled, they also drank a lot and consumed large quantities of rich food. Those who watched the percentages and counted the money knew it was bad for business if too many of them left Las Vegas feet first. So Las Vegas Memorial provided first-class medical care, good enough to get most of the out-of-towners home again. The circular drive that served the hospital's main entrance had a certain hotel-like quality to it; one almost expected to see a row of slots inside the automatic sliding-glass doors.

On the evening following Brandon Walker's ambulance ride from the Desert Flower Inn, an airport taxi swung up to the hospital entrance and delivered a very distraught woman. Her single travel bag rode on a strap off her shoulder. She stepped quickly to the entrance, paused a moment inside the doors, and then made straight for the reception desk, dodging several ficus trees and a large saltwater aquarium.

She was a tall woman with dark eyes and rich auburn hair. Her features were soft and regular, with high cheekbones that gave her a somewhat regal appearance. She eased her bag to the rich parquet floor and cleared her throat to speak. Behind the reception desk, an elderly woman, with a phone wedged between her shoulder and ear, raised her hand. The patch on the shoulder of her gray smock said she was a senior volunteer.

"I'll be with you in a moment," she said with a patient smile. "I'm holding for someone."

The younger woman responded in a well-modulated voice, but she was clearly struggling for control. "And I'll scream at the top of my lungs if you don't help me now—right this instant."

The older woman lowered the phone. She started to protest, but the woman standing in front of the desk had the look of someone who would not be easily put off.

"Well, then, if you must, Miss … ?"

"Walker. Mrs. Catherine Walker. My husband, Brandon Walker, was brought here sometime early this morning, and I understand he is in intensive care. I'd like to see him," she said, glancing at the gold name tag on the smock. "And, Mrs. Romano, I'd like to see him as soon as possible."

"Well, then, yes, let me see." She put down the phone and began to peck at the keyboard on her desk. "Ah, we have him—I mean, he's here. He's in the ICU on Four West."

There was a pause. "Four West?"

"Oh, down the hall to the right, I mean, your left, and take the first set of elevators. Go to the fourth floor. There's a nurses' station right when you get off the elevator. They'll be able to help you."

"Thank you, Mrs. Romano." She slung her bag over her shoulder and hurried down the corridor. The elevator was busy, so she pushed her way into the adjacent stairway and began taking the steps two at a time.

While the lobby was all show, Four West was strictly business. An imposing, tall-sided nurses' station was flanked by a large waiting area off to one side and a small chapel on the other. It was a sterile setting with lots of chrome and a strong smell of alcohol. Catherine Walker hurried across the highly polished vinyl to the nurses' station. Before she could speak, a nurse in green surgery garb and a hairnet rose to meet her.

"Mrs. Walker?"

"That's right." She paused to catch her breath. "I'm here to see my husband."

The nurse studied her for a second, then opened the hinged docket so she could step through and down from the raised station. She guided her over to the waiting area.

"Mrs. Walker, your husband is resting comfortably and doing just fine. But he's still in intensive care, and it'll be a few minutes before we can get you in to see him." Catherine started to speak, but the nurse placed a hand on her arm. It was a caring gesture, but it also carried authority. "I know you have a lot of questions and you need answers. When I heard you were coming, I notified your husband's doctor, and he'll be right out to see you. I know it's difficult to be told to wait, especially when you've rushed to get here, but that's what we're asking. Dr. Ward is one of our finest surgeons, and he'll be with you very shortly."

Catherine Walker stared at her, suddenly no longer in a hurry. *Intensive care, resting comfortably, a surgeon—my God, what is happening?* Since the telephone call early that morning notifying her that Brandon was in some kind of accident, she had barely been able to control her panic. Realizing there was nothing she could do but to get to Brandon as quickly as possible, she had focused all her energy to that end. Getting someone to come sit with the kids, then a quick pack, the race to the airport—she had been consumed by activity. During the short flight, she had gone on line trying to find out more. Now the race was over. She was here, and, suddenly, she began to fear the worst.

"Can I get you anything?"

"A cup of tea would be very nice," she replied, adding, "and thank you for your kindness."

A few moments later, she clutched a Styrofoam cup, trying to warm hands that had suddenly gone cold. When she raised her head, a young man in a shabby white hospital coat, who didn't look old enough to be an intern, let alone a doctor, was standing next to her.

"Mrs. Walker?"

"Yes." She rose, quickly setting the tea on the side table for fear she would spill it.

"Please, have a seat. I'm Chris Ward, your husband's doctor. I'm glad you could get here so quickly." Ward was tall and wiry and had an agreeable slouch. He wore clear-framed glasses. His red-brown hair was longish and neatly combed. He had a sparse mustache, probably there to make him look older, but it accomplished little in that regard. She studied him for a moment. Behind the glasses, she saw mild blue eyes that were both intelligent and kind—and very tired. She lowered back into her seat and never took her eyes from his.

"Doctor, what's going on? How is my husband?"

Ward tugged the fine hair at the corner of his mouth and furrowed his brow. He looked away momentarily, then met Cathy's intense gaze. "Your husband was brought in about seven thirty this morning. He was in pretty bad shape. We were in surgery for just under three hours, and, for the most part, we made progress—good progress. He's stable now and gaining ground. Another few hours and we may not have been so lucky. He'll be completely free of the anesthesia soon, and we'll begin treatments immediately. It won't be easy at first, but it's something we can deal with. A great deal of progress has been made in … Mrs. Walker, are you all right?"

Catherine Walker was unaware that she was holding her breath. A single tear had brimmed over from her right eye and run down her cheek. She had also been squeezing her nails into her palms, hoping the pain would keep her from screaming. All she knew was that she couldn't take much more of this.

"Please, Doctor! Just what exactly is wrong with my husband? Will someone please tell me?" Her voice rose, and several visitors and staff in the immediate area stopped to stare.

"You weren't told?" Ward asked. The look on her face told him she wasn't. "I'm so very sorry," he said softly, "I thought someone would have informed you by now. Your husband has lost both his kidneys."

"Oh my God!" Her hands shot up to her face, and the dark eyes widened in sheer terror. Then she closed them tightly and began to rock slowly in her seat.

"I'm sorry you had to find out like this; I thought someone would have told you before now. I just …" Ward shrugged helplessly. "Well, I'm very sorry. I thought you knew."

For several moments, she just sat there, her eyes closed, her mouth and nose buried in her hands. Suddenly, she stopped rocking and her breathing became even. She took her hands from her face and opened her eyes. It was a forced composure, but she was back in control. She was the same woman who'd stormed into the lobby twenty minutes earlier.

"Dr. Ward, I think you had better tell me everything that has happened to my husband since he came into your hospital. And please, start from the beginning."

Ward hadn't been out of surgical residency all that long. He was basically a technician, and a very good one. But he had quickly developed another faculty, perhaps more rare in his calling than his unusual ability in the operating room. He had learned to read the families of his patients—to separate the strong from the weak, the assertive from the meek. Many talented physicians practiced their whole lives and never learned this useful skill.

"Mrs. Walker," Ward began. "Catherine?"

"It's Cathy."

He nodded. "Okay, Cathy. Brandon was brought in here this morning with two large incisions across his back. They had been hastily closed with metal sutures—staples, if you will. He'd lost a lot of blood. He was somehow drugged while in his hotel room and"—a look of disgust passed across his face—"in a very crude surgical procedure, his kidneys were removed—both of them. I was just finishing an emergency appendectomy when they brought him in. He needed immediate attention, so I scrubbed and we went right into surgery. I spent a good part of the morning trimming and sewing tissue, repairing the vessels as best I could. He has good blood flow now and, hopefully, no internal bleeding. He appeared to be very fit so that was ... is ... in his favor. For the moment, he's stable. We've had to replace a great deal of his blood, but that blood will have to be treated through dialysis on a regular basis." He paused and watched her carefully a moment. "Cathy, are you with me? Do you understand what I've said so far?"

A shudder passed through her and she nodded grimly. "I think I understand. But why? W-why would someone"—she paused and closed her eyes, suddenly nauseous at the thought—"why would someone take a person's kidneys? I don't understand. And why Brandon's kidneys?"

"That's another issue." Ward ran his tongue across the skirt of his mustache. "You see," he said, carefully phrasing his words, "there's a demand, a very legitimate demand, for donor organs. The laws that govern organ donation and organ transplant activity are very specific and very strict. But the number of needy recipients far outnumbers potential donors, so this creates a backlog—a waiting list."

"So someone got tired of waiting? Is that what you're telling me?"

Ward made a helpless gesture. "It's possible; anything's possible. I suppose—"

Before he could continue, a man in soiled linen slacks, sunglasses, and a sport shirt approached them. He was short, balding, overweight, and hurtling through middle age. A toothpick peeked from the corner of a broad mouth that curled down in a fixed, insolent smirk. The few remaining strands of black hair on top of his head were pulled straight back. He hadn't shaved in several days.

"Excuse me, ma'am. Are you Mrs. Brandon Walker?"

Neither Ward nor Cathy moved.

"Mrs. Walker, right?"

"That's right," she managed.

"Good. I have just a few questions. Just when did your husband arrive here in Las Vegas?"

"Uh, Wednesday evening. Why?"

"And he went straight to his hotel when he arrived?"

"Well, I suppose … but just a minute. Just who are you?"

The smirk deepened, and he lifted his shirttail to reveal a gold badge pinned to a leather belt flap. "Detective Rucko, Las Vegas PD. I got just a few more questions." He took out a small spiral notebook and began flipping over the pages, but he was watching her carefully. He'd done this before—caught those close to an injured loved one off guard while they were still in shock.

"Your husband here on business, ma'am?"

She and Ward exchanged questioning looks. Over at the nurses' station, another man dressed like Rucko, younger and only slightly neater, was talking to the charge nurse.

"He was here to attend a medical convention."

"At the Desert Flower?"

"That's right," she said defensively.

Rucko cleaned the inside of his ear with his pencil stub and pretended to study his notes. "You ever have any reason to think that your husband would take the opportunity, while he's at one of these conventions, to spend time with another woman?" He looked down at her. "Maybe just a quick, one-night kind of thing?"

Cathy stared at him, openmouthed. Ward had finally had enough. He rose and stepped in front of Rucko.

"Now look here, Detective, this isn't the time or the place for these kinds of questions. I'm going to have to ask you to leave." Rucko regarded him coolly. "Right now, Detective!" Ward added.

"Look, Doc, you got a job to do; I got a job to do. You got a problem with that? I'm trying to be a nice guy here. We can always go downtown, y'know."

Cathy Walker couldn't believe what she was hearing. A part of her wanted to curl up and cry. Another part of her wanted to take her bag and strike out at this sleaze of a cop. All her pent-up fear and frustration and pain were quickly coming to a head. She was about to explode when a large, heavy hand dropped onto Rucko's shoulder.

"Yeah, what?" Rucko snarled.

"Detective, could I please have a word with you—over there."

The speaker was everything Rucko wasn't. He was tall, fit, polite, and well dressed in a dark-gray tailored suit, white shirt, and black wingtips. His smooth, black face was cut by even white teeth and bracketed by a touch of gray at his temples.

Rucko jerked his toothpick from the sneer. "Hey, buddy, do you mind?" He showed his badge. "I'm busy here."

The man never took his eyes from Rucko while he pulled a credential from his inside suit pocket and flipped it open to reveal a badge and a picture ID. He spoke in a low rumble, "FBI, *buddy.* Now, could I please have a word with you—*over there!*"

Rucko started to argue, but the menacing dark eyes continued to bore into him. Near the nurses' station, another suit was engaged with Rucko's partner. The detective snorted and tossed the toothpick to the floor, but he moved away. The FBI man followed him to the other side of the waiting area. Ward and Cathy watched while they talked in hushed whispers. Rucko was extremely animated; the black man was impassive, saying very little.

"Shit," Rucko spat out, raising his voice. His face was beet red. "You fuckin' feds really take the cake." He stomped out of the waiting area, collected his partner, and headed for the elevators.

"Hello, Mrs. Walker ... Doctor. Sorry to intrude at a time like this. I'm Agent Ray Stannick with the FBI. That's my partner over there, Agent Bateman. I was sorry to learn of the injury to Mr. Walker. We have a considerable interest in what has happened to your husband, Mrs. Walker." He handed her a card. "Please give me a call when you feel your husband's sufficiently recovered. We would very much like to speak with him." Cathy took the card and stared at it. "Again, I'm sorry for the interruption. Ma'am ... Doctor."

Stannick and the other agent left. Cathy Walker looked at the card in her hand, now more concerned than ever.

The San Ramon Hospice Clinic was a small facility in a fashionable part of Oakland. The clinic's original intent was to help a limited number of wealthy patients through the last few weeks of life. More recently, it had found its niche as a plush recovery facility for surgery patients rushed out of the hospital a little too quickly in the opinion of some, usually their families who had to care for them at home. Part clinic, part assisted-care facility, it was built to support a large staff and cater to a small clientele—individuals who wanted more amenities than Medicare or normal insurance coverage allowed. It was a private facility that could provide extended medical services—and, in some cases, nonstandard medical procedures—for those who could pay. The clinic had not fared as well as the initial investors had hoped. New laws that restricted physicians from accepting payment for care in excess of Medicare limits had nearly sent the San Ramon Hospice Clinic into bankruptcy. So the facility was always receptive when a wealthy client had a special request or required a specific fee-for-service surgical procedure. It was part of a growing underground care industry that catered to wealthy patients. If the money was right, few questions were asked.

In a private room near the rear entrance of the clinic, a man lay in a hospital bed while a white-coated attendant hovered nearby. The patient was hooked to several IVs. A heart monitor that hung on the wall nearby beeped patiently while a series of steep, alpine blips marched across the scope. The room was generous with large windows and was adjoined by a comfortable waiting alcove, complete with overstuffed furniture, coffee table, and large-screen TV. Two men in sport coats and slacks sat across from each other playing cards at the table.

The smaller of the two, who was not really small, turned a card facedown on the deck head and played his hand on the glass tabletop in threes.

"Gin." He looked up and smiled at his opponent, a large, coarse man with moles on his nose and chin.

The larger man stared at the other's play and surveyed all the cards in his own hand. "Son of bitch. You more than just lucky. I think you a fuckin' cheat."

The smaller man laughed. "Ivan, you may be a tough guy, but you're sure a lousy cardplayer. Let's see what you got left in your hand." He attempted to see the other man's cards, but the big man threw them facedown on the table. "No matter," the smaller man said, again laughing gently at the big man. "I only need a few more points. Let's see, that makes three bottles of vodka you owe me so far, Ivan."

"And I tell you," the big man said menacingly, "name is Kuznetzkof."

"Yeah, yeah, I know. But who can say such a mouthful, eh? So I call you Ivan. So, what's the big deal?"

"I tell you again, name is not Ivan. Is Kuznetzkof. Boris Kuznetzkof."

"Hell, why didn't you just say so? Boris is easy. I can say Boris as easy as Ivan."

The oak-paneled door swung open to admit a man in a crisp white coat with a stethoscope draped around his neck. He was short and intense with rich dark skin that complemented his regular, East Asian features. His glossy, straight black hair was parted neatly just left of center. The two men rose, their game forgotten.

"Good evening, gentlemen," he said pleasantly in a precise, English public school accent.

With that, he walked past them and over to the patient and began to examine him. He took a clipboard from the attendant and studied it. Then he pulled the sheet down. The form in the bed was lying on his belly, well bolstered by a series of pillows. He had broad shoulders and an unruly mop of black hair. Patches of black hair scurried across his back. His head was turned to one side, and there was a tube running from his nose. The doctor clipped on his stethoscope and listened carefully for several minutes. Then he placed a blood-pressure cuff on the limp arm, inflated it, and listened again. He nodded to the attendant, who drew a sample of blood and hurried from the room with it. Finally, he closely examined the two long incisions that ran from the middle of the patient's back around to the side of his rib cage. The gashes followed shaved furrows in the black hair, painted yellow with disinfectant. They were stitched together in a meticulous, workmanlike fashion. After a thorough inspection, the doctor carefully pulled the sheet up over the incisions. Finished with his examination, he stood back with his hands thrust in the front pockets of his coat.

"How's he doin', Doc?" asked the smaller of the two cardplayers.

"He's doing quite well, actually. We've a few tests to run to be absolutely certain, but all signs are positive. He'll be awake in an hour or so, and we'll turn him on his back. You can then ask him yourself."

"That's good to hear, Doc." The small man stepped over by the bed to better see the man resting on his stomach. "Hang in there, boss," he said to the inert form. "We'll have you out of here before you know it."

The second man, the large one, had positioned himself by the door, hands folded across his large bulk. He was clearly impatient. The doctor carefully skirted him on his way out, but he paused in the doorway.

"None of my business, of course, but I did have one question."

"*Da*?"

"Why two kidneys? One would have been most sufficient."

The big man shrugged. "Arrangement asked for two. Perhaps he is most important person and requires this."

"I see," the doctor replied, but he really didn't. "Well, good day, then."

The first man turned from the patient's bedside. "Well, it looks like he's going to be okay."

"Then work here is finished. You will soon get us rest of fee? Is good business to pay promptly."

"Don't worry, pal. You'll get your money. And Ivan, to show you the kind of guy I am, let's forget about the vodka. I'm strictly a scotch drinker."

The gruff man gave him an even stare and left without another word.

It was another two hours before Cathy Walker was able to see her husband. She stood with Dr. Ward watching Brandon through a viewing port of the intensive care unit. He was lying faceup on a dimpled mattress that had been overlaid with layered cotton half sheets. While they watched, a team of nurses came in and lifted him carefully to remove one of the top sheets. It was lightly stained with blood and yellow Betadine solution. Cathy finally had to turn her head.

"We were able to do a reasonable job of repairing the incisions, but they'll weep like this for a while. It's very normal."

She turned back toward Brandon. Even though he was sleeping, he had a very drawn and tired look about him. He breathed rhythmically, mouth partly open. His normally rich brown hair was dull and drifted listlessly across his ears to the pillow. Two IV-type tubes led from his right arm to a machine about the size of a console TV resting on a stainless-steel cart. Periodically, a technician came by to monitor the dials and inspect the connections to both man and machine.

Suddenly, Brandon Walker's eyes blinked. They closed for a short time, then the eyelids slowly raised and remained open.

Cathy caught her breath. "Dr. Ward, can I go to him? Please!"

Admittance to the ICU was severely restricted; infection from the outside was a constant worry. The doctor hesitated. "I think we can make an exception," he replied. "Let's get you a gown."

Minutes later, Ward led Cathy into the ICU. She was swathed in an oversized green surgical gown with a matching shower-like cap. Ward was dressed in a more tailored set of greens. She went to her husband's side and took his left hand.

"Brandon … Brandon," she said softly. "My poor darling, can you hear me?"

He rolled his head to look at her. For a moment, there was no reaction. She was just another hovering green figure. Then his eyes widened in recognition.

"Cath ... Cathy." He swallowed, trying to gain control of his speech. "Is that you?"

"Oh, yes—yes, darling, I'm right here."

Ward took up a position on the other side of the bed. He took Brandon's other hand, the one that was enclosed in a large, white boxing glove. He was careful not to disturb the attachments as he began to take his pulse. Brandon just lay there, gazing at his wife. Finally, he managed a crooked smile.

"Nice outfit, but it's not your color."

She leaned forward and pressed her cheek to the top of his hand. A white nylon band was stapled securely about his wrist. Tears rolled down across his hand and fingers.

"I was going to call you, Cathy. I was about to, and then I got sick. There were people in the room, but I couldn't do anything about it." He again swallowed hard. "I couldn't move."

"Shhh, it's okay. I'm here now."

"It was you, wasn't it? You tried to call me—kept trying to call me."

She nodded. "Every half hour. I was so worried when you didn't phone. I even tried the cell phone several times. I felt desperate to reach you; I guess I somehow knew that something had happened."

He closed his eyes briefly. "You did reach me. I couldn't answer, but you did reach me. I wouldn't have made it without those calls. You helped to keep me going."

He reopened his eyes and began to search the room, trying to come to grips with where he now was and what had happened. He felt nauseous, and his head ached. There was little feeling in the rest of his body, like the attached parts belonged to someone else. For a moment, he felt as if he were floating above the bed, watching himself lying between the two green figures. His eyes fell on the white volleyball that was his right hand. He remembered the pain in his hand, but that was gone now. With a wave of nausea, he remembered his pinkie turned out at an obscene angle. Then he saw the rubber tubes that exited his arm. He followed them to the machine that sat gurgling at the foot of the bed, like some fiend in a science-fiction movie. Brandon Walker had been in the medical software business long enough to know a CAT scanner from an X-ray machine. He also knew what a dialysis machine was; he'd seen them attached to *other* people.

"What's that doing here?" he said with some trepidation. He spoke slowly but clearly. "What the hell is going on?" His eyes flashed toward Ward, who stood erect by the side of the bed. "What's happened to me, Doctor? I think you'd better tell me exactly what's going on."

Ward took in the determined expression on Brandon's face and the tortured one on Cathy's. He plunged ahead. "There was an incident at your hotel, Mr. Walker. More to the point, you were robbed. You were drugged in your hotel room, and the people who drugged you have taken your kidneys. I know this sounds very implausible, even insane, but that's what has happened. We've been able to repair most of the tissue damage and repair the blood vessels in the area, but you are still a man with no kidneys."

"Both of them?" Brandon managed.

"Both of them."

Brandon closed his eyes, squeezing them tightly, and shook his head slowly in disbelief. When he opened them, Ward's expression had not changed, and the vile machine still sat bubbling at the end of the bed. He turned toward Cathy.

"Dear God, I can't believe this is happening—to me, to us."

She quickly leaned over him and laid her cheek gently on his. "We'll get through this, darling," she whispered. "You'll see; we'll get through it." Then, in a louder voice, she said, "If we have a little patience, we will find another kidney for you. We'll find a donor, right, Doctor?" She gave Ward a pleading look.

Ward stared at the floor, arms folded across his chest. "There's more." He looked up and met their eyes. "Normally, finding a healthy donor or terminally ill patient with an acceptable organ would be an option. However, it seems that you have a very unusual tissue type and some rather unique antigens. To be candid, it may be very hard to find a donor with your genetic construction. I … I wish I could be more encouraging." Ward genuinely liked these two, and he was almost overwhelmed with compassion for them. He paused to collect himself before continuing. "Naturally, we will do our best, but I have to tell you that it could be very difficult."

"You mean impossible, don't you, Doctor?" Brandon said weakly, looking at the dialysis machine. "What you really mean is that fucking thing will be attached to me for the rest of my miserable life."

Ward held his ground. "No, finding a replacement organ is not impossible, just very difficult in this case. But to expect anything close to a full recovery, you will need a donor with an exact tissue match."

Brandon stared at Ward for a long moment, then at the ceiling. He knew something of the cost and attention full-dialysis patients required. He also knew they had serious quality-of-life restrictions and seldom lived more than a few years. And he knew the burden he would be to his family. He closed his eyes, suddenly unable to contemplate what had happened to him, the changes that he would now face. *What have I done to Cathy and the kids? What will their life be like with me in this condition?* Suddenly, he was very, very tired.

Cathy Walker rose from the bedside and turned to Dr. Ward. "I know someone who is an exact tissue match," she said quietly. "In fact, it's an identical match."

"What?" Ward replied.

"I said I know someone who is an exact match, someone who has the same tissue type as Brandon—same everything."

"Oh no," Brandon said with unusual vigor. "There's no way in hell I can do that."

Ward ignored him, suddenly curious. "You do? Is this person a—"

"No," Brandon shouted. "Absolutely not! I forbid it!"

One of the technicians moved in to restrain him as he was about to disengage the dialysis leads, but Brandon fell back, spent. Before he could mount another objection, the nurse took one of the IVs and advanced the plunger on the painkiller hypo an increment or two.

"No … No, I can't ask him … I can't …," he said weakly, his voice trailing off to nothing.

"No, Brandon darling, I guess you can't, or won't" she said softly, "but I can." But he didn't hear her. He had returned to the oblivion of the white enveloping fog.

That morning, Master Chief Garrett Walker had flown by helo from Kandahar to the small NATO outpost just north of the village of Marja and west of the Helmand capital of Lashkar Gar. Earlier that evening, he had joined the small convoy of up-armored Humvees for the journey farther west of the outpost to the objective. Now he had to make the call, and it was not an easy one. It was not a go-no-go decision. They were fairly certain the Taliban cell leader was in the compound, but they were uncertain as to just how many others were with him in his security element. The cell leader was important enough for them to try to take him alive, and it was just as important to take his computer intact. The platoon officer was a good one, on his third combat tour, and the SEAL platoon chief was solid. The SEAL platoon was a seasoned group. But this was going to be a tricky assault. Their informant was not as well vetted as they would like, and the nature of these hard-core Taliban holdouts had changed. They fought to the death. And there was the issue of the Afghans. The SEAL-trained

Afghan commandos were good on patrol and on an assault, but this would probably turn into a shootout.

Helmand Province in southern Afghanistan had seen some of the heaviest fighting and most determined resurgence of the Taliban and their al-Qaeda allies. Thanks to the coalition-trained Afghan army, they had largely been driven from the major cities and into the countryside. But this rousting of insurgents had a Darwinian effect. Those who survived and had gone into hiding were smart, tough, and prepared to die for the cause. Rooting them out was not child's play. At this stage of this long-running war, Garrett wasn't sure whether it would not be more advisable to simply put a five-hundred-pound precision bomb into the compound and sort through the rubble rather than trying to take it intact. But the decision had been made to assault the compound and to try to capture the cell leader, along with any intelligence information. Everything depended on the reliability of their informant and the assault team's two best friends: the element of surprise and violence of action. Only the first of these was in serious doubt.

Garrett's only real decision was whether he would lead the assault. Even though the platoon leader was a lieutenant and he was an enlisted man, as command master chief, he carried the authority of the team commanding officer. If he said he would lead the assault, then the lieutenant and his platoon would follow his orders—reluctantly, as a matter of team pride, but they were all veteran SEALs, and they understood his position. And it wasn't as if Garret Walker had to invoke the authority of his commanding officer. In the SEAL teams, reputation is everything. Few in the teams were more experienced and respected than Master Chief Walker.

He stepped around behind the trailing Humvee where the platoon assault element had gathered—Navy SEALs and Afghan commandos.

"You all set, Lieutenant?"

"Roger that, Master Chief."

"Good. You'll be leading this assault. The Afghan commando element will follow you in and swing off to one side and serve as your blocking force. I'll be here with the rest of the headquarters element and serve as your QRF as needed." He extended his hand to the lieutenant. "Good luck, sir."

"Thanks, Master Chief. Nice to have you in the wings on this one."

The SEALs seldom went into the field without the support of the Afghan army. This was usually a platoon of SEAL-trained Afghan commandos or scouts. They spoke the language, and when they were in the field with an American unit, they were pretty good fighters. Whenever possible, a SEAL assault team went into action with a quick-reaction force standing by if needed. Should the SEAL lieutenant and his platoon run into trouble, Garrett and a light squad of SEALs and Afghans would serve as the QRF and be ready to lend a hand.

The SEAL element and the Afghan squad patrolled over the berm toward the enemy compound. Garrett didn't have a good feeling about this one; it could get difficult. But he wasn't one to second-guess his decision. What made him reluctant to step in was the confidence he knew the SEALs had in their lieutenant and in themselves. Walker himself had been a platoon SEAL for the better part of the last fifteen years. He knew how he would feel if someone had stepped into the leadership of one of his platoons. And, he had to admit to himself, there was little he could do better than the SEAL warriors who were now closing in on the objective. Perhaps the bad feeling he now had was something to do with being left behind while others went into battle.

Garrett and the four other SEALs, two from this SEAL platoon and two from his headquarters element in Kandahar, were kitted-up and ready to roll. The five of them manned a single

Humvee—a driver, three passengers, and a SEAL on the .50-caliber machine gun in the turret. They sat in the vehicle with doors open and waited. Just behind them was a similarly configured Humvee with their Afgan commandos. There was nothing for them to do until the assault element made its move, but they had a good idea of what was happening. All had MBITR squad radios on same line-of-sight frequency. Garrett could tell from the cryptic transmissions, in what was said as well as in the emotion of the voices, that it wouldn't be long. Suddenly, there was a burst of automatic-weapons fire from over the shallow berm separating them from the objective, then other machine guns began to bark into the night.

"Let's go," Garrett called to his driver, and a moment later, they were lurching over the berm toward the enemy compound. He could tell from the fire that something was wrong. SEALs seldom fired their weapons on full automatic fire, and when they did, they were short, disciplined bursts. There were simply too many sustained automatic bursts. As they got closer, Garrett could distinguish the sharp crack of M4 carbines from the *pop-pop-pop* of AK-47s. The SEALs were slugging it out with someone. Garrett wanted to ask what was happening, but he knew better than to bother a SEAL leader in the middle of a firefight. The lieutenant would know he was coming and would direct his small quick-reaction force when and where needed.

"QRF, you there?"

"This is Walker. We're inbound—go."

"I have two men down, and we're pinned down between the compound wall and the main building. Blocking force also engaged. Can you come in at nine o'clock from the main entrance and engage the muj from that side, over?"

Garrett saw the compound and pointed for his driver to bear to the left of the structure. "Roger that, El-Tee. Be there in thirty seconds. Will engage from entrance to main building to the rear."

To the .50 gunner, he yelled, "Work the building front to back, both stories." To the other SEALs, he barked, "You two on me—let's go!"

Like most residential compounds, there was a six-foot cinder-block wall that surrounded a large mud-and-stucco central structure. Once the Humvee reached the front corner of the compound, the gunner opened up with his heavy machine gun and began to chew into the building with rhythmic three-to-five-round bursts. The Humvee turret was just tall enough to reach over the wall and give the gunner a good field of fire. He worked the second floor, where the muj shooters would be. Then he shifted fire to the first floor and back to the second. The heavy .50-caliber rounds might or might not be punching through the walls of the main building, but those inside would know there was something more than a rifle platoon in the fight. Garrett leaped from the front passenger seat and sprinted ahead of the Humvee, which was rolling slowly along the left side of the compound wall. He reached the back corner of the compound, where he had a clear field of fire for anyone escaping out the back.

"Charlie, Rick—grenades, as fast as you can," he yelled at the two SEALs who were now a few steps to his rear. "From over there, and make 'em count."

Both SEALs had M203 grenade launchers under their M4 rifles. There was a small rise some twenty meters behind them, a good position from which to fire their 40-mm grenades. Soon Garrett could hear a *tonk*, followed a few seconds later by a *crump* as the high-explosive grenades crashed into the building. The loud bark of the .50 caliber told him the heavy machine gun was still in action. Garrett himself took a position where he could cover his two grenadiers and watch for anyone who might come out the back of the compound. A heavy iron-barred gate guarded a break in the wall nearby. There was no cover to be had, so Garrett took a knee near the wall and waited. For the SEALs, the world was green-tinted daylight with searing white eruptions that marked muzzle flashes. They were all wearing state-of-the-art night vision devices. A few of the muj had NVDs, but not many.

"QRF, cease fire! Cease fire!" The platoon lieutenant's voice came on the assault frequency. "We're moving into the building." All of the SEALs had earpieces and boom mikes as part of their combat load. Garrett paused a moment to ensure that his grenadiers and machine gunner had stopped firing.

"Copy cease fire. QRF standing by, rear left corner of compound."

A sudden silence fell across the entire compound, followed by a single, sharp explosion as the assault element took the door with an explosive breaching charge. For Garrett and his small QRF, there was nothing to do but hold their position and wait. Fratricide was on everyone's mind with two friendly forces in the same fight. He could hear tactical chatter over his radio earpiece and, from the building, an occasional two-shot burst. The assault element was clearing the building, room by room. Suddenly, the iron gate swung open, and three men burst through it. Garrett made a quick assessment. Through his NODs, he was surprised to see they were armed with M16 rifles, a standard American weapon, and that two of the three had night-vision goggles strapped to their heads. The rest of their kit was standard muj—sandals, baggy pants, collared shirts, and loose-fitting combat vests.

"QRF is engaged," he said evenly into the mike as he brought his M4 rifle level.

As with most SEALs, his weapon was set on semiautomatic fire. His first two-round burst caught the lead muj mid-torso, and he pitched forward. The second turned and dropped to one knee and brought his rifle to a firing position; he was a trained fighter. Garrett gave him two quick two-round bursts, and he slumped, dropping his rifle. As he shifted his attention to the third enemy fighter, he opened up on Garrett, spraying him with full automatic fire.

It all took place in a few seconds, but for Garrett, it played out in slow motion. The enemy muzzle flashes were like a slow strobe light as he swung his weapon to meet this threat. He knew he was being hit. Then, suddenly, his weapon was struck and exploded in his hands. He felt the bolt go partially home, blocked by a cocked round in the half-open chamber. He released the weapon and, with no conscious thought, went for the 9-mm Sig Sauer pistol on his right hip. His eyes never left the muj as the enemy fighter emptied his magazine. Garrett was aware that the enemy was firing from the hip, moving the muzzle of his rifle back and forth in fire-hose fashion. He was hit again, and he could feel the sonic snap of rounds going by. The Sig seemed to have a life of its own. It came level, just as the muj emptied his magazine, and Garrett then put three quick rounds into the man's torso. Garrett found himself moving forward. He put two rounds into each of the men on the ground, then peered carefully through the open gate to see if there were more enemy fighters. There were none.

He became aware that there was a SEAL beside him with a hand on his shoulder and another off to his left on one knee, giving him cover from the rear of the compound. He was also aware of the voices saying "clear" and "building clear" over the radio, followed by the normal after-action talk that came with giving orders for securing the compound. Garrett remembered it all in minute detail. He knew he had a fresh magazine in his pistol, but for the life of him, he could not recall dropping the old mag and inserting a new one.

"You okay, Tag?" said the SEAL at his elbow.

"I think so," he replied. But since he wasn't sure, he said, "Let me check. For now, you take charge of the QRF."

Garrett stepped back and began to inventory his body and equipment. His M4 had taken a round that had shattered the receiver. There was a cut in his right side, just above his belt where a round had sliced through, but no more than two inches of skin were damaged. There was a tear in the right sleeve of his blouse. On further inspection, he found a shallow furrow along his forearm that was more of a burn than a gunshot wound. Neither wound bled very much, but both burned, and it hurt when he breathed. His chest was bruised from the two rounds that had buried themselves in the chest plate of his body armor. He moved back to the gate opening.

"I got it, Charlie," he said to the QRF SEAL who waited by the gate while the assault element finished searching the building.

"You sure, Master Chief?" he replied.

"Sure as I can be," Garrett replied. This was not the first time he had been shot, nor the first time he'd experienced the euphoria of finding himself still alive after a close call. "Cheated death once again," he added with a grin.

"Roger that, Master Chief." The SEAL stepped back but stayed close by. He was concerned by the wild look in Garrett Walker's eyes.

Garrett Walker was back at the Kandahar base by late afternoon. He and the other two wounded SEALs from the assault element had been medevaced from the battle site to the medical facility within an hour of securing the compound. The American military was at its most efficient when it came to getting its wounded warriors off the battlefield. One of the SEALs would be held for a few days before being returned to duty. The other would be heading home to heal and prepare for the next combat rotation. Garrett Walker had a few stitches in his side, a wrap on his forearm, and some sore ribs. By all accounts, he had indeed cheated death. That evening, he and his commanding officer found themselves in the corner of the SEAL tactical operations center, camped over some very black coffee. There was a quiet buzz of activity as the watch team went about their duties, but they had what privacy they needed without being behind closed doors. The commander raised his cup to his command master chief.

"Good to have you back, Tag. If we were back on Coronado, I'd be hoisting a glass of Makers Mark to your good fortune." Alcohol was banned for US troops in Afghanistan, and though the SEALs were enterprising enough to avoid that restriction if they chose, they didn't.

"And if we were back in Coronado, I'd join you."

Garrett walked his commander through the operation with generous praise for the work of the assault SEALs and the Afghan blocking force. "And the medics on the Army choppers who took us out of there were the best." He paused for a reflective moment.

"Yes?" Commander Jim Toohey prompted.

"I made a mistake. After we were given the cease-fire by the assault force, I should have had Charlie and Rick move up to cover me and the back gate. Their job was over as soon as the others entered the main building. Tactical error on my part, and it almost got me killed." He shook his head as if to acknowledge his shortcomings. "I don't know, Jim. Maybe I'm getting too old for this shit."

Toohey regarded him a moment, then huffed. "Probably so. Maybe I should get you a fucking walker so you can get around the camp. And you can trade in that cup of mud for a nonfat latte."

Garrett grunted and said nothing, and they sat for several minutes in companionable silence.

"Oh, in all the excitement I almost forgot," said Toohey as he rose to his feet. "This came for you from the embassy in Kabul." He handed a message to Garrett. While Garrett read, he stepped away and returned with a thermos decanter to refill both their cups. Toohey had not really forgotten, but he wanted to give his command master chief some space before he brought the communication to his attention. "I was sorry to hear about your brother. When I saw the message, I readdressed it to the joint special operations commander with a request for airlift priority. You're good to go. I've booked you on the midnight helo to Kabul. There are three flights tomorrow from Kabul to Qatar, and then you can catch a commercial flight to the States." He noticed the color draining from Garrett's face. "I know this is kind of sudden, Tag, but are you all right?"

"So you've read this." It was not a question; it was an accusation.

"That's right."

"Sir, this was a personal message." There was suddenly an uncharacteristically aggressive tone in his voice. "It was none of your business."

Toohey stood immobile, coffee carafe in hand, and regarded him for a long moment. "Yes, it was a personal message, Command Master Chief, and this is a SEAL team—my SEAL team. You're my CMC and senior enlisted advisor. If it affects this team, then it damn well is my business."

Garrett, too, was now on his feet in front of his commander, and they glared at each other. "And I'm telling you, sir, this is my business, and it doesn't have a goddamn thing to do with this team or with you!" Toohey looked down at the finger that was now jabbing him in the middle of his chest, then up at his master chief. His face was expressionless. The operations watch team collectively stared at this unfolding spectacle, and then quickly returned to finding a task to busy themselves. Garrett finally dropped his hand and stepped back. "Anyway," he said in a more conciliatory tone, "I'm not going."

A silence hung between them. "You're not going! For Christ's sake, Tag, it's your brother—your *twin* brother. What do you mean, you're not going?"

"God damn it, sir, just leave it alone. I'm not going, and that's all there is to it!"

They glared at each other for a long moment before Toohey spoke in a quiet voice. "Hey, Tag, it's your call. I can't force you to go. But, man, think about it. He's your brother."

"That's right, sir. He's my brother, and it *is* my call," Garrett said with a little less force. "Subject closed."

He dropped his head and stared at the floor for a few seconds, hands on his hips. Then he brushed past his commander and out the door.

The Southwest Airlines 737 settled easily onto the tarmac at McCarran International Airport and hurried over to the terminal, anxious to discharge its boisterous load of gamblers and return to Los Angeles for another load of the same. Cathy Walker watched the boarding gate telescope forward, like some hungry, four-sided worm, and attach itself to the plane. Soon the boarding door was spewing passengers into the terminal. Cathy stood well back from the gate area. She resisted the urge to touch her hair and held her hands tightly in front of her. As the flood of new arrivals dropped to a trickle, a cold fear moved through her. *What if he isn't coming?* She felt a small surge of relief and then immediately felt guilty for it. *He has to come; it's Brandon's only chance.* Now she was beginning to feel panicky. Then, suddenly, there he was.

Garrett Walker slipped through the boarding gate and paused to get his bearings. He was in uniform because he was traveling under emergency military orders. He was dressed in a short-sleeved summer khaki uniform and wore a garrison cap low on his forehead. Rows of colored ribbons lined the space above his left shirt pocket just under the gold SEAL emblem. A fouled anchor with two stars, the device of a Navy master chief, was pinned to each collar point. He carried a small leather grip in one hand and an inexpensive garment bag slung over the opposite shoulder.

He picked Cathy out immediately and paused at the gate, oblivious of those behind him trying to get into the terminal. After the slight hesitation, he made his way over to her. He dropped his bags and they hugged, but it was an awkward embrace.

"Hello, Cath. We've got to quit meeting like this."

She smiled shyly, then responded, "Thanks for coming so quickly, Garrett."

He shrugged, not meeting her eyes. "Well, I'm here." He glanced around quickly before looking down at her. "I suppose we should talk—let you bring me up to speed on this thing. Is there somewhere we can go?"

"There's a coffee shop down the concourse, or a bar, if you prefer."

"How about the bar? I've been on and off planes for thirty-some hours now. I could use a drink." He grinned. "Come to think of it, I haven't had a drink in about four months. Now seems like as good a time as any."

They walked a moment in silence, then both spoke at once.

Garrett grinned again. "Sorry, go ahead."

"Oh, nothing. I was just going to ask if we should see to your luggage first."

He held up the bags as they walked. "This is it. I travel light, remember?"

She forced a smile. "Yes, I remember."

They found the bar and threaded their way to a table in the corner. It was a chrome and Naugahyde kind of place with TVs suspended from each corner of the room and the chimes and rattle of slot machines in the background. Garrett tossed his gear onto a vacant chair and waited until Cathy was seated. A chubby waitress in a short satin pinafore and net stockings followed them to the table and hovered nearby.

"What'll it be?" he asked Cathy lightly, trying not to look directly at her. It had been much the same last year in Arkansas when they buried Don. Garrett had kept his distance from her and Brandon then too. He had found it difficult to be anywhere close to Cathy, and they had spoken less than a dozen words. They had all made the effort to be there for the folks—and for Don.

"Could I have a glass of white wine?" she said to the waitress.

"And I'll have a double Johnnie Walker Black, neat." He stood to pull a fifty-dollar bill from his pocket and laid it on her tray. "We may be a little while." The waitress retreated, leaving Garrett and Cathy seated across from each other.

"You look terrific, Cathy. You really do," but as he said it, he quickly looked down. A heavy silence hung in the air until he made an attempt to clear his throat. He finally looked up from the table to meet her eyes. She started to speak, but he raised his hand. "Uh, Cathy … I have to say that … well, this is very hard for me. I almost didn't come, but when I thought about it, there really was no way I could not come. I'm just a little unnerved by this whole thing, about even being here. But now that I'm here, I'll do anything I can to help. Please understand that."

Cathy had taken this awkward opportunity to study him closely for the first time until he finally met and held her gaze. He was like Brandon in so many ways, but also very different. During their time together when the three of them were in college, she was one of the few people who could tell them apart at a glance. But the years now have marked them in many different ways. Garrett's hands, like Brandon's, were large, but his were rough and blunt, and had a powerful grace to them. His whole body looked leaner, harder, than she remembered. His arms were larger, too, but more sinewy, and there was a dragon tattooed on the inside of his right forearm that she tried not to stare at, to say nothing of the angry red scar on his left forearm. But it was his face that had changed the most. It was narrow and closed, where Brandon's near-identical features were more rounded and cordial. There was an intensity there as well—a fierce component under the surface that had always been there but now seemed more pronounced.

Then, suddenly, he smiled, and it was as if the two men were again identical. She looked away quickly.

"Hey," he said, chuckling, "go ahead and stare. It's what I've been wanting to do since I got off the plane—just to have a good look at you. So hell, let's get it over with." For the first time, they both smiled easily.

"Garrett, I'm sorry. It's just that ... well, this is difficult for me, too." She paused and drew a deep breath. "And I understand that it can't be easy for you. I ... I don't know what to say. If there were some other way, something else that could be done, I wouldn't have asked you to come."

He looked away from her strained features. "I can understand that, Cath. Believe me, I can. But here we are."

She looked at him, tears beginning to well. "He didn't want me to contact you, you know. In fact, he forbade me to call. But it's his only chance—our only chance." She paused and blotted her mouth with a table napkin. "I'm not making a very good show of this, I suppose."

"You're doing fine, but what about Brandon? Doesn't he have some say in this? Doesn't he have to agree to it?"

She nodded slowly. "He does. And he will." She recovered and gave him a determined look. "Like I said, it's our only chance."

Neither spoke for a few moments. Garrett, deep in thought, finally sighed and again met her eyes. "Well, maybe I can help with that. You see, I'm not going to give him one of my kidneys. I'm giving it to you, so it's yours to give to him. Let's see if he can turn *you* down." He paused and continued, "And as we well know, he could never say no to you."

Her eyes widened and she looked away quickly. It was as if he'd slapped her. He was immediately sorry.

"Oh hell, Cath, I shouldn't have said that—I had no right to say that. It's just that I'm ... well, it's just that it still hurts, that's all. I'm sorry. I truly am."

When she was finally able to look up at him again, he could see that the hurt was still there, but there was also a full measure of anger.

"Garrett, what do you want of me? What can I do to make this go away? It's a cancer that's been eating away at all three of us for too many years. At one time, I cared for you. Maybe I was even in love with you. It was so long ago I'm not sure what it was. But it *was* a long time ago—seventeen, eighteen years now! I'm married to Brandon. I'm in love with Brandon. My life is with him." She measured him, searching for the right words but knowing there was little she could say or do. "Garrett, you're just going to have to live with it. You have the ability now to save his life. Mine, too, for that matter. Maybe it will change things between you and Brandon; maybe not. But know that it will never change things between us; there's just no going back. Can you understand that?"

Suddenly, he looked very vulnerable. He drained his glass and signaled for another. "Yeah, you're right. I know that," he said evenly. "But tell me one thing if you can. Why him and not me? I've always wondered about that. We were both the same, everyone said so. We came from the same dirt patch down in Arkansas. We pledged the same fraternity; we both played football; we had the same major, even if he did get better grades. But why him?" he asked without rancor. "Why did you choose him?"

She twirled her glass by the stem. The wine was untouched. "I don't care what they all said. You weren't the same. Brandon was always much softer. Brandon was you, but without the hard edges. Like the way you played football. Brandon was a receiver; he loved to catch the ball, and he always tried to dodge the tacklers. You were on the defense; you hit people. There was an … an intensity to the way you played. And it always appeared that you really enjoyed it, playing rough and knocking people down. Brandon never played like that. It … it was like Brandon avoided hitting other players and you sought it out—you looked for it."

She made a helpless gesture. "There's a certain tenderness to Brandon. And it's that tenderness that's very important to me."

They were silent for a moment while the waitress delivered Garrett's drink. "People can change," he quietly offered.

"Have you? Over the years, Brandon and I have built a life together. He's a very caring man. He's been a good husband and father." She eyed him critically. "You were always the tougher one, Garrett. And, forgive me, but you don't look like you've mellowed all that much."

Garrett raised his eyebrows and nodded as he pulled on the fresh drink. She was right—at least partially right. *If there were a good reason*, he mused, *I could change*. But like Cathy, he knew there was little he could do or say to make things different. And, he was forced to admit to himself, he was trying to turn the clock back—not good for someone who had made it a practice to live in the present.

"Okay, let's do this thing, but first, tell me what happened. And start from the very beginning."

Cathy told Garrett what she knew—about the convention, Brandon's dizziness in the room, and the medical procedures, both in the hotel room and at the hospital. She had been at Brandon's side for most of the last three days. Between long periods of sleep, he spoke of little else, trying to come to grips with how this had happened and why it had happened to him. Garrett listened closely as he finished his third double, interrupting Cathy only to clarify a point. When she had finished, he set his glass down and thoughtfully rubbed the back of his neck. He knew he had to catch up on his sleep somewhere other than in a cramped airplane seat.

"Tell me again what he said about the girl, the one he saw at the meeting in the hotel and then again on the elevator."

She did, concluding, "He seemed to think that it was just a coincidence. He runs into a lot of people at these sales conventions."

"But he first met her at the software presentation, then she sent a drink to his table at dinner, then took the same elevator when he went to his room, and got off on the same floor."

"That's right." She looked at him coolly. "And if you think there was something else going on, forget it. I don't care what that slime from the police department may have been hinting at. I know Brandon, and that's just not him."

Garrett nodded. He and Brandon were estranged, but they were still twins. Garrett, too, knew it wasn't his way. "Well, he better not be out fooling around," he grinned. "Or he'll also need replacement arms for the two I'll rip off him to beat him over the head with."

For the first time since she received that terrible call three days ago, she smiled from the heart, and it felt good.

"C'mon," he said as he grabbed up his gear. "Brandon's kidney—excuse me, your kidney—doesn't need any more liquor, and neither does mine. You can drop me at a cheap motel on the Strip. Let me get some sleep, and then we can go to the hospital."

The waitress approached with the change tray, but he waved her off as they left.

Cathy Walker sat in Dr. Ward's office waiting for him to return from his rounds. She was very tired, and it showed. It had been almost two days since Garrett had arrived. When he wasn't sleeping off the jet lag, he was at the hospital undergoing a battery of tests. Cathy had taken Garrett in to see Brandon, but aside from a "Thanks for coming" and "No problem," they had very little to say to each other, or little they would say. It had been the longest two days of Cathy's life. Ward walked in and gave her a warm smile.

"Hi, Cathy. How're you holding up?"

She looked up at him and sighed. "To be honest, Doctor, I don't know how much more of this I can stand. I feel like I've been dragging two little boys around by their ears. How are things on your end?"

"We're all set. With identical twins, you don't really expect to find any problems, but we have to run the tests to be sure. As we expected, they are an exact tissue match. Both are healthy, and, in their own way, both are very fit. Aside from some calcium deposits from a leg that was broken twice and several dislocations, plus a few minor gunshot wounds, Garrett is in amazing condition. His resting heart rate is down around forty-five. Still, his body's had some hard use. I've never seen that many scars on someone who's not a member of a street gang, but he's got two very healthy kidneys. I've talked with the physician who'll be doing the operation, and he'd like to make the transplant tomorrow morning."

"Tomorrow? So soon?"

"That's right."

"I thought you'd be performing the operation, Doctor."

"Please, it's Chris, and I'll be assisting with the surgery. We have a specialist coming in from the Bay Area to perform the actual transplant. He's done this procedure numerous times, and I haven't. But I'll be there." Ward smiled easily. "I think this specialist just wants to increase his batting average. Siblings are good, but twins are even better. Fewer complications and the patients tend to live long, normal lives."

"Thanks, Doctor—I mean, Chris. I appreciate that, and I know Brandon does as well."

"Cathy, may I ask you a question?"

"Of course."

"This is not what you would call routine surgery, but we have the best of all worlds here. An exact tissue match, a healthy donor and healthy recipient, and a very competent and experienced surgeon. But it's obvious that your husband and his brother don't seem to be on the best of terms." He paused and sat on the edge of his desk. "You see, unless the donor is terminal or deceased, there's usually a very special bond between the recipient and his donor." Ward again paused, searching for the right words. "It's

... it's really one of the more beautiful things we do in medicine, to take a major organ from one human being and make it live in another. And it's one of the few ways we can include someone else in the saving of a life. We don't get too many chances to really cheat death in this business. When an organ gives out and we can replace it, we get one of these rare opportunities. I guess I just wish that the miracle we are about to perform was being a little better received." He laughed softly and shook his head. "I mean, we're pros—technically, we can make it happen. We don't need a lot of thanks; we get paid very well. But it would certainly be more rewarding if Brandon and Garrett had a better perspective on this. It's ... well, it's just very special, that's all."

"I know what you mean, Chris. Believe me, I know."

He again chuckled. "I feel like I've just arranged for the transfer of a spare blood-filtration component from one operational unit to another." Then he turned more serious. "Please stop me if I'm getting too personal, but it's about you, isn't it?"

She lowered her head. "Yes, it is." She hesitated, then the words tumbled out. "You see, I met Brandon and Garrett at a fraternity party at the beginning of our sophomore year at the University of Michigan." She looked up and pulled on a strand of hair at her neck. Ward listened patiently. "They were already the famous Walker twins. Well, semi-famous, perhaps. They both played football, and that was reason enough for celebrity status at Michigan. In those days, they were identical. Garrett asked me out, and we dated for most of the school year. But while I cared for him, there was something menacing about him. It was something difficult to put your finger on, but at times he would withdraw, and no one could reach him. I finally decided he was just an emotionally stingy person. While I was with Garrett, I saw a lot of Brandon. Finally, it dawned on me that I was dating the wrong twin. But I didn't know what to do. What could I do?" Ward smiled encouragingly. "So I broke up with Garrett and figured I'd had my fling with the Walker twins. Then the following semester, Brandon and I had a class together, and we became friends, then more than friends. End of story."

Ward pursed his lips. "I assume Garrett didn't take this too well."

"That's an understatement. At first, he avoided us whenever possible, and I suppose we avoided him. Garrett moved out of the fraternity house, and we saw little of him after that. When we did, it was all stiff smiles and mumbled greetings. I attempted to intervene, but as you can see by the way they're acting now, they can both be very stubborn. The following spring, when Brandon and I decided to get engaged, we knew we had to tell Garrett first. We met him one afternoon after class and told him we were getting married. He just stared at us and shook his head. 'I hope you both will be very happy.' That was all he said. He walked away, and that's the last we saw of him. Garrett left school that very afternoon and joined the Navy the next day. It's been that way since that May afternoon in Ann Arbor. And Chris, that was a very long time ago."

"You mean that you haven't seen him since … I mean, until now?"

"We saw him just once, and that was last year. Their younger brother, Don, was also a Navy SEAL like Garrett. He was killed in action. Garrett brought Don's body home for the funeral. He made no effort to talk to either one of us. And Brandon's just as bad as Garrett. Sometimes I feel so guilty—other times, angry. But most of the time, I just get so sick of it all." She began to dig for a handkerchief, but Ward quickly handed her a tissue. "I'm sorry, Chris. This must all seem just too strange. Isn't this strange … abnormal?"

"Sorry, Cathy, I'm a surgeon, not a shrink. I do know that most families can have their issues. I have a sister who I really can't stand, but I try to make a show of pretending I do." He slid off the desk and walked to a table in the corner. "Coffee? It's been here a while—pretty strong stuff."

"Yes, thank you, I would."

He poured two cups and handed her one. "Like all twins, these two share a great deal, no pun intended, and tomorrow, they'll share a part of each other. For Brandon, it'll be a lifesaver, literally. Maybe there'll be something in it for Garrett, too."

She forced a smile. "Let's hope so."

Brandon arrived first. The room had a lot in common with the stainless-steel kitchen of a fast-food chain, only the lighting was better and the smell was different. Garrett came through the double metal doors a few moments later. As they had with Brandon, the attendants lifted him gently from the gurney to the operating table, face down. The two surgical altars were positioned side by side with room for the gowned medical priests to move between them. The specialist from San Francisco was short, Jewish, animated, and very expensive.

"Okay, gentlemen, it's show time!" He stood at the head of the two tables, leaning over to look at one brother, then the other. His mouth and nose were covered with a surgical mask, but the kind, creased eyes above it said he was smiling broadly. Both Brandon and Garrett had their faces turned inboard so they could see him. "Now, help me out here, which one of you is the donor and which the donee?"

"One of us has two of them and the other doesn't," Garrett said thickly. On Dr. Ward's instruction, the anesthesiologist had given them both a strong preoperative injection. "You look like a smart guy," Brandon added with a slur, "you'll figure it out."

"Jeez, tough crowd in this theater," the surgeon responded. Then he looked past the two brothers. "Doctors, if you please."

The two attending anesthesiologists slipped clear plastic masks over each of the brothers' faces and began to study their metering devices.

"Okay, gents," one of them said. "You've seen the drill on the TV medical soaps. Start counting backward from one hundred. The best I've ever seen is sixty-three. How about you, Frank?"

"Had a lady go to fifty-five on me once. Long time ago, though. Go for it, guys."

Garrett and Brandon were each peering over their transparent mask at the other. When there was a break in the passing green forms, their eyes met and locked. In that moment, each saw himself in the other, and silently the long-extinguished bond between them was reestablished. Their old competitive spirit was also rekindled.

"Hey big brother, bet I'll count longer." Garrett was about twenty minutes younger than Brandon.

"We'll just see, little brother," Brandon replied.

They counted in unison, and both made it into the low seventies.

Part Three: THE HEALING

Garrett and Brandon stood looking at each other, each trying to read the other's face. Brandon leaned forward in a slight crouch, arms hanging straight down from his shoulders, one leg bent and well behind the other. Garrett, too, was well forward, his weight evenly distributed on the balls of his feet, hands on the tops of his thighs. They were both in sweat-streaked T-shirts and sneakers. Brandon wore tennis shorts, Garrett gray sweat pants with a hole in one knee.

"Hut one, hut two, HUT THREE!"

Tommy retreated from the line of scrimmage, marked by a knotted red bandanna on the grass. The two younger kids chased after him. On the third hut, Brandon charged straight at Garrett. After a quick stutter step, he dipped his right shoulder and looked toward the hedge, then broke left for Cathy's veggie garden. Garrett almost bit, but not quite. Still, Brandon had a step on him as they streaked across the middle of the backyard.

Tommy fired a tight spiral with the Nerf football, and, for a moment, it looked as if Brandon was going to take it on his fingertips. Then Garrett leaped to make the interception. He juggled it briefly, then turned the other way, Brandon racing in pursuit. Garrett juked past Tommy and into the end zone alongside the back deck.

"Touchdown!" screamed one of the younger kids. "We win!"

"Way to go, Uncle Garrett."

"Yeah, Uncle Garrett, we showed 'em!"

The two kids on Garrett's team practiced spiking the ball into the grass. The two brothers gasped for air, bracing themselves with their hands on their knees.

"Nice pick," Brandon managed.

"Thanks," Garrett replied. "Another game?"

"No way. I probably won't be able to get out of bed tomorrow morning as it is."

The deck was an expansive, multileveled structure that seemed to grow on the back of most semi-affluent California homes. Beyond the large deck stretched well-watered, manicured greenery guarded by a six-foot cedar privacy fence. Suburban Californians seemed to live much of their life on their decks, cordoned off from their neighbors and the rest of the world by wooden barricades. Cathy busied herself at a large redwood table with the meal preparation, laying out the condiments and pressing burgers between layers of wax paper. She paused to wipe her hands and take a drink of iced tea. Like most afternoons in San Jose, it was warm but not too hot, and there wasn't a cloud in the sky.

She watched the two men walking together around the yard, trying to catch their breath. It had been almost two months since the transplant operation. Their physical recovery had been remarkable. As Dr. Ward had taken the time to explain at length, kidneys in humans were redundant organs. The average person used less than half the capacity of a single kidney. So with an exact match and zero tissue rejection, there was every expectation that both Brandon and Garrett would achieve their normal life expectancy with no restriction on their activities. The backyard football game was certainly proof of that. The scars weren't pretty, but they were a small price to pay for a normal life.

Cathy was grateful for their physical recovery, but then she had expected it. They were resilient men, both physically gifted. And competitive! It was as if they were in a race to see who could get stronger faster. But the way they had mended their personal lives totally amazed her. It was as if the terrible rift and long period of silence between them had never existed. She didn't know if it was a twin thing or a guy thing. Sisters, especially twin sisters, would have talked it out with each other and probably with everyone else around them. The healing and reconciliation would have been shared, ongoing, prolonged, and emotional. Men didn't do it like that, she concluded. A painful episode was made closed business and off-limits for further discussion, like last year's tax return. They built a fence of silence around it, and both seemed to understand that the wound could only heal if the scabs were not picked.

When she brought it up with Brandon, he just said that they had an unspoken understanding. He said they both knew that any attempt at justification or apology or to "examine the relationship," a phrase he used with some disdain, would only lead to accusations and hostility. So they never spoke of it. Occasionally, one of the kids would bring it up in their presence, and either Garrett or Brandon would say something like "It was just a squabble between us, like you have with your brother, only it lasted a while."

As for she and Garrett, there was still a low level of tension between them, but it was a controlled and manageable presence. She would have been willing to talk more about it if he wanted to or needed to, but he clearly didn't. Before they'd left the hospital, Garrett had just simply said that he understood and accepted the way things were. On a rare occasion, she caught him looking at her in a melancholy way. He would smile sadly and look away, then usually find something to do. On balance, it was surprisingly easy to have them both at home. Now that Brandon had returned to the office, Garrett had busied himself working in the yard with such intensity that you would have thought he was preparing the grounds for a garden tour. Some psychologist could probably read something in to all of this, Cathy thought, but why bother. It was probably as good as it could be between all of them, and Cathy was thankful for that. On balance, it was far better than she could ever have hoped for.

After a circuit of the yard to cool down, they returned to the deck. Brandon dug into the ice chest and handed Garrett a beer. He pulled out a bottle of Gatorade for himself. Then he collapsed beside his brother on a wooden picnic bench, rolling the cold plastic bottle across his forehead.

"I gotta get back out on the golf course. This is too much like work." In spite of what he said, he was in better shape now than he had been in years. He and Garrett had been jogging every morning for close to a month. It began with long walks, then easy one-mile trots. Now they were crowding on the mileage. "You ever think about taking up golf?"

"Me? Go out and spank the egg? Maybe when I'm old, like you. I tried it a couple of times, but I don't have the patience for it. And since the Navy keeps me deployed overseas a lot, I couldn't stay with it for any length of time. Besides, it's not a warrior's game."

"The Navy starting to wonder where you are yet?"

"They know where I am, believe me. I still have a few weeks of convalescent leave, and can always get more. You'd be surprised how many SEALs are on extended time off to recuperate from injuries due to Iraq and Afghanistan. And I have sixty days of personal leave on the books. A few years back, we were lucky to get a few weeks off between deployments. With the draw-down in Afghanistan, that's no longer the case."

"Then what?"

Garrett shrugged. "Depends. My team is back from deployment, and most of the guys are out on leave. In three or four weeks, we'll begin another training cycle, and in sixteen or eighteen months, we'll go back out again. Sooner if the world turns to shit, which is always a possibility."

"No break from that? I thought the Navy had ... what do they call it, shore duty?"

"Oh, I had a few years of shore duty a while back. They assigned me to the training unit in San Diego. Didn't really sit too well with me. No, if I'm going to be in this business, I want to be operational, inasmuch as someone with my seniority can stay in the fight."

Brandon shrugged. *What do I know about what Navy SEALs do?*

"How's it going now that you've had a few weeks back at MedaSystems? Good to be back in the saddle?"

Brandon ran his hand under his shirt to the small of his back. The incisions had healed, but they still itched. "Yes and no. People are stumbling all over themselves being nice to me. And the company's doing well. The guys in the marketing department did a hell of a job while I was gone. I'm really proud of them. But there's something wrong or something missing, and I don't know what it is. Maybe it's just all I've been through—we've been through. It's nothing I can put my finger on, but I have a very odd feeling when I'm there." He chewed on his lower lip in thought. "I've been at MedaSystems for a long time. Now, suddenly, I feel like I'm just a visitor there."

Cathy watched them from the corner of her eye, just out of their hearing. Normally she let Brandon tend to the male ritual of cooking the burgers, but she decided not to interrupt. There had been a good deal more of that recently, the two of them sitting and talking quietly. It was a very exclusive club. Even the kids sensed this and left them alone. At first, Cathy had rejoiced at the reconciliation between the two. She was happy for both of them, especially for Brandon, whose guilt over Garrett's exile, she sensed, was greater than her own. But something more was happening between them, something very private.

It's a trade-off, she concluded as she laid the burgers on the grill. The glowing mesquite quickly attacked them. She had never known Brandon with Garrett in his life, not like this. She and Brandon were lovers, best friends, and confidants. When there were problems, triumphs, tragedies, concerns, whatever, she was the go-to person for him. They talked about everything. Now, she sensed, that had changed. Along with the relief that she felt with their reunion, she had to surrender a part of Brandon. With this came a sense of loss, and, she admitted, a little jealousy. *But do I want it back the way it was when I had all of Brandon and Garrett was a persistent, unpleasant memory—a distant specter of guilt?* She shook her head at the thought. *No way. No way in hell.*

"Any more from the cops?" Garrett asked, keeping his voice low.

"In Vegas?" Brandon snorted. "Give me a break. They were just going through the motions. Haven't you heard? Las Vegas is a safe town, a fun town. Bring the whole family. The cops, including that asshole Rucko, are only concerned that I don't stir the pot. They're afraid I might say something that would conflict with the Chamber of Commerce line of crap that Vegas is a swell place—a safe place. Rucko even said, in spite of what happened to me, that taking kidneys for profit is an urban legend in Las Vegas with no truth to it. Yeah, right!"

Garrett drained his beer. "Well, how about that guy Stannick? From what you said, he doesn't seem like the kind who would whitewash something like this. He seems like a pretty serious dude."

"He still calls every week. Always asks how I'm doing. Lately, though, he's been asking quite a few questions. Says it's still an active investigation."

"They come up with any leads?"

"I don't think so, but he's not a real talkative guy. He did tell me one thing last week. He said that my insurance company offered a reward to get one of my kidneys back the minute they learned I'd lost both of them."

"They what?" Garrett's outburst drew a look from Cathy, who was in the midst of turning the burgers.

"No shit. It seems that there's a way for them to do that—some underworld Internet, for all I know. Anyway, they offered a hundred thousand dollars for one of my kidneys to be returned, no questions asked—deliver the kidney, go past Go, collect the dough."

"Is that legal?"

Brandon shrugged. "Who knows—probably not. I do know one thing. Keeping someone on full dialysis for the rest of his life, along with the expected complications, makes a hundred thousand look like peanuts." He shuddered at the thought. "As long as they can find a good artery and a good vein, they just keep washing you out."

"And adding a quart when it gets low."

"That, too," Brandon replied. "And who knows where the money comes from for a kidney buyback. It'd be my guess that the liability carrier of that hotel in Las Vegas has some pretty deep pockets. But thanks to you, I have one very good kidney; I don't have to face that damned machine. Golden Western Insurance doesn't have to pay to have my blood flushed every other day, and I don't have to go walking around looking like the color of a banana."

Garrett pulled two beers from the cooler and offered one to Brandon. He shrugged and took it. "Looks like the Las Vegas PD and the insurance company have closed the books on you, big brother." Brandon again shrugged and sipped at his beer, but said nothing. "Tell me something, Brandon," Garrett continued. "Have you closed the books on this—on whoever it was who took your kidneys?"

Brandon looked at him for a long moment. "No fucking way, little brother."

"Hey, I cooked 'em," Cathy called from the grill, "but I'm not doing up your buns for you. Time to muster up. Front and center, guys."

They pushed themselves from the bench and joined the rest of the family. The three kids had already smothered their patties with catsup and mustard, and buried the loaded buns in a mound of potato chips. Brandon and Garrett got their plates and queued up to the grill.

"She doesn't do your buns for you, Brandon? What kind of a woman did you take up with, anyway?"

"She doesn't do buns or windows, but she does cook a mean burger."

Cathy eyed them suspiciously. "You guys look just a little too pleased with yourselves. If anyone's cooking something up, my guess is that it's the two of you!"

"Not us," Brandon replied sweetly. "Just wondering whose blood my kidneys are filtering this afternoon."

After dinner, they all went for a walk down to the local city park. While the kids chased with their friends, Cathy kept an eye on them. She also watched as Brandon and Garrett walked slowly around the edge of the park grounds, deep in conversation.

Cantello Construction, Inc. occupied a suite of offices that enjoyed full use of the entire top floor. The building itself was one of the newer glass and chrome medium-rise office buildings in Daly City. There was ample parking in an underground garage just below a modern lobby area complete with potted palms and a glassed tenant marquee. Most of the lessees were CPAs, consultants, software design firms, and attorneys—lots of attorneys. Cantello Construction was the only business in the building that served a traditionally blue-collar trade. Cantello Construction also owned the building.

A bank of three elevators opened onto a generous foyer with hardwood floors overlaid with Persian rugs and a well-appointed reception area. Modest gold leaf on black lettering neatly adorned the entry door glass:

CANTELLO CONSTRUCTION, INC
CORPORATE HEADQUARTERS

Two receptionists guarded the executive offices, which were segregated by an opaque, glass-encased oak partition.

The company dealt primarily in large-scale concrete and aggregate construction. Most of the firm's business was contract work for the state of California and local municipalities. It bid on the design, fabrication, and construction of freeways, highway overpasses, and bridges. It was one of several major contractors that repaired the Golden State's old infrastructure and struggled to build new roads to keep up with the growing needs of Californians and their love affair with their cars. The San Francisco earthquake of 1989, the one that flattened the elevated highway in the East Bay and damaged the San Francisco–Oakland Bay Bridge, had been a windfall for the company. State and federal dollars were made available for extensive reinforcement of overpasses, exit ramps, and bridging, and Cantello Construction had more than doubled in size since the big quake. State and federal contracts were always competitive and the margins traditionally slim. That was before. Following the earthquake, the politicians were held accountable by the voters for not being as prepared as they should have been. The voters wanted action, and elected officials wanted to be seen as responsive. As a result, most highway construction contractors had been able to build a comfortable profit into their construction bids. And for Cantello Construction, its cash flow was a little more predictable because the company, unlike many of its competitors, never seemed to be bothered by labor problems.

Frank Cantello's large office occupied a choice southwest-corner location. Most days he could see the ocean just four miles due west, and when it was clear, as far south as Pacifica. The office would be considered elegant for any company and opulent for a construction firm. But this had not always been the case. Frank's grandfather had worked as a stevedore in the Port of San Francisco and spoken almost no English. His father started the construction business in Oakland, and until just twelve years ago, the company leased office space in the end of a warehouse near the docks. The old man built a solid business, expanding the revenue base while keeping his overhead fixed. He married late in life, and when he died, he was younger than Frank was now. Yet he left his son a small, thriving company with little infrastructure and a great deal of cash. Since then, Frank had taken Cantello Construction to the next level. With several key acquisitions and a few shrewd political contributions, he had become a player in the multibillion-dollar California public construction industry, with branch offices in Sacramento, Bakersfield, and Long Beach.

The corporate offices were handsomely carpeted, but the pile of the rug in the corner office was especially plush. There was an abundance of light oak and soft tan leather. A wet bar near the window visibly stocked several brands of single-malt scotch attended by a row of cut crystal tumblers. Six upholstered armchairs surrounded an oak and leather-trimmed conference table. Frank's desk was a reflection of the man: It was massive, expensive, and orderly. Neat stacks of papers and files were arranged on top. Behind him on the credenza were rows of reference books along with a small television, two construction hard hats, and several cell phones patiently resting in their charging cradles. Alongside the credenza was a deep, custom-built rack, similar to a wine storage dais that held several dozen construction blueprints. While a man in tan cotton slacks and a short-sleeved shirt waited, Frank Cantello pored over a set of plans rolled out flat on the conference table.

"Jesus Christ, Manny. I can't believe we gotta use that much fuckin' rebar in those support columns. This is steel-reinforced concrete, not concrete-reinforced steel. What th' fuck's goin' on?"

Manny shrugged. "Hey, I know it's overkill as well as you do, but that's the new code. We got no choice."

"Bullshit. Who's the inspector on this job?"

"Guy named O'Bannon. He works out of—"

"Yeah, yeah, I know him—he's out of the Redwood City field office. Not a bad guy for a mick, but if he's not handled right, he can be a real prick." Cantello rolled up the plans and handed them to Manny.

"Go ahead with the forms, but don't set any rebar until I can have a talk with our friend, O'Bannon. Maybe I can get him to give us a special onetime variance."

"A what?"

"Never mind. Just wait until I can talk to him."

"Okay, Mr. C., but we're talking eighteen ton of rebar here. I need to know how it's gonna be pretty soon if we want to stay on schedule."

He snapped the construction foreman a sharp look. Falling behind schedule on a job was a mortal sin to Frank Cantello. Even the mention of it caused his heavy, dark eyebrows to pinch into a single line.

"You just keep your crews on the forms, and I'll take care of the inspector, got that, Manny?"

"Yes, sir." He tucked the plans under his arm and left without another word.

"Fuckin' O'Bannon," Cantello said under his breath as he moved across the office, headed for the bar. "Goddamn mick asshole bureaucrat." Cantello was well known within the company and his small circle of acquaintances as a man with little tolerance or time for anyone whose last name didn't end in a vowel. And he reserved a special contempt for the state and federal regulators and building inspectors—unless, of course, they could be bought. When encouraging an inspector to see his point of view, one of his favorite lines was "What can I do to make this an easier decision for you?"

Frank Cantello wore dark slacks, tasseled loafers, and a black knit shirt buttoned to the top, no tie. His gray sport coat was well tailored but still snug. He moved well for a big man. It was early afternoon, yet a heavy beard shaded his deeply tanned face. Cantello wore his thick hair pulled straight back over his head. He poured himself several fingers of scotch and carried it to his desk. There was a sharp knock on the door.

"Come," he shouted louder than necessary.

A man somewhat smaller than Cantello but dressed much the same entered the room carrying a dozen yellow roses in a clear glass vase. He set the flowers on the desk and handed a card to Cantello. An easy, familiar smile played across his lips.

"Flowers! You know something about this?"

"Search me, Mr. C. A messenger just delivered them and said they were for you. I signed for them—figured they were from a secret admirer."

Cantello snorted and deftly slit the envelope with a gold letter opener. He ran his hand along the stubble on his jaw and read aloud, "'Thank you for your remittance. With best wishes for your continued good health.' Signed 'S.'"

"So what's that mean, boss?"

"It means that the final payment has been safely deposited into a numbered account, probably in Turks and Caicos or the Caymans. And that they consider their business with us finished."

"What took so long?"

"Takes a while to launder money these days," Cantello replied as he studied the card. "The feds are after the druggies, and the

Hebes are after the Swiss. Moving money ain't like it used to be. Takes time."

"Yeah, but roses?"

Cantello shrugged and lit a cigar. "They ain't like us, Sal, they're commies. What do they know? I do a deal with someone and they pay me, sometimes I send them a good bottle of hootch. The Rooskies, they maybe send roses."

"Right. Say, boss, I got a question if you don't mind." Cantello eyed him over the cigar. "How come you wanted two of them? The doc at the clinic said that one of them would have been plenty. Why two?"

Cantello rose from the desk. He took out a folding Buck knife and clipped a bud from the bouquet on the desk. "Volume discount, Sally. When they finally found a match for me, they offered to give me both for only fifty percent more cost. How could I say no?" He chuckled and slipped the yellow bud in his lapel. "An' what the hell, I'm a belt-and-suspenders kind of guy, right?"

Sal smiled. "Yeah, but that left the other guy with none. So what's he gonna do?"

"Not my problem. Knowing the commies, they probably got 'em from some skid-row bum who was pretty far down on his luck anyway." Cantello tossed back the last of his scotch. "Now get the car and bring it around. We gotta go to Redwood City to see a mick."

"So why do we got to see a mick?"

"Never you mind, Sally, just get the fuckin' car."

Even though the elevator served the parking garage in the basement, Cantello liked to have the car brought around to the front entrance. Sal left, and Cantello punched the speakerphone on his desk.

"Hey, Claudia, you want to get the state highway department field office in Redwood City on the line for me ... Thanks, beautiful."

Garrett Walker held the Pontiac LeMans to just under the legal speed limit. He reasoned that there was no sense calling attention to himself, and the drive down from the Bay Area had given him time to think. Not that he was all that inconspicuous. As a kid, he'd always wanted a sixties-vintage convertible, a muscle car, and he'd found what he wanted. Red wasn't his favorite color, but it looked clean sitting there on the lot in Concord, and the price was right. The car came with a thirty-day/one-thousand-mile warranty, and he figured it would probably last him until his business was finished. Garrett and Brandon had made just one plan. To try to find out the who and the why. The "why" was Brandon's department. A key to the why was to find out whether the kidney theft was a random act or if Brandon had been singled out. The brothers shared a very rare tissue type and antigen composition, which suggested that the taking of Brandon's kidneys had not been an arbitrary act. Garrett was on his way to Las Vegas to see if he could learn the "who."

Garrett passed the small green "Welcome to Las Vegas" sign on 95 as he snaked his way down the Las Vegas Valley toward the city. Dusk was rapidly approaching, and the glow of the Strip was just beginning to dominate the horizon. He had been to Vegas years before on a gambling expedition with some of his SEAL teammates. A half dozen of them had checked into a suite and a couple of extra rooms at Caesars Palace. The Navymen had treated themselves to a long weekend of gambling, drinking, and chasing cocktail waitresses, with a couple of fights along the way. Regarding the latter, they quickly learned that a hardened group of Navy SEALs were less than a match for massed casino bouncers. But it was a fun town, one that tolerated a little rowdiness as long as the visitors spent money and didn't get too carried away. He saw little of the city, only the insides of casinos and the apron around the hotel swimming pool. When he arrived two months before for Brandon's transplant, it had been back and forth between the motel and the hospital, and they had left town as soon as they were sufficiently recovered from the operation. So he really knew very little about the town of Las Vegas. He also knew his first order of business was to learn the lay of the land. Navy SEALs call this special reconnaissance.

As soon as he was inside the city proper, he drove up and down the Strip several times slowly, pulling to the curb when possible to watch the hordes of gamblers and sightseers roaming the streets between different hotel casinos. There was more to Vegas now than the Strip; there was an Eiffel Tower, a Statue of Liberty, and even a mini-scale New York City. And people—lots and lots of people. *Where do they all come from?* They were in all shapes, sizes, and attire. He drove through the old part of town, the non-resort business part of Las Vegas where the work that made the city function got done. On his third trip past a parked police car, he knew that the two officers inside were beginning to keep an eye on him. He waved amiably to them and headed back toward the Strip, eventually finding his way from the city to an isolated bar on the outskirts of town. It was a few minutes before 10:00 p.m.

Garrett pulled the car to the edge of the potholed gravel parking area. He sat for a few minutes and studied the structure. The whitewashed, cinder-block building had seen better days and probably served as a warehouse or a light-manufacturing facility at some earlier time. It had a flat, hot-mopped roof that was poorly concealed by the cracked and faded fascia. There was a single window next to the metal door with a garishly-lit Lone Star Beer sign. The flashing neon was made fuzzy by the smoke etched on the inside of the glass. A single flood by the door opposite the window identified the establishment as Shorty's. This was not a watering hole that advertised itself or invited the passing traveler to stop for a beer. Garrett took his time and finished a bottle of water, then tossed it onto the passenger's seat. He left the top down, knowing that raising it would accomplish little. His bag was in the trunk, and the ragtop wouldn't keep anyone in this part of town from entering the car if they wanted to. He stepped onto the gravel and headed for the entrance, working his way through the parked motorcycles and an occasional pickup.

The inside of Shorty's held few surprises. The bar ran nearly the length of one wall abutting a crude plywood cubicle that housed a single toilet. Two pool tables with green shaded fluorescent lights lined the far wall. In the center of the dimly lit room, a patchwork of pedestal tables and wooden chairs dotted the linoleum. The floor was dirty and lightly sawdusted. The long mahogany bar was of surprising quality, but it was weather-checked and badly in need of repair. An ornate backbar looked as if it may have, at one time, seen duty in a more elegant setting, perhaps stocked with cognac and fine liqueurs rather than a dozen or more brands of tequila and at least that many of cheap whiskey.

Garrett stepped inside, pausing a moment to let his eyes adjust, then crossed the room to take a seat at the end of the bar. He was dressed in faded Levis, a green Windbreaker, and a pair of old hiking shoes Brandon had given him. This was odd for him, moving into an unknown and potentially dangerous situation as a civilian. On reflection, he realized just how naked he felt without his shotgun or submachine gun and a squad of SEALs around him. He slipped up onto the tall wooden stool and laid a twenty-dollar bill on the bar. The patrons of Shorty's were not what you would normally expect to find in a bar in the Southwest; they were more of an East LA crowd. Garrett spotted a few gang colors. The room and the bar were both about half full. A low undercurrent of conversation competed with a Charley Pride number on the jukebox. Both pool tables drew a crowd. The absence of slot machines said that Shorty's didn't want anything to do with the Nevada Gaming Commission, but through the smoky blue haze, Garrett could see folded bills wedged under the pool table rails. Nothing was said, nor was there any unusual movement, but several unfriendly glances came his way from the end of the bar. After several minutes, a sour-looking bartender in a soiled sweatshirt approached. He was a big man, but soft, with greasy hair rubber-banded in a tight ponytail. He wiped his hands on a soiled bar rag and stood across from Garrett.

"I'll have a longneck with a shot of Cuervo Gold alongside."

The bartender nodded slowly and ambled off. Garrett made a quarter turn away from the bar and surveyed the crowd. He was now starting to draw a few openly hostile looks from one table in particular. Shorty's was clearly a place that didn't see too many strangers. As far as the regular patrons were concerned, the fewer, the better. The bartender returned and pounded the beer bottle onto the bar, causing it to boil foam from the lip. The shot that slid next to it was well short of the pour line. He reached for the twenty, but Garrett's hand was there first, quickly covering the bill. Then, he carefully, sniffed the shot glass and set it down gently.

"Let's try this again. First, I want a beer that hasn't been mishandled. Then I want a shot, a full shot, of Cuervo—not this shit. And finally, I'm looking for a dude named Julio. He's about as wide as he is tall. I'm told he comes in here now and then."

"Oh yeah? What makes you think so?"

"Think what?" Garrett replied. "That Julio comes in here or that you're too stupid to get me a beer and a straight shot?"

The bartender's nostrils flared and he clenched his teeth, but Garrett met him with a hard stare. Neither man moved for a moment, then the bartender moved back down the bar. Garrett slid the shot off to one side but kept the beer in front of him. He didn't think he would have to wait too long, and he was right. A very large black man in motorcycle chaps and colors rose from a table and walked slowly across to him. He was big, but not soft like the man behind the bar. His head was shaved and he had a nose stud. A spider tattoo the size of a half dollar and a few shades darker than his skin clung to one of his cheeks. He stopped a few feet from Garrett as much of the conversation in Shorty's died away.

"What you be wanting with Julio?"

"That's my business, friend."

"I ain't yo' frien', and maybe I be makin' it my business."

The clack of pool balls had stopped; several shadowy figures had moved between Garrett and the door. Except for Bob Wills and "San Antonio Rose," the place had gone quiet. Garrett carefully eased himself down from the barstool. He casually grasped the beer bottle high on the neck, hand reversed, but he did not take the bottle from the bar.

"Just who the hell are you, anyway, his personal secretary or some kind of a fucking errand boy?"

There was a sliding of chairs, and a crowd surged behind the big man in leathers. Then another man stepped forward, much shorter but just as menacing. He was a barrel with arms sprouting from huge shoulders. His thick, smooth black hair was pulled back in a braid, while his mouth was framed with a sparse mustache and goatee. The high cheekbones and hickory complexion said that his ancestors were here when Cortés and his troop pushed their way up from Mexico to the southern Nevada border. He wore the same colors as the black wall who confronted Garrett, but there was an air of confidence and authority about him. He fixed the newcomer with an icy stare, then took a step forward.

"Chief Walker, is that you, man?"

"Hello, Julio. How's things?"

The two stared at each other a moment longer, then gripped each other in a fierce embrace. They separated, but each still held the other's forearms.

"This blows me away, man. I cannot believe it. You, here! Still senior chief?"

"I'm a master chief now, Julio. They upgraded me."

"I knew it—I knew it. *Bueno.* Man, it's good to see you." He turned to those gathered behind him. "This *hombre* is my brother; treat him with respect. And"—he shot a broad grin at Garrett—"without doubt, he's the meanest motha-fucker I've ever known—*es verdad*." Then he said to Garrett, "You're a long way from Coronado, Master Chief. What brings you slummin' in my neighborhood?"

"Need to talk, Julio, and maybe even ask a favor."

"Then let's us get to a table." He turned to the bartender. "You get the man whatever the man wants, *comprende*?"

Garrett eyed him coolly. "He knows what I want."

Julio led Garrett to a table against the back wall, midway between the bar and the pool tables. As they threaded their way past several tables, Garrett smiled when he saw the gold SEAL emblem pinned to the bottom of the sleeveless denim jacket. The crowd in Shorty's went back to what they were doing. Now and then, a curious glance was sent their way. The now not-so-surly bartender brought Garrett a tall, very cold Lone Star and a full tumbler of the right kind of tequila. He set a mug of coffee in front of Julio. Garrett eyed the coffee and then Julio, remembering him as a very-hard-drinking Navy SEAL.

"Had to give it up, man. It was getting the better of me." He lifted his mug. "To the teams."

"The teams." Garrett took a short pull on the tequila, then tossed it back. He then settled in around the beer.

"So what brings an ass-kickin' SEAL operator so far from the ocean? And hey, I was sorry to hear about your kid brother. Word had it he was a solid operator."

"Thanks, Julio, I appreciate that." The thought of Don caused a brief shadow to pass across his face. Garrett dug into the label on the sweating bottle with his thumbnail, then looked up. "Let me tell you why I'm here in Vegas. A few months ago, someone close to me had something taken from him. Now I want to find out who took it."

For the better part of the next hour, Garrett told him the story. The furrows on the ex-SEAL's broad forehead deepened as he listened. If he were surprised or shocked at what had happened to Garrett's twin, he didn't show it.

"So there you have it, Julio. We were robbed by some very dangerous and ruthless people. I'm a little out of my element here, but it would seem that no one does that kind of business in this town unless they have some kind of permission—or protection."

"Or paid the right people to look the other way. What is it that I can do for you, man? Tell me, Master Chief, and it's yours."

"Ask a few questions. Nose around and see what you can learn. You know the territory; I don't. I know that just about anything you want is for sale here. Apparently, even human organs."

Julio was quiet for a moment. "Give me a few days, Master Chief. I'll see what I can do."

"Thanks, Julio, and the name's Garrett. You're not in the Navy anymore."

"Y'know, the Navy was pretty good to me, man, but I'm glad to be back here with my homeys." He gave his Anglo friend a broad smile. "*Lo siento mucho, mi amigo*, but to me you will always be a Navy chief—and now a Navy master chief."

Garrett thanked him again and left. On the way out, he tossed a ten spot on the bar.

The bartender's hostility had lessened, but he still wore a sour expression. He pushed it back. "Sorry, bud, your money's no good here tonight."

"Then you keep it. And next time some guy off the road tumbles in here with a thirst, give him a cold beer instead of a ration of shit."

It was well past midnight when he guided the LeMans out of the parking lot. He found a cheap motel and was asleep in the stale, air-conditioned single just before one.

Garrett was out early the next morning for a short run, wanting to avoid the heat of the day. His recovery from the surgery was nearly complete, but he still lacked endurance. Normally, he might have been a little hung over after an evening in a bar with an old teammate, but this was not the case. While he was a long way from Julio's commitment to temperance, he was now careful about how much he drank. If he had learned one thing from the transplant operation, it was that he now had to live with one, irreplaceable kidney. He drove to a blue-collar grill not far from the motel and found something on the menu that was only semi-greasy. It was close to ten o'clock when he hit the Strip.

Las Vegas truly was a town that never slept. Because of the nighttime glitter and the shows, the sheer numbers were greater in the evening. But there were crowds of people at all hours—coming, going, walking, eating, gambling. Garrett gave the Strip a second pass and pulled to the curb across from the Desert Flower Inn. It was the kind of cloudless day the casino owners loved, one that would be hot enough to drive everyone inside to the air-conditioning and their tables. He watched the activity around the entrance for about a half hour, admiring the efficiency of the doormen and porters. A steady stream of limousines, shuttle buses, and taxis competed with private cars for the shaded area under the portico. A uniformed bell captain who could have passed for a Mexican army staff officer directed traffic with the aid of a shrill, two-toned whistle. It was a well-choreographed drill: Get the fleeced lambs back out to pasture, and get the unshorn lambs into the sheering pens.

"This's a fifteen-minute-only parking area, sir. You'll have to move."

The policeman standing on the curb by the passenger's door had an easy smile and courteous manner. They were trained to be nice to visitors in Las Vegas. He also had a long nightstick with a blocking bar and what Garrett took at a glance to be a Browning Hi Power 9-mm automatic in a Velcro-fastened, quick-draw holster. Garrett glanced at other cars parked along the yellow curb, but they were newer, more expensive cars, and their drivers were absent.

"Would it make a difference if I just parked and left it for a while—like the others?"

"You could," the cop said, smiling, "but I'd have to write you out a ticket."

"And the other cars parked here? Then you'd have to give them all tickets, too?"

"If they haven't been moved in fifteen minutes, I may do just that."

"But what if I just got here? Don't I get fifteen minutes?"

Again the smile, still courteous but with a forced show of patience. "Hey, look, sir, you're going to have better luck in there on the tables than you're going to have with me. Why don't you just move along?"

"That's a great idea, officer." Garrett started the car and returned the policeman's synthetic smile. "You have a nice day."

The patrolman touched the bill of his combination cap with his index finger and watched the Pontiac crawl away from the curb and up the street.

Garrett drove to the building that housed the Las Vegas Police Department and Clark County Sheriff. He was surprised at how clean and modern it was, with none of the bustle or chaos often found at an urban police complex. But then it should be a little different, Garrett reasoned, in a city where sin is not only legal but a regulated and highly profitable industry.

"May I help you, sir?" The woman at the counter was in uniform and had a ready smile. She reminded him a little of the policeman who had shooed him away from the Desert Flower.

"I hope so, officer. I'd like to speak to Detective Rucko, if he's in."

"I'll check for you. Could I have your name, please?"

"Yes, tell him Mr. Walker is here to see him."

Garrett took a seat and began to sort through the offerings in the magazine rack. *More like a doctor's office than a police station*, he noted, as he began to thumb through an old copy of *Arizona Highways.*

Garrett Walker looked much different now than he had when he arrived in Las Vegas just over two months before. His hair was still not long, but it was parted neatly and brushed back on the sides. He was now dressed in an oxford cloth shirt, tan cotton slacks, and, thanks to Brandon, a blue sport coat that was only a little tight in the shoulders. It had taken awhile, but he was starting to enjoy his civilian disguise. Before this, even when he was not in uniform, most people took him for someone in the military. Or a cop. Garrett had served more than one tour with the SEAL special missions units, direct-action teams that often operated in civilian clothes. During that time, he and his fellow SEALs had been encouraged to allow their hair to exceed military standards. Garrett smiled to himself as he recalled those days. He and his fellow SEALs only succeeded in looking like a bunch of shaggy military guys. It takes a while to again become a civilian, he thought. *You can take the SEAL out of the Navy, but it takes some doing to get the Navy out of the SEAL. And,* he wondered, *can you ever get the SEAL out of the man? Fortunately, I still have one good kidney, and the nation still needs Navy SEALs who are willing to go to the trouble spots in the world and take care of business.*

After fifteen minutes with the magazines, a man emerged from a door beside the counter and approached.

"Mr. Walker?"

"That's right."

Garrett stood and offered his hand. Rucko took it, but there was little warmth in the greeting. Brandon had never met Rucko, but the detective had seen Brandon in the hospital. And Cathy had described him to Garrett as a slimy little shit out of central casting for a grade-B gangster movie. Garrett would have had to suppress a smile at the accuracy of this characterization but for one thing Cathy had failed to tell him. Rucko was very dangerous; he could see it in his eyes. Garrett instantly disliked him.

"Well, Mr. Walker, it looks like you're doing much better. Sorry about your accident here a few months ago. I'm a little surprised to see you back in our city so soon."

Like most twins, Garrett was always a little startled when people took him for his brother. More so since they had been apart for so long. "Thank you for your concern, Detective. I'm here because I have a few questions about my ... uh ... my accident. Is there someplace we can talk?"

Rucko shrugged impassively as he drove a pinkie into his ear canal and wiggled it. "Sure, c'mon back to the office." Garrett followed him through the door. They threaded their way past a patchwork of desks to a cubicle near the exit at the rear of the building. "Can I get you a cup of coffee, Mr. Walker?"

"A glass of water would be great. I'm on a high fluid intake these days." Rucko made a neutral gesture and disappeared. Garrett looked around the small box of an office. It looked like the sweat-cubicle of a telemarketer on shift work—telephone, phone books, a scattering of metal office chairs, and a locked filing cabinet. There were no pictures or personal items on the desk, only a shabby raincoat that hung on a metal coatrack. Rucko returned with a small Styrofoam cup of tepid tap water and handed it to Garrett. He himself had a stained, semi-white porcelain mug with black coffee.

"Have a seat, Mr. Walker." Rucko hiked one cheek onto the corner of the desk and folded his hands in a patient manner. "So how can I be of help?"

"Well, for starters," Garrett said pleasantly, "I was wondering if there had been any progress in the investigation of what you call my accident."

Rucko assumed a professional tone. "I'm afraid not. It was a very unusual incident. We investigate a lot of burglaries, assaults, and an occasional homicide, but nothing like this has ever happened before. We have no idea who the perpetrators might be or where to look for suspects. Naturally, we gave it a great deal of attention, questioned people at the hotel, made inquiries around town, and so on but nothing has turned up. There was very little to go on. And there's the urban legend thing. A lot of people we speak to think we're kidding—that we're putting them on. Go figure."

Garrett was well versed on the Las Vegas hotel-kidney-removal scenario that was a well-documented urban legend. It was the kind of thing that thrived on the Web—a far-fetched fable until now.

"So urban legend aside, you have no idea at all who might have done this?"

Rucko lifted his shoulders in a helpless gesture. "There's not a lot more we can do. As much as we'd like to apprehend whoever did this, right now they're probably a long way from Las Vegas. Of course, we'll keep the file open."

I'll just bet you will, Garrett thought. He had a sudden urge to take Rucko to the floor and kick the living shit out of him. *Not the time, not the place.* Garrett forced a smile.

"I'm sure you've been most thorough. Tell me something, Detective Rucko, do your investigations always entail the rude interrogation of the victim's wife? Do you regularly question women at the hospital when their husbands are in intensive care? And is it your usual policy to harass them about their husband being with another woman? Is this how you do business, Detective Rucko?"

"Now look, pal, I did nothing of the sort. In a crime like this, you gotta move fast, get the information as quickly as you can. I was just doing my job." He rose and tugged at the bottom of his sport coat. "You got a problem with that, Mr. Walker?"

Garrett stared up at him, the urge to take him down almost overpowering. "Naw, I don't have a problem with that, Detective," he said easily. "It's just that I think you're probably as incompetent and stupid as you look. And your police work is apparently as sloppy as your personal habits. I do have a question, though. Since you're no doubt on somebody's payroll, why don't you dress better? You look like an advertisement for a thirdhand store."

Rucko's eyes narrowed, and he rocked forward on the balls of his feet, hands clenched at his sides. Then he forced himself to relax. Rucko really wanted a piece of this smart-mouthed prick; he needed to be taught a lesson. But he had been around the block, and he knew he was being baited. There was also something in this guy's manner that suggested there might be more to him than some computer geek who got rolled for his kidneys.

"Why, Mr. Walker, I'm surprised at you. Here I am, an honest, hardworking public servant, and you're treating me with no respect—no respect at all. You should be ashamed of yourself."

"Hardworking? Honest?" Garrett scoffed as he glanced out the door of the room. "This looks like a pretty well run police department. How do they let the likes of you work here?"

"Because I get results, pal," Rucko said tightly, working to keep his voice even.

"Right. Rucko, I think there's as much of a chance of you solving this case as there is of me breaking the bank at Harrah's this afternoon."

Rucko regarded him coolly. "You don't look like a gambler to me, Walker. Just what are you doing here in Las Vegas, anyway?"

"Like I said, I just thought I'd see how you were coming with your investigation, Detective," Garrett said, his voice laced with sarcasm. "I just came in to check on your progress."

"You didn't need to go to all that trouble, Mr. Walker. You could have just picked up a phone," Rucko replied.

"Well, maybe I wanted to take a look around for myself. Some people come here and lose money; I came here and lost a lot more."

"You could have lost more than that, pal, like your life. We still have an active file on this. You don't want me to have to bust you for interfering with an ongoing investigation, do you? And, if you do know anything, you'd be wise to pass it on, understand? Withholding information is against the law."

Garrett watched him closely. "I told everything I knew to that FBI agent who came to see me when I was here. Seems they have an active file, too."

Rucko's face turned sour. "Goddamn feds. What did you tell them?"

"Why don't you ask them? Your name did come up, though, but they didn't speak too highly of you."

"They got no business here," Rucko snarled. "This isn't a federal case."

"If my kidneys have left the state, which I'll bet they have, then it is a federal case. They seem to think so, anyway."

Rucko pulled a toothpick from his shirt pocket and slid it into the corner of his mouth. "Walker, I'm going to give you some good advice. Go on back to San Francisco and—"

"It's San Jose, Detective." More sarcasm.

"Whatever. Just go on home—play with your kids, make love to your pretty wife. Do yourself a favor and get your nose outta things here in Vegas." He lowered his voice. "You're over your head here. You just might find it a little too dangerous and not so good for your health."

Garrett stared at him a long moment. "Y'know, Rucko, that's probably the only thing you've said since I walked in here that isn't a lot of bullshit." Garrett rose, looked down at the shorter man, then stepped from the cubicle. Rucko moved to follow, but Garrett held up his hand.

"Don't bother, *pal*, I'll find my own way out."

George Grant was a man between two generations. The world had changed around him, but he was blessed with an ego that allowed him to concede that fact. In his day, he had been one of the young Turks at IBM, back when Big Blue spent more money on computer research than all of its competitors combined. He had come out of MIT with one of the first degrees in computer science. While other students on campus were protesting the war in Vietnam, he was writing early programs in Fortran and Cobol on computers the size of minivans, machines considered almost medieval by today's standards. Grant couldn't keep up with today's young software wizards, but then he didn't really have to. Out in the office bays of his company, he had several dozen of the new young Turks who conversed in Linux, HTML, and Java with an ease and fluency of rap musicians talking street trash. It wasn't that George Grant was unintelligent—far from it. Grant simply came of age intellectually when computers were novel, high-speed electronic idiots. He never quite made the transition to the fast-forward, competitive world of modern programming and systems applications. He was technologically obsolete, but at least he was willing to admit it.

Twenty some years before, when his working knowledge was still state of the art, he used his skill, his contacts, and a second mortgage on his home to put together a pool of capital to start MedaSystems. At first, he worked from his home office in Cupertino, then expanded into the building in San Jose that he now owned and MedaSystems leased from him. He knew then that medical science had far outstripped the cumbersome manual data entry and tracking systems that drove both the clinical and administrative sides of the health-care business. And the growing involvement of the federal and state governments in medicine slowed the process even further. Then there was the greed and independence of the doctors. All this contributed to complex and decentralized health-care systems and an industry with huge margins. Next to the federal government, health care was the largest business in the United States, accounting for close to 15 percent of the gross domestic product. Health care in the 1970s and '80s was run like a government bureaucracy—without competitive forces and a ripe target for software developers who could make those fat margins even fatter. At that time, Grant had estimated that there was an hour of processing for every ten minutes a doctor spent with a patient.

MedaSystems had gone public in 1996, and quickly became one of the dominant players in the medical software business. By 2005, MedaSystems was a cash cow serving a large network of clinics and small hospitals nationwide. Its clients initially enjoyed good profits and could afford to be loyal. But now things were different. MedaSystems fought for market share along with a number of very aggressive and capable competitors. There were no more sweetheart deals with independent clinics and sole practitioners. The insurance companies now controlled health care. The Affordable Care Act was creating changes daily. The big health-care providers were highly focused on the bottom line, and margins continued to shrink. Or, more to the point, the healthy margins were now on the side of the insurers. It was now a business in which either you grew market share and shaved your profit margins, or you went out of business. All this was being accelerated by an avalanche of new technologies and government regulation.

MedaSystems had not only survived, but it had also achieved modest growth. Grant knew its line of medical management software was among the best in the industry. The company's stock prices were also up, but recent acquisitions of smaller competitors and huge R & D expenditures had put the firm in debt. He lived in almost daily fear that one of his existing competitors would come out with a better product that would seriously erode his company's market share. The medical software business was a whore's market; even long-standing clients would drop them in a heartbeat if they could get a better product or your same product at a better price. The competitors didn't necessarily have to develop a better system. They could copy a MedaSystems program, make a few revisions, and market it under their own brand. Then MedaSystems would have to decide whether it was worth the time and money to take them to court for licensing infringement. Either way, he lost. *That's where the money is these days*, Grant mused. Legal firms that represented software companies in licensing disputes were springing up like cell-phone kiosks. Grant's thoughts again drifted back to the old days at IBM, before the arrival of Bill Gates and Steven Jobs. *Back then, we owned the market, the hardware, and the software.* The soft buzzing of his phone brought him back to the present.

"Yes?"

"George, Brandon's here. You wanted to see him?"

"Yes, yes, I did. Have him come in."

The heads of most software firms, even very large ones, seldom had a secretary guarding their office, but Grant was old school. He pushed himself from the desk and rose, adjusting his striped Guards tie. George Grant was the only person at MedaSystems who regularly wore a tie. The starched white shirt and conservative suit were also relics of his industry's past. Had he come to work in a short-sleeved, open-collared shirt like most of his engineers did, no one would recognize him.

"Brandon, come on in. How are Cathy and the rest of the tribe?" Grant had grandkids the approximate ages of Brandon's children.

"They're terrific, George. Thanks for asking."

Grant motioned him to a chair. "By the way, great job with that order from the HMO in Tampa. I'm tickled that we're finally getting some systems into the Southeast. It's a fast-growing market."

Brandon nodded his thanks, knowing that was not why Grant wanted to see him. Brandon and Grant had labored under a strained relationship since Brandon joined MedaSystems more than ten years ago. Apart from their difference in age, George was a systems man and Brandon was a marketing man. For Grant, the system was everything. He worked under the "If you build it, they will come" philosophy. Brandon's world was one of features and benefits. No matter how good the system was, unless the client could clearly see how the system benefitted him and how it solved his problems, he would not buy.

As director of marketing, Brandon had to understand the client's needs and see that those requirements were built into the systems the company developed. So he had cultivated a good rapport with the engineers and programmers at MedaSystems. Grant was not unaware of customer service and response to the marketplace, having watched IBM fall on its sword in those areas. Still, he had difficulty in running an organization that had to be nimble, often discarding an idea or concept in which the company had invested time and money. In the medical software business, the survivors were those who were most adaptive. But Grant feared failure like a pensioner fears debt. So along with Brandon and his strong marketing department, he had surrounded himself with the best people he could find. This included a well-paid group of programmers and a twenty-five-year-old director of engineering who was so smart he was scary. For the most part, he let them do their jobs and backed them up.

"Brandon, I'm going to be direct. I couldn't help but notice that you exercised most of your stock options this past week.

Some of those options were pennies on the dollar, so you're going to have a big capital-gains hit. I hope you're not thinking of leaving us."

Brandon decided against pushing Grant's paranoia button; the capricious engineering director threatened to quit every other week just to pull his chain. "No, George, of course not. It's just that I have a lot of my net worth tied up in those options, and I thought it would just be prudent to convert some of them to cash. I'm a little more comfortable now that I'm more diversified."

"I see," Grant replied. "Not a reaction to this kidney business, is it?"

"Perhaps it is, at least to some degree. Life is short—and fragile, as I've recently found out. I still believe in MedaSystems and MedaSystems stock, but I can't put my family's financial future in a single company—even this one. We don't live in a certain world." Brandon knew Grant had watched a fortune in IBM warrants expire worthless. "Besides, I still have plenty of shares in the employee stock purchase plan." He gave Grant a reassuring smile. "Enough to keep my shoulder to the wheel."

Grant nodded, apparently satisfied. "I got a call from an insurance investigator yesterday. He wanted to talk about the episode in Las Vegas. I told him that you were almost fully recovered, thanks to the transplant operation, and that the worst of it was behind us."

Us? thought Brandon. *Us?* George Grant had been as shocked as anyone when he learned of the "episode" and that Brandon had lost his kidneys. To his credit, George had done all a good employer could, and more, flying to Las Vegas to visit him during his hospital stay there and getting someone to come and help Cathy's mom with the kids. Time off, with full pay, had been no problem. The company health insurance carrier had paid out well over a quarter million in medical bills. But now Brandon sensed an impatience in Grant, like he had no more time for it and wanted it behind him.

"Was this insurance investigator from our carrier?"

"No, he was an independent investigator. Said he was just gathering background on the matter to decide if there were sufficient expenses incurred to justify him trying to recover the expenditures. When I told him the status of your recovery, he seemed to lose interest."

"Who did he think he would go after for the money? It's not like I got mugged by a corporation with deep pockets. And I sure as hell didn't fake the injury."

Grant shrugged. "Maybe he felt the hotel has extended liability."

"Did you get his name?"

Grant ran a finger down his daybook. "Right here … a David Baker, Southbay Insurance Investigators. You want his number?"

Brandon noted the number and rose to leave. "George, I'm pretty much a hundred percent recovered, and the workload is caught up. But since I've had to put in some long days, I may take a day here and there to make sure I don't overdo it."

"By all means. We want you healthy and at your desk for a long time to come. Again, great job with the new account in Tampa."

Brandon thanked him and slipped out. He closed his eyes and drew a deep breath, which brought a sympathetic chuckle from Grant's secretary. He then headed through a series of cubicles and workstations to his office. It was near the programmers' bays, where there was always a comfortable hum of activity in the air.

While Brandon and the CEO had not always seen eye to eye, he rather liked George Grant and often defended him when some of the senior staff, many younger than Brandon, made fun of Grant's stiff manner. George was an entrepreneur, Brandon would always point out, and he mortgaged his house to start a company—the company that now paid their salaries. These talented software engineers and programmers were the heart of the company, but they were generally introverted souls, usually capable of no more than an occasional intellectual gamble. Away from the office, they led narrow personal lives with little tolerance for financial adventure. They lived in condos, drove Volvos, and went about in Rockport walking shoes. Few of them had the stomach or the vision to go into business on their own. When Brandon got to his office, Richard was there waiting for him.

"Hello, Brandon. I hear you've been in with the rector. How is old Lonesome George this morning?"

Brandon gave him a tolerant look, but smiled in spite of himself. "Doing quite well, and I know he'd be tickled that you asked about him. How about you, Richard? How're you this morning?"

"Except that I think I may be coming down with another nasty cold, perfectly marvelous." Richard made a show of crossing his legs and leaning forward, hand guardedly alongside his mouth. "I told my section chief I was going out for a latte. You wanted to talk?"

Richard was thirty-something, fastidious, balding, and gay. He loved gossip and intrigue. He was also a software genius, one who had been a key player in the development of MedaSystems' patient tracking systems. The company software engineers referred to him as "the Franchise." Richard had received more than a few serious six-figure offers from competing firms, but he had remained loyal to MedaSystems. Brandon found that refreshing. He assumed that Richard stayed on because he liked the way the firm treated him. He was highly respected, and no one in the company took him for granted. And there were the stock options. In Brandon's world of marketing, money talked and loyalty walked. His sales reps came and went depending on what they earned working for him or what they could make somewhere else.

"This isn't a big conspiracy or anything like that, Richard. I just wanted to ask you to do me a favor, and for now, I'd like it not to go any further than the two of us." Brandon walked over and closed the door. "This has to do with what happened to me in Las Vegas a few months ago."

Richard nodded, "I understand, and you know I've been very worried for you. I get goose bumps just thinking about it." He made an exaggerated show of a shiver passing through his lanky frame.

"Thanks, Richard," Brandon said, quickly adding, "but I'm a lot better now—fully recovered and with every prospect for a long and healthy life." Richard was visibly relieved. "But there's something I think we had better check out, and it's probably a good idea to do it quietly. Now, I want this thing with my kidneys behind me. I want my life back to normal. Only it may not be that simple." Brandon got up and began to pace behind his desk. "Specifically, I've had to ask myself a hard question: Why me? Why did someone take my kidneys? Was I simply a target of opportunity or was I selected? Since I have a rare, hard-to-match tissue type, I'm worried that it might be the latter."

"Oh my God," Richard whispered. "You think that perhaps someone … rather, that some *creature* might have targeted you personally!"

"It's a possibility—only that. Now, consider this," Brandon replied, wanting to get Richard from the emotional to the technical. "Our medical insurance plan allows for self-directed care or a health maintenance organization. I've always been satisfied with Bay Area Cooperative, so I chose the HMO option."

"So did I," Richard added. "They're very caring people."

"Now, Bay Area is one of our clients—one of our biggest clients. They use our Universal Patient Manager system, which, as you well know, provides integration for all of their clinical applications. Well, I was wondering if it were possible—and I mean, just remotely possible—that someone could have gained access to the system. I mean," he said gently as he returned to his seat, "is there any way someone could have hacked their way into our database to do a search by blood and tissue type, then single me out as a potential, unwilling donor?" Richard looked as if Brandon had slapped him. "Richard, I'm merely suggesting it as a possibility, one I think we need to check out."

Richard rose and looked sternly at Brandon. "Our systems are *very* secure. I've gone to great lengths to see that no unauthorized person, no *hacker*"—he paused as if the term were a vulgar word—"could gain unauthorized entry into one of our systems. Brandon, that was cruel. You really know how to hurt a person—you really do."

Brandon would have smiled except the matter was too serious, and he knew Richard to be as sensitive as he was brilliant. He also knew Richard had a flare for the dramatic. "Look, Richard, I know you're the best in the business. This is no reflection on you or your ability. But my wife almost became a widow, and my kids almost lost their father. If someone did harvest my kidneys, then they had to have typed my tissue without my authorization. Now, if it isn't a system problem, and I'm not saying it is," he added quickly, "then someone who has legal access to the system has done something very wrong. Shouldn't we look into it, just to make sure it never happens again?"

Richard appeared a little mollified. "Well, I suppose you have a point there," he said with a sniff, "if for no other reason than to reconfirm the integrity of my security system, which I already know is totally tamper-proof."

"Thanks, Richard. I knew I could count on you. And again, let's keep this just between us. I don't want anyone getting upset for no reason."

"I can run some standard diagnostic programs," Richard said, beginning to warm up to the intrigue of the venture, "then slip in a few utility routines of my own. If any of our programs have been tampered with or changed since we installed them, or if we have had an unauthorized entry into the database, I'll know it." He rose to leave. Richard often became restless when he was away from his keyboard for too long.

"Thanks, Richard. Thanks for doing this," Brandon said as he came around the desk to see Richard to the door. "I really appreciate it. Let me know if you come up with anything. And look, you're pretty important around here, so don't take too much time away from any of your ongoing work."

Richard gave him a sly, conspiratorial look. "Don't worry, you can count on me." He turned, peeking around the doorjamb. "And mum's the word." Then he slipped out.

Brandon returned to his desk and sat lost in thought for several minutes. The desk was neat with several stacks of files on one corner. There was a framed picture of Cathy in a print dress out by the garden and another of her with the kids. Next to them was one of Tommy, the oldest, in his soccer uniform and cleats. And a fourth frame, a new addition, was one that Cathy had recently given him. It was a picture of him and Garrett sitting together on the steps of the Delta Theta house. They were both smiling, relaxed, and happy; Brandon remembered the day Cathy took it. It was one of the few pictures he recalled in which Garrett was smiling. Normally, he had a somber look for the camera. Brandon reached for the phone next to the photos and dialed out.

"Southbay Insurance Investigators," said the voice on the other end of the line. "How may I direct your call?"

"Yes, I'd like to speak with a Mr. David Baker. He's one of your investigators."

"One moment, please. I'll see if he's in." Brandon leafed through a short stack of phone messages until a man's voice came on the line. "This is David Baker, how can I help you?"

"Uh, Mr. Baker, this is Brandon Walker at MedaSystems. You called here yesterday about investigating a medical mishap I had a few months ago."

There was a pause. "I did? I'm sorry, but I don't recall your name or the phone call."

"This is David Baker, right?"

"For the last forty-five years," he said with a chuckle. "Are you sure you have the right David Baker? This is Southbay Insurance Investigators?"

"And you didn't talk to a George Grant here at MedaSystems yesterday regarding an accident I had in Las Vegas?"

"No, Mr. Walker, I did not. Perhaps it was another one of our investigators. Forgive me, sir, but I don't recognize your name or the name of your firm as being one of our clients. I could check it out if you like."

"No, Mr. Baker, that won't be necessary. I seem to have got it wrong. Thank you for your time."

Brandon hung up, but he didn't immediately release the handset after he had returned it to the console.

Garrett relaxed in the parking lot of the Desert Flower Inn, leaning against the LeMans while he took in the enormity of the big hotel. The Desert Flower Inn was not as large as some of the grander hotel-casinos and tended to cater to the convention crowd as much as the gamblers. Still, it was huge. From what he could see, the pool appeared to be large and well attended. Many of the Las Vegas hotels, like the Desert Flower, also billed themselves as family-oriented establishments with video arcades and miniature golf—somewhere for the kids to spend money while the parents gambled. Garrett noticed that most of the cars were large, American-made four-doors from Iowa, Kansas, Illinois, and other non-California places. He was a little unsure how he was going to proceed from here, but thought the best approach was to continue being Brandon and gauging others' reactions to him being back in Las Vegas. That meant pulling a few people's chains.

A well-starched, uniformed attendant pulled open the door for him. "Good afternoon, sir. Have yourself a lucky day."

Yeah, right, Garrett thought. He smiled at the doorman and strolled inside, then took a slow circuit around the lobby and reception area. The room was generous, with high ceilings and tasteful decor, not to blatantly garish as was normally the case in most Las Vegas hotels. The gaming areas were visible but well away from the reception desk and concierge. A guest could actually get to a bank of elevators without having to walk through the casino. Garrett wandered into a bar near one of the casino rooms and ordered a beer.

It was a small watering hole with a dozen or so stools along the bar and as many tables scattered across a red, plush-pile carpeted area nearby. Only two stools and a single table were occupied. There was an electronic poker game embedded in the top of the bar at every other stool. Two cocktail waitresses stood talking with each other at the other end of the bar.

"Slow shift?" Garrett asked the bartender as he set the mug down in front of him.

"Yeah, so far. Things will probably start to pick up in another hour or so. We have a pharmaceutical convention starting tomorrow. Be real busy then." The bartender was friendly, but he had one eye glued on the TV over his shoulder. Oakland was playing the Angels.

"Who do you like in the American League?" Garrett asked casually.

"Who's to say? Probably the Angels. They got the arms in the pen now, but now they need some consistent hitting."

Garrett nodded at the wisdom of this assessment. They watched the game for some time. Garrett had a second beer, and the bartender left him occasionally to build a drink for one of the waitresses.

"Say, buddy," Garrett said, glancing around as he rubbed his chin with the side of his index finger. "I'm here for a few days to unwind—just got in. I haven't been here in a long time. What's the best way to find some action?"

The bartender lifted an eyebrow. "Depends on what you want. This is Vegas; whatever it is, it's probably here."

Garrett moved the bottle in small wet circles on the bar. "If I wanted a good piece of ass at a reasonable price, where would I go? Nothing kinky, just want to clip my horns."

"Depends," the barman said guardedly. "You staying here?"

"I sure could be." He tapped his glass.

The bartender set a full one down and swept up the empty. "I'm not sure I can be of much help. Try one of the escort services. From what I know, they're all pretty much the same. Some say Dolly's, others say Doreen's. My advice is to stay with one of the established services. Pay a little more maybe, but it's safer."

"Nothing here at the hotel?" Garrett asked, again glancing around. "This looks like a pretty well-run place."

He shook his head. "Too much liability. The convention trade is our bread and butter. Some guest has a problem with a girl who works here and files a complaint with the convention bureau, we're in big trouble. Occasionally a freelancer will wander in. I usually buy 'em a drink and send 'em along. The girls know our policy; they don't want any trouble."

Garrett finished his beer. "Thanks, friend. I appreciate the advice." He tossed a twenty on the bar and left.

He took a long, slow walk around the casino area. There were all the standards—blackjack, roulette, craps—but half of the floor space was devoted to slot machines. Rows and rows of them. Fred and Wilma from Des Moines were sometimes intimidated by the gaming tables, but they could play the slots forever. They came here with five or six hundred dollars to gamble away and felt like they were winners if they could make it last through the weekend. Often it didn't, and then they had to play the cash machines with their credit cards.

Garrett thought about what the bartender had told him and concluded he was probably telling the truth. He also had to consider that the bartender could have made him out for a cop. His hair was still fairly short, and he moved with a sense of purpose that suggested he might not be in town just for fun. He also knew he probably didn't fit the profile of the kind of a guy who had to pay for sex. Still, it made sense. A place like the Desert Flower could stand to lose a great deal if it became known that they were in the business of providing women. Garrett found himself back in the lobby and went to the concierge desk.

"Yes, sir, how may I help you?"

"I was here a few months ago and something was stolen from my room, something quite valuable. I had some questions about it. Could you tell me where your security office is?"

"Of course, sir. Our business offices are down that hall. Go to the end and turn right. You can't miss them, and I'm sorry to hear about your loss. I hope it wasn't too valuable."

"Well, you might say it was irreplaceable, but thanks for asking."

The security office at the Desert Flower began with a solid oak door marked Guest Protective Services in modest black lettering. Garrett stepped inside and asked to see the director of security. Again, he said only that something of value was taken while he was a guest a few months back.

"Hello, I'm Brent Williams, director of guest protection," he announced pleasantly. "How may I be of service?"

Williams was stout, affable, and outgoing; he could have been taken for a politician. He wore the security person's civilian uniform—gray slacks, blue blazer with the hotel logo on the breast pocket, and a white shirt with a solid-colored tie. There was a slight bulge from the radio on his belt. He was probably armed, but Garrett couldn't tell for sure, which marked him as a professional.

"You may not remember me. I was a guest here a few months ago. My name is Walker."

"Oh, Mr. Walker, yes, of course. I'm happy to see that you're up and around. Won't you please come in? Liz, honey," he said to the receptionist, "please hold any calls."

It was a small, no-nonsense office—a cop's office. Most people in Williams's position had put in three decades with a badge on some city's force yet somehow retained the ability to put on a good public face. He showed Garrett a seat and returned to his desk. Garrett had the distinct impression that somehow Williams was expecting him. *Maybe a call from my pal, Detective Rucko.*

"Let me first of all say how shocked and sorry I was about what happened to you while you were here with us. That something so tragic could happen to a guest in our hotel was ... well, it was a shock to all of us here at the Desert Flower. Again, my apologies." Williams shifted smoothly from empathy to hotel employee. "Now, what can I do for you, Mr. Walker?"

"I suppose it is a little upsetting for you when a guest has to be hauled out of here on a gurney after a criminal assault." Garrett was pleasant, but there was a slight edge to his voice. "I was wondering if anything had surfaced to shed some light on what happened to me."

"No, I'm sorry, Mr. Walker, but there's nothing more I can tell you. We've had no new information come to light. It's also my understanding that the authorities have nothing new, but you should probably check with them." He paused to muster a measure of compassion. "It was a terrible thing, to be sure, but I'm glad to see that you appear to be doing well."

"Look, Brent—can I call you Brent?—just how many of your guests have had major organs stolen while they were a guest in your hotel? I'd be real anxious to hear just how often this kind of thing goes on at the Desert Flower."

"Uh, Mr. Walker, I can assure you that this was the first and only occurrence." Williams was struggling, but he remained civil. "Again, I'm truly sorry it had to happen to you." He flushed slightly and continued, "What more can I say?" Another empathetic pause. "Actually, around the Desert Flower, we still refer to it as a heart attack. It's ... well ... it's not the kind of thing that reflects well on the hotel, as you can imagine."

"Are you shitting me?" Garrett was incredulous. "A heart attack! This was hardly the kind of thing that you can easily sweep under the carpet—to pretend that it just didn't happen. The room, for God's sake, must have looked like someone butchered a hog in there. I was more than a few quarts low by the time they got me to the hospital. What about the hotel staff? If nothing else, you'd think the papers would get wind of it."

"Well, it's the standard policy of this hotel that our staff is to ignore a single incident or the rare personal tragedy of one of our guests. As for the press, well, candidly, they refrain from reporting on isolated incidents which reflect poorly on the city's tourist image."

Garrett was doing a slow burn. *Is this whole town just one big conspiracy—or one big casino payroll?* "Tell me something, Brent. You look like a decent fellow. Doesn't what happened to me seem pretty damned bizarre, even for Vegas, and maybe a little too nasty to just look the other way?"

Williams made a helpless gesture. "Mr. Walker, as I've already said, I'm sorry for what happened to you; I truly am. No one is intentionally sweeping this thing under the rug, but what can we do? It could have happened in any hotel in this city, but it happened in ours. Our security precautions are as good as any on the Strip. I'd like to think better. The police investigated the incident; we cooperated fully. The federal agents had some questions, and we answered them as best we could. Your medical insurance people talked to our liability insurance people, and I'm told they came to an understanding. What more can I do?"

"I know you have some pretty sophisticated surveillance equipment built into these casino operations. Any chance I could look at some of the video footage on the day I was nearly hacked to death in your hotel?"

For the first time since they met, Williams's voice took on a hard edge. "Not without written authorization from the owners of the Desert Flower or a court order."

"Fat chance of getting either of those, right?"

"Look, I know this is frustrating for you, but there's nothing I can do. Anyway, the police reviewed all our video logs for that day and the one previous. They didn't find anything."

"Yeah, I'll bet they didn't. Tell me something, Brent, what did you do before you became head of security here?"

Williams hesitated, but just for an instant. "I was a Las Vegas PD detective."

Garrett snorted. "Why doesn't that surprise me?"

"Mr. Walker, I've been as patient with you as I know how to be." The hard edge was back. "But I don't appreciate the inference you're making. This is a good hotel. A very bad thing happened to you here, but there is nothing we can do about that. Go on home; there's nothing for you here."

Garrett stared at him for a long moment. "Y'know, you're not the first person to tell me that today." He rose. "Thanks for nothing, Brent."

Williams rose and walked him through the door to the outer office. "Have a safe trip back to California, Mr. Walker." Garrett gave him an even stare and walked out.

Outside the office, Garrett paused, not sure what his next move was going to be. Navy SEAL work was different, and in some ways easier—locate the target, scout the target, attack the target, destroy the target, get the hell out of the area. Right now,

Garrett wasn't sure he could even get past the locating-the-target part. He walked back out into the lobby and made another circuit of the casino. On the way out, he stopped and dropped a quarter into one of the slots—fruit salad. As he turned to leave, a woman came up to him. He recognized her as the woman from Williams's office.

"Oh, Mr. Walker, there you are. You forgot your sunglasses."

Garrett hesitated momentarily, then took the glasses from her and casually slipped them on. He sensed that it was what she wanted him to do, even though they were not his glasses. "Why, thank you, Miss—"

"Never mind that," she said as she quickly slipped him a small, flat package. "Just get this back to me by eight o'clock tomorrow morning." Garrett gave her a questioning look. "It was a terrible thing that happened to you here, that's all," she said and then walked away.

Garrett slid the packet into his jacket and clamped it to his side with one elbow. He removed the glasses, dusted them off on the front of his shirt, and put them back on. Then he walked easily out of the Desert Flower Inn.

Minutes later, he was back out cruising the Strip. He knew exactly what he was looking for, and it didn't take him long to find it. A few blocks off the main row of casinos, he pulled into a seedy-looking video emporium that offered erotic tapes and DVDs as well as a do-it-yourself capability. He parked on the street and walked inside. A beaded curtain segregated a small countered area and store office in front from a larger space in the rear of the building. Garrett seemed to be the only patron in the place. Behind the counter, a vacant youth, probably in his late twenties but looking much younger, was reading a crotch novel and sucking on the last half inch of a cigarette. The kid had stringy unwashed hair, a ring in his nose, and a drawn, anemic look. He tore himself away from the book and gave Garrett an irritated, unfriendly stare.

"Yeah, what can I do for you, man?"

"Need the use of some video equipment," Garrett replied. "I want to view this DVD and maybe isolate a few stills. You can make prints from a DVD, right?"

"No problem, man—copies, freeze-frames, full-color enlargements, whatever you like. Got some good stuff, huh?"

"Perhaps."

Garrett took the disc from its sleeve and handed it to him. The young man slid behind a video workstation and dropped the DVD into the tray of a sophisticated-looking machine. Garrett leaned across the counter and watched. There was a flicker on the monitor, then an overhead shot of the lobby of the Desert Flower with people crossing through the field of view. The image was made with a wide-angle lens. At the edges, there was a great deal of distortion, but the activity in the center of the screen was of remarkable clarity. A moment into the disk, he watched Brandon check in. Then, from another angle, it was Brandon waiting for an elevator, then Brandon picking up a message at the front desk, then Brandon talking with a prospect in the lobby. Someone had edited the security-camera video feed and made a clip of those parts in which his brother appeared.

"Is that hard to do, take several hours or days of video and patch together a few minutes here and there?"

"Not really—we do it all the time. Someone just has to know what they're looking for and push the record button to transfer that section of video to a second DVD. It's no big deal. Say, this is pretty boring shit. I thought you had some good stuff."

Garrett shot him a cold look. The kid shrugged and turned back to his equipment.

"There, right there, hold it … now back up … right there, now go forward."

It was Brandon leaving the restaurant and walking across a portion of the casino toward a bank of elevators. His image was not too clear in the distance, but recognizable to Garrett. Brandon became quite clear as he approached the elevator, as did a well-dressed woman who hurried after him. She glanced quickly to either side as she stepped up next to him. A big smile appeared the instant Brandon turned to look at her.

"There, stop. I want to see the woman."

The video jock deftly reversed the DVD slowly and froze the frame, then enlarged it. A full facial view of a very stylish, dark-haired woman waiting for the elevator door to open filled the center of the screen. Brandon stood partially visible, nearby and to one side.

"Nice babe. Hey, that's you, man." He wondered what the angle was. Everyone had their clothes on. Then he brightened. "The babe's married, right? So pretty soon we get to see the two of you go at it, huh?" He was visibly disappointed when the screen went blank.

"Can you make me a print of that enlargement? Exactly like that, so I can see her face?"

"Yeah, no problem, man."

"I'll want another few prints that show her walking up to the elevator, and a copy of the disc."

"Sure, but it'll cost more."

Garrett pulled a money clip from his trousers and slipped a fifty-dollar bill onto the counter. "Great. How soon can I have them?"

"Well, y'see, man, I was just about to take my break . . ." Garrett dealt another twenty onto the counter.

"And since that's probably a hotel security disk, it may cost even more."

"That's right," Garrett said evenly. "It could cost you a broken leg. Now, why don't you just do what I asked and quit fucking with me, *man*?"

The kid looked at Garrett and made a quick decision. "Hey, sure, mister, whatever you say."

While he busied himself with the video equipment, Garrett roamed about the foyer. He paused at a color photograph on the wall, tilting his head over to one side, then the other, trying to figure just how two naked women and one naked man could get themselves intertwined in such a curious position.

Brandon was at a table in the small café with a cup of coffee and the *San Francisco Examiner* when Ray Stannick arrived. It was just past midmorning, so the breakfast crowd had, for the most part, come and gone. Stannick had called two days earlier and said in his easy rambling way that he would appreciate a few minutes of Brandon's time. Brandon had suggested he come to the office, but the FBI man deferred, wanting to meet someplace else. Stannick had called on several occasions, but Brandon had yet to meet him in person. He had always been courteous on the phone, asking about his health and the progress of his recovery. And while he was stingy with any details of the government's progress in finding out what happened in Las Vegas, he seemed to be the only one who didn't want to let the matter drop. If nothing else, Brandon wanted to thank him in person for his courtesy to Cathy during that first day at the hospital.

"Mr. Walker, I'm Ray Stannick. I'm happy to finally get the chance to meet you face-to-face." He extended a hand as Brandon rose to greet him. "Thank you for making time in your day to meet me like this."

"Not a problem. I'd like to help any way I can, and as you can probably guess, I have a few questions of my own. Please, have a seat."

"Thanks."

Ray Stannick was as tall as Brandon but much broader. He wore an expensive dark suit, a yellow button-down dress shirt, and a tasteful paisley tie. His hands were massive, yet he handled the coffee and creamer when they arrived in a correct, almost feminine manner. But it was his speech that caught Brandon's attention. His diction was very precise, like that of a radio announcer. The quality of his voice was rich and full, like a strong barbershop bass vocalist, yet he used it in a considerate, persuasive way, not unlike James Earl Jones, the actor. Stannick gave the impression of a powerful man skilled in discipline and restraint.

"I guessed that you would have a question or two, so let me give you some background on this matter. Perhaps that will provide a few answers. Are you aware of the laws that govern live-organ transplants in this country?" Brandon nodded. "Then you understand that here in the United States, like most Western nations, we forbid the sale of human organs under any conditions. The Supreme Court recently upheld this in a decision involving a North Carolina man with a failing heart who had less than a year to live. He was penniless and wanted to sell one of his kidneys so he could leave his wife with a little something. The Supreme Court said no and strictly upheld the existing provisions of Title 42 of the Code. There are no exceptions; human organs cannot be sold under any circumstances."

Brandon smiled. "So then it must really be against the law to steal someone's kidneys without their permission and sell them."

"True enough. But the fact of the matter is that there's a growing demand for organs, and the availability is shrinking. There's still a robust black market overseas, but some of the foreign underground sources are drying up. Interpol helped the Pakistanis close down a large clinic in Lahore recently. And there have been several closures in Thailand. There has been a succession of rumors about the Chinese taking organs from prisoners for the wealthy and the politically connected, but not so much recently. China is very image conscious, and they want to be seen as a civilized nation. Bottom line, it's getting harder to get on an airplane and go overseas for a new kidney or heart." Stannick paused, watching Brandon closely. "I would assume that you've looked into all this?"

Brandon again nodded. "I have. And I've done some research on the subject on the Internet. There're lots of stories about organ theft, but none of them are documented. Most of the information comes under the topic of urban legend. But I can assure you, I'm not an urban legend."

"No, you're not," Stannick conceded, "and as far as we know, excluding possibly yourself, there are virtually no known instances of organs actually being taken from a live, unwilling donor, at least in this country. And the urban legend thing kind of gets in the way—makes people want to write off what happened to you as some kind of a fictional event. What we know about black-market activity in Pakistan, India, and Thailand is sketchy, but we know it exists. We do know that in this hemisphere, there's an emerging organs-for-sale market in Rio de Janeiro. Where you have new wealth along with a great deal of poverty, anything is possible. Voluntary or involuntary donor activity is inevitable, given the capability of modern medical science and the inequality of wealth. In these situations, specifically in a lawless, free-market economy, money can get just about anything done. My apologies ... I hope I'm not going into too much detail here."

"Not at all, Agent Stannick. It's become an area of keen interest for me."

Stannick smiled, generating laugh lines at the corners of his eyes. Otherwise, his face was smooth and unlined. Only a touch of gray at his temples suggested that he was on the long side of forty, but he was very fit.

"Please, just call me Ray," he said easily as he signaled for more coffee. "We keep an eye on what goes on overseas, but only as it affects demand here; our primary concern is domestic organ trafficking. Of course, there are problems if you simply go out on the street to randomly look for organs. Unless there is a close and careful matching of blood and tissue, a successful transplant is rare. The key is to know your exact requirements in the way of tissue and blood type, as well as the complex antigen characteristics. You see, if you have a captive population like in a large prison, you can conduct selective testing, and the problem gets easier. When an organ is needed, you can sort through your inmate population and find someone with the right medical typing."

"Then encourage a prisoner to step forward and give up one of his organs," Brandon interjected.

"Or just eliminate the inmate and take the organs you want, as we think may be taking place in China. Modern-day China is a nation that is rapidly developing a class of wealthy citizens that can afford to buy what they want, including organs. Now, in this country, we have laws and a very advanced medical delivery system that make live-donor transplants under illegal circumstances nearly impossible. There has been, however, illegal activity on the part of disreputable donor banks and brokers. This activity is still very rare and has to do with taking organs from the deceased without their consent."

"I'm not sure I understand that one," Brandon said.

"A patient goes into the hospital with a terminal injury or illness. Usually his stay is accompanied by a full medical workup, as surgery or drug therapy may be involved. The patient dies, and his remains are given over for cremation. In more than ninety percent of these cases, there is no permission in place for organ donation, so a great many usable spare parts head for the crematorium. We've uncovered several cases where money is paid for viable organs, and those organs are removed and recycled without the individual's consent. The rest of the remains are cremated, and no one is the wiser. Some would say this is not a crime; the law says differently. And because it is against the law, it creates a black-market dynamic. Money and those who can pay for a lifesaving organ become an issue. A fully usable warm cadaver might be worth as much as four hundred thousand dollars on the black market. And there are those who see the use of these organs as a humane and compassionate enterprise. There are over fifty million uninsured people in this country, Obamacare notwithstanding. Many of them need organs but have no access to the system, legal or otherwise.

"And then there's the issue of timing. The best transplants happen when they are planned well ahead of time. When done illegally, this means organs are best moved from a donor to a recipient with a minimum of paperwork, bureaucracy, and family interference. None of those were issues when they took your kidneys."

Stannick was not a frivolous man, but very affable and easy to be with. Suddenly, he was deadly serious. "Mr. Walker, our nation is not—"

"Please, it's Brandon."

"As I was about to say, Brandon, this country is not China or some other developing nation where prison populations are a source of slave labor or a depot for organs for high government officials or the affluent. And we are a nation of laws. But the United States does present an opportunity that is unique, even among Western nations." Stannick paused and sipped cautiously at his coffee. "In this country, we have an advanced health-care system, and, most recently, an interconnected patient database that serves hospitals, health-care providers, and insurance companies. It has its flaws, but on balance, it's quite an efficient system. But then I imagine you already know that, Mr. Walker—uh, sorry, I mean, Brandon."

"That's right, I do. My company helped to develop it."

"Then you must also know that this database is very well suited to sift through a large segment of the population for all kinds of useful and legal information, including typing potential organ donors. I would even bet that you've probably given some thought to this, am I right?"

"Right again, Ray, but you've overlooked one key problem. Those of us who design these systems have made sure that redundant safeguards are built into our programs such that we virtually guarantee the privacy of these files. It's well beyond a simple privacy issue for us. The confidentiality of patient files is the cornerstone of our business—the prime directive, if you will."

"But," Stannick replied, "you do have the ability to go into the database, including individual patient files, and search for general statistical information like, say for instance, the incidence of breast cancer in women under fifty or diabetes in teenagers."

"True, we can use the database for demographic and group medical statistics. The access to an individual patient's file by name, however, is severely restricted." Brandon was beginning to like Stannick. "You seem rather well informed for a policeman, Ray."

"Well, we do our best. With the explosive growth of the communications industry and the Internet, we've had to hire our own programmers and software experts." Stannick smiled. "We call them cybercops. It's a fast-growing segment of law enforcement. Of course, when it comes to state-of-the-art software design and systems application, we're certainly not in your league. We simply can't pay our people what you pay yours. I would expect that one of your experienced programmers takes home a lot more money than an underpaid federal agent like myself?"

Brandon chuckled. "As a taxpayer, I sure hope so. We pay those guys a lot of money. But your point is well taken, Ray. I would have to think that our people are a lot better than yours. And it's not always the money. We give them a great deal of creative freedom. It's a cutting-edge environment—an intellectual challenge for them."

"But the bonuses and the stock options certainly don't hurt, do they? It's still a money-driven business." Suddenly, the twinkle that had briefly returned to Stannick's eyes was gone. "We noticed that you sold a fairly large block of options on MedaSystems stock. That's interesting, since the company seems to be doing very well."

Brandon measured him carefully. "My selling of those options and my reason for selling them are personal, Ray. I reported the sale to the Securities and Exchange Commission, as I'm required to do. Past that it's really none of your business."

"Brandon, you're considered a control person at MedaSystems by the SEC, and your sale of MedaSystems stock was properly disclosed. Your reason for doing so is, of course, your own affair."

"So what can I do for you, Ray? Somehow, I don't think you wanted to see me just to compare the compensation of government software programmers with those in the private sector."

"No, no, I didn't. Brandon, I can't help but think that you were somehow individually typed and that your kidneys were taken for a specific recipient. Someone just like you with a rare tissue type—someone whose kidneys were failing. This hypothetical recipient left you to face a slow death while waiting for that rare donor who might legally provide you with a workable kidney." Stannick paused a moment, then continued softly, "This theoretical someone probably had a lot of money and strong desire to live. He, or she, must have felt his right to life was far more precious than your own, since he took both of your kidneys when one would have probably done the job." Stannick folded his big hands in front of him and studied Brandon carefully. "My guess is that you've been more than a little curious about this thief yourself. Am I right?"

Brandon shrugged. "Yes, you are, but I still don't see how someone could have hacked their way into a health-care system, let alone into individual patient records. We're not the only software vendor out there, but they all have controls similar to ours. That still doesn't tell me what you want from me."

"Quite simply, Brandon, I want you to look into this from your position inside MedaSystems. See if there is some way that you can discreetly find out if this may indeed have happened, even though you say it's impossible. We could really use your help."

Brandon sat back and regarded the man seated across from him. There was a part of him that wanted to confide in Stannick—to tell this G-man that he had already reached the same conclusion and begun his own inquiries. But he wasn't sure that was the proper thing to do at this stage of the game. At any rate, he would do nothing until he had talked it over with Garrett. *Talk it over with Garrett*, he mused. He had forgotten how really important that used to be.

Throughout their childhood and into their first years at Michigan, whenever a decision or a major choice had to be made, each always sought out the other's counsel before making a commitment. *It's nice to know Garrett's there again*, he thought. *Maybe that's why the split was so dramatic and irrevocable. How do you seek your brother's advice about marrying the woman he loves?* While these thoughts flashed through his mind, Stannick patiently sat across from him, his large features impassive, unreadable.

"Why are you coming to me with this, Ray? You're asking me, in effect, to spy on my industry from inside my own company. I'd like to know why you haven't gone to George Grant. Seems like he should be brought into this, wouldn't you think?"

Stannick pursed his lips. "In the first place, I can only *ask* for your help. You can turn me down flat, no questions asked. You're under no obligation, and no pressure will be applied. I just thought that you may have a personal interest in seeing if we can find out who did this heinous thing. Me? I want to nail these people; they're crooks. I assume you do, too." Stannick rubbed his large hands together. "But since you asked, there are several reasons I came directly to you, Brandon. First of all, if we come through the front door and go straight to the president and CEO, which is how we usually do business, we might spook someone who had something to do with the incident. There are no secrets in a small company. They may go back and electronically cover their tracks and erase a potential lead. And there's always the chance that a CEO, since his first loyalty is to the company and the shareholders, will refuse to cooperate. As of this moment, we don't have enough to justify a warrant, and even if we did, it might prove counterproductive. Tossing a software company isn't exactly like charging into a smuggling operation or even raiding a bank. It's just that we really don't have that much to go on."

Stannick now seemed pensive, as if he were undecided whether to proceed. Brandon started to say something but held back, sensing that the big FBI man needed time to resolve something for himself before continuing.

"There's another thing," Stannick said slowly. "I have no reason to think George Grant has any connection at all to what happened to you, wittingly or unwittingly. His reputation in your industry is impeccable, and, in his own way, the man is a pioneer in the development of medical management software. But right now, I don't trust anyone in your company or, for that matter, in your business—only you. Can you understand that?"

Brandon paused before he answered. "Yes, I think so."

"Good. And there's one more thing. I want you to know that this organ-theft business has become a priority with us. Yours is the first clear-cut case we've had. We're reasonably sure that a few transients or street people have been picked up and tested to see if they were suitable as a donor. Again, we have no proof. One or two of them have even disappeared in a way that suggests they were relieved of one or two of their functional parts, then had their bodies disposed of. The street people don't easily talk to us, and few average citizens care if an occasional piece of street trash turns up missing. Your wife was looking for you in a matter of hours. Some of these indigents won't be missed for months or even years, if at all." Stannick paused, trying to choose his words carefully. "You're a first, Brandon. In some ways, I've wondered why it took so long. After all, that's what America is all about: a demand arises, and the entrepreneurs step up to satisfy that demand. It's what the illegal drug business is all about. The organ-theft market may have just become an industry. Demand has driven margins to the point to where legal brokers and organ bank suppliers know exactly what the market needs and are doing their best to find and obtain organs. Most of them are scrupulous about observing the law. But given the demand and the money available for a hard-to-find organ, the rats have come out of the sewer. Maybe I'm overreacting or being a little dramatic, but I don't think it's an exaggeration. I think we have to stop these guys—that we need to send a message that this kind of conduct just isn't going to be tolerated in our country."

He pinned Brandon to his seat with a forceful stare. Neither man spoke for several moments. Brandon concluded that the earnest man sitting across from him either had a genuine passion about finding the people responsible for taking his kidneys, or he was an actor with Oscar-quality talent.

"Ray, I'll do what I can. Believe me, I'm with you on this; I want these people in a way that even you may not be able to understand. Let me see what, if anything, I can do, and I'll get back to you."

Stannick laid his hands on the table, palms down. "That's all I can ask. I appreciate any information you have or can generate to help us solve this case. Is there anything I can do for you?"

Brandon shrugged. "No, not really, but I'll let you know if there is. And, before I forget, thanks for stepping in when that jerk Rucko hassled my wife at the hospital. She really appreciated it, and so did I."

"It was no big deal. The Las Vegas department isn't bad by big-city standards. But I do have questions about the clown who tried to question your wife. We think he might be dirty. Whether he had anything to do with what happened to you, I couldn't really say. But I do have some real questions about him which I plan to follow through on."

"Anyway, thanks. I'll let you know if I come up with anything or have questions, fair enough?"

"Fair enough. By the way, I saw you and your brother play at Michigan a few times. You guys were pretty good."

"Oh, really? You play ball?"

"A little. I graduated from Purdue a few years ahead of you, but I've always followed Big Ten football. Your brother was a real headhunter." Stannick smiled easily. "Do they still call him Tag?"

Brandon lifted an eyebrow, surprised that Stannick would know his nickname. "I suppose so. It even followed him into the Navy."

"That was a terrible hit he put on that Ohio State receiver. That kid was a good pro prospect, but he didn't play much after that."

"It was a clean hit," Brandon said, sounding more defensive than he intended. "Garrett met him head on."

"Oh, there was nothing illegal about the play," Stannick said, adding quickly, "and I've never heard anyone say otherwise. But it's always a shame when someone gets hurt. Especially a career-ending injury. By the way, where is your brother?"

"He went back to San Diego to take care of some personal business. I guess he's got a lot of vacation—they call it leave in the military—coming to him. So you played ball, too," Brandon said, wanting to get away from the topic of Garrett. "What position did you play, tight end?"

Stannick chuckled. "No, I was a quarterback. I backed up the starter for a couple of years. Didn't see a lot of playing time, but I got my degree in four years."

"Engineering?" Purdue is the Big Ten engineering school.

"No, psychology. Then I got my law degree at Indiana."

Brandon gave him a broad smile. "Ray, why do I not find that hard to believe?"

Now they both had a laugh. Brandon took his leave first; Ray Stannick followed about five minutes later.

Brandon reached MedaSystems some twenty minutes after he left the FBI man and went straight to his office. He had just logged on to his computer and started to go through his messages when the phone rang.

"This is Brandon."

"Hey, big brother, how's it going?"

"Going well, little brother. I just had coffee with our FBI friend." While talking, he stretched the coiled phone cord to its limit and kicked his office door closed. "He's asked me to help him with his investigation, see if there's any connection with our medical database and what happened to me."

"What'd you tell him?"

"I said I'd do what I could, but I didn't make any promises. Personally, I'd be surprised if there is a connection. Hacking into one of our systems is no small feat."

"Nothing else? You didn't say anything about having your genius programmer working on it?"

"Nope. I just said I'd do what I could and keep him posted. He did ask where you were, though. I told him you were in San Diego. He seemed satisfied, but I'll tell you one thing, Garrett, this guy's no dummy—far from it. We may want him on our team somewhere along the way."

"Maybe at some point, but not now. You checked your faxes yet?"

"No, but they should be here on my terminal." Brandon paged through his messages and e-mails to his faxes. They were automatically scanned and routed to his PC—no hard copy unless he chose to print one. He quickly tabbed through three routine fax transmissions and froze when he hit number four.

"Jesus, Garrett, that's her. How did you find her? I mean, how did you get a picture of her? That's incredible!"

"A little bit of shoe leather and a lot of luck. That's the one, huh?"

"That's her, all right. Still hard to believe she was involved, though. Can you find her? Do you know where she is?"

"No, but I have someone working on it."

"You mean, like I have someone working on our database to see if our system's been compromised?"

"Well, something like that, but maybe a little different. I'll let you know what I come up with."

"Take care of yourself, Garrett."

"You, too, Brandon," he said. Then rang off.

Garrett had stopped by a steak house after he spoke with Brandon and treated himself to a generous porterhouse. Afterward, he went to Shorty's, where he had a few beers and dropped off a picture of the mystery lady to Julio. He had no idea who she was, but he told Garrett to stop by the following evening and he'd try to have something. Garrett was in no hurry to get back to his motel since it was little more than a crash pad with TV, so he stayed at the bar until eleven thirty. He had paid for a week in advance, in cash, and registered under a phony name. It wasn't the kind of place that asked a lot of questions.

He slept late the following day and found a coffee shop for a bran muffin and some fresh fruit. There wasn't much for him to do in Las Vegas, especially since he had no interest in the casinos. He'd heard that Las Vegas had a world-class water park, so he found his way there and settled in beside one of the arcade pools with a good book. Between chapters, he took a few laps, and it was like tonic for his soul. A Navy SEAL, he realized, simply can't go too long without some time in the water, even if it was inland in a concrete tank and treated with chlorine. *Strange thing though,* he mused, *we never seemed to miss the water when we were in Iraq or Afghanistan. Maybe that's because we had things to occupy our spare time.*

It was about ten o'clock that evening when he arrived back at Shorty's. Julio was waiting for him. Garrett collected a Lone Star from his petulant friend behind the bar and found his teammate at one of the back tables.

"*Julio, mi amigo, qué pasa?*" Garrett could make himself understood in Spanish, but it was not one of his better languages. For some reason, he was more at ease and fluent in Asian tongues.

"Not too much, bro. Have a seat."

"How do you stand this heat day after day? And no water. Guys like us shouldn't be this far from the ocean."

"Maybe you, Master Chief; you're a lifer. Me, I like it hot and dry. This is my kind of country."

"Don't you miss it—the beaches, diving off San Clemente, poaching lobsters out near the Coronados?"

"I miss the guys—the teams—I guess, but I don't miss the coast. This is my place, man. My people are here."

"Julio, I don't mean to pry, but just what the hell do you do here? How do you make a living?"

"I got a piece of this place, a big piece. It pays the rent, and it's a place for my friends to hang out."

Garrett looked around. "Kind of a Tex-Mex, biker version of a yuppie bar," he observed.

Julio smiled, showing a row of white teeth with a single gold cap. "I guess you could say that, Master Chief. Not a bad fit. I also got a chopper shop up the road a few miles. I got a couple homeboys there that know how to fix just about any kind of motorcycle. An' it's someplace to hang out during the day."

"And a place to fix bikes for your friends." When he was on active duty at SEAL Team One in San Diego, Julio was always tuning motorcycles for the other SEALs.

"Yeah, that, too. An' I also got a consulting business." He watched the look on Garrett's face with some amusement. "Yeah, man, *es verdad.* The casinos hire me to sit at the bar to see that their bartenders aren't working the wrong side of the till."

"How can you do that? You don't drink."

"Don't have to drink, Master Chief, just have to order it. Then I watch them while they wait on others. If they're stealing, they usually do it by ringing up a short order from a cocktail waitress. Not always, but usually." He again flashed the gold tooth. "An' I'm the last person they think would be working for the house. You know what they say: It takes a thief to catch a thief."

"Well, hell, Julio, you're just a regular little one-man industry, aren't you?"

"A man's got to work—got to pull his load. I learned that in the Navy and in the teams. Who knows what mischief I might have got into if I hadn't joined the Navy—or had a few Navy chiefs who put me in line when I needed it."

"You were never out of line, Julio. You're a stand-up guy, always were. The Navy and I may have had a hand in guiding you along at times, but you always got the job done. A go-to guy in a SEAL platoon." He regarded the blocky man across the table with an equal measure of respect and affection. "You were a good man to go to war with, Julio. And, my guess is, you probably still are."

He snorted. "Let's hope it doesn't get to that, Master Chief, but I gotta say that I smell some trouble ahead." He pulled a scrap of paper from the inside of his denim colors and handed it to Garrett. It was a name and a drawing. "As for the chick, her name's Dawn Smallwood, or that's one of her names. Been around here, on and off, for about ten years. She's a looker, but she's also a junkie. She was a blackjack dealer a while back, but junkies don't last long on the tables—too unreliable. Been a hooker, and in and out of the drug scene—basically a loser. Seems that she's had a couple of kids along the way, girls I'm told. I've heard that when she needs bread, she gets straight and comes to town to turn tricks. Like in that picture you gave me, she can clean up pretty well."

Garrett looked at the crude map that Julio had given him. "This where I can find her?"

Julio nodded. "About twenty miles outside of town, up Dayroad Canyon. Lot of people up there living on the edge—folks up there do a lot of peyote and who knows what all. The county Mounties leave them alone as long as they don't bother anyone. If you go up there, watch your back. They look out for each other in Dayroad Canyon. You carryin'?" Garrett shook his head. "Then you probably ought to have this."

He passed Garrett a folded newspaper with a heavy metal centerfold. Garrett slid it to his lap and pulled it from the wrapper. He unzipped the nylon holster just enough to reveal the butt of a heavy automatic pistol. There were two additional magazines in Velcro pouches on the side of the holster.

"If I remember right, you were partial to a Sig Sauer."

"You might say that Mr. Sauer and I have a passing acquaintance," Garrett said as he refolded the paper with its contents and set it on the empty chair next to him. "Nine millimeter?"

"No way, Master Chief," he chuckled. "This is the real world; you need to get with the program. It's a forty-five, and it's untraceable."

"Thanks, Julio, I owe you one—maybe more than one."

"I don't think so. I still remember the day we went into Iraq ahead of the Third Infantry Division, and we stumbled into that company of Republican Guards on the Faw Peninsula. My ass would have been Iraqi grass if you hadn't been there. I won't ever forget that day, *hombre*. If we're keeping score, I'll probably owe you for the rest of my sorry-ass life."

Garrett smiled and rubbed his chin. "We did kick some raghead butt that day, didn't we?"

"Yeah, Master Chief, I suppose we did. For a while, it looked as if it were our butts that were going to get kicked. There were more of them than we had bullets. 'Run and shoot,' you kept yellin', 'run and shoot.' It was like a pop-up range; they kept popping up, and we kept knocking them down. I didn't have a chance to notice much else. All I remember was that there was a trail of Republican Guard guys facedown across that dry wash by the time we pulled outta there." Julio smiled sadly and lit a cigarette. "I don't miss the water and the parachuting and the explosives, and all that other shit. But I do miss the shooting. Those days out on the range with an automatic weapon and all the ammunition in the world—that I miss. Melt the fuckin' barrels down if you wanted to. Man, could we shoot. Nobody shoots like Navy SEALs. God, I do miss that part of it, I really do."

"You could always re-up, Julio. Course, you'd have to lose a few pounds and shave off that womb broom."

Julio fingered his goatee. "No way, Master Chief." Then he pulled at the lapel of his denim colors. "This is my uniform now. Besides, I got responsibilities here; people count on me. I guess you might say that here, I'm a master chief—just like you are in the teams."

"I'm sure you are." Garrett said seriously as he reached across the table and squeezed his shoulder. It was the size of a dinner ham. "And a damn good master chief at that." He started to get up, but Julio waved him back to his seat.

"You better take this along." He tossed Garrett a ziplock bag with a few grams of white powder sealed inside. "When you've got to deal with these people, sometimes it helps to have the currency they deal in. If she's gonna be helpful at all, you may have to bribe her. You lay some of this on her and she might not even remember you were there."

Garrett pocketed the plastic bag and scooped up the folded newspaper, tucking it securely under his arm. "Thanks again, teammate. You've been more than just an *amigo*, Julio." He turned to leave, but stopped midstride. Julio was smiling from ear to ear, his eyes just slits of mirth. "Okay, so what's with the shit-eating grin?"

"Nothin', man. I jes' never thought the day would come when I'd pass a bag of shit to Chief Garrett Walker—an' a master chief, no less." Suddenly, he turned serious. "You watch your ass up there, Chief."

Garrett nodded. "I will. Thanks again, old friend."

It was a little past one o'clock in the afternoon by the time Garrett swung the LeMans off the paved secondary road and headed into Dayroad Canyon. His progress up the canyon was marked by a rooster tail of fine dust that rose from the gravel behind him. The temperature was well into the nineties, but the dry heat made it bearable. He was glad he had purchased the cream fleece seat covers for the convertible and didn't have to deal with the black vinyl. He passed two vehicles going the other direction, both old pickup trucks. The drivers gave him hard looks as they passed and disappeared into his cloud of dust.

Julio's directions said the mobile home was just over three and a half miles from the turnoff. He slowed at the three-mile point and began to look for a drive on the left-hand side. The entrance was marked by a battered mailbox with faded, indistinguishable numbering. Access to the property was little more than two ruts between the sage and tumbleweed. A dusty, dated Ford Pinto and a single-wide waited on a shallow rise some forty yards from the road. The trailer, once white, was blocked in place and sat rust-streaked in the hot sun without wheels or skirting. At one time, someone had tried their hand at a yard, but the desert had won back most of its own.

Garrett pulled cautiously up to the Pinto. The only evidence that the little car had been recently driven was two streaked arcs made by the wipers across the dusty windshield. Garrett tapped the horn politely to announce himself and waited a few moments. He eased himself from the car, and as he did, he pushed the automatic into the waistband in the small of his back. He was dressed in jeans, a T-shirt, and a light cotton jacket. As he walked up to the front door, he had the same naked feeling as walking the streets of Ramadi or Kandahar in the bad old days. Only on those occasions, he had an assault weapon and a squad of heavily armed SEALs with him. Garrett stepped up to the crude, unpainted platform that served the front door and knocked lightly. He stood off to one side close to the doorjamb.

"Hello, anyone home?"

He knocked again, louder this time, and waited. Nothing. He thought about trying the door but decided against it. Instead, he went back down the steps and slowly moved around the side of the trailer house to the back. The rear door had a slightly larger, but no less primitive, porch and wooden steps that landed on a ten-by-twelve cracked concrete slab that served as a patio. She was lying on a plastic-webbed chaise lounge, partly shaded by a faded umbrella that rose through the center of a rusted patio table. A bottle of Gordon's gin and a tumbler rested on the tabletop within reach. Several rumpled glamour magazines were scattered about the lounger. She looked up at him with one hand over her eyes to shield them from the glare.

"Y'know, mister, if I was home, I would have answered the door."

"And if you had a phone, I would have called first." Garrett had made note that the mobile was served only by a single power line, no phone connection. He also knew that most druggies used cell phones.

"Yeah, and if I did, I might not answer it, just like I didn't answer the door." She stared defiantly at him and took a sip of clear liquid from the glass.

Garrett stared at her for a long moment before he finally convinced himself that it was the same girl in the video from the Desert Flower. She wore only short, cutoff jeans and a pink bikini top. The black hair in the picture had been replaced by a bleach-streaked light brown mane pulled back to a single ponytail. She had good bone structure, but she was thin, and her skin had a translucent, alabaster quality. Without makeup, her lips and eyes had a washed-out, lifeless look to them. She had no eyebrows.

Garrett could see that she had been very attractive at one time but that was now on the decline.

"What the hell do you want? I'm not working today."

"Day off, huh?" Garrett said as he eased himself into a folding aluminum chair across the table from her. The wooden handles were cracked and weather-checked.

"You could say that." She was watching him carefully now, trying to decide if he was a cop. "Why don't you have a seat; just make yourself right at home."

He took a pack of Camels from the table and studied them a moment.

"Help yourself."

He hesitated for a long moment, then shook two of them from the pack. There was an old Zippo lighter on the table. He pushed the cigarettes into his mouth and lit them with a practiced motion. Garrett had taken up smoking shortly after he joined the Navy. After 9/11, beginning with the long combat patrols in Afghanistan, he had quit. In close combat, a warrior needed all his senses, including his sense of smell, and that had been enough for Garrett to put them away. He quit cold. Suddenly, he wanted a cigarette. Perhaps because of what he was about to do, he felt he needed one. At least it was his old brand, Camel straights.

Garrett felt the rush from the tobacco immediately, and it calmed him. He gazed at her through the exhaled smoke and brushed a piece of tobacco from his tongue with his ring finger. She drew the smoke deeply into her lungs from the cigarette that he had handed her, held it, and exhaled slowly, in a halfhearted attempt to be sensual. "So, what is it I can do for you? You don't look like someone who wandered out here and got lost."

"Well, now, that's where you're wrong. I am a little lost, and I thought you might be able to help me. First of all, do I call you Dawn, or do you prefer Linda?"

At the mention of Linda, her eyes narrowed. She leaned forward seeing him clearly for the first time. Her inquisitive look took on an expression of disbelief, as if she had just seen a ghost. With a trembling hand, she took a couple of short, nervous puffs on her cigarette and flicked an imaginary ash to one side. Garrett waited for her to speak.

"I don't know what you mean. My name is Dawn. W-who the hell are you, anyway?"

"Ah, Linda, I'm hurt, I really am. You mean to say that you don't recognize me?" Garrett said evenly, holding her with his eyes. "Must be that I don't have on my business suit. Or maybe it's that I'm wearing my hair shorter." He pulled his sunglasses from one ear, then the other. "That better? Maybe you remember me now. It was only three months ago."

She stared at him, motionless save for a steady flicking at the end of her cigarette with a thumbnail. But her mind was racing, and Garrett could see that she was desperately searching for a response. He continued to prod her with a steady mocking smile, waiting for her to speak.

"Oh yeah, now I remember. They said it was a big joke—said that they were your college chums and were going to play a trick on you. Y'know, tie you up, bring in the hookers, and take a few wild pictures. They gave me a few bucks to slip you a mickey and get them into your room, but I left right after that." Her hand was shaking so hard now she had difficulty getting the cigarette to her mouth. "And besides, you don't look too worse for the wear. Matter of fact"—she was talking quickly now—"matter of fact, you look pretty damn good. We could go inside if you want. The bedroom's air-conditioned."

Garrett smiled again, a little sadly this time. "I don't think so. We've already had our fun and games. And like you said, it was just a little grown-up grab-ass at the Desert Flower—big boys' horseplay. No harm done, right?"

"Yeah, sure, whatever you say. You want a drink?"

She knew something about this conversation was terribly wrong. This man made her extremely uncomfortable, like she had just been cornered by a big cat. She felt desperate, trapped, and she fought to clear her thoughts. It had been a special job, but then most of them were. She couldn't turn it down, the money was too good—had been good. Most of it was gone now. There had been a lot of pills and powder since that day she dressed herself up and played her role at the Desert Flower. But maybe it was, after all, just a prank—a big practical joke.

Dawn Smallwood was no stranger to the seedier side of life. At one time or another, she'd seen most of it—done most of it. Now she sometimes had difficulty separating the sordid reality from the more pleasant ones that she created for herself on the patio with a bottle of gin and a vial of pills. She really wasn't sure if it was last month or last year she had played her bit and let that big, vulgar gorilla into this guy's room. Did it really go down like she remembered, or was it just a bad dream? She simply wasn't sure.

Garrett watched her closely. She wasn't drunk, he concluded; she just needed some alcohol to get through the day, or to take a break from the chemicals and the peyote. She swung her legs from the chaise lounge and crossed them as she sat upright, elbow on the table, holding the cigarette high. Garrett continued his fixed scrutiny of her.

"No? Okay, then, mind if I do?" She reached for the bottle but was trembling so badly that he had to take it from her and pour.

"Thanks, mister. Sure you don't want to have one with me?" She was now trying to act composed, even poised, as if some show of sophistication or charm would save her from the cool, penetrating stare from across the table. But she couldn't quite carry it off.

Garrett regarded her with a sadness bordering on pity. In her own way, she was pleading with him, but the dark shadows under her eyes and the thin features only reminded him of a wistful, dark-eyed child in a Keane painting. He'd seen the same poignant look on the faces of child prostitutes in poor Asian and African nations. It was the look of despair and hopelessness. This pathos only made what he was now about to do that much more painful.

"No, Dawn, a drink is not what I need from you."

Garrett dropped his half-smoked cigarette to the concrete and crushed it underfoot as he rose. She watched as he looked down at her, then he leaned across the table. With a lightning swift move, he slapped her hard across the face with the open part of his hand, causing her head to snap back and to one side. The force of the blow spun her off the lounger, causing it to roll on its side. She hit the concrete and sprawled out facedown amid the gin and broken glass. In passing, he hoped he hadn't unhinged her jaw. It was a calculated blow, but he hadn't expected her to be so frail or that light. He was on her in an instant, heaving her to her feet and pinning her roughly to the side of the mobile home. She was limp and dazed; a small trickle of blood seeped from the corner of her mouth. One elbow and a knee were starting to weep from skidding along the concrete.

"Now listen carefully, because I'm not going to repeat myself. I want to know who it was that hired you to become a career girl for a day and get me to pass out in my hotel room. And who were the sons of bitches you let into my room at the Desert Flower?"

She started to sob and tried to turn her head away, but he had her by the hair and kept her facing him.

"Talk to me. Tell me what I want to know and I'll go away." He slapped her again, not hard this time. "If you don't talk to me, I won't go away. It's as simple as that."

"I don't know," she pleaded. Her lips were beginning to swell, causing her to slur. "I was working a john down off the Strip, and this guy asked if I wanted to make a quick grand. Sometimes I do special gigs to make an extra buck. I thought it was some kind of a prank, honest."

She tried to look away, but he snapped her head back, tugging hard at the wad of hair held tight in his fist. "I want a name, and I want to know what he looked like."

"I don't know, honest, I don't." She was nearly hysterical, her eyes wild, but Garrett presumed that hysteria came easy for her. He considered hitting her again, but he sensed that she could probably take more than he wanted to dish out. The Dawn Smallwoods of the world get knocked around a bit, and she was probably no stranger to physical violence. For all he knew, she might even like it.

Garrett stepped closer, releasing her hair and grasping her throat in a choke hold under the jaw. He pulled a six-inch switchblade from his trouser pocket and sprung it open in front of her face. Her eyes widened in pure terror. He dragged the knife slowly down her chest, not cutting her but allowing her to know the touch of the metal. With a flick of his wrist, he sliced through the front string of the bikini top, allowing it to fall away and bare her breasts. Garrett locked on to her terrified stare, then laid the cold blade alongside one of her breasts.

"You're going to tell me what I want to know or I'm going to cut your tits off. You'll be stuffing foam rubber into your bra for the rest of your miserable fucking life. Now give me a name."

She was silent for a moment, but only until he rolled the blade from the flat side up onto a sharpened edge.

"Boris," she managed to say. "That's all I know—Boris." Garrett put a little pressure to the knife. "Big ugly guy," she choked out, "spoke with an accent. That's all, honest! Oh God, don't cut me!" Garrett held her without moving. "You've got to believe me, that's all I ... no, wait ... wait, his face," she stammered, her voice weak. "He had black moles on his face—two of them, big enough to see. That's all I know." She closed her eyes and began to weep softly, like a puppy having a nightmare. "Please, don't cut me ... please!"

Garrett snapped the knife closed and pulled her roughly into the chair at the table. "Here." He pushed the bottle of gin over to her and swept up the cigarettes and lighter, stuffing them in his jeans. She stared at him with a mixture of fear and hatred. He stood looking down at her.

"I'm not going to cut you, not now, but if I find out you've been lying to me, I'll be back. If you've told me the truth, you'll never see me again."

"It's the truth, you bastard," she spat out as she struggled to bring her top back up to cover herself, "and it's all I know."

Garrett leaned over her with his hands gripping the arms of the folding chair. Their faces were about twelve inches apart. She winced involuntarily, but she held his gaze.

"I hear that you have a couple of kids, girls, I'm told. Or is that just more of your bullshit dreamed up by a junkie?"

Her eyes widened briefly, then her whole face became a mask of hatred. "Don't you dare bring them into this. Goddamn you to hell. I'll kill you if you do, you son of a bitch!" She started to rise, but he shoved her back into the chair.

Garrett nodded and gave her a cruel smile. "Good—very good. I believe you would, or that at least you'd try. Now you listen to me, *Mommy*. Because of what you did to get the money to stuff up your nose, three little kids in California almost lost their dad. And, just like you, I'll do anything to protect them—*anything*. That's where I'm coming from—the same place as you if I harmed your girls. That wasn't some john you took down a few months ago; you were almost responsible for killing those kids' father."

She just stared at him. The hatred was still there, but Garrett thought he saw some spark of comprehension. Maybe it was just wishful thinking on his part.

"Anything else you want to tell me? Because believe me, you won't like it if I have to come back out to this hellhole and pay you another visit. You really won't."

She shook her head. He studied her for a moment longer, then released the chair, sensing that there was nothing more he could do here. Well, almost nothing. He was, he told himself, about to do something worse to this poor wretch than slapping her around and threatening her. His only consolation was that it was a sound tactical move, and Garrett Walker was a superb tactician.

"Here," he said as he tossed the ziplock bag on the table. "Forget I was ever here."

After he disappeared around the corner of the mobile, she took several gulps from the bottle. She listened to the engine roar and then heard a spray of gravel as he did a brodie out front and sped away. When it was quiet, she staggered up the back steps into the trailer clutching the plastic bag in one hand and the bottle in the other.

"I can't believe it. It's just not possible! I mean, who would *do* such an awful thing? This just can't be happening. Oh my God … it's … it's all just *too* diabolical."

Richard was pacing in Brandon's office, totally inconsolable. Brandon listened patiently, knowing that he would play himself out in a few minutes, and then he could learn what his talented programmer had found out. Being able to judge the actual level of Richard's distress was difficult since he could become theatrical over trivial matters. Finally, his degree of animation abated, and Brandon was able to get him to sit down. His tone with Richard was that of a consoling parent.

"Richard, calm down and tell me what's wrong. Does it have to do with your security systems? You found out who's been tampering with our medical database, is that it?"

"Oh it's so much more! You just don't understand. Nobody understands. We're dealing with a devil here, a sorcerer. It will take some time to pull the sheet from this corpse! Or we may never learn who he is. But you can bet I'm going to shake the bushes until I've exhausted every possibility! Whoever he is, he's a very, very bad person."

"Why do you think it's a he?"

"Has to be. I can tell. He's very insensitive—and very devious."

Brandon tried another tact. "But you're sure that someone has been into our system? You know for certain that someone's tampered with it?"

Brandon knew about software applications, but he was a marketing guy. He could use the system and, more importantly, he could demonstrate it, but he really didn't know the intricate details of the programming that created the system. It was a lot like selling cars. A good car salesman has to know something about what's under the hood, but he doesn't necessarily have to be a mechanic. Richard was a master mechanic in his area of expertise, perhaps one without equal.

"Oh, he's tampered with it all right. If I didn't feel so violated, I could almost admire what he's done. In his own twisted way, he's really quite accomplished."

"So we know someone is into our system, but it may take a little time to find out who?"

"Oh dear me, we may never know that, unless he gets very careless or we get very lucky." Brandon gave him a puzzled look. "You see, the architecture of a software program is rather like a three-dimensional road map, with all kinds of signals and gates, sidings and routing instructions." Brandon understood much of this, but he knew Richard had to work through this in his own way. "Think of this giant three-D map as a series of links designed to allow information to pass or not pass, or to reroute the information to a different part of the structure. When we build one of these programs, we try to use rigid but replaceable modules, like the erector-set bridge you built when you were a boy. Somehow, Brandon, I can see you as a kid with an erector set." Brandon smiled in appreciation of the little joke. "Then we can make alterations and modifications to fine-tune the architecture of the program or to make the application more responsive to the customer's needs. We do this by refining or replacing one of these modules, or a series of components." He continued to nod, wanting to move Richard to the bottom line. "The system is designed to be user-friendly, but we also want it to allow us to monitor who uses the system. This benefits us in a number of ways. We can track program usage and monitor high-demand modules within the system, but it's also an important component in how we ensure the confidentiality of our software and database. We designed it so we could monitor not only system usage but also who uses which applications and when. All inquiries and retrieval of data are meticulously recorded. The design of the architecture uses sophisticated data access filters that restrict certain users from certain portions of the database. We do that with a series of user passwords and internal codings that are very explicit. We even know if someone is persistent in trying to obtain information that is off-limits to them. At least that's how it's supposed to work. That's how it *has* worked except for this one exception."

Richard drew a deep breath and plunged ahead. "Somehow, someone—some fiend—has been able to get into our clinic and patient tracking software and gain access to our database." He drew himself up indignantly. "We have been violated."

"So someone has been, ah, reading our mail if you will, and we don't know who it is. Could it be one of our users?"

"Could be. I don't know for certain, but I doubt it."

"Well, since our programs are able to track who uses them, isn't there some way we could track our illegal friend and identify him?"

Richard gave Brandon an exasperated look. "This … this … hacker is too clever. First, he has found a way into our system and is able to roam freely in our database, taking what he wants and changing what he wants. Then, somehow, he is able to leave and we can't follow."

"Can't follow him? I don't follow you, no pun intended."

"Remember I said that our software is an architecture of rigid, replaceable components?"

"Yes, I remember."

"Well, this ingenious criminal has been able to replace our design components with some of his own. I ran one of my diagnostics that is designed to find unauthorized access to information in a very subtle and sophisticated way. It's a very elegant utility program that is absolutely state of the art. Well, I've found several incidents of unauthorized entry. When I attempted to learn who it was or where he had gone with my diagnostic program, disaster—a house of cards. This hacker had replaced our steel girders with rotten timbers. When I try to follow him, the floor falls from beneath me, the walls cave in. *The system crashes.* I was here until three in the morning fixing the damage this devil brought about, or that I brought about when I tried to follow him." Richard was in physical pain, like some parents ache when their children are very sick. "It's like Indiana Jones in the Temple of Doom. Who knows what hidden rockslides or snake pits are going to be in my path if I try to go after him. I can't believe what he's done to my program. I feel so betrayed. Brandon, this is very difficult for me."

"Tell me something," Brandon asked carefully, not wanting to seem indifferent to Richard's pain. "Did you happen to see if this invader had been into my medical records?"

Richard looked away, unable to meet his eyes. "Yes, Brandon, several times. I was trying to track him from that entry point when the roof fell in. I'm sorry. There was nothing for me to do but retreat and begin to repair the program."

"I understand, Richard. You did what you could. Is there any way we can get a list of hits that this guy made, maybe find a pattern of what he was looking for?"

"Possibly," Richard replied, "but we have to be especially careful now."

"Why is that?"

"Why? Because now he *knows* we're looking for him. He's covered his trail well up to this point; now he'll really be hiding his tracks."

Brandon was silent for a moment, then said gently, "You know, Richard, that if we can't seal this leak and do it soon, I'll have to ask George to recall the program."

For Richard, recalling one of his programs was like putting one's dog down. "Not yet, please," he pleaded. "I'll work round the clock. Like I said, he may get careless and we might catch him. Even so, that still won't stop him. He'll just come after me again. I can design a more secure system, but from what he knows from breaking into the Clinic Manager and Patient Manager programs, he'll probably be able to get into a new or redesigned system. Give me a few more days, Brandon. Maybe I can get this guy for you."

"Okay, but only a few days. If what happened to me happens to someone else, it'll be on our heads." Richard nodded, visibly relieved to have a reprieve. "But first, I want you to try to get me a list of the unauthorized entries. Specifically, the names of those individual files that may have been called up by this hacker."

Richard thought for a moment. "I'll do what I can. A lot of those individual files have been legally accessed by authorized users like doctors and hospitals. Unauthorized access won't show on our system management software. I'll have to design another diagnostic program, one that can safely screen for this intruder—one that won't crash the system while it searches for where he's been. No promises, but I have a few ideas on how we might be able to do it."

Brandon could see his mind beginning to work. "Okay, Richard, do what you can. Keep me posted, and don't hesitate to call me at home. Oh, by the way, what have you told your boss about the time you're giving to this?"

"I just said that I'd found a flaw in the system, maybe a critical flaw. Clinic Manager and Patient Manager are sacred cash cows here at MedaSystems. He said to take all the time I needed."

"Good luck, Richard, and keep me updated. You're doing splendid work."

It was after six o'clock, and most of the MedaSystems employees had gone for the day. Brandon was at his PC setting his appointment schedule for the next day when the phone rang. He wouldn't have bothered, but it was his personal inside line.

"This is Brandon."

"Brandon, Garrett. Can you talk?"

"Sure, go ahead. What's up? Did you find her?" He could hear traffic noise in the background and correctly assumed that Garrett was on his cell in the convertible.

"Yeah, I found her. She as good as admitted helping to drug you and steal your hotel key. But she says she was paid by some guy to just slip you a mickey and then get them into your room, nothing else."

"You believe her?"

"Maybe. It sounds reasonable. If someone's paying big bucks for kidneys, she didn't see too much of it. She gave me a name, so I'm going to see where it leads. How about you?"

"My guy here found out that someone very clever has hacked their way into two of our programs. We don't know who or how, but we're working on it."

"Sounds like progress. Keep up the good work, big brother. I'll be in touch."

"I'm on it here, and you be careful out there."

Brandon quickly finished his scheduling and headed home. He lived only fifteen miles from the office, but on a normal day that was still a forty-five-minute commute. Since he was running late and the traffic was light, he made it home in half an hour. He entered by the inside garage door, through the mudroom and into the kitchen.

"Honey, kids, I'm home," he called to no one in particular as he draped his jacket over his briefcase. Since he had made a sales presentation that day, he was wearing a suit.

Something was odd, and it took him only an instant to realize what it was. The house was dead silent. This time of day, it should be anything but. *Where were the kids? Cathy was normally in the kitchen fixing dinner this time of day. Where was she?* A stab of cold fear ran through him as he ran through the plausible scenarios—soccer game, school play, birthday party—but none of them worked. He kept a log of family activities on his computer at the office, so he knew there was nothing on for this evening. The loss of his kidneys had taught him that disaster could strike suddenly and without warning. *Had something terrible happened to his family?* He bolted out of the kitchen and into the dining room.

"Hi, stranger. I wondered when you were going to find your way home."

He paused to catch his breath, then swallowed and smiled. "Where are the kids?"

"I sent them to spend the night with the Clautice kids. I figured we could use a night alone, just the two of us. We haven't had all that much time to ourselves lately."

"No, no, we sure haven't."

Cathy was dressed in a simple black dress, pearls, and earrings, with her hair pulled back. Two tall candles were lit at the end of the table. The two settings were simple and elegant. A bottle of Kendall-Jackson Grand Reserve Chardonnay was chilling in a pottery wine caddie on the table while a second bottle, a vintage Rex Hill pinot, sat breathing on the side table. The dinner plates rested on chargers and featured a lightly glazed halibut. Alongside the glistening white fish was a small mound of rice and herb pilaf, with blanched asparagus spears, bisected by a splash of hollandaise sauce, nearby. She must have pulled them from the oven, he reflected, when she heard the garage door go up. The salad was fresh endive and greens with a sprinkling of feta and olive oil.

"If *madam* will excuse me, I'll be right back."

He returned a moment later with his coat on and his tie cinched back into place. They both treasured these stolen opportunities. They came infrequently now, always after the kids had gone to bed or like tonight, when they could be conveniently farmed out. He drew the chardonnay from its chilled cooler and poured a small amount into her glass. She tasted it and smiled. He filled their glasses, kissed her on the back of the neck, then took his place beside her at the head of the table. They raised their glasses.

"To a magnificent woman with an impeccable sense of timing."

"And to us."

"And to us."

As was their custom, they talked about anything but day-to-day office or household matters—California politics, music, skiing, vacation plans, old friends, new friends, and the like. It was their way of reconnecting, not that they were ever very much apart. They were soul mates. The kidney business and the reappearance of Garrett had only validated that. The kids and the trust and sharing over the years had all but joined them at the hip. The love was always there, but it was especially strong and explicit during these private, romantic dinners. The Kendall-Jackson was nose down in the caddie, and they were well into the pinot when they finished the main course and salad.

"If you'll take the wine in by the living-room fire, I'll get the dessert and coffee."

"You are nothing short of fantastic."

"You're not such a bad deal yourself."

They sat on the floor by the fire, finished the wine, and shared a slice of decadent cheesecake. Soon they were working on the coffee and a nice cognac, and Brandon was feeling very relaxed—more so than he had in many months. His tie was again loosened, and his shoes and coat were off. Cathy had kicked off her shoes as well, but she was not so relaxed. She needed to talk.

"Brandon, I don't want to change the mood of this beautiful evening, but we need to talk. Do you mind?" Their eyes met and both smiled. "Maybe this is something of bait and switch, but I've felt a great need to be alone with you and for us to have this time together. We've been through such an ordeal these past months. I've felt very close to you since this all began, maybe even closer than before, and yet"—she paused, searching for the right words—"and yet, it seems, to me at least, that we need to get ourselves realigned—to get ourselves centered again. Does that make sense?"

"It makes a lot of sense."

She looked into the fire. "You and I have been so fortunate—not just the lifestyle and the kids, but us. We have that special connection that few couples have. Do you know any of our married friends who are as close as we are?" Brandon, now watching her carefully, shook his head. "Then I hope you'll understand when I ask that I need you to be very clear with me about what you and Garrett are doing. I know what you've told me—that you and Garrett are making inquiries on your own—but I sense that there's more to it. My intuition tells me that there's cause for concern." She lowered her head. "I'm scared. I love you so much, Brandon. I can handle just about anything, but you must talk to me—include me. It's not about honesty; it's about clarity." She looked up into his face. "Is this a strange conversation? Am I still making any sense?"

"You're doing just fine." He put another dash of cognac in her glass as a sign of encouragement.

"I'm a little uneasy about Garrett and what he may be up to. I know we owe him a lot; in fact, we owe him our life together. The kids and I would have a very tough go of it without you." She shivered visibly at the thought. "But, thank God, that's all behind us. The only positive thing that came out of all this is that Garrett is back in your life, our lives. I know you've always said that it didn't matter—that it was his choice, and you no longer had a twin brother. But it seems that you're very glad to have him back, am I right?"

Brandon stared into the fire as he spoke, "It was never Garrett that I had a problem with. It was his inability to give you up, to accept the fact that you and I were together. I guess I've always resented the fact that he made me choose between him and you." He swirled the amber liquid in his snifter, pausing to clear his thoughts. "Yet it was never really a choice." He now looked into her eyes. "I was too much in love with you. Now it seems I have a chance to have you both—my life's partner and my brother. I'm a very lucky guy. He's my brother and I love him, but if he were to force me to choose again, I'd choose you. It was almost worth a kidney to have him back, but you can be very certain of one thing: I'll never let him come between me and you and the kids—never."

She gave him a pained smile. "Oh, darling, I know that; I've always known that. Sometimes I just need time with you, like right now, for reassurance, but in my heart, I know you love me and that you'll always be there for us. I also know that to make a place for Garrett in your life again, it may even take some of you away from us." He started to object, but she brushed his lips with her fingertips. "It's okay; that's as it should be. I understand that, and I accept it. I know that it's possible for you to make room for Garrett and still not let anything important between us slip away. But that's not what has me concerned."

"What is it then? What are you worried about?"

"Brandon, I'm not worried; I'm frightened—terrified, actually. I'm afraid of this … this quest that you and Garrett are on, this hunt for the people who took your kidneys. I'm afraid that, well … that I'm going to lose you—that I'll lose the person that is Brandon. To be honest, what really scares me is that you'll become like Garrett, the dark side of him." She took his hand and held it tight. "You see, what I love most about you is that you have a softness, a loving manner. You're willing to share things with me; you allow me into your heart. It's the caring side of you that I love. I've never seen any of that in Garrett; I don't think it's in him. For some reason, Garrett doesn't seem to have those qualities, certainly not the way you do." She paused, her eyes welling up. "I'm not afraid of losing you to Garrett; I'm afraid of you becoming Garrett. I don't want this obsession the two of you seem to share to cost me the husband I know and love, and the father my kids adore."

"Hey, hey," he said gently, taking her into his arms, "I'm not going to change. Garrett's Garrett, I'm me. I'll always be just who I am, the guy you married, okay?"

"But Brandon, it's happening. You've already started to change. Maybe it's because a part of him now lives in you; maybe it's because he's back in your life. I don't know, but you have changed."

He pushed her away to arm's length and looked at her. "I can't tell you that you're wrong; you know me too well, and I've too much respect for what you see and what you feel. I don't want anything to be different, certainly not between us. I—we've been through one hell of an ordeal. But this quest, as you call it, is something I have to do, something I have to see through to the end—with Garrett. Can you understand that? I have to do this."

She nodded slowly. "I'm not sure I like it, but I do understand it. Or at least I'll accept it. Just talk to me—tell me what you're doing. I won't hold you back. It's just that if I know … if I can at least share that much of it, then maybe I can help you get through this. All I want to do is hang on to you, the Brandon that I know and love, okay? Is that asking too much?"

"No, dear, that's not asking too much."

They held one another in silence by the fire, each lost in their own thoughts before slowly ascending the stairs to their room. They didn't make love that night but fell asleep closely intertwined in each other's arms.

Part Four:
THE SEEKING

Garrett contacted Julio and asked that they meet somewhere away from Shorty's. Garrett knew he was now moving into an area that could attract attention, either from the law or from those well outside the law, and he didn't want Julio involved. Garrett understood that Julio could take care of himself; he was street-smart and then some. But Garrett also knew that if he didn't want his friend mixed up in this, he would have to be very careful. Julio would come to his aid no matter what the personal risk. That's what Navy SEALs did. In their short, combat-rich history beginning with Vietnam, the SEALs had fought in wars and nonwars around the world. It was a part of their culture to leave no one behind. It didn't matter that Julio was a full-time civilian and Garrett a temporary one; it made no difference at all.

Julio had recommended a roadside service plaza on U.S. 15, a little more than thirty miles from Las Vegas. It was one of the few places out of town where Julio's Harley and Garrett's convertible would be lost in the shuffle of a transient parking area. Julio was waiting when he arrived. They both ordered coffee.

"*Hola, mi jefe*, how goes it?"

"Not so bad, Julio, how about you?"

He shrugged with an easy smile. "My bike has been running a little rough. It was good to get it out on the freeway and wind it up a bit. It's still not right, though. I need to put some time in on it."

"And you run a bike shop?" Garrett replied with a smile. "Just like the cobbler's kids that have no shoes."

"Say what?"

"Never mind—Anglo humor. Thanks for coming out to meet me like this."

"No problem, man; I'm here to help. Speaking of Anglos, you're starting to look less like one."

Garrett was still too tall to be taken for anything but a *norteamericano*, but he had acquired a deep tan, and his thick hair was now pushing around his ears. If nothing else, he had that healthy, unkept, outdoor look of a construction worker. Only the way in which he carried himself suggested he might be something more.

"Lying out by the pool and riding around in a convertible is a pretty soft life. Maybe I'll take it up full-time one of these days."

"Yeah, right, Master Chief, and maybe I'll go back in the Navy. So how was your trip up Dayroad Canyon? Find your girl?"

"I found her, all right." A shadow seemed to pass over his face. "She tried to stonewall me, so I had to lean on her some to get her to talk."

Julio looked at him thoughtfully. "Don't give it a second thought, man. A lot of these Strip ladies don't know it any other way."

"Yeah, well, easy to say. I really don't think she knows much. She told me someone paid her to set up my brother. Then they must have let her clear out once her part was done. She did tell me something about the guy who hired her. Said he was a big dude with moles on his face. Called himself Boris. That mean anything to you?"

Julio sat back, and a worried look crossed his brow. "Uh-huh, that means something to me. It means trouble—the worst kind of trouble. You ever heard of the Russian Mafia?"

"Sure, who hasn't?" Garrett said with a shrug. "Bunch of Sicilian wannabes. So you're saying this Boris guy is one of them?"

"He's one of them, all right. And these Russians aren't just a bunch of thugs who watch gangster movies. They're organized, and they're mean. The Sicilians may be bad, but they have a little class. They have respect and a moral code among themselves. And some rules, like messing with someone's family is off-limits. They're even willing to share their territory up to a point. Sure, they're into extortion, but only for a percentage. Not these Russians. They play by their own rules. These guys are very bad news—*muy malo.*"

"How are these Russians so different, Julio? Tell me."

Julio tugged gently on the fine hair of his goatee. "Master Chief, who were the baddest dudes we ever came up against? Who were the meanest of the really mean motherfuckers?"

Garrett hesitated, but only for an instant. "The Sammys."

"Right, the Somalis. An' why were the Sammys so bad?"

"Well, they had no fear, and they were fanatically loyal to their clan. And cruel beyond all reason—totally ruthless. Worse than the Taliban. They not only liked to kill people but liked to mutilate the corpse. Yeah, they were as mean as they come."

Julio nodded. "Believe me, the Russian Mafia is just as bad. They're not Muslims, so they don't look for a reason to die; they're just cunning and smart. Their religion is money and power. They deal in drugs, but very few of them are users. And they're arrogant as camels. Master Chief, these guys are very scary. My advice is to stay clear of 'em; they'll cut your heart out."

"Well, I guess we already know what they're willing to do along those lines, don't we?" Garrett replied with a tight smile. "I have no choice in this, Julio. I'm going to have to find this Boris dude and have a serious talk with him." Julio gave him a very troubled look. "Talk to me, Julio. Tell me about Boris."

Julio leaned across the table on his elbows and spoke non-stop for close to ten minutes. In those few minutes, Garrett learned something of how the Russian Mafia had earned their ugly and vicious reputation in Las Vegas. They were feared as much by rival underworld elements as by law enforcement. Even the hired casino muscle, which was formidable, gave them a wide berth. Garrett flipped open a notebook and questioned Julio for close to an hour more. He was gathering intelligence, and his ex-teammate, understanding this, gave him all the cooperation he could. Finally, Garrett stopped and was silent for several moments.

"Okay, Julio, you've been more than helpful. I don't want to push our friendship, but I may need some additional support."

"If I can get it for you, man, it's yours."

Garrett nodded. "Before I tell you what I'm going to need, I want your word on something?"

"Sure, Master Chief, name it."

"I have to do this myself; you can have no part in it. I don't want any of this traced back to you, understand? I'm leaving town soon, but you have to live here. If you can help me and stay clean, fine. If there's any chance that you'll become involved, I'll find another way. Is that clear?"

"I hear you, Master Chief. We may go back a ways, and I may owe you, but I ain't stupid. Tell me what you want, and if it's doable, I'll get it for you." Garrett gave him an understanding nod of acceptance. "Trust me on this one, Master Chief. This is my town, and I know how to get things done quietly."

They had another cup of coffee and talked for another half hour. Then Julio climbed back onto his Harley and roared up the highway back toward Las Vegas. Garrett ordered a sandwich and followed in his convertible a short time later.

Boris Kuznetzkov was a blunt man; there was nothing sophisticated or oblique about him. He was neither well educated nor particularly intelligent, but he was gifted with a low animal cunning that more than compensated for his intellectual deficiencies. Boris was a predator by nature, one who could turn ruthless and savage without warning, but he was loyal within his organization. He was deferential and obedient to the alpha wolf, his Mafia boss, but otherwise accepted no other authority or limitation. Since his boss was not in Las Vegas, he considered the town his own and did pretty much what he wanted. He ruled those under him in the organization with an iron fist, and they lived in terror of him. Boris Kuznetzkov was a man no one really liked and most feared, which was just as he wanted it.

Boris and his thugs worked the edges of the Las Vegas gambling empire—prostitution, extortion, and drugs. He was particularly good at terrorizing cocktail waitresses and taking a percentage of their tips. For some of them, he arranged jobs. For others with jobs, he convinced them it was easier to pay him a percentage of their till than to try to wait tables with a broken leg. He extorted sexual favors as well as cash. Boris wasn't as interested in the sex as he was in the pleasure he took in the domination of women. It provided him a small measure of physical release, and it totally demeaned the women he was extorting. Usually, this took place in the early morning hours when they came off the busy evening shift. And while he had others to do it for him, Boris liked to make the collections personally. No one knew when Boris would show up, which added to his mystique and created a terror in those who he forced to work for him. It kept him in touch with his organization and ensured that he could keep up with his own payments—those he had to send to his Russian Mafia boss in San Francisco.

Lilly MacIntyre had come to Las Vegas out of desperation to earn money to care for the son and daughter she had left with her mother in Los Angeles. A good cocktail waitress could make decent money in Las Vegas, and Lilly hoped that if she lived frugally, she could put enough money aside to soon be with her kids again. Lilly was a seasoned cocktail waitress, but she was black and a little overweight, making it difficult at times to find a job. Someone had told her to talk with a man named Boris; he could always find jobs for new girls in town. Lilly made the mistake of following that lead and found herself working for Boris in one of the casinos on the Strip. Lilly never knew when Boris or one of his associates would be around to collect, but she did know it was all too frequent.

It was early morning, and she'd just come off her shift feeling dead tired and anxious to get home. When Lilly arrived at her apartment, the first thing she saw was the Buick parked in the alleyway. Just the sight of the car caused an immediate shudder through her entire being. These visits were costing her more than a cut of the money she earned. Boris had also found the apartment for her, extorting a fee from both Lilly and the apartment owner. By his rules, this allowed him his own key, and he used it whenever it suited him. Lilly knew what was waiting for her inside. She briefly considered not going into her apartment, but there was no place to go, no place to hide.

"Ah, you are here. Good work this night at casino?" Boris was reclined on the couch with a drink in his hand. He would use one of her glasses but always brought his own vodka.

"Yeah, I done okay."

He smiled cruelly. "Then let's see how much, okay?" She passed him two twenties. He grunted and slipped them into his coat pocket as he rose from her couch. "Now, Boris is ready for rest of payment."

"Please! You got your money. Why can't you just leave me alone?" she pleaded.

He slapped her hard, but not too hard. She usually protested, and he usually hit her. For Lilly, it made what he was about to do a little more bearable. She was like a POW who felt a little less guilty if the signed confession were preceded by a period of torture. For Boris, it was simply how you treated women. His father always hit his mother, and while he was with his wife in Russia before he abandoned her, he had always hit her. It was the way things were done.

"*Da,* is one of my few pleasures. Would you deny me? I believe you like it, too."

Boris pushed her face down over the arm of an overstuffed chair. He yanked her skirt up across her back and roughly pulled her panties down just past her rear. Lilly was round and ripe, and he quickly had an erection. She stayed motionless, holding back her anger and tears while Boris unbuttoned his coat and dropped his trousers to his knees. He pushed his big hairy body hard against her and mounted her from behind. He kept his soiled white boxer shorts in place. Like many large men who run to fat easily, his penis was disproportionately small for his bulk. He came immediately, almost as if he wanted it over with as quickly as Lilly. Boris finished his business with the same satisfaction as if he had just taken a good piss. Wiping himself with the hem of her dress, he then whacked her playfully on the backside and reached down for his pants.

"You make Boris happy. Other girls maybe more pretty, but I like to fuck you. Is good for you, too, no?"

She wanted to tell him how he disgusted her, that his inept and clumsy performance made her sick, but she knew it wasn't worth taking a punch. Lilly had learned that once he was finished and no longer needed to rut, his cuffs could be considerably harder. Boris left her apartment without another word. Lilly took her hatred for Boris into the shower, attempting to cleanse herself of him even before he managed to walk the short distance to his car. It would not be light for another two hours, and the street was deserted.

Boris settled his bulk into the car and began to sort through his many keys for the one to the ignition. It was only then that he noticed the small U-Haul-type van parked in front of his car. It was probably there when he arrived to see the girl, but he hadn't noticed it. He smiled to himself, acknowledging that when he was horny, he didn't always notice things as well as he should.

Boris had again turned his attention to the ring of keys when he felt the cold steel muzzle of a gun pushed into the back of his head. He immediately froze, attempting only to steal a glance at the rearview mirror. It had been turned up to shield the identity of whoever was behind him.

"Put your hands on top of the steering wheel." Boris didn't respond right away to the voice behind him, but after a hard nudge from the snout of the automatic, he did as he was told.

"That's better, friend." The man spoke low and slow so Boris had no trouble understanding him. "Now, I want you to sit there quietly and don't even think about doing something stupid. Make one wrong move and I'll paint the windshield with your brains." Boris felt the muzzle of the gun slide from the back of his head slowly around to the side until it was pushed hard up behind his ear. An arm reached from behind him and a hand moved to the inside of his jacket.

"You here to rob me?" Boris asked in genuine surprise. "Do you know who I am?"

The hammer of the big .45 came back and resonated in his ear—*ka-CLICK*! Boris held his breath. With a gloved hand, Garrett eased a pistol, a Walther P-38, from the big man's shoulder holster. With the automatic still resting behind Boris's ear, Garrett leaned forward, close enough to smell the borscht and sauerkraut Boris had eaten the evening before.

"Listen very carefully, my friend. I have some questions for you, and I advise that you give me your full cooperation. Now, do not move, not so much as an inch, and pay very close attention."

Garrett spoke very slowly and deliberately into the back of Boris's head. "Answer my questions and we go our separate ways; nobody gets hurt. If you don't, then I will have to hurt you, and I promise, I will hurt you very badly. Even you can't imagine just how badly. Do you understand?"

"*Da.*"

"Good. Several months ago, you took some human organs, two kidneys to be exact, from a man staying at the Desert Flower Inn. I want to know who paid you and who those two kidneys were for. I want to know everything about that night at the Desert Flower. Do you understand?" Again, the prod with the nose of the automatic. The front sight was now beginning to carve a notch in the skin behind Boris's ear, yet he was silent.

"I asked you a question and I want an answer. Do you understand me?"

"*Da*, understand. But know nothing. You maybe have wrong person. Do you know who it is you talk to, who I am?"

"I'm talking to the man who removed two kidneys in the Desert Flower a few months ago and sold them."

"You wrong. I know nothing of kidneys."

"I was afraid you were going to go stupid on me, Boris. That really is unfortunate."

Boris was listening very carefully; all his senses were focused on the man behind him. He understood little about these Americans, yet he thought that he detected a trace of resignation, even sadness in the man's voice. That was his last thought as his head exploded—then there was nothing.

Garrett had wrapped a brick in a towel so as not to cut him or tear his scalp. He needed to strike a blow to the side of Boris's head with enough force to effectively knock him unconscious, but just for a short while. Aware that Boris was a very large man with a massive head, he was cocked and ready to deal another blow, but the big man was out cold. Garrett slipped from the rear of the

Buick and raised the rear garage-type door of the van. He checked the street to make sure it was still empty, then hauled Boris from his car in a fireman's carry and rolled him onto the wooden deck of the van. With another quick look around, he jumped aboard and pulled the door down behind him. Five minutes later, he raised the door a few feet and dropped back down to the street. He walked quickly around to the cab and drove slowly away.

It was now well past two in the afternoon, close to ten hours after Garrett had clubbed Boris and put him in the back of the van. After leaving Lilly's street that morning, Garrett had driven to Sloan, Nevada. Then some twelve miles west of Sloan, he left the pavement. After close to a half hour on an old dirt road, he pulled the van into a dry wash, taking care that the sand and gravel were firm enough to hold the weight of the vehicle. It was difficult hiding a moving van in the desert, even a small one with all markings of the previous leasing company painted out. However, it was relatively sheltered from view, parked low in the ravine with a berm between the vehicle and the seldom-used road. He had arrived midmorning, and there he waited. Garrett climbed onto the roof of the cab every half hour or so. He could see for miles, and there was no sign of life. He had arrived at his destination about five hours earlier and was beginning to feel comfortable with his choice of location.

Garrett sat in the shade of the van's box, leaning against the rear tire and drinking from a plastic quart bottle of store-bought water. It was his fourth bottle. In keeping with his desert training, he wore a light, long-sleeved shirt, a floppy hat, loose trousers, and sand boots. He finished the water and reluctantly looked at his watch. Slowly, he climbed to the top of the cab for a last look around. Nothing. Garrett moved gingerly across the hood of the van, which radiated enough heat to fry an egg. He thought about cracking open another bottle of water but decided not to. It was time. He walked around to the rear of the van and raised the door quickly. Inside, Boris was lashed spread-eagle fashion to the side of the box, the side that had been exposed to the sun. His wrists and ankles were tightly bound with stout nylon slip-ties, each restraint drawing a limb away from the torso by means of a thick nylon web strap. The Russian was essentially drawn and quartered to the wall of the van. Both wrists were bleeding from the snap-ties.

Boris jerked his head away from the door as the bright daylight overtook him. He had been in darkness for close to fourteen hours. He had awakened shortly after daylight to the pain of his bonds and the pounding in his head. Soon, the heat overtook the pain. His lips were parched and cracked, and the side of his face around one eye and cheekbone was purple and gray from the collision with the padded brick. The temperature inside was close to 130, and the van reeked of feces and stale urine. While Boris's eyes became adjusted to the light, Garrett carefully took off his shirt, folded it neatly, and laid it on the wooden van deck. Then he removed the .45 from his belt and laid it on the shirt. Dressed in a sleeveless undershirt, he carefully pulled on a pair of leather gloves and cinched them tightly with the draw strap on the top of the wrists. None of this was lost on Boris, nor was it the first time he had seen this preparation. Garrett stepped to the middle of the van and faced the parched and tethered man.

Garrett stared at Boris a long while. The Russian glared back defiantly while his pinched red face seemed about to pop the large dark moles from their attachment points. At the best of times, Boris was not a handsome man. He looked much worse now. Garrett took a bottle of water and splashed it on the big man's face. For a brief moment, this cooled the fires of Boris's hell. He sucked greedily at the sweat and water runoff from his face, but it did little to quell his raging thirst.

"Mr. Kuznetzkov, we are well outside of Las Vegas. There isn't a soul around for miles except for you and me. On second thought, I take that back. I'm convinced that you are without a soul, and right now, I'm not so sure that I have one, either. In any case, it's only you and me—no one else. A few hours ago, I asked you a few simple questions, and you refused to answer me. Do you remember?"

Boris nodded; it was the only physical move he could make. When he had regained consciousness, he could at least move his hands and feet, but that was hours ago. He had long since lost feeling in his limbs. It took several moments for him to work enough moisture to his mouth so he could speak. Garrett waited patiently.

"And I asked you question," he gasped. "You remember?"

"Yes, I remember."

"You know who I am? And what you deal with?" Boris labored to speak, his tongue thick.

"Yes, I know," Garrett answered in an even voice. "I know all about you and your organization—your Mafia."

Garrett watched him carefully and saw some relief in the man's eyes, as if his ability to convey what and who he was would somehow protect him. Julio had told him that these people were arrogant, and Garrett was just now beginning to grasp what he meant.

"And you feel this makes a difference—out here. No one saw me put you in the van; no one knows where you are. And when you don't appear, do you believe the men who work for you will really want to find you?" Garrett forced a laugh. "Out here, you have no organization. You want to call for help, go ahead; be my guest." He waited several moments. "Like I said, it's just you and me, my Russian friend. There is no one else. You have no Mafia now."

Boris tried to moisten his lips, but there was no moisture left in his mouth. He swallowed bile and eyed Garrett carefully. Boris desperately wanted more water, but he was not going to ask for it. "You know … I can tell you nothing. Is … is not allowed. I do not talk."

Garrett shrugged. It was not what he wanted to hear, but he expected as much. He removed his sunglasses and stepped closer to Boris.

"I know who you are, Boris, but do you know who I am?"

He peered at Garrett through eyes that had now become slits above his puffed cheeks. As his eyes adjusted to the light, Boris, for a moment, had the feeling that he had seen this lean, purposeful man before. Yes, there was something vaguely familiar about his captor who had lashed him to the wall of this portable hell. Now, without the glasses, he knew exactly who he was.

"You are he," he managed to say, "the one with the kidneys."

"Wrong, you scumbag," Garrett spat out, again playing the Brandon card. "I'm the one without the kidneys, thanks to you. And do you know what I'm going to do to you?"

Boris didn't answer, but he watched Garrett carefully. Garrett brought out the switchblade and snapped it open in front of his face, causing Boris to blink rapidly. Suddenly, the sadness and reluctance that accompanied Garrett to this point quickly deserted him. He was consumed with rage—a carefully controlled fury but very transparent. It was a rage born by what this man had done to Brandon and nurtured by what it now forced him to do. It suddenly became a very personal, deep-seated, and focused rage. Boris instantly recognized this sudden ferocity, but he was helpless to do anything but watch and wait.

Garrett took the knife and made a shallow slice in his own shoulder. The blade was very sharp; it required little effort, and he felt nothing. The cut was a superficial wound, and the blood seeped slowly down and across his biceps. He smeared the blood from his shoulder onto his gloved hand and then brushed it onto both of his own cheeks. Garrett then passed his glove over the wound again and bloodied both of Boris's cheeks as the Russian instinctively tried to recoil. In the case of the Russian, it simply made him look more pathetic, more vulnerable. But in the eyes of the defenseless man tied to the van rack, it transformed Garrett into a sinister, nightmarish avenger, one capable of unspeakable things. Boris Kuznetzkov was not a man who terrified easily, but he was that now, and more.

"I'm going to do to you what you did to me, only no drugs—no painkillers. And if you pass out from the pain, I'll revive you, and we'll continue until I'm holding one of *your* kidneys in front of that ugly, melon face of yours. And if you haven't bled to death by then, I'll start on the other one. Do you understand me, Boris?" He paused and held the big Russian in a fierce stare for a long moment. Then he smiled cruelly. "And do you know what? You're going to squeal like a pig, and I'm going to enjoy it."

Garrett released one of Boris's wrist and ankle restraints. Even with this partial freedom, he could do nothing but hang drunkenly from one wrist. Garrett quickly swung him around and reattached him to the wall with his back exposed. This effectively heightened his terror, for he could no longer see his tormentor. Next, Garrett dipped the stiletto into the collar of Boris's shirt and, in one motion, parted his suit coat and shirt, exposing a sweaty, fleshy back. It was the bleached, hairy flab of an albino boar. Garrett began to run a bloodied glove over the Russian's rib cage and across the small of this back, testing for the best point of entry. Boris choked and said something, but Garrett could not hear what it was.

"Are you speaking to me, Boris?"

"*D-da.*"

"Well, speak up! What is it you want to say?"

"If I answer questions, what is to happen?"

Garrett hesitated a moment, then spoke. "I will give you water and I will set you free, this I promise."

"You say you promise?" His voice was barely a whisper.

"You have my oath on it. Now, other than yourself, who were the people who took my kidneys?" Garrett leaned close to hear him. It took awhile for the Russian to be able to get it out. "And where are they now, the kidneys?" Again, a barely audible response. "Both kidneys, the same man?" Boris nodded.

Garrett stood back and considered what the Russian had told him. It made sense, seemed logical. And if he were lying, there was nothing more he could do, or more he would do at this stage. He had to accept it as the truth. Garrett pulled a handkerchief from his trousers, wetted it down, and began to carefully wipe Boris's face. He loosened the straps but did not release him, allowing him a slack, slumping stance supported by the bonds still on his arms. Boris leaned back, still facing the wall but away from it. Then, little by little, Garrett allowed his captive to drink, still splashing water onto the cloth and wiping his face. Boris gained a measure of relief and began to recover somewhat. Garrett was careful not to give him too much water so he wouldn't founder. All the while, he washed and cooled him. It was a caring, almost soothing act, one that was a surprise to both men.

"Danka," Boris managed to say, but Garrett did not reply. He kept swabbing him and giving him short drinks.

Finally, he poured the remaining water over his head and let it soak down into his clothing. Boris began to breathe regularly.

"I'll take you home now," Garrett said.

Without another word, he covered Boris's head and shoulders with a large quilted furniture pad and secured the covering about his neck and waist with several bungee cords. Boris made no protest. He himself had moved hooded men in trucks and cars so they could not know where they were going or where they had been. In one slow, even movement, Garrett retrieved the Sig Sauer .45.

"Dos Vadalek da mamkea vekik. Sukos es de pak," Garrett said. His Russian was very passable, but in case Boris did not understand, he added, "And the truth will set you free. Go in peace."

Garrett placed the muzzle of the big automatic against Boris's temple and fired. He aimed the weapon so that in case the bullet managed to penetrate the breadth of the large, thick head, it would exit his skull with a good chance of going out the open door of the rear of the truck. Yet Garrett knew that since the big .45 rounds were soft-nosed hollow points, there was probably little chance of the bullet passing through his skull cleanly. The sound inside the box was deafening. Boris made no sound and slumped as far as the arm restraints would allow. Garrett put a second round into his head, rebound him with another furniture pad, and lowered him carefully to the deck of the van. He stood over the inert form for almost a full minute, slowly removing his bloodstained gloves. Then he began to move quickly, purposefully. From that instant forward, Garrett was mechanical; he was again a SEAL, on a mission where time was a factor.

He rolled Boris unceremoniously from the deck of the van out onto the desert floor. He checked the decking for blood and found none, but still wiped it quickly with a wet towel soaked in bleach. In the process, he found both expended shell casings and pocketed them. He grabbed his shirt, noting that his self-inflicted shoulder wound had already begun to clot. Pulling the door down behind him, he jumped to the ground, stepped over Boris, and walked to the driver's door. He opened it and took a bottle of water and a towel from the cab. He cleaned himself up and replaced his shirt. He moved swiftly, economically, but yet there was nothing hurried or frantic in his movements. After a quick look around to be sure he was still alone, he drove slowly away from the dry creek bed, careful not to raise a dust plume.

While he concentrated on his driving and putting distance between himself and the scene, Garrett began to review the events of the last eighteen hours. Tactically, things had gone exactly as planned. Given the short period of time he had to plan the mission, it had been a textbook operation. But then, that was what Master

Chief Tag Walker did best—plan and execute combat operations. He hadn't wanted to underestimate Boris; the task simply had been distasteful but not difficult. The success of most organized thugs was the result of terrorizing ordinary citizens—people who couldn't defend themselves. Or dealing with law enforcement that was restricted by constitutional rights and the rules of evidence. They were unprepared for a challenge by a dedicated and capable opponent. The Borises of the world believed themselves to be at the top of a vicious food chain—that no one else could be as completely ruthless as they. Once he was trussed up in the van and cut off from the world he knew, Boris's reaction and cooperation were predictable, if not inevitable. Garrett knew all this; he had planned on it.

And that's basically what I am, he thought pensively, *a highly trained, low-paid, government thug*. He had thought of everything. Well, almost everything. Shortly before he reached a paved secondary road, he pulled the van off to the side of the road. He stepped down and slowly walked around the van to a nearby ditch. Dropping to the desert floor on all fours, he began to wretch uncontrollably. Garrett stayed there until everything in his stomach was in the ditch. He finally stood erect, pulled himself back into the cab, and sat there for a few moments, his forehead resting on his hands on the steering wheel. While he had terminated life many times and in many situations, for reasons he himself could not articulate, this was a new experience. He had just killed a man in a way that was far different from anything he had done previously. No one deserved a bullet more than this man, he told himself. Yet, in ways he found hard to ignore, he had just committed murder. After another moment's sober reflection, he started the van and headed back to Las Vegas.

Ray Stannick was as close to a hired gun as the Federal Bureau of Investigation allows. Earlier in his career, when he was a promising young agent and the special agent in charge of a small field office, he made a momentous decision. He left the career path that would one day surely have made him the SAIC of a big FBI field office in a large city. After that, perhaps a deputy directorship. Stannick abandoned this fast-track course to join the Bureau's Special Investigations Team. That was eight years ago; he was now the team's chief. The SIT was a small unit that reported directly to the Bureau's executive director. More important, it had a very generous budget. When he joined the team, he was told that he was being selected to join an elite task force. They were to be the new Untouchables—the FBI's Jedi warriors. Stannick knew it was a load of crap, but he didn't care; he had still volunteered. Even though the pay was the same, his career-advancement opportunities would be limited, and he would spend more time away from his family than a merchant seaman. But he rightly understood that the Bureau's new Special Investigations Team—or Sitters, as they called themselves—would have the highest ratio of police work to administrative work in the FBI. Stannick had joined the FBI to chase crooks, not push papers. The Bureau, like many government agencies, was always looking to promote capable minorities. He knew they would have him in a senior position, behind a desk, and buried in paperwork in record time if he let them. Several mentors at the deputy-director level had tried to change his mind, saying he was committing career suicide. Stannick didn't care. He wanted to catch crooks—the bigger and nastier they were, the more he wanted to catch them.

San Francisco was just another place for crooks to hide. Stannick would be just as happy out in Montana tracking some rogue militia group or prowling the docks in Boston looking for smugglers. He lived for those rare and exciting moments when, with a gun in one hand and badge in the other, he could shout, "FBI! Get your hands over your head!"

Stannick's small team of Sitters had been grudgingly allowed the use of two small rooms in the San Francisco field office. The

SAIC of the San Francisco office, a bland man named Osborne, didn't want them there. Osborne himself didn't want to be there; he considered the San Francisco SAIC job as just a stepping-stone to a senior administrative position back at headquarters in D.C. But Osborne wasn't stupid. He was fully aware that Stannick and his team really were untouchable. All field offices had been ordered by the director himself to cooperate with them fully. The Sitters—or Shitters, as many working agents now called them—had clout. For Osborne, a career bureaucrat, Stannick's presence was particularly distasteful. While he had to make room for the SIT team and provide them with unlimited administrative support, he had absolutely no control over them. For men like Osborne, control over those around you was what the FBI was all about. Osborne's career in the Bureau represented everything Stannick wanted to avoid.

Ray Stannick was in his office diligently going over some psychological profiles from the FBI's Assessment Group in Quantico when Agent Judy Burks burst in. Stannick allowed only the members of his team to enter without knocking. On occasion, like now, he regretted that allowance.

"Good mornin', Chief. How're you this fine day? Hey, and let me say that you're looking pretty spiffy this morning—well turned out, as usual."

Stannick made a habit of looking like the centerfold for *GQ*. He was wearing a crisp, heavily starched white shirt and a hand-painted silk tie. The Bureau mandated conservative dress, but Stannick took some liberty with his ties.

"Thanks for the observation, Agent Burks. Now, what can I do for you?"

"*Au contraire, ma capitaine*, this morning, it's what I can do for you."

Agent Judy Burks was an unusual assignee to the SIT in that she came directly from the FBI Academy. Like many seasoned FBI agents, Stannick was leery of rookies from the academy. He was also skeptical about the worth of female agents in chasing crooks. He wasn't particularly sexist; it was just that most of the bad guys that they were looking for were just that—guys. He could use female agents in certain roles, but Stannick saw the demanding and often seedy work of investigating crimes and catching crooks as a guy thing. He actually didn't dislike Agent Burks—far from it. She was cheerful, hardworking, pretty, and very, very smart.

Agent Burks had an undergraduate degree in computer science from Caltech and an MBA from Stanford, which made her arguably more educated than her boss. This also meant she had a solid understanding of sophisticated business computer applications. She had also worked for a software firm in Silicon Valley for a few years before coming to the Bureau, so she had been out in the real world collecting some serious money. None of this particularly endeared her to the man she worked for. Stannick's contempt for education and money rivaled that which he normally reserved for rookie female agents. What made him tolerate Agent Burks, even like her, was the fact that Agent Burks wanted to catch crooks almost as badly as he did. He was also well aware that Deloitte & Touche had a standing offer to triple her government salary if she ever chose to leave the Bureau. But here she was, standing across the desk from him, chomping at the bit to catch crooks.

"Okay," he said, laying the psych assessments on the corner of the desk, "what do you have for me?"

"We got another kidney heist. Confirmed." She handed him a faxed copy of a police report. "This one went down in Venice—Venice, California."

"Thank you, Agent Burks. I happen to know where Venice is in these United States."

"Actually, Chief, there are six cities or incorporated entities in the U.S. named Venice. But our kidney theft did take place in the one here in California."

Stannick gave her an irritated look. He began to study the report while Agent Burks waited, studying him. She had begun to regard Stannick as an idol of sorts, big and bad, and on her side, thank God. This was natural since, as a new G-person, she had yet to meet any really bad people. Judy was from a small town in eastern Oregon where someone occasionally stole a car or broke into a home while the owners were on vacation. Ray Stannick was probably the first real working cop she had ever known personally. She knew she was developing a crush on him. She also knew she could pull his chain, which she enjoyed doing whenever possible.

"This guy was street trash," he said, "or the next thing to it. So they took a kidney and dumped him in the park. They do a lot of weird things in Venice. Maybe it was a cult thing. And besides, you know that someone taken off the street at random seldom, if ever, makes an acceptable donor."

"C'mon, Chief. Look at the investigating officer's report. The street people watch out for each other and keep an eye on their neighborhood. Someone saw him being thrown in the back of a car just after dark. The county coroner put the time of death at about four in the morning. Allowing for the few hours it would take for him to bleed out and die, they probably cut into him sometime between one and two."

"So?"

"Jeez, do I have to draw a picture? I think they snatched him and took him someplace to type his tissue. In that amount of time, they could do a quick medical workup on him. In this case, they found an organ they could use and took it. Could be our illegal organ suppliers have multiple recipients on the line and they're out trolling for parts."

Stannick raised his eyebrows at the possibility. "Yeah, but what if the guy they grab is no good to them? If the tissue type is wrong, as it usually is, then what do they do with him?"

"If he doesn't work out, they pack his nose and turn him loose back on the street. Nobody's the wiser. These people don't talk to the cops; but if the guy were to talk, he'd probably say he was abducted by aliens."

"Yeah, but this guy in Venice wasn't abducted by aliens. He was murdered."

"After they took his kidney. But check the report. Looks like they did a crude but effective job of sewing him up, just like in the Walker case. Only this guy didn't make it. He probably wasn't in the best shape to start with. Thirty-five-year-old Rollerbladers in Venice are usually not good candidates for surgery. And did you see what else is in the report?" Stannick continued to watch her and waited. "They found a rose in his mouth. That might mean something—something really important. I did some research on the Web. The rose in the mouth thing isn't too common, but it has been done, and it usually means the Russian mob. So, the plot thickens. Why don't I run down there and check it out? We could learn something that may tie this guy to the Walker case." Stannick hesitated. "C'mon, Chief. It'll get me out of the office for a day or two so you can have a little peace and quiet."

"All right, all right. See what you can find out, but don't do anything stupid. You're still a rookie and not a full-fledged field agent yet."

"Yes, Dad."

"No more than two days, and Judy, be careful down there—there are a lot of creeps in that town. Now get out of here."

"Why, Chief, you called me by my Christian name. You really do care!"

"Out! And how many times do I have to tell you to quit calling me 'Chief?'"

Garrett had been at the roadside lookout for about a half hour, drinking black coffee and smoking, nursing the remnants of a hangover. The California border was less than five miles farther west. He had checked out of the motel early that morning. Actually, checked out was not really the term for it. Since he had registered under a name other than his own and was still paid up in advance for another three days, he simply tossed the keys on the dresser. They'd figure it out.

Late the day before, he had parked the van in a lot near Julio's garage and walked the six blocks to where he had left the LeMans. He made a few inquiries earlier that evening and then proceeded to get very drunk. Too much tequila, he concluded, is not the best prescription for a man with one kidney, and he vowed not to let it happen again. Earlier that morning, he had met a showgirl who wanted to take him home with her, but she didn't seem too disappointed when he suggested they just go and have breakfast together. Neither of them, it seemed, wanted to be alone.

Garrett heard the Harley coming up the grade before he saw it. Julio eased the big bike off the freeway, downshifting smoothly as he cruised through the turnoff to where Garrett waited.

"Qué pasa, jefe?" Julio said after he had shut down his machine. He kicked out the stand arm and swung himself from the bike. "You look like shit, man. Too much cactus juice?"

Garrett nodded. "I'll live. Thanks for coming out to see me off." He offered Julio a cigarette, lighting it for him and another for himself. "I want you to know how much I appreciate what you've done for me," he began. "I can't begin to thank you, my friend."

"*De nada*," Julio said with a wave of his hand. "That's what teammates are for. I may get back to San Diego one of these days and need a favor in return."

"Just say the word. You're sure I can't pay you something for any of this? The van and all?"

"Don't insult me, man," he replied with a trace of hurt feelings. "So your business here is finished?"

Garrett nodded. "Ah, Julio, about the van. I had some unpleasant business to take care of in the desert. I cleaned it up and covered my tracks pretty well, but you never know, understand?"

"Hey, man, don't worry about that van." He pulled out an old-fashioned pocket watch held by a gold chain that snaked across his vest. "It seems about a half hour ago, the van, she is no longer a van. It's now a lowboy flatbed—new tires, new look. One of my homeboys will use it to transport the customized lowriders he builds here for the bros out in LA." He looked carefully at Garrett, not wanting to pry but sensing his friend might need to talk about the ordeal. "Not to be nosy, *amigo*, but from what I gather, our friend Boris will no longer be shaking down cocktail waitresses or hassling pimps."

"Yeah, you got that right," Garrett replied. "Boris is definitely out of that business. You might say he's permanently retired."

"You left him out there?" Garrett nodded. "You figure they'll find him anytime soon?"

"Hard to say. I took him as far out as I could. Maybe in a few days, but probably a week or more. He won't be very pretty by then."

"He'll be found. First by the buzzards, then the coyotes, and then by the sheriff's deputies." Julio paused and put a hand on Garrett's shoulder. "You having a hard time with this one, brother?"

He nodded slowly and looked up at Julio. "Yeah ... yeah, I guess I am."

"Hey, man, ain't nobody goin' to miss this guy, believe me. And it's not like this was the first guy you ever dusted. It's been done before, man."

"I know that, Julio, but somehow this was a whole lot different. He wasn't shooting at me or guarding something or even trying to get away. He caved in and told me what I wanted to know. It was just impossible for me to let him walk away. There wasn't any choice. I had to take him out or risk having him and his people after me, after my brother and his family."

"And neither one of you had a uniform on, right? He was not 'the enemy,' right?"

Garrett snorted. "Yeah … that, too."

"Look at it this way, Chief. How many guys have you wasted just because they were on the other side—because they had on the wrong uniform or they happen to read the Koran a little too closely. A few? Maybe more than a few?" Garrett nodded. "And some of these guys were probably foot soldiers, insurgents who were just in the wrong place at the wrong time an' got waxed, *comprende*? Hell, some of them may have even been religious fanatics, patriots in their own way, who thought they were doing the right thing."

"So?"

"So Master Chief, this ain't the Navy—this's the real world. The guy you just put away was big-time bad. He was the enemy as much as any one of those dead Iraqis or Afghans we left out there in the desert or the al-Qaeda scum who attacked us. An' he's a Russian Mafia asshole; they're screwin' things up in our country. Naw, man, you just took out the trash. Ain't nobody gonna be sad that dude ain't back out on the street. Certainly not me."

Garrett smiled grimly. "You're probably right. Thanks for the pep talk, Julio."

"*De nada*. You get your butt back in the Navy, Master Chief, back in the teams where you belong." He smiled, and the noon sun glinted off the polished gold tooth. "Back where you get a license and a paycheck to do this kind of shit."

Garrett smiled genuinely this time. The two men shook hands, then embraced. He watched as Julio popped into the air and came down hard on the kick-starter. No electric starter on this man's machine. The Harley roared to life. It was an old hard-tail hog—a real man's bike. Garrett waited until Julio was out of sight before he climbed back into the LeMans and headed up 95 into the hills, toward California and the Bay Area.

The warehouse was a two-story cinder-block, postwar construction to which the designer awarded very few amenities or style points. The structure crowded the lot lines to maximize interior storage space. A recessed entryway in the front of the building emptied out onto a cracked sidewalk. It was blanked with a solid metal door that had neither window nor door handle. The entryway itself bisected two windows built halfway up the first story. Both had metal bars bolted into the cracked wooden casings and were boarded up from the inside. It was a concrete fortress with a loading dock attached to the rear, one of several dozen such structures near the docks in Oakland.

Inside, the cement floor formed the base of a dimly lit cavern stacked with boxes and shipping crates strung about in a reasonably orderly fashion to create aisles for the forklifts that wandered about. Caged storage bays lined one wall. Above them, served by crude wooden stairs and a catwalk, were the offices of Pacific Rim Freight Expediters. In reality, it was only one office—the second office space was little more than a lunchroom with a dirty Formica table and an assortment of rusted folding chairs. The office was an unpainted plywood cubicle that held a gray metal desk with dated black Bakelite phones, two rusted metal file cabinets, and an old refrigerator. A small, closet-sized space with a grungy sink and toilet connected the two larger rooms. A single door led to a back entrance.

This was the office of Dimitri Stolichnaya, a Russian expatriate who had somehow managed to gain political asylum in the United States. Once here, he quickly faded into the underworld. He arrived at the warehouse early each morning and usually didn't leave until well into the evening. There was a canvas army cot in the corner where he occasionally took an afternoon nap or spent the night if he wanted to remain near the phone. Stolichnaya was the undisputed leader of Russian Mafia activity in Northern California and Nevada, and one of the more ruthless individuals to leave Russia after détente with the West. He operated out of the Bay Area and represented perhaps one of the most barbaric and corrupt subcultures ever to arrive in America. From his native Russia, where organized crime under the communists became a well-developed art form, Stolichnaya and his kind brought a whole new kind of criminal organization to the United States.

Back in the old Soviet Union and the new Russian Federation, there were two kinds of criminals: those who had official status within the government and those who didn't. Both preyed on the long-suffering Russian people. The few honest government officials and bureaucrats were treated with contempt by those on the take both in and out of government. The nongovernment criminals like Stolichnaya had to, one way or another, pay a portion of their revenue for protection. In Russia, they call this protection a "roof." They paid public officials to look the other way or paid more powerful thugs who had purchased the protection from a corrupt government. In the Soviet Union, as in Russia, you couldn't stay in business unless you had a roof. Sometimes Stolichnaya had to pay government officials *and* some underworld boss for the right to work—or, in his case, the right to steal. When he arrived in San Francisco and set up business, he swore that he would never again pay protection money to anyone. A few corrupt officials and one or two from the local mafioso had tried to put him on a payment schedule. They quickly found that it was like trying to pet a wolverine. Across America, corrupt policemen and the local gangs were learning that they were well advised to just leave this new breed of criminal alone. Aside from that, they had little competition in the traditional sense, as they kept to themselves and preyed, for the most part, on other expatriate Russians and eastern Europeans. But with the criminal organizations being built by men like Stolichnaya, that was changing. The Russian mobs were expanding and becoming more diverse. One thing that had not changed was the bedrock philosophy they brought with them from the Motherland: Always be prepared to be more brutal and more vicious than anyone who challenges you—always.

Stolichnaya, or Stoli as he was universally known except to his face, was amazed at how easy it was to do business in America. His name was not really Stolichnaya, but seeing the popularity of this famous brand of Russian vodka in his new country, he took the name as his own. Back in Russia, he could never afford to drink it.

From the beginning, Stolichnaya felt like a feral cat on an island populated with rabbits. At first, he was perplexed at just how easy it was to come to America, even for someone like him who had an extensive police record. For a while, he even thought it was some kind of a trap. Then he realized the stupid Americans had been so brainwashed with the evils of the Soviet system, they could not distinguish between dissident behavior and criminal behavior. They just assumed that all Russians, even the good ones, had a rap sheet. The liberal administration in Washington lifted the emigration restrictions and freely allowed most Russians to come to America. Stoli had merely stated on his visa application that he was a victim of religious persecution. In reality, he had not stepped inside a Russian Orthodox Church since he grew too big for his mother to force him to attend mass. He had in his youth, however, broken into a few synagogues looking for something to steal. The religious persecution angle had also allowed Stoli to bring over several of his trusted lieutenants. America was truly the land of opportunity, and he planned to take full advantage. There was so much money and, by comparison to the land of his birth, so little vice. Like most Russians of his generation, he grew up and came of age under communism, so he never knew a Russia without massive, unchecked government corruption and street crime.

Stoli sat at his desk going over his accounts, which he still did in his native Cyrillic script. He was dressed in a gray T-shirt and a baggy, soiled pair of dark cotton trousers. Stoli chain-smoked one cigarette after another and never failed to marvel at the quality and affordability of American cigarettes. If the Soviets had been able to make cigarettes like these, he often thought, they might not have lost the cold war. Such was his appreciation, and his frugal nature that demanded he smoked each down to half an inch. He then lit the next one with the expended butt as it singed his callused fingers. There was a soft knock at the door.

"Enter!"

"Excuse me, Mr. Stolichnaya, but you wanted a report on the last transfer operation as soon as it was completed."

"*Da.* Come sit, Alexei; tell me about it. You would like something to drink?"

"Uh, no, thank you, sir."

Stoli snorted as he rose from the desk and made his way over to the refrigerator. He took a pint jar from the freezer compartment and poured a measure into a tumbler. It had an amber cast, like antifreeze, but it was much thicker. He could now afford a much better brand of vodka, but Stoli was careful about just what pleasures he allowed himself. *"Prost,"* he said, as much to himself as to Alexei. He regarded the younger man. In the old days, it would have been unthinkable for a young man not to join his superior when offered a drink. But things change, including the new breed of young Russians like the one who sat before him. They drank scotch or bourbon or one of the fancy drinks unheard of in the Russia of his time. As much as Stoli represented the old-line Moscow mobster, Alexei was the prototype of the new Russian hoodlum in America. They dressed well, drove plush cars, and carried cell phones. They wanted money, and they wanted it to show—the cars, the houses, the expensive jewelry, the mistresses. These young men yearned for the flashy side of what America offered, and they were getting it. They had lost none of the viciousness or predatory nature of Stoli's generation, and showed an arrogance that was not as prevalent among their mentors. Most of them still understood Russian, but few of them spoke it. Nonetheless, while they might not totally respect their seniors in the New World, they still feared them, and with good reason. They would wait their turn, albeit impatiently.

"So," Stoli continued after he had returned to his desk, "we had a successful transaction?"

"Yes, sir."

"And a satisfied client, I presume."

"Yes, sir. Apparently very satisfied." He pulled a fat envelope from the inside of his Versace suit and handed it to Stoli. "I understand that they were a little pressed to make the second half of the payment in cash, but it's all there."

"You counted it?"

"Yes, sir."

"Good," Stoli replied, "then I won't have to."

Alexei swallowed uncomfortably as he watched his boss put the envelope into a small floor safe by his desk. He knew Stoli would count it later, and while he himself had ensured the payment was made in full and had taken nothing, a simple error in arithmetic would most certainly cost him his life.

"And the volunteer who provided us with this product, I understand there was a problem?"

Alexei shrugged. "Not really, sir. He was just some vagrant we found on the street, someone who pushes the powder up his nose—not very healthy, I'm afraid. After we removed the part we needed, he died, so we tossed him back where we found him." Alexei smiled. "We even put a rose in his teeth, to show some gratitude for his contribution."

Stoli pulled his hand over the stubble on his head. "American police maybe have been castrated by silly laws and procedures,

Alexei, but they are not stupid. Nor do they appreciate having someone thumb their nose at them. Next time we lose a donor, take him somewhere and dispose of him properly—somewhere more decent, like a construction dumpster." He sipped the vodka and sniffed at the impudence of the young man. "The ones that live are enough liability. Don't provoke authorities more than necessary, do you understand?"

"Yes, sir."

Stoli drummed his lower lip with an index finger while he studied Alexei. He probably should have put one of his older people on this assignment. They were more reliable and less likely to do something stupid. A rose, indeed! But he knew there simply weren't enough old hands to go around. Those of his generation wanted a territory of their own. Many of them had moved on to other cities. In some ways, that was not so bad, since they regularly sent him a small percentage of their business—a token of respect. *Fortunately*, Stoli admitted to himself, *the young ones like my impetuous Alexei are content to stay and do as they are told, so long as the money is there.*

"Tell me, Alexei, what do you think of this business—this service that we provide people who have enough money so they don't have to get sick and die?"

"I think it is an excellent business," Alexei said without hesitation.

"Why? Why is it such good business?"

"Well, the person who is sick and has the money pays all of the costs and takes most of the risk. All we have to do is deliver a small ice chest with a body part in it." He paused a moment, wanting to give his boss a thoughtful reply. "The doctors we get to do the work can sometimes be difficult, especially on the removal side. However, it seems their greed to turn a nice profit prevents any real problems. And if they do it once, they can't really say no if we ask them again, can they?" He gave Stoli a greedy smile.

"Two hundred thousand American dollars for a cooler with a slab of human flesh in it. Our costs to make this happen, paying the doctors and our pilots, are under fifty grand. I'd say it was a very good business."

Stoli nodded thoughtfully. "Very well. Next time, do it without the theatrical improvisation. Get the job done, nothing more."

"Yes, sir."

Stoli nodded his dismissal and Alexei rose. He made a short bow, and the older man inclined his head to acknowledge this sign of respect. But he watched with a measure of disgust as he noted Alexei's immaculately tailored suit and expensive shoes. He frowned, then knocked back the rest of the vodka and lit another cigarette.

He, too, liked the organ traffic business, but for different reasons. As Alexei noted, it was certainly a profitable business, but there was more to it. The people who he provided with organs, those who needed this service to stay alive, were wealthy individuals who violated the law. More important, they had a lot to lose if it were ever brought to light that they had done business with him. Stoli was not above extortion, and he felt this modest but growing list of satisfied clients was a bankable resource. He would not blackmail them, nor would he go to them on any kind of recurring basis; these were successful people with means and resources of their own. They were to be treated with respect. Nonetheless, if they had other options, they would not have come to him in the first place. He, Stoli, had a hold on them. If the need arose, they would become part of his roof. If threatened, he wouldn't hesitate to sacrifice them for his own purposes, but he would not use his advantage capriciously. That was not good business.

Still and all, this new enterprise was not without risk, and it was bound to attract the wrong kind of attention. Stoli didn't like to attract attention; he just wanted to pursue a livelihood and take care of his organization. He may not be in Moscow, but he still had responsibilities. That meant he had to be careful. He regarded the cigarette fondly for a moment, then treated himself to another three fingers of vodka.

Garrett wasted little time driving back to the Bay Area. He drove north through western Nevada, stopping only at a Motel 6 on the outskirts of Reno late that evening to eat and sleep. He was up early the next morning and had a quick workout, after which he headed west on I-80 for San Francisco. He felt the need to purge himself of the desert, the cheap motels, and the plastic, crowded Las Vegas scene. Sensing that an upscale accommodation and some refinement might do him some good, he drove around the North Bay through Napa to Marin County and checked into The Inn Above the Tide in Sausalito. If the stuffy-looking bell captain thought the lanky man in blue jeans and faded cowboy shirt who drove up in a dusty old convertible was anything out of the ordinary, he had the good taste not to show it. Late that afternoon, Garrett sat on his private veranda that looked out over the Bay toward San Francisco and scanned the newspapers. After a shower and a fresh shave, he found a wonderful bistro down on the waterfront for dinner. The following morning, he had a leisurely breakfast on the veranda with a pot of coffee, eggs benedict, and the specialty of the house—a superb Ramos fizz. The commuter traffic heading into the city began to thin out about midmorning as he set out on his rounds.

It took Garrett another two days to complete his inquiries and another three nights at the The Inn to quiet his spirit. The last few months marked the first time in a long while that he was away from the Navy. And the past few weeks, with the exception of Julio, he had been on his own—alone. Over the years, he'd grabbed a week's leave here and there from the teams, but he had never really been out of uniform for any extended period of time. It felt strange and, in many ways, very good. In the Navy and in the teams, he was a leader—he was always "on." People counted on him and looked to him for direction. And he took these responsibilities very seriously. He was recognized as one of the best and most experienced combat leaders in the teams. The Navy SEALs put great stock in their chief petty officers. Being a master chief, even a new master chief, made him the best of the best. Garrett now clutched the top operational rung of the enlisted-ranks ladder. Along the way, he had resisted the efforts of several of his commanders to make him an officer. Officers, even those in the SEAL teams, had extended administrative duties. There was enough paperwork in being a master chief, but not the deskbound load carried by the team officers. Garrett was an operator, and he wanted to stay that way.

In the evenings at The Inn, he sat quietly on his veranda and looked out over the city. He limited himself to two tequilas, neat, and then switched to coffee. Garrett Walker was the kind of man for whom a personal crisis would have been a very rare occurrence. Yet he fully realized that the events of the past several months had changed him—changed him forever. He also understood that the most dramatic changes, both for himself and for Brandon, might lie ahead.

When he began to check the information he had extracted from Boris, he was afraid that the burly Russian might have lied to him. He had moved cautiously, stopping at convenience stores and neighborhood taverns, carefully asking questions. There were several occasions on which a fifty-dollar bill was needed in order to refresh the memory of those reluctant to give information to strangers. By day three, his inquiries convinced him that Boris had, in fact, told him the truth, which was an immense relief. It was like being given a clean bill of health after a diagnosis of cancer. Garrett didn't think he had the stomach for another trip to Las Vegas. He also didn't want to think that he had killed a man, even a man like Boris, for nothing. Midmorning on the fourth day, he finally called Brandon.

"Garrett, where are you? Are you all right?"

"I'm fine. Sorry to be out of touch, but I had a few things to get out of the way before I called. I'm here in the city and will probably head down to San Jose this afternoon. Why don't we meet somewhere after work and I'll bring you up to date?" What Garrett was saying, and Brandon immediately understood, was that he wanted to talk before they went back to Brandon's home that evening. Brandon gave him directions to a hotel bar close to the freeway and rang off. Since he always traveled light, it took Garrett only a few moments to pack and check out.

"How was your stay with us, sir?" the bell captain inquired while Garrett's LeMans was brought around. He was older than Garrett, with a friendly, refined manner.

"More therapeutic than you can imagine."

"Excellent," he said as he held open the car door for Garrett. "Nice car. Sixty-six, right?" Garrett nodded. "When I was a kid," the bell captain continued, "I had a sixty-four GTO 445 automatic that I bored out and rebuilt with a competition cam. When you got on it, that puppy would bark in all four gears. They just don't make cars like that anymore."

"No," Garrett replied as he handed him a five-dollar tip, "indeed, they don't."

Garrett was waiting at a table in the bar when Brandon arrived. He saw Garrett and hurried over. Garrett rose to meet his brother, and they embraced.

"It was good to get your call, Garrett. I was beginning to worry about you," Brandon said as he took the chair across from him. He ordered coffee from the waitress, who had trailed him to the table.

"Give me a double scotch—neat, Johnnie Walker Black if you have it, and a water back."

"A double it is," she smiled, noticing they were twins. She dealt two cocktail napkins and left.

Brandon watched him carefully. After their transplant operation, Garrett still drank, but sparingly for the most part. "I'm glad to have you out of Las Vegas. I never liked the town in the first place—less so now. And I don't think I ever relaxed the whole time you were there."

"I can understand that. Fortunately, I found an old teammate living there who was willing to help us out. It made all the difference. You can't do business in that town unless you have connections. It was a real piece of luck."

"So tell me what you found out. What happened after you IDed the lady who drugged me?"

Garrett looked at Brandon, not knowing the best way to tell him that his brother was a murderer, or that Brandon could possibly be indicted as a coconspirator. He was just getting to know Brandon again, and he wasn't so sure how he would handle this kind of information.

Garrett was painfully aware that he still wasn't handling it particularly well himself. The killing of Boris had taken a great deal out of him. As a Navy SEAL, he had killed many times, at close range if not in cold blood. He was as well schooled in the taking of life as the armed forces of the United States could make a man. But in many respects, this training was not only immaterial, it was also irrelevant. All of his background and experience had only served to make the killing of Boris a mechanical task. The moral implications were quite another matter, in spite of Julio's kind words. He had not considered the huge chasm between taking a life for your country and taking a life for yourself. The difference was between uniformed service and a personal execution—between being a patriot and being a murderer. Garrett's professional discipline and SEAL training did not allow him to rationalize or quibble about killing. He knew full well that it was Garrett Walker, private citizen—not Garrett Walker, Navy SEAL—who had tortured and murdered a fellow human being. The caliber of the life he had taken and the threat this twisted individual represented to his brother and his brother's family were compelling but separate issues. Within the tight, rational framework he allowed himself, Garrett Walker had just killed his first man.

The drinks arrived, and Garrett took half of his in a long, single pull. Brandon was rapidly becoming aware of Garrett's frame of mind.

"That bad?"

Garrett shrugged. "Depends on your point of view."

"I'm interested in your point of view." Brandon immediately sensed his brother was struggling. "Why don't you tell me what happened?" he said gently. "Start at the beginning."

For the next forty-five minutes, Garrett toured Brandon through Shorty's, his meeting with Detective Rucko, his time at the Desert Flower, and the visit with Dawn Smallwood. He finished with his trip into the desert with Boris. Garrett kept to the facts and said nothing about the way he felt, but Brandon could sense the emotion in his twin brother.

"And that's about it. He finally told me what I wanted to know, and then I killed him. I tried to do it as humanely as possible and not let him know what was coming, but he probably had an idea. I'm not really entirely sure why I tried to make it easy for him in the end." He gave Brandon a twisted smile. "Boris was a world-class asshole, and he sure as hell deserved worse."

"Garrett, you didn't do it like that, with the blankets and all, to make it easy for him," Brandon said gently, "You did it for you—for us."

Garrett finished his drink in a single swallow. "So what do you think about all this? I blew a man's brains out, and I didn't even have the courage to look him in the face—to tell him he was about to die." He fingered the empty glass. "What do you think of your little brother now?"

"I think he's a helluva guy." Brandon looked away from Garrett and down at his coffee. "This guy Boris hurt me pretty bad, almost killed me. You did what I wish I had the skill and courage to do. There's no way I would have been good enough to take him off the street like you did and get him out to the desert in that van. And I'll tell you something else. If it had been me out there in that van with him, out where no one could see us or hear us, he would have died much slower. He'd have died in all the pain and terror I could create for him. One of the last things he would have seen on this earth would have been the satisfied look on my face."

Garrett's first reaction was that his brother was just playing out a vengeful fantasy—an emotional reaction to the suffering he'd endured at the hands of Boris. But the composed, measured look on Brandon's suddenly hardened features told Garrett that his brother was more than capable of making good on his words.

"Then you're a tougher man than I," Garrett said. There was a melancholy tone in his voice over which he had no control.

Brandon replied, choosing his words carefully, "This guy took something from me; he took a part of me. I don't know quite how to say it, but I'm not the same person I was before this happened. I don't like the way it feels—the meanness inside me that wants to strike back." He lowered his voice. "I'm ashamed to admit this, but I'm a little jealous in that you were able to take care of that bastard and I wasn't. Does that surprise you?"

"Maybe. Maybe not. Perhaps it's just how we are—how we react when someone steps over some sacred, internal boundary."

"You almost have to experience it firsthand—to have something cut away from inside of you to really understand how I feel, not to mention the extended pain he almost inflicted on Cathy and the kids."

Garrett smiled sadly, remembering rubbing his own blood on his face and then on Boris. "Oh, you'd be surprised, big brother. You just might be surprised."

Brandon, lost in his own thoughts, continued. "Do you think it will pass—this meanness I feel? Do you think it will ever leave me?"

"Time will tell, Brandon. Time will tell for both of us."

Ray Stannick was working late that evening. He did this often when he was on assignment, preferring to do his police work during the day and defer the administrative part of the job as long as possible. The San Francisco field office was a large and busy operation, so he was seldom alone, but the resident agents and support staff quickly learned to avoid him. In the short time Stannick and his SIT agents had been there, the locals had concluded that the team's senior agent was by nature a gruff and taciturn man—someone to stay clear of when possible. This was especially true on those evenings when he stayed late to wrestle with the Bureau's paperwork. So they gave him a wide berth rather than taking a chance of getting snapped at. Agent Burks was not one of those people. She pushed into his office unannounced and unceremoniously dropped her overnighter and briefcase onto the floor. She then pulled off her suit jacket and slung it across her bags.

"Jeez, what a trip," she said as she slouched into one of the straight-backed office chairs attending Stannick's desk. "Southern California is full of lunatics and degenerates. I had to take one of those cattle cars that Southwest flies up the coast. Since I just barely made the flight, I got to sit in the very back with a bunch of Koreans who brought little boxes of kimchi takeout to eat on the plane. I feel like I just got spritzed with fish oil and duck shit. Then, on the way into the city from the airport, the cabdriver turned out to be some asshole in a turban who tells me he wants to have sex with me but I must wear a veil. Go figure. I flashed him my badge and he clammed up in a hurry, I can tell you that! I shoulda pulled my piece on him."

Stannick regarded her coolly. She was wearing a shoulder holster that was well concealed when under her jacket, but now, without the jacket, she looked ridiculous. The large leather holster strap practically covered one shoulder, and the elastic back strap around the other shoulder had a tendency to pull the fabric of her blouse tightly across her breasts. This was not missed by Stannick, but he easily ignored it. He thought the Bureau should consider issuing smaller-caliber guns for the female agents. The regulation Glock 23 .40 caliber automatic looked like a small howitzer under her armpit. She crossed her legs and smiled sweetly at him, fingering a strand of her short, straight, blonde hair back behind one ear. He tolerated the theatrics; he knew she had something good or she wouldn't be baiting him like this.

"Please, come right on in, Agent Burks. Have a seat. Tell me, did you have a pleasant trip?"

"Oh, it could have been a lot worse, Chief, but I don't want to get into a rant over it. Thanks for asking, though."

"And what did we learn on our trip to Venice, California?"

"*We* learned that *our* California Venice is a gigantic black hole that sucks in the worst of the perverts and weirdos from the greater LA area. As it turned out, the local cops down there really aren't such a bad bunch. Still, I had to play the dumb blonde federal agent who was lost, bewildered, and afraid. Told them that I worked for a mean senior agent who was looking for an excuse to can me if I didn't make good on this assignment."

"You do, and I might," Stannick interjected.

"It's demeaning," she continued, without breaking stride, "but it works. I had the local boys falling all over themselves to help out." She flipped open a small spiral notebook. "Our John Doe, sans one kidney, turns out to be one Harold Eisenbach, age thirty-five and a member of the beach scene for about the last three years.

Not really what I would classify as street trash, and believe me, I saw some world-class garbage down there. Harold was a quiet guy. He hung out at the coffeehouses, did a bit of pottery work and sold it around the beach. I saw some of his stuff, and it wasn't all that bad. Lived with some guy in a studio a few blocks off the beach. He was very distressed over Harold's untimely death."

"How distressed?" Stannick intoned.

"About as worked up as a fella can get when his sweetheart gets whacked."

"Wonderful."

"Seems Harold and his paramour had only been shacked up for a short while. They met at a bathhouse about six months ago. He must have made an honest man out of Harold. According to the local fuzz, he hadn't been picked up for loitering around the public toilets along the boardwalk for quite some time."

"Uh-oh, not good. I assume you talked with the county coroner about this?"

She nodded. "Nice guy—reminded me a lot of my dad. The job looked very similar to the work done on Brandon Walker. I got the surgeon from Vegas, a Dr. Ward, on the phone with the coroner, and they concluded it was a similar cut-and-run operation. Only Harold was different from our guy Walker; Harold was sick."

"How sick?" Stannick asked, knowing the answer.

"Sick to death, Chief. He had AIDS."

"Shit," he said softly. Then he was silent for close to a minute. "We've got to put a stop to this," he said out loud to himself. He rose from the desk and began to pace. Agent Burks knew when to hold her tongue, and she let him prowl the office in silence. "Okay, we can only work from what we have. Where does this Eisenbach come from? Has anyone claimed the body?"

"Funny you should ask, Chief. The boyfriend needed to talk, so I spent some time with him. Said I was so much more understanding than those beasts down at city hall. He gave me this card."

Stannick read it. "Eisenbach, Sanchez, and Thompson, LLC—specialists in personal injury and liability, Phoenix, Arizona. And?"

"That's his father's card. Seems Harold also has a law degree from Berkeley, just like his dear old dad. I guess he was in practice for a while with his father. When the senior Eisenbach learned that Harold acquired a different sexual outlook while at Berkeley, as well as a law degree, he tossed him out on his ear—disowned him. Didn't want to claim the body, according to the live-in. Didn't want anything to do with his dead son. Very insensitive, according to the boyfriend's account."

"But there's more, yes?" Stannick was now back at his desk, watching her over steepled fingers.

"Yep, it looks as if Dad did care a little bit for junior, or at least he used to. As the senior and managing partner of the law firm he founded, he called the shots. He was able to keep Harold on the books as an employee and"—she paused for effect—"he was also able to keep Harold on the firm's health insurance plan. Not totally legal, but it shows Dad's heart was in the right place. Or it was until a short while ago, when the coverage was canceled."

"Really. Now that is interesting. And just how did you find all this out?"

"Well, there was a health benefits card in his personal effects, but it was so drenched in blood I couldn't make it out. I called the dad, but he refused to talk to me. So I went back over to visit the boyfriend. Walked into the middle of an honest-to-goodness wake. You ever been to a gay wake, Chief? On the level, it was a very sensitive and moving affair." Stannick moved his hand in a forward rolling motion, urging her to get on with it. "Anyway, I finally got him alone, and he tells me all about it. Seems the boys had a spat a few weeks back, and, in a gesture of reconciliation,

Harold told this guy that he would try to get him on the health plan as his dependent. I guess that's when Dad finally pulled the plug."

"I suppose a father's love does have its limits. I wish we knew which insurance company or could get a copy of the policy. We might learn something."

Burks reached over to her briefcase and pulled out a legal-sized envelope. She opened it and tossed a benefits statement and policy description on the desk. Stannick took each one in turn, inspected them briefly, and then lifted his eyebrows toward Burks.

She shrugged. "I was there with the grieving spouse to lend solace. I felt his pain. I told him there was a possibility that he might have been named as a beneficiary—said I'd look into it for him."

Stannick looked up from the portfolio packet, lifting an eyebrow. "A death benefit—from a health insurance policy?"

"Well, it seemed the right thing to say at the time."

"Burks, you're too damn much. Good work. As a matter of fact, great work. Could be a coincidence that the guy they grabbed off the street just happened to have insurance coverage—i.e., a medical history on file with an insurance carrier. But I don't believe in coincidences. You were down there along the boardwalk. How many of those street creeps do you think carry health insurance?"

"Except for the occasional duffer on Medicare, I'd say one in a hundred, maybe one in a thousand."

"Uh-huh, and I'd say you're probably right." He tossed the policy in his top drawer and locked it. "I want you to check this out tomorrow, but now go get some rest. You look like you could use it." She nodded and retrieved her jacket from atop the bags. Stannick glanced at his watch. "Say, you hungry?"

"Well, the Koreans offered, but I had to pass on the kimchi. Yeah, I could use something to eat."

"Great. Let's go down to the Fog City Diner and get a steak. My treat; you've earned it."

"Why, Agent Stannick, a dinner date. Then maybe a drink at some out-of-the-way spot, and then who knows? I accept."

"Burks, sometimes I don't know whether to write you up for insubordination or just give you a good spanking."

"Well, it's not really my thing, but if *you're* into it, I guess I'll take the spanking?"

"Don't push it."

"Yes, Chief."

"And don't call me 'Chief.'"

"Yessir."

"C'mon, Mr. C., reach! Now four more … three more, go for it … just two, reach … now one more. You can do it, deep inside, reach for it!" The huge young man shouted encouragement as he stood over the teetering bar, his hands hovering just a few inches from the metal but not touching it. Finally, the older man on the bench under the weights managed to lock his arms straight, and the bar stabilized.

"Good job, Mr. C. That was awesome. Way to hang tough."

After the weights were safely back on the cradle, he offered the man on the bench a towel. The older man took it as he rolled up into a sitting position. He carefully wiped his forehead and blotted his mouth, pressing the towel to his face with leather gloves that had the fingers cut off at the second knuckle. He had a broad leather belt support strapped to his midsection.

"Fuck me, Bernie, but I didn't think I was gonna be able to finish that last set. Whatta wimp."

"Don't be so hard on yourself, Mr. C. You've just been back on regular workouts what, maybe five weeks? We really only started to crowd the weight here in the last ten days."

"Yeah, maybe, but I'm still a wimp."

Frank Cantello wasn't a wimp, but he was a man fighting the clock. He would be fifty-five in another year, and he had the genes of an Italian baker. As he was fond of saying, he could put on weight if he sat next to a bowl of pasta. Yet he had a remarkable physique for a man his age, still broad across the shoulders with a relatively small waist. But while the Gold's Gym workout shirt fit snugly around his chest and hung loose about his lower torso, he was still an aging beefcake fighting a holding action at best. The muscles he had so carefully sculpted as a younger man were still big, but they were now smooth, sheathed in a layer of skin fat. No amount of Bernie's admonitions could change that. And unless he watched his diet very carefully, the rolls of flesh that pouched out from the belt on either side were also permanent attachments.

Bernie waited patiently for Cantello to catch his breath. "Okay, what's next?"

"Lats and pecs, Mr. C. We have some ground to make up there since you got out of the hospital, so we might as well get to it." Bernie was consulting Cantello's chart when his attention was drawn to a man in a suit who walked into the weight room. The weight room was just one venue of an extensive and very exclusive health club not far from Cantello's Daly City office. Bernie didn't recognize the stranger.

"Excuse me, Mr. Cantello, but I need to see you for a moment." Cantello gave him an irritated look. "It's important," he added.

"It better be, Sally. You know how important my workouts are."

"Uh, yessir, I do."

Cantello pulled the towel around his neck. "Gotta take a break, Bernie. I'll be back in a few minutes."

"No problem, Mr. C. I'll be right here when you're ready."

Cantello led Sal from the weight room to a juice bar that serviced a bank of racquetball courts as well as the weight room on this level of the club.

"Jesus, boss, is that guy some kinda wall or what?"

"Who, Bernie? Yeah, I know—he's big and rock solid. I'd kill to have definition like that."

Sal was about to comment that for his age, Cantello was doing pretty well, but thought better of it. He had learned from experience that Frank Cantello was very sensitive when it came to the issue of age, however flattering the remark.

"He's a big boy, all right," Sal concluded.

"Let me have a Gatorade and a PowerBar, honey, an' the same for my sedentary friend here. He hardly ever does anything good for his body."

"Hey, boss, I do sixteen-ounce curls every night." He chuckled. "Budweiser curls. How about you, gorgeous, you want to come and work out with me sometime?"

She served them and blushed. "Sorry, I work out every day after I finish my shift, right here in the gym."

"See there, you schmuck. You could learn something from her. Thanks, sweetheart." Sal followed him to a small, high table without stools. "You ought to be ashamed of yourself, Sally. You're old enough to be her father."

"Good-lookin' kid. Who knows, maybe I am."

"Maybe, but I kinda fucking doubt it. So what you got?"

"Remember you said to keep an eye on that Russian hood in Vegas who brought you the filters, the one who called himself Boris."

"Yeah, of course I remember. Why, something going on?"

Only two of Cantello's people knew the true nature of his "gallbladder surgery," and only because they had seen to the transplant arrangements. He seldom talked about his replacement kidneys, as if the need to have new ones made him appear inadequate or less of a man. When he did, he always referred to them as his new filters.

"You see, we got this materials supplier over in Vegas who has some connections down at city hall. We used him when we were trying to get the bid on that county bypass contract." Cantello nodded. "Our man has a nephew in the police department. He says our Russian deliveryman just turned up dead. They found him yesterday."

"Dead? You sure it was the same guy?"

"That's what he says—big guy, connected, went by the name of Boris Kuznetzkof. Can't be too many of them. He was well known around town as organized muscle—Russian Mafia. I'm working to confirm all this, but I don't want to come on like I'm too interested, know what I mean? Seems they found him out in the desert—been there a couple of days, and the buzzards and animals had done a number on him. Not pretty. Our helpful supplier says it was a hit. He was murdered."

Cantello was quiet for a moment, lost in thought. Finally, he looked up and spoke in a low voice to Sal. "What's your take on all this, Sally?"

"I don't think it has anything to do with us. This Boris guy was into the rackets in a big way in Vegas. He was a bottom-feeder, but he ran a sizable operation—probably had a lot of enemies. Looks like maybe he got into the wrong rice bowl and someone whacked him. Word is there are very few tears being shed on account of his untimely passing."

"Okay, you're probably right, but keep your ear to the ground. These Russians are not guys to take lightly. And just in case someone thinks we may have had something to do with this, I want an extra man with me when I'm out traveling to job sites. I don't trust these guys. Hire some local talent and charge it to the Bayshore off-ramp contract."

"Right, boss. You want I should tip off the local guy in Oakland that we know about this, kinda like a favor to them? They may not know about it yet."

Cantello turned this over in his mind before answering. "I don't think so. If we know, they know or they soon will, and we don't want to call attention to ourselves. No, Sal, we do nothing. Just lay low and wait for this thing to blow over." Cantello gulped the last of his Gatorade and pulled the towel around his neck. "I gotta get back to the gym before I cool down too much. See you back at the office."

"Sure thing, boss. Have a good workout."

Stolichnaya had just ordered a steak sandwich, potato salad, and a six-pack of German beer from one of the local delicatessens. A black youth, barely in his teens, rang the bell next to the metal door in front of the building and looked suspiciously up and down the dark street. Delivery boys were fair game in this neighborhood, but he knew he had temporary asylum while he waited in the alcove of the warehouse door. Word was out that the occupants tolerated no trouble around their property. For the local gangs, this particular warehouse was off-limits.

Not long after Stoli moved his operation into the building, some of the homeboys forced one of the doors in the back by the loading dock and made off with several crates of televisions and stereos. Stoli fronted his operation with a semi-legitimate freight-forwarding business and had a few bona fide commercial contracts. After the break-in, he sent some of his young Cossacks out to ask questions around the neighborhood. The information led them to a local gang leader. One morning about three o'clock, Stoli's people yanked the young chieftain from his sleep at his girlfriend's apartment. They brought him, bound and gagged, to the warehouse. There, in his halting English, Stoli carefully explained the gang's critical error in assuming that since they weren't Italian, it necessarily followed that they weren't organized and dangerous. Stoli further explained to the young man that his business interests were wide ranging, even international, and had little to do with the neighborhood and the local gang's operations. Since they were not competitors, Stoli explained, there was no reason they could not live and let live. He treated the youth with respect, as an equal, but he also assured the young gangbanger that he would personally hold him accountable for any future problems. As a show of respect, Stoli offered him a drink of vodka and then personally escorted him to the front door. If the young gang leader had any second thoughts about this proposed armistice, he forgot them immediately upon learning that while he was sipping vodka with this strange and powerful man, the two break-in artists were having their ring fingers removed.

"You have my order, boy?" Stoli confronted the young man in his doorway.

"You order th' steak sandwich an' beer ... sir?"

"*Da.*" He took the bag and handed the kid three tens, then closed the door without another word. While he made his way back through the warehouse to his office, the delivery boy faded quickly into the shadows. He took an alternate route back to the deli since he now carried the monetary equivalent of six nickel bags of heroin.

The warehouse was scheduled for another delivery that night. Stoli had bought the freight-forwarding business soon after he arrived in America to legitimize his ownership of the warehouse for a base of operations. Actually, he had forced the owner of the business, a Lithuanian immigrant, to sell it to him for next to nothing. But tonight's delivery was not part of the legal side of his business. It was the result of tribute that had been brutally extracted from a group of Asian longshoremen. The delivery would be broken down and reshipped before daylight. Stoli didn't need to be present, but he often was. On occasion, he would unexpectedly take a crowbar and jump in the middle of the activity. Alongside others, he would tear into shipping crates and wrestle goods from one part of the warehouse to the other. He didn't do this as some sort of top-down managerial tool or to maintain a personal touch with his organization. He just simply enjoyed wielding a crowbar and tearing things apart.

In his office, Stoli had finished one of the beers and was beginning on the steak sandwich and a second beer when Alexei knocked on the open door. Stoli looked up, surprised, as Alexei was not connected with the shipping part of the business. With a mouthful of steak, he motioned him to enter and have a seat.

"Alexei," he said as he dragged a sleeve across his mouth, "what brings you here at this uncivilized hour?" He fully expected Alexei to be out with his friends at some upscale supper club.

"I just got a call from one of our people in Las Vegas. He tells me that Boris Kuznetzkof is no longer among the missing."

"Oh?"

"No, sir. He is among the dead. They found him out in the desert, half eaten by coyotes and a bullet in his brain."

Stoli cautiously sipped at the beer, then lit a cigarette. The sandwich lay partially eaten on the desk. "There is more that you can tell me about this?"

"Not a lot, I'm afraid. As you know, we haven't heard from him in several days. No one thought to look for him until he missed a couple of collections. His people out there just figured he was shacked up with a showgirl or had to make an unexpected trip out of town for some reason. Then some desert varmint shooter finds him and calls the cops. From what our people in Las Vegas say, the police don't know what to make of it. The cops certainly know who he is, but they have no idea who shot him or why." Alexei shrugged. "Boris always liked the ladies. Maybe it was a jealous husband."

"Maybe." Stoli pulled heavily on the cigarette, holding the smoke deep in his lungs before exhaling.

Boris did like the ladies, Stoli thought, but he was as reliable as celestial mechanics in making his collection rounds. He was one of the old guard, like Stoli. Business always came first, even if he did occasionally mix business with pleasure. When he first learned that Boris was missing, he expected something like this. But there was nothing to be done. Boris was not a man you could easily find if he failed to appear. Either he would show up and explain the nature of his absence himself, or he would be found as he was—dead. Now he, Stoli, would have to try to learn what happened. A hit on someone in his organization had to be resolved and vindicated. One thing he was sure of, Boris must have been totally fooled, for he was a cunning man who usually sensed danger. He may have played the lumbering bear, but he was very difficult to surprise. Whoever lured or forced Boris out into the desert and killed him must have been exceptionally good. Or he must have planned his attack very carefully. Or both.

"Who is now looking after our interests out there?"

"Andrei Dmitriev."

"I see," Stoli replied. Another of the younger ones, he mused—a reliable man, but young. "I want you to go out there and look into this. Andrei is a good man, but he now has a business to run, a business in which I have an interest. See if you can find out who did this and why. Then we will see what needs to be done from there. Do you understand?"

"Yes, sir."

Alexei was turning to leave when Stoli stopped him. "Have someone claim the body and have it cremated."

"Cremated?"

Stoli lashed him with a murderous look. "You heard me," he said angrily. "And bring the ashes back to me. We will send Boris back to rest along the banks of the Volga."

"Yes, sir. I'll see to it."

When he was gone, Stoli lit another cigarette from the stub of the old one. He pushed the beer aside and retrieved the jar from the refrigerator. He had a bad feeling about all this and wanted to give it some serious thought. For that, one needed vodka.

Outside the warehouse, Alexei paused to consider his next move. Naturally, he would leave for Las Vegas that night. He had worked with Stoli for several years and had seen his mercurial temper on occasion. It was like the wrath of the devil himself, and to be the focus of this rage was a near-death experience. But this business with Boris's ashes? This was the first time he had ever seen Stoli say or do anything that could have been thought of as charitable or compassionate.

Cathy knew that Garrett had been in Las Vegas for some time. She also assumed that he was probably skirting the law as he tried to piece together what happened to Brandon on that tragic night. Even though Brandon had agreed to share what he and Garrett were trying to do, and they talked about it almost every day, she was still unnerved by Garrett's sudden appearance. She had to admit that Brandon had been as candid with her as he knew how. Yet she also knew she would not be fully included in what actually went on between the two of them. During the weeks of their recovery, she had watched as the bond of unspoken understanding began to again grow between them. There was simply a private channel of communication, some covenant of insight, that was theirs alone, and she knew she would never be a part of it. All she could do was watch and listen carefully, and trust Brandon to interpret things for her. But no matter how much Brandon worked at the translation, she was still an outsider. She would never be privy to their innermost, collective feelings.

Occasionally, she would allow herself to drift back to the time when she had met Garrett. He was an exciting, unpredictable, and unsettling man—quite unlike anyone she had ever met. Both he and Brandon were wild and carefree, but Garrett took it past their shared youthful exuberance. There was an energy and an aura to him that was different—more highly charged and explosive. It was as if Garrett had some hidden reservoir of desire and passion that was his alone. This was a subtle, well-masked side of Garrett and was dormant much of the time. But when it showed itself, they were no longer the Walker twins; Garrett was a man apart.

On the football field, Garrett made a lot of tackles, but occasionally he would take a ball carrier head-on with a hit so vicious that it could be heard in a crowded stadium. It didn't happen often, but the few times it did, it made her nauseous. She would never forget that Ohio State game—the Tag incident. It was hard to be close to someone so mercurial and violent; for that reason, she never referred to him as Tag. If it had been confined to the football field, she might have been able to live with it. But it wasn't.

One evening, a group of townies from Ann Arbor decided to come out to the Michigan campus bar for a few beers. A young, burly construction worker made a pass at her. He was boorish but harmless. Garrett was immediately on his feet, challenging the big man and making it awkward for him to back away. When he stood his ground, Garrett hit him three or four times—blows that came too fast to count. He was on his way down after the first punch, but Garrett followed him to the floor, pummeling him. When one of the man's friends tried to intervene, Garrett dropped him cleanly with a single blow. Cathy never forgot the awful silence that followed as the two men lay motionless on the floor, nor the speed with which it had happened. And she never forgot the cold look on Garrett's face as the two unconscious men were carried by their friends from the bar.

Briefly, she and Garrett had been lovers. She always tried never to make comparisons between Garrett and Brandon—that wasn't fair. Each was a different time and place. But when she did, she was forced to admit that her affair with Garrett Walker had been like no other—a unique and meteoric memory that she had buried in her past. Here, too, there was that fierceness and abandonment and a strength that was almost overwhelming. It was like riding the wind—intoxicating, euphoric, and scary. More often than she would like to admit, she found herself trying not to remember what it was like to be the focus of Garrett Walker's passion.

The Garrett Walker she had met that day at the Las Vegas airport was a mature, tempered version of the one she had known in Ann Arbor—physically stronger, perhaps, but somehow more measured. She couldn't help but notice that he had changed over the past weeks, yet it was a subtle evolution. He was now more thoughtful, more contemplative than she remembered, but still a very hard-edged man. As she watched him interact with her husband, she saw him as a comforting yet frightening influence. Aside from the kidney transplant, she knew that Brandon needed to reconnect with his brother, but there was a price to pay. She was apprehensive and could only continue to hope that the cost wasn't too great—for both her and Brandon.

Garrett's stay with them had not been as disruptive as she had expected. At first, his presence was lost in the aftermath of their surgery and the physical healing. There was a steady stream of friends and family through the house. Garrett was regarded as a savior and a prodigal returned, and a bit of a curiosity. Finally, they had settled into some semblance of a family routine. Brandon had finished a room over the garage that was someday to be a home office. It was served by a small bath and an outside entrance, and functioned well as a studio apartment. Garrett was more like a frequent visitor than a guest—part family, part neighbor. He seemed to meld easily into the household without changing the family chemistry. He was more than helpful, and he seemed to have a sixth sense in knowing what might need to be done around the house and yard without seeming presumptuous or intrusive. Occasionally, when she and Brandon felt the need to be alone, they had no more than thought about it when Garrett seemed to vanish.

The kids loved him. At first, Garrett was overwhelmed by their attention—this stranger who looked just like Dad. But he wasn't their dad, nor did he try to parent them. Yet he drew firm lines and insisted they behave. He hadn't the baggage of having raised them and was immune from the seemingly arbitrary parental inconsistencies that invariably come with bringing up three children. As a newcomer, he carried the big stick—the ultimate weapon. If they behaved badly, he could quietly withdraw his affection and approval. This gave him near absolute control over them, and he used this power judiciously. So Garrett had settled comfortably into the role of favorite uncle. Cathy did feel badly for her own brother, as Garrett had raised the bar and would be a tough act for anyone else to follow.

When Garrett left for Las Vegas, Cathy had felt a measure of relief. More than anything else, she wanted to get back to some sense of normalcy, although she was hard-pressed to define just what exactly that meant. Yet it was clear that Garrett's leaving created a fissure in the fabric of the household, like the death of a pet or the unexpected passing of a kindly neighbor's wife. There were lapses in the conversation around the dinner table, the kids fought a more aggressive holding action at bedtime, and the grass needed to be cut. No one talked about it, but there was a different dynamic in the Walker home after Garrett left. They would adjust, they already had, but she was forced to admit that in one way or another, they had all missed him—even her. Now he was back.

The lasagna and bread were in the oven warming. When she heard the garage door go up, she started the water for the vegetables and began to drag out salad makings from the fridge. Cathy had found the perfect mom-job at a frame shop near Palo Alto. It was piecework, and she was very good at it. She could drop the kids at school, do her five hours or so in the shop, and collect them on the way home with time for errands and shopping squeezed in at both ends. All it took was organization, discipline, and a lot of energy. Fortunately, Brandon had always helped with the kids as much as his work and travel schedule allowed. He had reached her at the shop that morning to say that Garrett would be coming home with him. She had just enough time to grab the kids and stop by the store for a quick pass by the frozen foods and produce department.

"Hi, Cath."

She dried her hands on a dishtowel and kissed him. "Hi, honey." Not seeing Garrett, she asked, "How was it—how is he? Can you tell me now or should we wait?"

Brandon tossed his briefcase on the counter and gently pulled her to him. "He's fine; he went up to the apartment to change. It's a long story and not a particularly nice one. Garrett knows about our agreement—that you're a part of this whole thing. He says he understands, but I'm not sure he does. At any rate, he asked if he could tell you about his trip to Las Vegas himself. It's his story, so I said that would be fine. Once the kids are in bed, we can talk then, okay?"

"That's fine with me. Are you okay with this, the three of us talking about it?"

A shadow passed across Brandon's strained features. "I don't know. This thing will probably get messy before it's done with—it already has. I don't ever want to lose contact with Garrett again, but I also want to be back where we were, just you and I and the kids." He released her and folded his arms, leaning against a counter. "But for right now, we are all in this together; I need his help to finish this damn business. So it'll be the three of us for a little while longer. Do you think you can handle that, Cath?"

"How much longer?"

"I don't know—a week, two weeks, not much more than that."

"And then what?"

"Hopefully, back to the way we were, just that papa bear has only one kidney. Garrett has to get back to the Navy; we have to move on. He'll probably remember the kids' birthdays, and we may see him occasionally on a Christmas and Thanksgiving if he's not overseas on some assignment."

"You think we can get there from here, back to normal?"

He shrugged. "We have to; there's no place else for us to go. We owe it to the kids and to each other."

He again took her in his arms and they hugged fiercely.

When the kids learned that Uncle Garrett was back, they stormed the apartment over the garage. A short time later, they dragged their prize to the dinner table. The setting was formal, but the dinner was anything but decorous. Brandon had chopped a little of everything he found in the refrigerator salad drawer and tossed it all in a large wooden bowl with two medieval-looking serving tools. The lasagna was served at the table in the factory aluminum packaging. They said grace and attacked the food. Initially, the three adults occasionally exchanged wary glances, but they were soon lost in the family feeding—more salad, seconds on lasagna, and what happened at school today.

This is good, Brandon thought as he watched his kids and their uncle. *It helps us to focus on what's really at stake here—three wonderful kids. That's what's on the line.* He had, of late, found himself doing this a lot, quietly observing his kids. It helped cool the rage inside when his thoughts flashed back to what those animals had done to him in Las Vegas. It was much, much more than two kidneys. Their brutal theft had threatened his family, and he was finding it nearly impossible to forgive or forget. Recently, he often felt his only sane reference point was Cathy and the kids.

"When I get outta high school, I'm gonna join the Navy and become a SEAL," Tommy announced. "College is for dopes."

"But you won't be in high school for another year," Garrett observed. "I think you might do very well in high school and then want to go to college."

"Yeah, but why wait? You can join up right out of high school, can't you?"

"Yes, you can, but if you finish college and then join the Navy, they make you an officer."

"You didn't finish college. Dad said that if you did you might have played pro ball, right, Dad?"

"That's what I said," Brandon replied, enjoying the interchange.

Garrett eyed his brother. "Your dad's right about one thing. If you don't stay in school, you can lose out on some good things in life."

"I'm going to be a SEAL in the Navy, too."

"Uh, Amy, sweetheart," Garrett said kindly, "I don't think they allow girls to be SEALs."

"They will when I get there," she said confidently. "My mom says girls can be anything they want, and I want to be a Navy SEAL."

Garrett considered the logic and shrugged. "Well, that's good enough for me. You can be on my team anytime." He glanced down at Tim, the youngest. He was a fifth-grader and more under Garrett's spell than the others. "There's only two helpings of broccoli left, shipmate. What say the two of us finish them off?" Tim nodded enthusiastically. Garrett served the boy, then himself.

"I didn't think Timmy was all that fond of broccoli," Cathy observed.

"It's a guy thing," Garrett replied.

"That's what I suspected. Okay, gang, the ice cream comes out when the table is cleared and the dishwasher loaded."

Brandon organized the bussing of the table and the kitchen cleanup. It was done in a matter of minutes. Soon, they were all camped in silence over vanilla ice cream and fresh raspberries. While the older kids did their homework, Garrett broke out the riding mower and cut the grass with Tim on his lap steering. Brandon and Cathy took a long walk together. That evening, she joined the two of them on the deck. Brandon was drinking a cup of decaf and Garrett was smoking. She thought for a minute that he was drinking a beer, but it turned out to be a soda. The smoking was something new, but she withheld comment.

"Okay, guys," she said as she sat next to Brandon and took his hand. "The kids are in bed, and I declare the Walker council of war now in session."

Garrett studied her with open admiration. Everyone had been quick to point to Brandon's suffering and his own noble mission in rushing halfway around the world with the missing organ. But what about Catherine Walker? She had stood like a rock amid all this turmoil and held her family together. Her husband was handed a death sentence. Cathy was the one who had the courage to summon her outlaw brother-in-law back home to save him. Family, friends, and co-workers—they all called, stopped by, asked questions, offered sympathy. It was chaos. Cathy stood in the middle of all this and directed traffic. She made decisions and explained what was difficult for those around them to understand. She answered all the hard questions. It would have been so much simpler if Brandon had been in a car wreck or been mugged and had his wallet stolen instead of his kidneys. Garrett had watched as she had been both mother and father to those three wild Indians until Brandon was back on his feet. She kept the family centered and together during the entire debacle. She was magnificent.

As he recovered from the operation and became a part-time member of the Brandon Walker family, Garrett had watched Cathy and Brandon carefully. The hurt he took with him when he sent himself into exile from Michigan, he now realized, had long since faded. He had nursed that bitterness for years, often having to resort to the mental gymnastics of self-pity to nurture the pain in order to keep it alive. He had found some twisted comfort in the role of the exiled rogue, the lone wolf; it gave him direction. Being a Navy SEAL helped, for it was the domestic equivalent of the French Foreign Legion. He was tough, self-sufficient, aggressive, and a natural leader. To his adopted military family, the Navy SEAL teams, these were highly prized virtues. They welcomed him with open arms.

Very soon after the operation, Garrett found that Cathy Walker, his brother's wife, and Cathy Simpson, the Michigan coed whom he had been in love with, were two different people. When he finally understood this, his reconciliation of the girl she was then and with the woman she was now had been surprisingly easy. He and Cathy had been lovers; that they were young and in another time and place didn't alter that fact. For a while, he had nursed the image of this intimacy as a symbol of her betrayal. Time and distance assuaged what he had thought of as a deception on her part, yet it could still cause him anguish if he thought about it long enough. But it was all so long ago, he admitted. The years of marriage and child rearing had distilled the pretty sorority girl he remembered into the beautiful woman that now sat across from him, clutching his brother's hand as if to declare herself firmly in his camp. He still loved her, of course, but in a very different way. Since his return, he had groped with these feelings, trying to reconcile the past with the current reality. Garrett sensed that the grief and loneliness that drove him from Ann Arbor into the Navy was a personal space he just simply could not go back to; it was a dishonest world based on a long-dead perception of duplicity. When he began to reconnect with Brandon, the old wounds he was so afraid would open had begun to heal. A sense of well-being had begun to take root inside of him, and he savored it like vintage wine. He was tasting the first measure of tranquility that he had known in a very long while, and he wanted more.

As for Cathy, she was his brother's wife. It had taken awhile for him to get his pride in check—to see her for what she now was today. Finally, during those long hours in the Nevada desert while he waited by the moving van for the sun to do its work on Boris, it had come to him, as sharp and clear as a distant mountain on a cloudless winter morning. He could now love Cathy *because* she was his brother's wife.

"So, who's going to begin first? Brandon? Garrett?"

"I suppose I should," Garrett answered with a sad smile. "To begin with, I'm reasonably sure I know who took Brandon's kidneys, why they took them, and exactly where they are at this very minute."

"You what?" she exclaimed.

Garrett raised his hand in a calming manner. "A lot has happened since the last time I had supper here. Perhaps I should tell you how I came to learn all of this."

I know you're one tough lady, Garrett said to himself, *but let's see if you really know how to take a punch*. Then he told her exactly what he had told Brandon that afternoon, sparing none of the details.

Part Five:
SETTLING ACCOUNTS

Garrett, Brandon, and Cathy had talked into the night. Cathy had mostly listened while the two brothers discussed what they had learned and what they felt they could do about it. As she listened, she was again reminded of just how much the two of them were alike—and different. In the weeks following their return from Las Vegas after the operation, she learned there was a balanced and sensitive side to Garrett. Since his recent return from Las Vegas, it was more noticeable. She watched him closely as he described in detail the killing of the Russian. As Garrett talked about what he had done, she could see it had been a very difficult thing for him, something in which he took no pleasure. Perhaps his life as a Navy SEAL made him more circumspect about violence. The need to find and punish those responsible for taking Brandon's kidneys was business—difficult and distasteful, but still business. The one she worried about was Brandon. He seemed bent on revenge. For him, there was almost an obsession about settling the score. At first, she thought that it was because of the physical pain he suffered at the hands of those butchers. Now, she was not so sure. She knew her husband well, but this was a side of him she had never seen, and it worried her.

There was a strange dynamic at work between Brandon and Garrett. When one twin overreacted or took an extreme position, the other typically would move opposite of that center, almost in a counter move. There was no friction between them; they just seemed to balance each other. She had let them talk, content to be an observer for most of the evening, but when Brandon asked her what she thought, she was quick to answer.

"I think you should call Ray Stannick."

They had all been up late, but both Garrett and Brandon were down on the deck at eight o'clock in their sweats and running shoes when she emerged from the kitchen.

"This should get you two heroes down the road and back," she said as she set the tray on the patio table. There was orange juice and a stack of buttered English muffins.

"Thanks, hon." Brandon poured a glass of juice for her and then one for Garrett and himself. "Kids still in bed?" She nodded.

The two younger kids slept in on Saturday. Tommy was already out delivering papers. Garrett had just taken Brandon through twenty minutes of stretching and upper-body exercises. After the juice and a muffin, they would be out for a long, easy run.

"Well, we took your advice," Garrett said with a grin. "Brandon called Ray Stannick a few minutes ago."

"Really? On Saturday?"

"That's right," Brandon replied. "He gave me a private number to his office, but I guess it also rings through to his cell phone. He was having breakfast down at the Marina."

"So you've already talked with him?"

Brandon nodded. "Just briefly. He wants to see us, so we said we'd meet him this morning"—he glanced at his watch—"in about forty-five minutes. He's probably on the road by now."

"Now?" Cathy replied. "This morning? Is he meeting you here?"

"No, not here," Brandon said. He chuckled. "You don't have to worry about federal agents in the living room this morning. We're meeting him over at Starbucks for coffee."

"Which means," Garrett said, "we better be on the road if we're going to get our five miles in by then."

"Maybe six if we leave right now." Brandon was on his feet, draining the last of his juice. He turned to Cathy, suddenly serious. "You want to meet us there?"

"No, but thanks for asking. This is probably a good time for a guy meeting. I have to feed the kids anyway."

Cathy watched as they trotted across the yard to the back gate that opened onto a jogging trail that ran through the development. Brandon was talking while Garrett set his watch to clock the time of their run.

Ray Stannick was waiting for them at an outside table, tucked in behind a double Americano. The dark suit was gone, but he was well turned out in light-gray slacks, cabled socks in Dockers, a charcoal turtleneck, and blue blazer—off-duty federal agent attire. He waited while they went inside for an iced coffee and a bottle of water. The regular Saturday morning coffee klatches, mostly women in their late thirties or early forties, gathered at the scattered tables. They chatted incessantly, occasionally casting a glance at the two fit, tanned look-alikes and the handsome, well-dressed black man who had been waiting for them.

"You look pretty good for a couple of guys who recently had major surgery."

"Long and slow, Ray. We're not back into wind sprints just yet. Ray, I'd like you to meet my brother Garrett. Garrett, Ray Stannick."

They shook hands. "Pleasure to meet you, Ray. Brandon's told me a lot about you."

"Has he now? Well, I hope it hasn't all been bad. I should probably follow your lead and try to get a few miles in, at least on the weekends. Seems like there's just never enough hours in the day."

"Make time, Ray," Garrett said agreeably. "A guy like you should know that you have to take care of yourself."

"Point taken. I'll try to do better."

"We didn't mean for you to drop everything and drive down here," Brandon interjected. "I wanted you to meet Garrett, and Monday or sometime during the week would have been soon enough. I really only called to make an appointment."

Stannick smiled easily. "Not a problem. When I'm on assignment, I work seven days a week and then some." He folded his hands in front of him as if to signify he was ready to talk business. "And I was glad you called, Brandon, because I wanted to bring you up to date. We've had a development in a related incident that could be significant. It appears there has been another kidney taken from an unwilling donor." Stannick paused to sip at his drink and gauge their reaction. "This one occurred down in Venice. The victim was one of the locals. He turned up at the county morgue missing one of his kidneys. I sent an agent down there to check on it. We've been in touch with the surgeon who first operated on you, Brandon, and he agreed that it sounds like the same handiwork—or butchery, if you like."

"Was he in a hotel like me, packed in ice?"

"We're not sure what happened or where. The autopsy suggests that he died during the procedure or a short time later. After he was relieved of his kidney, his body was dumped in the park, so he wasn't on ice. Chances are he died during the removal so there was no need to cool him down."

"That brings up something I've been curious about, Ray," Garrett asked. "Why the ice? Why do these people want their organ donors cold?"

"Well," Stannick replied, "the medical folks tell me that under the crude operating conditions, if they can keep the patient cold, there is less bleeding and they can make cleaner work of it. It makes the procedure easier under those conditions. But I have my own theory. The fact that the victim is cold, which can keep him from bleeding to death as in Brandon's case, serves another purpose. I think they do it so that if we ever do get the sons of bitches in front of a jury, they can escape the death penalty. They'll try to cop a plea to aggravated assault."

"Can they do that? I mean, is that a viable defense?" Garrett persisted.

Stannick shrugged. "This is California. It's hard to get anyone into the chair in California. And the jails are crowded. They won't walk, but they might do less time."

"But my kidneys were taken in Nevada. They still fry them in Nevada, don't they?" Without realizing it, Brandon had allowed his voice to become harsh.

"As a matter of fact," Stannick said, smiling, "they do. But you need a dead body, even in Nevada. I'm glad you didn't give them an opportunity for a first-degree murder rap. The guy in Venice wasn't so lucky." He sat back and regarded the two brothers. *These are a tough pair*, he thought, *and I'll bet they're holding cards they aren't showing.* He had shared the incident about the missing kidney in Venice as a show of good faith. *Now*, he thought, *I'm going to have to prod them a little.*

"Garrett, Brandon," he began, "I drove down here because I wanted you guys to know about this; I wanted to keep you fully informed. Now, while I was driving, I had this overwhelming premonition that you two fellows had something you wanted to tell me. Maybe it's just the cop in me. Or maybe I sense that you guys know something I don't, am I right?" Stannick paused and looked directly at Garrett, then Brandon. "While you're giving that some thought, can I get you a brioche or one of those delicious scones they have here? It's on the government. Brandon? How about you, Tag, can I get you something?"

Ray Stannick gave them a patient, easy smile and waited. His use of Garrett's nickname told both of the brothers that he had done his homework. He gave every indication that he was prepared to sip coffee there in San Jose indefinitely until they told him something. Brandon and Garrett exchanged a glance, and they both laughed. Then Brandon leaned onto the table with his elbows.

"You're a piece of work, Ray, you really are. Okay, remember when we met last, and I said I'd do what I could to see if someone was hacking into our systems?"

Stannick nodded. "And you assured me that such a thing was next to impossible. Something about confidentiality being the prime directive is how you put it, I believe."

"Something like that," Brandon admitted. "Well, I was wrong. I asked one of our programmers to study the problem. Actually, he led the design team that put together our patient and clinic management systems. The guy's the best there is. Anyway, he found that someone had managed to gain access to our systems—unauthorized access—and had interrogated several individual patient records. We don't know much more, other than it was evident that this intruder had definitely called up my medical file."

"And you don't know who did it?"

"No, we don't. This may sound strange, since you're not in the software business, but this hacker was able to break into the system, read my file, and then cover his tracks when he left."

"I see," Stannick said gravely. "It does seem peculiar, but one of my agents is a software engineer. She said that an illegal entry into a database is often hard to trace, especially if the hacker is highly sophisticated."

"Well, my guy says this intruder is very good at software manipulation. He's working on it now, but it's going to take a little time to track this rogue hacker, perhaps more time than I can give him. Since the software programs have been corrupted, who knows how many patient files are being rifled through for information. It could be hundreds."

"Just who has access to your systems from a user standpoint?"

"Any number of people. Physicians, clinics, hospitals, insurance companies, billing services, even the National Institutes of Health."

"The NIH?" Stannick asked. "Why them?"

"Lots of reasons. They track patterns of disease and sickness, like various strains of the flu, as well as prescription drug usage, HIV statistics, lead poisoning, birth defects, you name it. They're also looking for indicators that could signal a major epidemic, like some new virulent strain of hepatitis."

"Does the NIH have access to individual patient files?"

"No, but they have access to the system, just like all the other users. At this stage, we can't rule out anyone."

"You said that your programmer only has a short time to find the hacker. Why is that?"

"Ray, we're up against the wall. If our systems are compromised, my company has tremendous liability. And I'm not talking just a recall of software; I mean extended liability. The fact that our systems are approved by the FDA will mean little or nothing in court. I gave my guy a few days to see if he can find out where this illegal entry originated. But come Tuesday, I'm going to have to pull the plug—or recommend that the plug get pulled. That means a product recall. The system is compromised."

"Meaning, you'll have to take this to George Grant."

"Exactly."

"When did you actually learn that your systems were … ah … as you said, compromised?"

"About a week ago—the Friday before last, to be exact."

"Brandon, I have to ask you this." Stannick had suddenly become very measured, almost formal. "The recall of your two biggest software lines will devastate MedaSystems. Share prices will fall dramatically. Did you have any direct knowledge of this before you exercised your options in the company stock?"

Brandon looked dumbstruck. "Jesus, Ray, you don't think I learned about this and then sold the stock options? I don't believe you said that!"

"Easy, man." Garrett said, placing a hand on his brother's arm.

"Easy, my ass. You tell me, Ray, you think I bailed on the options after I found out we had a problem?"

"No, Brandon, I don't. But this has the potential to send the stock into the toilet, and you'll be questioned about trading on insider information. After all, you are an officer of the company. If the damage is bad enough, you could be named in a class-action suit. I'm sorry. I'm thinking like a cop or a prosecutor, but that's the reality of it."

"Well, number one, I sold well ahead of learning about the flaws in our system. My programmer will testify to that. And number two, I was asked by a federal agent to quietly look into the matter to see what I could find out." Brandon did not mention that he had initiated his inquiry *before* Stannick asked him to check into it.

"And I'll testify that I asked for your cooperation," Stannick said. "I just wanted you to know what's on the table. I'm on your side, remember."

"Sorry, Ray." Brandon replied. "Guess I'm a little sensitive about all this. I just want it over and done with. So what's the next move?"

"The next move is yours. I certainly hope your programmer comes through, but I think you're right. You have an obligation to tell Grant about the problem. And if you have no objection, I'd like to be there when you do. I'd like to see his reaction." He hesitated, then said, "I may even be able to help out. I could say you were keeping us advised while you ran a check on your software products. And that I requested your confidentiality while you were doing it as part of an ongoing criminal investigation."

Brandon shook his head. "This is going to be hard on George. It could ruin his company, and the company has been his life's work."

"Don't worry about it, big brother," Garrett said, this time with his hand on his shoulder. "Easier to lose a company than to lose your kidneys—or your life."

"He's right about that," Stannick added. He then turned to Garrett and asked, "How was San Diego?"

Garrett shrugged. "Sunny and warm."

"I'm sure. But then it's usually always warm and sunny in San Diego." Stannick gave him a neutral look. "Interesting. I had a report that someone who fits your description, actually fitting both of your descriptions, was asking questions in Las Vegas about what happened to Brandon. Does there happen to be more than two of you?"

Garrett measured him. "It's hard to say, Ray. Could be someone else out there who looks like us, I suppose."

"Uh-huh. Well, if it's not a terrible imposition, I hope you two junior G-Men will keep me informed if there's anything you think I need to know."

"Absolutely, Ray."

"Yeah, Ray, you'll be the first to know."

He looked from one to the other and then rose, taking his cup. "I think I'll get myself a traveler for the trip back to the city. You want a lift?"

"You go on ahead; we'll run back to the house," Garrett replied. "It's not all that far from here, but then I'll bet you already know that."

"Thanks anyway," Brandon added.

"You gentlemen behave yourselves. And give my regards to Mrs. Walker."

While he was inside for more coffee, Brandon and Garrett bused the table and trotted off down the street. It took them about fifteen minutes to reach the house. They walked the last few hundred meters so they could talk. Cathy was waiting for them when they arrived.

"Good run?"

"Not bad for a couple of old guys. The FBI said hello."

"Really? Oh, before I forget, Richard called from the office. He wanted you to call him as soon as you arrived—says it's urgent."

They walked out onto the patio, Brandon grabbing the portable phone on the way. He dialed in a leisurely manner; with Richard, everything was urgent.

"So what did you think of Agent Stannick?" she asked Garrett while Brandon rang through.

"Seems like a solid guy. Told us there was another incident of a missing kidney."

"Oh God, no! Where?"

"Down in Venice. Only when they found this guy, he was dead. They're still investigating it, but it looks similar to what happened to Brandon."

Cathy folded her arms about herself and shivered involuntarily. "Is this ever going to end?"

"I hope so. But you do see why we have to stay involved, why we have to do what we can to bring an end to this dirty business?" She just looked at him, frowning. "When I say 'we,' that also includes you, Cathy."

Reluctantly, she nodded. "That's right, it does include me. It also includes Tommy, Amy, and Tim. How much longer? Brandon says a week or two; what do you say?"

"I don't know, but things are going to start happening pretty quickly in another day or two. Hang in there, Cath."

She gave him a sad smile as Brandon turned from the phone. "That was Richard. Looks like he's found something, but I couldn't get it out of him over the phone. We're going to have to go down there, the sooner the better."

"Do we have time for a shower?"

"I don't think so. He's really in a snit."

Garrett looked to Cathy. "A snit?"

There was always a low level of activity at MedaSystems on Saturday. Few from Brandon's marketing group came in, but many of the techs and the engineers gathered on Saturday mornings. The excuse was that they were there to catch up on work or get a jump on the coming week. Basically, they came in on Saturdays to hang out. These were people who had little interest in sports or cars or politics; they liked to talk shop. They were very gifted, highly focused supernerds. If intelligence were a skin color, they would be consummate racists. When they wanted to relax with others of their kind, they came to work. The company paid them overtime for this quasi-social weekend work, but some of the boldest concepts in software design came from these Saturday sessions.

When Brandon and Garrett arrived, there were several loose conversation groups in progress in the engineering department. As they made their way to Brandon's office, they passed a little blonde girl on a tricycle. Outside one of the cubicles, a half-dozing Labrador retriever managed to thump his tail a few times as they passed. Richard was pacing the office when they arrived.

"Brandon, thank God you're here. I don't know what I'd have done if you hadn't called back." Richard did a double-take in Garrett's direction. "Well, hullo there."

"Richard, this is my brother, Garrett. Garrett, Richard Rogers."

They shook hands. "Hullo, again. Brandon told me he had a twin brother, but I had no idea! I hear you're in the Nav-ee."

"Uh, that's right, Rich. And Brandon's told me a lot about you. Understand you've found out something for us."

"Well, yes, I have—at least I think I have. And it's Richard, if you please. Well, first of all, you have to understand that this has truly been a very trying experience. I'm very distraught."

"Garrett," Brandon interrupted, as he shot his brother a look of caution, "Richard has been working very hard on this, and I—we—appreciate just how difficult this has been for him. Richard, why don't you sit down, take a deep breath, and start from the beginning."

Richard dropped dramatically into a chair and tried to compose himself. "All right, Brandon. I developed some new diagnostic programs to use with our commercial applications, specifically with our patient tracking software. I had to be very subtle and interrogate our access points and data transmission sites with the greatest care. I could do nothing overt or straightforward; all inquiries had to be, well, oblique—indirect. I was," he rose and began to pace the room, "looking for fingerprints, some way to recognize this intruder without revealing my position to him or causing the system to crash. It has been very tedious work."

"But you did it." Garrett interrupted. "You caught the son of a bitch, right?"

Richard stopped pacing and glared at him.

"Garrett, please," Brandon warned. "Let Richard tell us in his own way." Then to Richard, he said gently, "Try to relax and tell us what happened. This is all very fascinating."

"Yes, if I may continue!" Richard said as he folded himself back into the chair. "I found nothing. I tell you, the man is an absolute ghost, a phantom. But," he exclaimed, brandishing an index finger over his head, "I was haunted by this feeling that I was overlooking something, some key that would unlock the puzzle. Then it came to me; I was looking in the wrong place."

"Really?"

"Yes, Brandon. It would have taken months to dissect our systems and try to track the intruder from an illegal entry point or a corrupted access code. Months! And God knows what mayhem or unknown viruses I would have unleashed along the way. So I said to myself, *Richard, hello, you're overthinking the problem.*

Kiss, kiss—keep it simple, stupid!" He gave them a sly smile. "First, I developed a utility program that would simply check each of our clinic and HMO clients for the number of times individual patient files were accessed—a simple count of the number of files entered. This is a routine request. Then I went a step further; I scanned the files for the user who had accessed the file. Our hacker friend, being a clever fellow, is not going to show up on this routine search, nor tip his hand by blocking us from checking file users with legal access. So, I now know whose files were looked at, legally, by those who could legally access them. Well, duh, what does that tell us? Nothing, right? Well, almost nothing. *Then*, I went to our list of clients and non-client users who routinely enter patient files for information. I used a variation of our old billing software." He was again up and pacing. "I hoped and prayed that our devious friend would spend his time trying to defeat my attempts to find him by manipulating our MedaSystems standard security software. And to keep him thinking this, I occasionally tinkered with our security programs, at some risk to our own software, just to keep him on the defense. I want him to think that's how we would come after any intruder, by using our standard security protocols."

"But that's not what you were doing, was it, Richard?" Brandon prompted.

"No indeed. While I had him looking for me to come at him through our proprietary software, I quietly checked each and every one who has access to our systems. And once again, I prayed that while he had done a shamefully thorough job of getting in and out of our database, he had not covered his tracks so well from his own entry-point system. You know what I found?"

"I couldn't begin to hazard a guess, Richard," said Garrett, getting in on the game. "Please, don't stop now. What happened?"

"The number of inquiries by users matched the number of patient file interrogations *exactly* … except for one entry point."

He turned to face the two brothers like a priest about to offer the Eucharist. "There have been a number of requests for information from Golden Western Insurance Company, a number far *in excess* of the legal file interrogations I counted from the diagnostic I developed to count the file entries."

"Let me see if I understand this." Brandon said. "You just counted the legal file requests, then found another clandestine way to count the number of times each legal user made a request for information. So for each legal user, the number of times they requested information should exactly equal the number of times they legally entered individual patient files."

"Precisely, Brandon." Richard was beaming. "Except for this one entry point, every user who has access to our system had a matching number of legal access requests to patient files."

Garrett leaned forward with his forearms on his knees. "So let me make sure I understand this. The total medical file requests from a user, minus your count of the times medical files were legally accessed by the same user, should equal the authorized entries by the user. And only Golden Western had more entries than your count of entries that legally accessed files?"

"Exactly."

"See, Richard," Brandon said, smiling broadly at Garrett, "my twin brother's not as stupid as he looks." He rose and walked around the desk to give Richard a hug. Garrett simply rose and shook his hand.

"Richard, I can't tell you what a breakthrough this is," Brandon continued, very deferentially, "and you're sure of this. Our hacker is at Golden Western?"

"Positively."

"And if we cut Golden Western's access to the database, we eliminate the problem—the system's intact, right?"

"Possibly."

"Possibly?"

"You see, Brandon, you block Golden Western—terminate their access—and all you do is plug the leak. But this fellow is very good. He may have left behind a virus or something worse that gets triggered if we revoke his user access codes. If I were the ungodly fiend this person is, it's what I'd do. What I'm saying is, if we terminate Golden Western, he will know that *we know* where he lives. In an attempt to keep us from following him, or just to spite us, he could crash our system, possibly even our other user systems, and then escape in the confusion. He could ruin us, and we would never know who this monster was—other than he was someone who worked at Golden Western. Or had access to Golden Western's database."

Brandon was in his seat now, hands together in front of his face, deep in thought. It was a chess game, and his next move could lead to checkmate—or disaster.

"So knowing where this bastard is, and exactly who he is, are two very different problems."

"That's right. I can still try to go after him, but it'll be slow and dangerous. He frightens me, Brandon."

Brandon was again silent for a moment, considering the options. "Let's do nothing for the present. Keep probing the edges of our programs so he'll think we're still in the dark. The only thing we really have going for us is that we know he's at Golden Western and he doesn't know we know. Richard, why don't you go home and get some rest. You've earned it. We'll pick this up in the morning. And again, great work. I can't tell you how much I appreciate and admire what you've been able to accomplish."

After he left, the two brothers sat looking at each other. After their morning run, the meeting with Ray Stannick, and more than an hour with Richard, they looked rumpled and defeated.

"What's next, big brother?"

"I don't know. I think we better take this to Stannick—tell him what Richard's come up with. Maybe he'll have some ideas."

Brandon stared at his desk for a moment, then looked up at Garrett. "And when do we tell him about Stolichnaya? Now, or do we hold that information back?"

Garrett considered this. "Let's tell him what Richard came up with and that we think someone at Golden Western is dirty. Let's hold off on Stolichnaya—and who told us about Stolichnaya."

"So you don't think he'll buy a story that we got an anonymous tip from a rival mobster who told us Stolichnaya was dealing in organs?"

"I doubt it, and he probably needs proof, anyway. Besides, I don't want to get subpoenaed and have to testify under oath. It looks like our best bet is the guy at Golden Western who's been supplying the information for potential organ donors. Maybe he will lead us to Stolichnaya, and Boris and I can stay out of it. Otherwise, we'll have to try to pick the right time to tell Stannick about the Russians." Garrett paused and pursed his lips, as if he were reluctant to speak. "As for the other matter, when do you want to do it?"

"I don't know yet, but soon. Maybe even later on this week. I'd like to get this software business resolved first."

Garrett lifted his eyebrows. "If it's that soon, then I better get to it. I've got a lot of work to do. And Cathy?"

A look of pain passed over Brandon's face. "I've been wrestling with that one. I don't like secrets, but I think we have to keep her in the dark on this part of the plan. At least for now. What do you think?"

"It's your call, Brandon."

"I know it's my call, but I want to know what you think."

Garrett sighed and nodded his head slowly. "You're probably right. Let's keep her out of it for now. When are you going to call Stannick?"

"Right now," Brandon replied as he reached for the phone.

"That Richard, what a piece of work," Garrett said as he propped his feet on Brandon's desk. "And smart. Wouldn't mind having a few guys like him in the teams. Old SEAL proverb: Good mission intelligence is essential to operational success. How many gay guys like him do you have around here, anyway?"

"Probably less than you might expect. Those that are gay are pretty open about it, like Richard." Brandon punched two numbers and wedged the phone to his ear with a shoulder. He had Stannick's number on his autodialer. "How many gay guys do you have in the SEAL teams?"

Garrett lifted an eyebrow. "I dunno. Probably more than I might expect, but they keep it to themselves. A good teammate is a good teammate. But I really have no idea."

"Hello, Ray, Brandon Walker again … Nice to see you as well. Got a minute to talk?"

Judy Burks had been waiting in the MedaSystems reception area for more than a half hour when Brandon arrived Monday morning. She was dressed in a business suit and heels, and she carried a padded, computer shoulder bag. There was a visitor's tag clipped to her lapel, so she had already been signed in as his guest. She rose to meet him and handed him a card. Brandon wore chinos, an oxford cloth shirt, and a corduroy sport coat that had seen better days. He recognized her name on the card but not the company.

"Acme Computer Design?"

"Yes, Mr. Walker. I believe you were expecting me," she said. Then, in a whisper, she added, "Had 'em printed up myself last night. What do you think?"

Brandon looked up from the card. "Uh, sure … they're just fine, ah … Judith. Why don't we go into my office?"

She gave him a quick, mischievous smile. "It's okay, sir, you can call me Judy."

"All right then, Judy, this way."

Once in the office, Brandon closed the door and offered her a chair. "Judy, this is a pretty informal place. We have a lot of consultants through here and many of our clients come here for training. I'm not so sure you really needed to go to the trouble of printing up business cards. You're my guest here."

"I understand that, Mr. Walker; I've visited software houses before. About the card, well, you see, this is actually my first undercover assignment, so I wanted to do everything by the book." She handed him her FBI shield and credential. He studied them briefly and handed them back to her. The photo looked like it had been taken for a piece of student ID.

"And you really work for Ray Stannick?" He couldn't keep a tone of reservation from his voice.

"Yes, I really do. Great guy, isn't he? So when can I talk with your programmer?"

"Well, I guess right now. I'll see if he's in."

When Stannick had informed him that he was sending another agent over to meet with Richard, Brandon had readily agreed. On one hand, he felt it would be helpful to have another person with a background in computers read into the problem—one that was a federal agent. He had been glad it was someone other than Stannick. Brandon felt Ray's presence would prove much too intimidating for Richard. However, he was now surprised and more than a little concerned that Stannick would send someone who was this young and inexperienced.

Brandon started to reach for the phone, but she raised a hand. "Before you call your programmer in here, we need to get clear on a couple things." Suddenly, she seemed more professional. "Would you prefer that I continue to pose as an outside consultant that you brought in to help with this matter? I know the business, and I can pull it off. Or do you simply want to introduce me as a federal agent? I'd prefer we go the federal-agent route, if only to your programmer; nobody else has to know. If your man is worth his salt, it probably won't take him long to smoke me out. But Ray says, it's your call."

Brandon hesitated a moment. "I agree; stay in the consultant role around the office, but let's play it straight with Richard. Only let me tell him. Richard's … well, as you will see, Richard's a little sensitive."

A few minutes later, Richard entered and closed the door behind him.

"You wanted to see me, Brandon." He glanced at Judy but chose to ignore her.

"Richard, I'd like you to meet Judy Burks. Judy, this is Richard Rogers, the programmer that I've been telling you about. He's probably more talented than all the other programmers here at MedaSystems combined."

"Oh, Brandon, stop it. I'm pleased to meet you, Miss Burks."

"Have a seat, Richard. Richard, Miss Burks is with the federal government. She has a special interest in what happened to me and any connection that may exist as to a problem with our clinic and patient management systems. I've told her about some of the things we've learned this past week."

"Oh my!"

"It's okay, Richard. She's just here to try to learn more about what we're up against."

"Oh my, my—a federal person. Brandon, I had no idea." He now eyed Judy suspiciously.

"Richard, she's had some experience in these matters, and I think she can help us out."

"Well, I thought you and I were doing pretty darn well, Brandon. I really did."

Judy smiled and swung in her chair to face Richard. He was now sitting with his legs crossed and his arms folded and turned to one side away from her. Richard did hurt feelings very well. He treated her as if she had some exotic, contagious disease.

"Richard, I'm with the FBI." At the mention of FBI, he visibly winced. She continued in a very soothing voice, "I'm one of a new kind of special agent. I have an undergraduate degree from Caltech in computer science and an MBA from Stanford. Now, that means two things. First of all, it helps me to understand some of the problems you've been up against. Second, it takes a degree in computers from Caltech just to recognize the brilliant way you're handling this. It doesn't take a tremendous amount of ability to be a hacker, although Brandon's told us that this one is not your run-of-the-mill variety. Your ability to tease him with one of your utility programs while tracking him to his user site was nothing short of genius. If you should ever get bored with your job here, there's always one waiting for you with us."

"Well, it was quite an interesting challenge, so I took my best stab at it. I just got lucky."

"I doubt that luck had much to do with it. A really good programmer has to have intuition as well as brains. I can see that you have both. And I can just imagine how you must have felt after this … this criminal tampered with your work, after he contaminated your programs. It must have been just dreadful."

"You simply have no idea. I was absolutely crushed."

Brandon sat back and quietly watched the scenario develop before him. Judy Burks was treating Richard with the empathy of a social worker rather than an FBI agent who worked for Ray Stannick. He had been more than a little worried about how Richard was going to accept a federal investigator prying into his private domain. Richard was a very complex person, and he often let his emotions overrule his intellect. But she was handling him like a fine wine, gently and with great care.

"Richard, I think I have a vague idea of what you've been through so far, but could I ask you to quickly go over this terrible ordeal just one more time? It might help me to better understand the full impact of what you're up against here. That is, if it's not too painful for you."

She listened and took notes, but asked no questions. Mostly, she played the role of the empathetic listener; on two occasions, she reached out and gently touched his arm. Richard was able to manage a shorter and less emotional explanation than Brandon received on Saturday. When he had finished, she flipped her notebook closed and sighed.

"You've had quite an experience, Richard, and it's obvious that you've done a marvelous job. I had some really talented professors at Caltech, but none of them would have been up to this task. Now, if you can just continue to keep this malicious hacker on the defensive by probing for him with your normal security protocols, we may be able to crack this case." She shot Brandon a hard look. "I hope you appreciate what a splendid individual you have working for you."

"Absolutely. No one appreciates what Richard does for us around here more than I do."

"Tell me, Richard, do you have some hard copy that could document what you've told me—some printouts that would summarize how you deduced that the unauthorized entries are coming from Golden Western?"

Richard hesitated. "Well, I suppose so ... I mean, it could be done."

Highly computer-literate individuals like Richard often distrusted printed text. They felt it was like communicating with quill and ink. People like Richard lived in an electronic data transfer world. She again placed a hand on his arm.

"You see, we have these old-fashioned laws about probable cause that we have to deal with. And my boss is positively barbaric about these stupid legal details. It would really help me out if you could generate some text for us. It helps"—she shot Brandon another glance—"in dealing with some of the illiterates in our world." Brandon stared at the ceiling.

"Oh, not a problem. I deal with those kinds of people more than you might imagine—present company excluded, of course."

Brandon looked down and smiled, but said nothing. "Why don't you come with me, Judy, and we'll see what we can do. Is that all right with you, Brandon?"

"Absolutely. And take whatever time you need."

They rose, and Judy Burks followed him out. "Richard, I just love the fabric in your shirt. It's very unusual."

"Isn't it, though? I found it in the city last summer; it was such a bargain."

Brandon stared after them for a moment and allowed himself a quiet chuckle, then reached for the phone to call Garrett.

The offices of the Golden Western Insurance Company occupied one entire building of the Madrona Business Park in San Mateo. It was a sprawling complex of brick and glass with neat parking lots and a perimeter jogging trail. Golden Western was one of the survivors in the California medical insurance free-for-all. They were a tier down from the big national insurers like Kaiser Permanente or MetraHealth, but they had a solid regional business that served a large piece of the California market with inroads into Oregon, Nevada, and Arizona. Their premiums weren't any lower than their competitors; in fact, their pricing structure was slightly more than what many other insurers charged. But Golden Western had combined an aggressive marketing and client service strategy with strict internal cost controls. They enjoyed solid, if not spectacular, margins, and were gaining market share in the competitive West Coast medical insurance market. And they were proficient in integrating internal systems with the Affordable Care Act.

Jon Sterling was the driving force behind Golden Western. The company reflected the strong personality of its young president and CEO. Sterling had degrees in management and finance from Wharton and was considered something of a prodigy. He was a financial technocrat with the charisma of a marketing exec, and he enjoyed the complete confidence of his board of directors.

The company's business plan was ambitious and exacting, and each department within the company was held to specific performance goals. At Golden Western, there was a single vision: Jon Sterling's. For those who worked there, it was his way or it was the highway—in this case, Bayshore Freeway.

Ray Stannick was unable to get an appointment with him the afternoon of Judy Burks's visit to MedaSystems, but Sterling's secretary was able to squeeze him in from nine to nine fifteen the next morning, between Sterling's other appointments. Stannick had said they were from the federal Occupational Safety and Health Administration. He and Judy were there promptly at eight fifty-five and were kept waiting for close to an hour. When Jon Sterling was later to review the events of the morning, he would deeply regret having made Ray Stannick cool his heels for so long in his outer office.

"Excuse me, sir, ma'am, you may go in. Mr. Sterling will see you now." An attractive, older woman in half-glasses left the reception desk to guide them into his office. She had an efficient, arrogant air about her, like she was granting them an audience with the pope.

"Thank you, Ms. Watson. That will be all." Sterling rose and reached across the oak desk to offer Stannick his hand. He was an impressive man—tall, dressed in a crisp, pale-yellow shirt and floral silk tie. His suit coat remained on a hanger on a brass coat-tree by the door, as if to convey that Jon Sterling was a shirtsleeves kind of guy.

He favored them with a smile. "It's been a busy morning, but then aren't they all." He remained standing and did not ask them to sit. "Forgive me, but I do have another appointment in about five minutes." Jon Sterling didn't get where he was by the inefficient use of his time or failing to manage his schedule to his own advantage. He glanced at his appointment book. "You people are here from OSHA, right? Perhaps this is something that could be handled by our in-house legal counsel?"

"No, Mr. Sterling, I think you'll want to deal with this one yourself." Stannick pulled his FBI credential from the inside of his jacket and held it for Sterling's inspection.

Sterling glanced at it briefly and regarded them with patient civility. "So you're with the FBI. I'm not sure I understand this charade, Mr. Stannick. I'm a very busy man. Perhaps if you and Miss Burks here could please get to the point."

Stannick regarded him coolly. *What an asshole.* If he hadn't needed his cooperation, he would have cuffed him and read him his rights, just for the sport of it.

"The point. Okay, *Mr.* Sterling, the point is that *Agent* Burks has in her briefcase a subpoena that allows us to close down Golden Western and suspend your operations pending an investigation into your company's alleged involvement in criminal activities. These activities include conspiracy, aggravated assault, and murder. If I choose to serve this subpoena and you resist, an army of federal marshals will be here within the hour to empty the building and impound all your records. And you, sir, will be led out of here in handcuffs and arraigned before the Honorable Felix Alvarez, the federal judge who signed this subpoena. Are you getting all this, *Mr.* Sterling?"

Sterling flicked his tongue over his lips to moisten them but remained poised. "You've got to be joking."

Stannick put both hands in the middle of the desktop and leaned across it. "Do I look like someone who's got the time to wait in your reception room for an hour and then walk in here and joke with you?" A part of him wanted Sterling to be uncooperative; he wanted a piece of this prick.

Sterling did his best to remain composed, but he was beginning to look apprehensive. "I need to know what this is all about … and just what is it that you want?"

"What I want, Mr. Sterling, is for you to call the good *Ms.* Watson out there and tell her we're not to be disturbed for at least a half hour. Then we'll tell you what this is all about."

"You know, I really do have an important appointment."

"Look, either we sit down right here, right now, or we take you downtown. Tell your appointment to wait. There's an empty chair out there that I just finished warming for the better part of an hour. It will do nicely for your important appointment." Stannick regarded him closely and saw that fear was beginning to replace indecision. "I suggest we have a little talk, Mr. Sterling, and if you refuse"—Stannick's hard face suddenly split into a broad smile—"then I get to read you your rights and take you in."

Judy Burks said nothing, but quietly slipped the subpoena onto the corner of the desk. It was one of those trifolded documents in a light-blue cover that strike fear into the hearts of the highly regulated. Sterling sank into his swivel, signaling his submission. He waved Stannick and Burks to the two chairs in front of the desk, then called his receptionist and told her to hold his calls until further notice.

"All right, then. Now, tell me exactly what is going on here."

Stannick turned to Agent Burks and nodded for her to proceed.

She pulled a legal-sized file from her briefcase and slipped on a pair of reading glasses. "Mr. Sterling, we have compelling evidence that someone here at Golden Western has been hacking into multiple proprietary medical databases to obtain information that has led to the murder and aggravated assault of people insured by your company. The underlying purpose of this misuse of information by person or persons here at Golden Western is to identify unwilling organ donors for the purpose of removing said organs for sale on the black market." She looked up from the file and watched his eyes go sunny-side up. She gave him a warm smile. "The extended liability of a situation like this sort of gets your attention, wouldn't you say?"

He started to speak, but Stannick held up his hand, then motioned for Burks to continue. She outlined the detective work of the programmer at MedaSystems and the evidence that pointed to Golden Western.

"B-but isn't this a MedaSystems problem? It's their software that's been corrupted."

"A few days ago, a Mr. Harold Eisenbach down in Venice turned up in the morgue missing one kidney," Stannick said in a cold voice. "We traced him through his father's business to a clinic where he had been treated. The clinic uses a medical management system called Patientsfirst. They are a competitor of MedaSystems, so the problem is not confined to MedaSystems programs. But your company, Golden Western, is the insurance carrier for the business that insured Mr. Eisenbach. That tells us that the data leak is here at Golden Western. Now, our Mr. Eisenbach was HIV positive. What do you think the chances are that whoever got Eisenbach's kidney also got the AIDs virus along with it? Some people would call that just desserts for the person who illegally received the stolen organ. But I think a jury might see your role differently."

"I still can't believe this."

"Believe it," Stannick said. "We have a very convincing chain of physical evidence. We haven't identified the person or persons who are doing this, but we do know that they are here. It's someone inside your company."

"All right, Stannick, enough! What is it you want from me?"

"My name is *Agent* Stannick, Mr. Sterling. Remember that. And I'll tell you exactly what I want. I want unlimited access to your files, telephone records, computer records, billing records, and online systems. Agent Burks and a Mr. Richard Rogers are going to be working here at Golden Western for a few days. I have a connection with the state insurance commission, and they'll provide documentation for them as insurance inspectors. You just let it be known that they are here on regulatory business—strictly a routine visit."

Sterling reluctantly made a note of their names. He sighed. "Anything else?"

"Just this. You are to tell no one who they are or why they are here. Not your board of directors, not your wife, not the good Ms. Watson out there guarding your door—no one. I'll sign a memo that your silence was requested as a part of this investigation. We have every reason to believe this is a single individual who is acting alone. You do anything to tip our hand and spook this person, and I'll have you up on obstruction of justice charges. Is that clear?"

"Very."

"Good. Your best course of action is to help us nail this guy. We'll do this as quietly as possible, because we don't want him to know we're this close. Now you can understand why we said we were from OSHA, not the Bureau. This hacker-employee on your payroll can do a great deal of damage in a short period of time if he knows we're on to him. Judy?"

"I think you've covered it, Chief. Mr. Rogers and myself will be back later this afternoon as documented state insurance auditors, with a backup cover story in place with the California state insurance commissioner." She shot him a youthful grin. "We'll even have some personalized, authentic-looking business cards to hand out."

Dimitri Stolichnaya was sitting in his Oakland warehouse office, sucking yet another cigarette down between his nicotine-stained fingers. The room was hot and hazy. It was as if Stolichnaya was determined to replicate the pollution of his native Moscow but wanted none of the bitter cold he remembered from his youth. The phone purred on the corner of the desk. It was his private line, which he had checked periodically to ensure that it wasn't tapped. He let it ring several times before answering. He was too old school to have caller ID installed, or a phone with a digital readout.

"Da?"

"Good evening, Mr. Stolichnaya. I hope this is a convenient time for me to call?"

"As good as any, Alexei. What do you have for me?"

"Nothing good, I'm afraid. I've made arrangements for Boris to be cremated, and I will bring the ashes back with me when I return. As to what happened to him, that still remains unclear."

"Tell me what you know."

"Boris was most certainly murdered. He was taken out into the desert and executed. He had been bound, and there was evidence of torture before he was killed."

"And how do we know this?"

"We have a contact in the police department, part of our roof here. He saw the results of the autopsy."

"So Boris was interrogated?"

"That would seem to be a strong possibility."

"And this contact we pay to keep watch on events. Does he know anything?"

"Not anything definite. He did say that one of our providers was here in Las Vegas when Boris was killed and disappeared soon after the approximate time of his death."

"Do you mean the one that provided us with the two identical replacement parts? He was in Las Vegas?"

"That's what he told me. The man was asking questions and trying to learn what had happened to him. He is a businessman with a family; it's hard to believe a man like that could have done this to Boris."

"And you believe our source there is telling the truth?"

"He is a corrupt policeman. I do not trust him, but I believe him. He has an appetite for what we pay him."

Stoli nodded to himself. He liked Alexei's response; perhaps he was going to learn the business after all. But he didn't like the fact that someone whose organs they had taken was traveling about asking questions. He clearly recalled this incident. The construction man with the rare blood type and the failing kidneys had paid them well. He needed, or rather he wanted, two special kidneys. Stoli had been pleased that this man could not only pay a good price, but that he had connections as well. They had not expected this provider to live, or live long without both kidneys. Yet he seemed to be making inquiries about his lost organs in Las Vegas.

Stoli had not been all that keen on allowing those who provided the organs to live. A dead body could be disposed of in a number of ways to prevent it from being traced back to those responsible. But as Alexei and some of the other young men had pointed out, they needed the cooperation of doctors and private clinics to accomplish the removals and the transplant operations. These people were willing to operate outside the law if the money was right, but they would balk at knowingly being accessories to murder. There were also the American courts to consider. For anything less than first-degree murder, you could be back out on the street in ten years. Prison life in America held advantages for someone from the streets of Moscow. The food was decidedly better than normal Russian fare, and the cells were often roomier than a one-room flat in one of the decaying Moscow high-rises. But that was Alexei's reasoning, not his. He could do the time if he had to; he had spent a considerable portion of his life in prison—real prisons in a communist state that had no concept of inmate rights or humane treatment. Now here was this man, presumably without his two special kidneys, traveling about and asking questions. This was a bad turn of events.

"What are your instructions, Mr. Stolichnaya?"

"Get back to our helpful policeman and learn all you can about our inquisitive friend who is looking for his missing parts. Have Andrei Dmitriev make the inquiries; you stay out of it. Does this man who is asking questions have a name?"

"Yes, sir. It's Walker, Brandon Walker."

"I see. Bring the information on our Mr. Walker and the remains of Boris back to me as soon as possible. And treat Boris with respect. He was a lion in his day."

"Yes, sir. Anything else?"

Stoli pulled a hand along the side of his jaw, then swept it back across his bald head. He quickly made his decision.

"Tell Andrei Dmitriev that Las Vegas is now his territory. Say that I expect the same consideration from him as rendered on a regular and timely basis by my late friend Boris. Tell him I expect him to run low-key and profitable business. Also tell him that until he gives me reason to believe differently, he has my complete confidence."

"Yes, sir."

Stoli put the phone down and lit another cigarette. This was troubling business. It was hard to imagine that a man who had both of his kidneys ripped out of him just a few months ago could have kidnapped Boris, interrogated him, and then killed him. But Stoli didn't get to where he was by overlooking details. Improbable as it might be that this man could be stalking them, he would have to check it out. This, and the business in Venice, could attract more attention than they needed. Perhaps it was time for them to hold off any further procurement and sale of organs until things quieted down. It would do well to alert those in his organization that unwanted inquiries were being made. And perhaps, he reflected, some of those outside his organization. He sat there for another fifteen minutes—smoking, thinking about this stranger who could prove dangerous to them, and sipping carefully at the tumbler of vodka on his desk. He pulled a tattered, leather-bound notebook from a desk drawer. Then he reached for his private phone.

"Cantello Construction, how may I direct your call?"

"Mr. Cantello, please."

"I'll see if he's in. May I say who is calling?"

"Just tell him it is the man who sent him the yellow roses."

"Yellow roses?"

"Exactly. He will understand."

After more than a minute, another voice came on the line. "This is Frank Cantello."

"Mr. Cantello, this is Mr. Smith. It was my organization that assisted you with the merchandise you needed to feel better. I hope everything is all right."

On the other end of the line, Frank Cantello sat at his desk and listened carefully. He had been concerned ever since he learned of the murder of this Boris in Las Vegas. He had paid them well for the two organs that were, from his perspective, priceless. He could only hope that he would never hear from these people again, but he was not naive enough to think that he wouldn't. He was not a fool, nor would he allow himself to be taken for one. Certainly not by this Mr. Smith who spoke with a thick accent. Still, these people were very dangerous and had to be treated with caution.

"Everything is just fine, Mr. Smith. Your concern is noted. The roses were lovely, but I understood that with their delivery, our business was finished. Was there some misunderstanding on my part?"

"None at all, Mr. Cantello. It's just that there has been a complication—a lingering problem that came up. I was calling to alert you to a potential situation."

"I was under the impression that we paid you not only for the merchandise, but also to see that there were no complications."

"*Da*, that is true, but occasionally situations can develop that lead to complications, and maybe has to be dealt with—in proper manner, of course."

"Just what is it you want?" Cantello asked coldly. He sensed that he was about to be shaken down for more money.

"For now, Mr. Cantello, just your attention. It would seem that former owner of your merchandise has been nosing about—he asks questions. He was in Las Vegas short while ago, trying to find out what happened to his property. We are keeping close watch on this, but at this time, we are not sure how much information he has. His name is Brandon Walker. In event should he contact you, please let me know. We will deal with it, you understand?"

"Are the police involved?"

"Not yet—not to our knowing. We think this Walker, he is acting alone."

"I see," Cantello replied.

Cantello had known nothing of the man who provided his kidneys, nor, until now, did he want to. However, he did know that dealing with these Russian thugs was dangerous business, as was his accepting the stolen organs. But there was no alternative. All the drug therapy, the dieting, and the vitamins had done nothing to halt the degeneration of his kidneys. He faced the same painful death that had taken his father before he was fifty. With the dialysis that would have soon begun, his would have only been a slower death. His rare tissue and antigen typing made finding a replacement a long shot. Then six months ago, he received a phone call. The caller said they had a service that could find him a suitable kidney, but that it would be expensive. Cantello had moved carefully but quickly; he had no choice. The result had been a complete recovery. Physically, he had never felt better. But now this.

"Tell me something, Mr. Smith. Could this Walker fellow have had something to do with the death of your associate in Las Vegas?"

There was a long pause on the other end of the line. "That is possibility; however, is also of no concern to you. We ask only you notify us if Walker or anyone else contacts you. Please to let us handle this. Do I make myself clear?"

"Perfectly clear, Mr. Smith. I'll leave this matter in your capable hands."

Stoli replaced the receiver and sat without moving for several minutes. He was clearly surprised that Cantello knew about Boris. Yet that was not unreasonable. Cantello had a large business organization, and he was not without connections. Still, if he knew about Boris, what else did he know? Could he have had something to do with Boris's death? Unlikely, Stoli thought. He pushed himself from the desk and opened the refrigerator. Very deliberately, he took the glass jar from the freezer and poured himself another generous portion. He again picked up the phone and dialed.

"Let me speak to Anatoli ... Hello? Anatoli? ... Yes, I am well, *danka*. I want you to do something for me. Contact our friend at the insurance company and ask him to pull the file on Brandon Walker ... *Nyet*, no more medical data; this time I want personal information—home address, business address, that sort of thing ... Just as soon as you can ... I'll wait for your call, Anatoli."

Stoli lit another cigarette and considered just how he was going to deal with this annoying organ donor. For now, he would wait to see what developed.

In Daly City, Frank Cantello sat at his desk and studied the Pacific Ocean in the distance. He was more than a little concerned. The last thing he wanted was a confrontation with the former owner of his kidneys. Cantello considered the possibilities. It seemed almost inconceivable that this Walker guy could even travel to Las Vegas without kidneys, let alone kill some Russian thug. Or could he have found what he, Cantello, had been unable to find—a willing donor with a perfect tissue match? The more he thought about it, the more the hair on the back of his neck bristled. A man who had his kidneys taken from him without his permission could be a formidable enemy. Still, there was nothing he could do but watch and wait. Well, almost nothing. He pressed the intercom.

"Sal, get in here."

Cantello was up and pacing behind his desk when his lieutenant came in.

"What's up, boss?"

"We got a problem, Sally. That guy who provided my filters is out looking for them."

"You mean the big Russian? I thought he was dead."

"No, not him—the guy who had 'em before me! The former owner!"

"Jesus, boss, I thought he was dead, too."

"Yeah, well, he's not. He was over in Las Vegas asking questions. Our Russian friends just called to warn me to be on the lookout for him. His name is Walker—Brandon Walker. I'd like to get a line on this guy. Talk to our people in Vegas and see what they know about him."

Sal gave him a somber look. "Are we gonna take some serious action with this Walker guy, boss?"

"Not right now, but I want to know as much about him as possible, just in case. We'll let the Russians deal with him." Cantello frowned. He wasn't sure which he found more menacing, a man looking for his stolen kidneys or the Russian Mafia, to whom life meant nothing. "And I want you or Lou with me whenever I'm not home or in the office, *capisce*?"

"Understood, boss. And I'll get on this Walker guy right away."

Ray Stannick was eating at his desk in his San Francisco office, and he was not in a good mood. Although he headed a special task force, he still had to account for the activity and expenses of his agents, and to file time and work reports on their activities. Once again, Stannick had put his accounting and reporting duties off until the last possible moment. These weekly reports were due every Friday and had to be at FBI headquarters by the close of business—as if the bean counters were going to come in and work on them over the weekend. That meant he had less than a half hour to get them finished and e-mailed to Washington. He couldn't afford any interruptions, so he ignored the phone when it rang. It was his private line, so there was no secretary to pick it up or voice mail to take a message. On about the fifteenth ring, he snatched the receiver from the cradle.

"What!"

"You sound a little on edge, Chief. Did I get you at a bad time?"

"Damn it, Burks, I'm busy. What the hell do you want?"

"We got him."

"Listen Burks, I'm up to my armpits in these damn ... wait a second, what do you mean, you got him? You mean *him*?"

"Yep, *him*. Got him cold as a polar bear's tush. Richard and I are outside the central data processing center watching the creep as I speak. This guy's dirty, Chief, and we can prove it."

"You're sure about this? There's no doubt?"

"None. His name's Wilbur Dannahey—been with Golden Western for about eighteen months. Richard hacked into their computer—excuse me, I meant that Richard entered their database from this end—and tracked him down."

Agent Judy Burks sat on the corner of a desk in the small office that had been assigned to the "state insurance inspection team." She was wearing a short suit skirt and silk blouse. Richard, seated at his laptop computer, gave her a hurt look. Comparing him to a hacker was like calling a Muslim a pig. Richard and she had stormed into Golden Western with their version of good cop/bad cop. She played the part of the incompetent flirt, all sugary and helpless, while Richard went for the database like a gundog to a covey of quail. State insurance inspectors were a fact of life in the industry. These two were a little strange, but no one at Golden Western gave them a second thought. After the first day, most of the employees ignored them, save for several of the men who continued to ogle Judy.

"Richard has managed to reconstruct some erased files," Judy continued. "We can prove that the requests for Brandon Walker's medical record were made by Dannahey almost six months ago. We can tie these requests to Dannahey's login ID, from his personal terminal."

"Could someone else have used his login?"

"No way. The company time-log entries have him signed into the data processing center each time there was an unauthorized patient record entry. Only one person can use a login ID at one time. It's him, Chief, we got—hold on a second."

Richard was gesturing frantically to her, pointing to the screen of his computer. She stepped behind him and put a hand on his shoulder, leaning close to read the text.

"Holy shit, he's at it again. He's into a patient file without authorization."

Ray Stannick was frustrated; he wanted to be there. Reports be damned; if there was a takedown, he wanted to be in on it. "Maybe it's a routine, legal entry."

"Oh yeah! Then why the hell's he looking at Brandon Walker's file this very second? That's it! I'm gonna bust his ass right now!"

"No, wait, you need backup. Agent Burks, I forbid you to … hello … hello … Judy … you there?" He was talking to a dial tone.

Stannick slammed the receiver down. "Goddamn rookie agent. She's going to give me my first heart attack." *Or get herself killed*, he thought immediately. He quickly sifted through several alternate courses of action, then roared, "Bateman!"

"Yessir."

"That chopper on standby?"

"Yessir."

"Tell the pilot I want to be airborne in less than five minutes. Have him file an emergency flight plan for San Mateo. I want you and Prouty on board with me."

"Yessir, but don't we have to clear with the SAIC here? After all, it's his helo."

"Is he in the building?" The agent in charge of the San Francisco office hardly ever stayed late.

"No, sir."

"Then I guess the SAIC won't be needing his helicopter," Stannick said as he pulled on his jacket. He took the Browning Hi Power from his desk drawer and jammed it into his shoulder holster. Then he hit the intercom.

"Yes, Mr. Stannick?"

"Brenda, please run a flash background check on a convicted felon named Wilbur Dannahey. Have it relayed to me once I'm airborne."

"Yes, Mr. Stannick."

Ten minutes later, the FBI Bell JetRanger was screaming south at a thousand feet and close to two hundred knots, just a little over the maximum-rated airspeed. They would be there in fifteen minutes. Behind the two pilots, Stannick and his two agents were strapped into the passenger compartment. They were all wearing large plastic Mickey Mouse ears with boom lip mikes. The copilot turned and handed Stannick a sheet of paper.

"Sir, here's that background you were waiting for." The helo was equipped with a cell-phone fax capability.

"Thanks," Stannick replied. He studied the report with a deep frown and turned to one of the junior agents. "Look at this! Our man Dannahey at Golden Western was in Joliet for embezzlement and fraud. Prior to that, he did time for armed robbery. Damn that Burks; she's just a rookie agent! If she blows this one, I'm gonna have her ass."

Bateman rolled his eyes and Prouty coughed, trying to suppress a smile. The issue of Judy Burks's ass was not an infrequent topic among the younger agents on Stannick's team.

"Sir, we'll be there in just a few minutes. Where do you want me to land?"

"As close to the front door as possible, and as quickly as possible."

The two pilots, both former Army helo drivers, exchanged a knowing look. That meant they could go in hot and fast, something they thoroughly enjoyed but were seldom allowed to do. They had Golden Western's location dialed into the GPS navigation system. About a mile out, the pilot took the aircraft off autopilot and dipped the nose.

"Okay, back there, hang on. We're going in tactical."

The Ranger dropped from the sky, then tail-walked across the parking lot, skimming the tops of cars as it shed speed and altitude. The pilot skillfully planted the skids in the middle of the road in front of the covered portico entrance. Two women leaving the building raced back inside to escape the noise and the driving wind, covering their heads as they desperately tried to hold down their skirts.

"Let's go, people," Stannick shouted. He tore off the headset and leaped from the cabin to the blacktop. The other two agents raced after him for the front door. Once inside, Stannick flashed his shield at the terrified receptionist.

"FBI! Which way to the data processing center?" She sat there, openmouthed, unable to speak. "The data processing center, which way?"

She pointed across a bay of cubicles, still unable to speak. A young actuary with a passion for detective novels came racing from his office.

"Down this hallway," he shouted, eyes shining, "second door on your left!"

Ray Stannick burst through the door and into a room humming with servers, computer terminals, and high-speed printers. He now had his gun drawn, which added to the effect. The other two agents crowded in behind him. Three people sat comfortably in the corner; two of them rose.

"Oh, hello, Chief. Say, that was a pretty fast trip." She gave him a reproachful look. "Shame on you; I'll bet you missed your weekly reports deadline again."

Stannick slowly took in the scene as he eased the Browning back into his shoulder holster. Burks was on her feet, along with a young man in jeans and a sport coat next to her who was wide-eyed and frozen in place. Seated between them was a middle-aged, overweight, balding man with tinted glasses. He looked like a sloppy accountant. While everyone gathered around him, he calmly remained seated, smoking a cigarette. He had a patient, bovine expression—somewhere between resignation and amusement.

"Hi, guys," she continued, nodding to the other agents. She then said to Stannick, "Chief, this is Richard Rogers, the programmer from MedaSystems. He's the one who cracked this case." The man in the jeans and sport coat, still unable to speak, swallowed and bobbed his head. "And this"—she smiled and placed a hand on the seated man's shoulder—"this is Wilbur Dannahey. I've already read him his rights. Now that we're all here, it might be a good idea to have a little chat. Wilbur, this is my boss, Special Agent Ray Stannick."

"Good to meet you, Ray," he said, regarding his cigarette with some interest. "Y'know, I'm really not supposed to smoke in here, but at this point, what th' fuck, right?"

Stannick fixed Dannahey with a cold stare, then turned to the agents behind him. "Bateman, go and see if you can find a gentleman by the name of Jon Sterling, and tell him we're here and we'll be using his data processing center for a little while. Prouty, wait outside the door and see that we're not disturbed. Tell the chopper crew they can shut down and wait, but that we shouldn't be too long."

The two agents nodded and hurried out. Stannick leaned against one of the computer tables and folded his arms. He lifted an eyebrow and regarded Burks suspiciously.

"Wilbur, why don't you tell Agent Stannick about your little operation here and how you came to be at Golden Western. I'm sure he'd be just as interested as I was in your fascinating story."

Stannick turned his attention to the seated man. "All right, Mr. Dannahey," he said with a forced sweetness. "I'm all ears."

Dannahey regarded him warily and pulled on his smoke, pausing to flick an ash on the polished vinyl floor. "Yeah, I bet you are. Well, it all started when I went to the joint for the second time. As you probably know by now, I've done a little time. Most guys in the joint pass the time watching TV or lifting weights." He grinned and spread his arms. "I obviously wasn't into weight lifting. But as a second offender, I had eight years of hard time ahead of me. So I started studying computers—found I had an aptitude for them. I got really good. Toward the end of my stretch, I was managing the prison database and payroll records. A real model prisoner, I was. Course, that didn't keep me from getting buggered a time or two by those weight-lifting assholes. That's why I ain't going back."

Stannick pursed his lips and pushed his hands into his pants pockets. "Oh, I wouldn't count on that if I were you, Mr. Dannahey."

He ignored Stannick's comment. "After I hired on here at Golden Western," he continued as he lit another cigarette, "I was approached by a group of very nasty people. You might say they made me an offer I couldn't refuse. So what could I do? Tell my parole officer—that uptight, stupid social-worker wannabe? What a prick," he spat out. "No, I couldn't very well do that." He paused to pull on the cigarette. "I didn't tell Golden Western I had a record, and they never bothered to check. They were hungry for programmers and too shoddy to do a decent background on me.

So I was hired on. The guys who contacted me after I was on the job here wanted me to identify individuals by certain blood type and medical traits. I designed a program that allowed me to invade the existing databases and search for what I wanted. And it was a damn good piece of programming, if I do say so myself. If it hadn't been for him"—he gestured toward Richard—"you and your posse sure wouldn't be storming in here now." Richard stared at him, his hatred plainly showing. To have corrupted his programs, this man might as well have physically just raped him. Dannahey chuckled to himself and continued. "No, Ray, I didn't really have a choice in this matter. And these guys paid me very well, not like the cheap bastards here at Golden Western. And if you were to start checking for green cards around here, you'd be in for a real surprise. This place is a fucking sweatshop, pardon my French."

"It's okay, Wilbur, you're among friends," Judy Burks said.

"Yeah, right," Dannahey replied, "I'm sure you're all concerned about my welfare. Look, I want a deal. You're gonna want these guys I'm working for, and I can give 'em to you on a silver platter. I always thought this day would come, so I've been planning for it. I got names, dates, records, addresses—the whole works. I even got taped conversations."

"Taped conversations? You mean you were wearing a wire?"

"Naw, nothing like that. I did it here. Know when you call an insurance company and they say 'this conversation may be recorded to ensure better service'? Well, I never play that stupid message on my line, but I record everything. I can help you put these guys away, big-time. But I want the full witness protection deal: new name, relocation, new ID, and a new job—the whole enchilada. And these guys are nasty; if they find me, I'm toast."

"We got you cold, Wilbur. We don't need to deal," said Stannick.

"You got shit, Agent Stannick. Look, I'm a three-time loser. You prosecute me, and I go away for keeps. If I clam up, which is the only way I'm going to stay alive in the joint, you get me and no one else. And who knows with these animals; they might just wack me anyway. On the other hand, if we deal, I'll give you the whole organization. You'll be a hero. The Bureau'll think you're another Elliott fucking Ness. And another thing, I've formulated some very ugly viruses here at Golden Western and in the MedaSystems database as well as other medical software providers. I don't have to *do* anything; if I fail to log on to the system for a few days and fail to enter some very specific codes, the medical databases of a number of health-care organizations go into the toilet. Golden Western has interconnected databases with their software providers, clinics, and HMOs. You see, I'm not just a criminal; I'm a full-fledged cyberterrorist." Richard did his best to stifle a gasp. "You fuck with me and I'll toast thousands of valuable medical files up and down the West Coast. It'll take an army of guys like ol' Richard here to salvage them—if they can be salvaged at all."

Stannick and Burks looked at Richard, and the terrified look on his face said that Dannahey was telling the truth.

But Stannick wasn't ready to throw in the towel. "I think you're bluffing, Dannahey. You can do hard time or *really* hard time. That's a call I can make if you want to be uncooperative."

"Look, Stannick, I'm not going back inside and be boy-butter for a bunch of thugs at Victorville. No fuckin' way. The people who recruited me are very connected in the joint. Even if I keep my mouth shut, the very best I can expect is to become joint boy-toy. They can promise me that. Can you guarantee me it won't happen? Y'see, Stannick, I'm scared shitless. So get real. We do the deal my way, or let the chips fall where they may. I gotta cover my ass one way or another, if you get my meanin'."

Stannick stared at Dannahey for a full minute. Then he reached over and opened the door. Bateman and Prouty were standing just outside.

"Put the bracelets on this son of a bitch and get him out of here," Stannick growled.

"Yessir," they both chimed.

Dannahey rose, cigarette dangling from the side of his mouth. "Hey, Richard, baby, you okay? Y'know, I thought I was pretty good, but I'm not in your league, darlin'. No hard feelings, huh?"

Richard glared at him. "No hard feelings?" he sputtered. "No hard feelings! Well, Mr. Computer Hacker, you can just kiss my ass!" With that, Richard swept past the two agents and Dannahey and out of the room.

Ray Stannick was the last to leave the data processing center. He was no more than a few steps from the door when a hand grabbed his arm.

"You said you'd handle this as quietly as possible. You call this quiet? A goddamn helicopter at the main entrance ... racing through my company with guns drawn. You better have a good explanation."

Stannick took the hand on his arm and peeled it from his jacket. The force of his grip caused the man to wince. "Mr. Sterling, you hired a man here who was a convicted felon. You failed to adequately check his background before you allowed him access to confidential information that you had a responsibility to safeguard. Given the damage he was able to do while in your employ, I think you, personally, are in a very tenuous situation. Once the full extent of the destruction is known, we may be back here with a warrant for your arrest."

Stannick started to turn away, then hesitated. "And, *Mr.* Sterling, you ever grab me like that again, I'll kick your butt right up between your shoulder blades."

He followed the others out of the main entrance to the waiting helicopter.

"Bateman!"

"Yessir."

"When we get back to the office, give a call to Immigration and say that we have a solid tip that Golden Western Insurance has been hiring undocumented workers."

"Yessir."

Brandon and Garrett had been at Liverpool Lil's for about a half hour. They were well ahead of the dinner crowd and sat at one of the back tables drinking a beer with a plate of calamari between them. It had been a sparkling afternoon, and the two of them had jogged along the San Francisco waterfront and through the Marina District to Lil's. Until this business with the kidneys was finally completed, they had decided to stay in the city. Cathy had said little when Brandon told her they'd be gone for a few days. Get it over with, she had told him, then come home. That was yesterday, a Sunday. They had left San Jose shortly after breakfast and taken a room in the city.

"So you think we have everything in place?"

"As well as it can be," Garrett replied. "Anything can happen, but I'd say we have a good chance to pull it off. How's Richard handling all this?"

"Better than I thought. At first, he was reluctant, but it was a chance to get back at the people responsible, not just Dannahey. This whole business almost sent him over the edge. He feels very responsible."

Garrett shrugged. "He'll get over it. With a little luck, we'll all get over it."

"Then here's to tomorrow."

"To tomorrow," Garrett answered. They raised their glasses and looked each other in the eye, then both sipped quietly at their beer for a moment.

"So where do you think Ray is on all this?" Garrett asked.

"I don't know. Richard is scared to death that he won't cut a deal with our man Dannahey and there'll be further damage to our systems. My guess is that Ray will do the deal. Anyway, I hope so. Then maybe we can stay out of it."

"Possibly. Hey, heads up. He just walked in, so maybe we'll find out."

"Don't you guys ever wear anything but sweats?" Stannick was in his standard dark suit, white shirt, and tie. The waitress came over and he ordered coffee. "You're also hard to track down. I left several messages at your office before you finally called."

"We're in the city for a few days," Brandon said neutrally. "You seem a little anxious, Ray. Getting closer?"

"I think so. We did a deal with that piece of trash today. Had no choice." He looked at Brandon. "Dannahey's agreed to turn over all his computer files and access codes. Our people think he could really have wreaked havoc with your company and a whole bunch of others. I think he gave us everything, but I still want your guy Richard to do some follow-up work and check things out. Especially when it comes to neutralizing any virus programs he may have set up as booby traps."

"No problem, Ray. I'm sure Richard will be glad to help. Just like Garrett and me."

Stannick gave him a skeptical look. "That's what you keep telling me, but why do I always get the feeling that you two are holding back on me?" He looked from one brother to the other. They mirrored the same blank look. "At any rate," Stannick continued, "our cooperative friend gave up what we think is the big dog in this organ-theft operation. But it's still based just on his testimony and the electronic evidence he's provided. The phone conversations he taped probably won't be admissible in court. I think he'll make a good witness on the stand, but you never know. A good defense attorney could get to him. After all, he's an ex-con and a three-time loser." Stannick sipped his coffee, studying Garrett and Brandon over his cup. "We're going to take this guy's operation down this evening, but I'd feel a lot better if I had another source—something to confirm what Dannahey's telling us. The Bureau gets a little upset if we go storming into a legitimate business with guns drawn."

Stannick looked from Garrett to Brandon, then back to Garrett. He held him in a steady gaze and said nothing.

Garrett smiled. "Tell you what, Ray. If your hacker stooge is sending you after a guy in Oakland named Stolichnaya, I'd say he's probably giving you good information."

Stannick regarded him for a long moment. "Any reason why you waited so long to tell me this?"

Garrett shrugged. "Just a name I picked up while I was out of town for a few days. I had no way of knowing whether my source was telling the truth or giving me a line of crap."

"This source who gave you the name. You wouldn't by any chance happen to remember his name?"

Garrett again shrugged. "No … no, I don't believe I can recall a name. I seem to recollect he had a thick accent. Might have been eastern European or something like that."

"Could it have been a Russian accent? Might his name have been Boris Kuznetzkof?"

"Maybe," Garrett replied, giving the impression of searching his memory, "but I really don't remember. I couldn't say for certain." He met Stannick's even gaze without as much as a blink. "Look, Ray, you want to catch the bad guys; we want all this behind us so we can go back to our lives. Why don't we just focus on that?"

"Now you look here, Garrett, this isn't the Wild West anymore," Stannick said softly, "and you're not off in Afghanistan or Iraq where you can take out a bad guy when you feel like it. This is America, and we play by American rules. If you make a habit of this vigilante justice, then *you* are the bad guys. You simply can't go around killing people. It's against the law."

"So is taking people's organs," Brandon said. "And you wouldn't even be close to nailing the guy who's behind all this without our help—and Richard's. Your job's to chase bad guys, Ray. So, have at it."

Stannick sat back and looked from one Walker to the other. *A couple of hard nuts*, he conceded. There was little chance he could actually prove they were connected to the death of the Russian in Las Vegas. And as much as he opposed the killing, personally and professionally, he wasn't sure it was in his heart to even try.

"Okay, let's concentrate on the local Russians. Is there anything else you can tell me?"

"Not really," Garrett said seriously. "Only that these are very nasty people, but then you should already know that. They're arrogant and the taking of a life means nothing to them. This guy over in Oakland probably got to where he is because he's very smart and very brutal. Don't underestimate them."

Stannick nodded his acknowledgment and was again silent for a moment. "Fair enough, we'll take it from here." He gave them a hint of a smile. "And I suppose I ought to thank you two concerned citizens for all your help and cooperation."

"So you're going to move against these guys tonight?" Brandon asked.

"That's right."

"If you'd really like to thank us, Ray, why not let us be there when it goes down? As citizen observers, of course. Well away from the action."

The big black man lifted his eyebrows as he considered this. Might be a good way to keep track of these two characters until this business is done, he reasoned.

"Okay, fellas. This is strictly against Bureau procedure, but I'll bend the rules just this once. I'll send a car around for you. Where are you staying?"

"At the Marines' Memorial Club downtown. You know where it is?"

"We'll find it. Be in the lobby at nine thirty sharp." He rose to leave. "Can I drop you someplace? Or no—don't tell me, you're going to run back to the hotel."

Garrett glanced at Brandon and then smiled at Stannick. "You're always one step ahead of us, Ray."

"Right," Stannick snorted as he turned and left.

Brandon and Garrett were collected by an unmarked government sedan at their hotel. Two FBI men rode up front while Brandon and Garrett rode in the back. A half hour later, they met with another sedan at a convenience store in Oakland about a mile from Stolichnaya's warehouse. Garrett and Brandon left the first car and slid into the backseat of the second. Stannick sat behind the wheel, drinking coffee. Judy Burks occupied the passenger's seat across from him. She was dressed in slacks, turtleneck, and blazer while Stannick wore a black set of coveralls.

"Brandon, I think you know this young lady. Garrett, this is Agent Judy Burks. Judy, Garrett Walker."

"Happy to meet you, Garrett. Jeez, you two really do look alike."

"Yep, that's why they call us twins," Garrett said pleasantly. "Do I address you as Agent Burks, or can I call you Judy?"

She turned and eyed him critically. "As long as he'll vouch for you," she replied, nodding to Brandon, "you can call me Judy."

There was a burst of static from the radio under the dash, then a brief, cryptic exchange between two men. The car occupants quickly fell silent to listen.

"We've been filtering people into the neighborhood for the last several hours," Stannick said when the radio went silent. His voice was a soft rumble. "The subject has a warehouse not too far from the docks. Not a particularly nice part of town, so we can't have too many people in the area until we're ready to move." He gave them a wink. "Some of us would look a little out of place. Also, we know Stolichnaya is usually there at night, and the streets are deserted—less chance of harming some innocent civilian if things get out of hand. Although there are very few innocent civilians on these particular streets at night, or any other time, for that matter."

"How do you plan to do this, Ray?" Garrett asked in a professional tone.

"We have six SWAT-trained agents standing by, plus a special weapons detachment from the San Francisco field office. Also, we have a few agents from the Oakland field office who know the area. They managed to find an identical vacant warehouse in Alameda for a walk-through drill. We were able to do a few practice runs there this morning. When we're sure Stolichnaya is there, we'll move into position."

As if on cue, there was another burst of static, followed by a scratchy voice.

"Got the pizza delivery boy at your three o'clock, over."

"Roger, I have him."

"You in position to get a look, Tony?"

"That's affirm. Stand by."

Stannick turned to the two in back and said quietly, "Our Russian friend seems to love American pizza and deli sandwiches. He orders regularly from a twenty-four-hour pizza joint a few blocks from the warehouse."

They waited in silence, then a voice came over the radio. "Control, this is Tony. I got a positive visual ID. Subject is on the premises. How copy, over?"

Stannick spoke into a small Motorola transceiver. "This is Control. Understand positive ID and that subject is on the premises. All units, move to your staging area, report when in position, over."

"Unit one, roger."

"Unit two, rolling."

"Unit three, roger, we're moving."

Stannick started the car and pulled swiftly from the convenience store, followed by the other sedan. Five minutes later, with lights out, they pulled silently to the curb, half a block and around the corner from the warehouse. The other sedan slid in behind them. They waited without speaking as each of the three other units reported that they were in place. Now the voices on the radio were speaking in hushed tones. The exchanges were very professional but charged with tension. Stannick acknowledged them and told them to stand by. The four of them sat without speaking for about ten minutes. Then a black man in faded blue jeans, an old sweatshirt, and a tattered knit stocking cap turned the corner and shuffled up to the car. Judy Burks rolled down her window. The man glanced around and bent to the car sill.

"What do you think, Tony?" Stannick asked.

"Everything looks normal, sir. A step van backed into the loading dock about forty-five minutes ago. Otherwise, no other activity."

"Let's do it, then."

Tony nodded and shuffled off. It was very difficult to see in the dim light, but Garrett's practiced eye picked up the coiled communications cord that led from the cap to the neckline of the man's shirt. Garrett also saw an outline from the handle of the automatic pushed into the waist of his jeans.

Stannick pulled a heavy black vest from the seat between Burks and himself and struggled into it. Stenciled in big white letters on the front and back were the letters "FBI." He spoke quietly into the Motorola transceiver.

"Okay, gentlemen, we move in two minutes from my mark." He studied the illuminated dial of his watch. "Stand by ... three, two, one ... mark!"

"Unit one, roger two minutes."

"Unit two, a go in two mikes."

"Unit three here, copy two."

Stannick squeezed his transmit key twice to acknowledge the replies. He clipped the Motorola to his vest. Then he slipped on a headset and boom mike and attached the lead to the radio. Finally, he pulled on a black baseball cap and dragged a big .45 automatic from his shoulder holster.

"Agent Burks," he said as he checked the action of the pistol, "you can follow the progress of the operation on the car radio. I want you to remain in the car with our guests until the building is completely secure." He turned to Garrett and Brandon. "It's against regulations for you to even be here, so stay in the car." The two in back nodded. Then he looked at Judy Burks. "Understood?"

"Understood, Chief," she replied sullenly, "but I still don't see why I can't be in on this. I've been with this investigation from the beginning."

"One last time, Burks, you're still a rookie on probation, and you're not SWAT qualified. Those aren't my rules; it's Bureau policy." He glanced at his watch. "I've got to move. Stay here until the building is cleared and reported secure—no exceptions. And that's an order. Got it?"

"Loud and clear, Chief."

With that, Stannick slipped from the car. He moved to the corner and dropped to one knee. Two dark forms joined him. The two agents from the trailing car were dressed like Stannick, the white letters just visible against the dark background. Garrett watched closely, noting that one agent was carrying a shotgun and the other had what looked like an M16 assault rifle with a night-vision scope. In the car, the three of them waited, scarcely breathing.

Stannick's gravelly voice came in over the radio. "This is Control. Move to assault positions; move to assault positions. I say again, move to assault positions. Control, out."

The three dark figures rose, and the one with the shotgun led them across the street at a brisk walking pace. Two vans approached from either direction. They drove at normal speed, but their lights were out. One pulled to the curb in front of the building, the other directly across the street. Doors opened and more black forms poured silently from the vehicles. Each seemed to know where he was going. Their movements were brisk, yet there was no running; everyone walked quickly. Two pairs detached from the group and moved down each side of the building toward the rear. A file of six men lined the front of the building to one side of the door. They formed a tight stack; all were armed with MP5 submachine guns, each with a long flashlight fixed below the barrel. Stannick and his two agents positioned themselves to the other side of the main door.

"This is Control, stand by to go." He nodded, and two men wielding a heavy battering ram stepped to the door. The ram was a six-inch-diameter solid-steel bar with metal handles on either side of the shaft so it could be swung between them. Both men had assault rifles slung across their backs.

"Take it down," Stannick said quietly. Then he spoke into his radio. "Go, go, go!"

The metal warehouse door yielded on the second swing of the ram with a loud crash. The black file poured through the lit opening, weapons shouldered.

Upstairs in the office, the first loud metal report brought Stolichnaya up from his racing form. He cocked his head to one side, a string of mozzarella dripping from his lower lip. The second crash was much louder as the locks gave way and the doors banged open. Seconds later, he had rounded the desk and gained the overlook in front of the office. Black-suited forms streamed across the warehouse floor toward the loading dock and the stairs to the offices. Others were taking positions behind packing crates to gain a field of fire. A half dozen of Stoli's men had been busy moving boxes in from the step van at the loading dock in the rear of the building. Others worked to repackage the contents and prepare them for reshipment. All of them were now fleeing for the loading dock. Stoli knew that none of them had a chance when he saw the first of his men reach the loading platform and raise their hands. They were surrounded.

Two of Stoli's men burst onto the catwalk from the office next door, guns drawn. Before he could intervene, one of them fired at the forms below. The shooter had just let loose his second round when several well-directed streams of automatic fire tore into both men. One pitched forward through the catwalk rail and onto the warehouse floor. The second man was blown back through the office door as windows in both offices shattered in a hail of 9-mm fire. There was shouting and more firing.

Stoli ducked and raced back to the relative safety of his office. He'd always known a day like this might come, so he was prepared. He grabbed his coat as he passed the desk, slipped through the rear office door, and started down the back stairs. Halfway down, there was a crash and a splintering of wood as the door to his private entrance was kicked in. "Go!" he heard a man cry as they began to leapfrog up the stairs. He hesitated, but only for an instant. The odds were not in his favor. Stoli turned quietly, walked back into the office, and tossed his coat over the back of his chair. He sat down and lit a cigarette.

Outside, there were shouted orders and the sounds of men being pushed about, but the firing had ceased. Stoli had just poured himself a measure from the jar on his desk when the back door blew open.

"Freeze! Put your hands on top of the desk and don't move!"

One of the men moved to the side wall, watching over the trained muzzle of his submachine gun. The other stood behind, guarding the door and avoiding the chance for a cross fire.

Very professional, Stoli noted. They were probably feds, which made sense. If the local police were involved, he would have been tipped off. "What are you going to do? Shoot me because I take a drink?" He sipped at his glass, then knocked it back contemptuously.

"Control," the man on the side wall said. He never took his eyes off Stolichnaya. A boom mike swept down from his Kevlar helmet to the corner of his mouth. "I think I have the alpha wolf, second-level office complex."

"Understood, I'm on my way. Control, out."

Moments later, Stannick and Bateman came through the door. The two agents who had come up the back way moved to the front of the office near the shattered windows and positioned themselves in the corners to either side of the door. Stannick stepped to the desk and looked down at the Russian.

"Mr. Stolichnaya?"

He looked up at the big man towering over him. "*Da.* Would you like a drink?"

"I don't think so," Stannick replied. Stoli reached for the jar to refill his glass, but Stannick swatted it from the top of the desk, sending it crashing to the floor. "I think you've had your last drink of vodka for a long while." He flashed his credential. "You, my Russian friend, are under arrest."

Stolichnaya regarded the pool of vodka seeping into the cheap carpet, then brought his attention back to Stannick. "That was good vodka, from Ukraine. Difficult to get here, but not impossible if you have right connections. Why you come here like this—destroy my property, kill those who work for me? I am honest businessman, good American."

"You are neither, and we have a star witness who will swear to that under oath. I'm sure you know a Mr. Wilbur Dannahey, and he certainly knows you. He will testify in court that you are guilty, among other things, of murder and aggravated assault." Stannick leaned across the desk. "You're going down, Stoli. Your vodka-drinking days are over." Then he read him his rights.

Stoli stared up at him, showing no emotion. The warehouse operation, he thought— receiving stolen property, bribery, extortion—was three to five in one of their comfortable prisons. However, it was yet another story if they really did have this programmer named Dannahey. The big black federal cop could be right. Stoli frowned. A life sentence, even in an American prison, was not something he wanted anything to do with. As he contemplated this disagreeable turn of events, Alexei stepped from behind a curtain that masked the alcove that held the commode and washbasin. He leveled an Uzi submachine gun at Stannick.

"If anyone moves, I kill the big black one first." The two agents in the room corners started to react, but Alexei shouted, "Go ahead, but the black man dies if you so much as raise your weapons!" No one in the room moved. In the background, they could hear sirens as police cars and ambulances converged on the warehouse.

Stannick glanced at Alexei, then back at Stoli. "This isn't going to do you any good. The building is surrounded. And if you do manage to get away, we'll find you. You know that."

"Perhaps," Stoli replied with a frown, "perhaps not. But is a chance I must take." He opened the drawer and removed a heavy Makarov machine pistol and leveled it at Stannick. "In America, like Russia, is not good to kill a policeman, but as you say here, I have not much to lose, eh? Tell your men to lay down their guns, and we will go. No one gets hurt."

Stannick regarded him a moment, then said to those behind him, "Put your weapons on the floor." The two SWAT agents slowly laid their MP5s on the carpet; Bateman and Stannick also tossed aside their weapons.

"Good," Stoli said as he backed to the door. Alexei still commanded the room with his Uzi. He flipped the catch on the doorknob, which would lock it behind them and give them a few seconds head start on their pursuers. That might be enough, Stoli reasoned. In the darkness and the confusion that were sure to follow, they had a chance. He knew the neighborhood well, and they probably did not.

"*Dos vadanya*, pigs," he said.

As he started to turn to descend the stairs, the muzzle of a Glock 23 automatic was rammed under the corner of his jaw, just below his ear.

"If you so much as blink, I'll blow the top of your goddamn head off." It was a female voice, but a serious female voice. Stoli froze.

"Now, lower your weapons."

Stoli did as commanded, but his eyes were moving; he knew he was losing precious seconds.

When the automatic-weapons fire stopped from inside the warehouse, Judy Burks had bounded from the car. Garrett Walker raced after her. The agent responsible for security in front of the building let her pass but held him up. They were starting to bring out the warehouse workers, cuffed and with their hands on their heads. She had decided to avoid the exodus and enter by the side door, quietly ascending the stairs.

Stoli's machine pistol was now along his trouser seam. Alexei had the Uzi pointed down at a forty-five-degree angle. Stoli shot a knowing look at his lieutenant. Ray Stannick, for the first time since the standoff began, was scared, and his face showed it.

"Okay, asshole, now release the pistol. Let it fall to the floor."

"Is very sensitive gun; it will discharge," Stoli said carefully.

"So is this one. Just do it!" she said, pushing the 9-mm hard under his jaw, forcing his head to one side. Her free hand was on the collar of his shirt.

"As you wish," Stoli replied as he cast another furtive look at Alexei. Judy, sensing this, glanced down. She saw the Russian slide his index finger into the trigger guard of the pistol and the barrel move back in her direction. Her next move was instinctual.

She squeezed off a round and whirled to a shooter's crouch to face the Russian with the Uzi. Her combat range instructors at Quantico would have been proud of her. The report of her pistol startled Alexei for an instant, as did the small eruption of blood and tissue from the top of Stoli's head. He recovered quickly, but not quickly enough. Her first round caught Alexei full in the chest; the second went through his hand and shattered the pistol grip of the Uzi. He managed to raise the weapon but got off only a short burst that stitched the far wall and walked across the ceiling. Alexei was vaguely aware of the jolts pelting his body and that this woman was walking toward him. Then a round to his forehead brought darkness.

The sound was deafening, then it was over. Judy remembered only squeezing off the first round and feeling the man she was holding go limp, then turning to the man with the Uzi. *Sight picture and trigger squeeze—sight picture and trigger squeeze.* The next thing she knew, she was standing over the man, the slide of the Glock locked to the rear, indicating that she had emptied the magazine—all thirteen rounds. A large black hand now closed over hers and the top of her weapon.

"It's okay, Judy, it's all over," Stannick said in a soothing voice as he peeled her fingers from the pistol. "You're all right … it's all over now." He laid the Browning on the desk and put a reassuring arm around her. She was shaking, welded to the floor next to the second man she had just killed. He had taken all thirteen rounds. Armed men in black coveralls stormed into the room. The air was still thick with the stench of cordite. Stannick continued in a calming tone. "You did just fine … it's going to be all right, Judy."

It was another twenty minutes before Garrett and Brandon were escorted into the warehouse by Agent Prouty. By that time, there were police lines being established and yellow barrier tape everywhere. The first of the body bags were just being wheeled to waiting ambulances. A chorus of rotating red and yellow lights swept the warehouse and surrounding buildings.

Inside, Ray Stannick stood near a packing crate on the main floor of the building. He had a radio in one hand and a cell phone in the other. FBI agents and policemen came and went, delivering information and receiving instructions. Nearby, a glassy-eyed Judy Burks sat on a metal folding chair.

"What happened?" Brandon asked as he surveyed the activity in the warehouse.

Stannick sighed. "We missed one of them on our initial sweep of the building. He had a weapon and caught us by surprise. He and Stolichnaya were about to make a break for it when Agent Burks appeared on the scene."

"She killed them both?" Brandon asked, looking from Judy Burks back to Stannick. Stannick nodded. "Good God," he replied with some reverence.

Stannick replied. "Yeah, I'm still not sure whether she realizes yet exactly what happened. But, I'll have to say, I've never seen a better piece of clutch shooting." He forced a smile. "I don't know whether to give her a reprimand or a commendation, or both. She scared the hell out of me." At that moment, an Oakland police lieutenant approached, and Stannick turned to speak with him.

Garrett surveyed the building professionally. *Fire superiority didn't always buy you a free ride*, he mused. *Violence of action and the element of surprise were your best bet.* It was as true in military combat as in police combat. In the 1980s and '90s, few military special operators could match actual gunfight history with the SWAT team from a major American city. Nine-eleven changed all that. Judging from what little he saw, there was probably more than a few military combat veterans on this operation. Then his eyes fell on the young woman seated alone on the folding chair. At a glance, he knew exactly what she was going through. He'd seen that same look on the faces of tougher customers than Agent

Judy Burks. He walked up to where she was sitting, dropped to a crouch, and looked directly into her distant stare.

"Hey, Judy, it's Garrett Walker. How're you doing?" he said softly. She registered on him for a moment, then her focus shifted back to somewhere on the horizon. "Hey," he said a little louder, "stay right here with me." Again, there was a glimmer of recognition but no response. Garrett gently slapped her on the cheek, urging her back to the here and now.

"Hey, man," Stannick said, turning from the Oakland officer. "Take it easy; she's been through a lot!"

Garrett rose quickly and took Stannick by the elbow. The firmness of Garrett's grip surprised him. He moved the big FBI man a few steps away, still clamped to his elbow.

"I know what she's going through, Ray. Do you?" Stannick said nothing. "How many men have you killed, up close and personal?" Again, Stannick was silent. "I know about this kind of thing; it's what I do for a living. You've got business to clean up here; let me spend a few minutes with her. I can help her get through this."

Stannick saw the compassion in Garrett's hard features. "Sure thing, Garrett," he said quietly. "Do what you can for her."

Garrett again crouched down in front of her, only this time he took both her hands in his. She now looked at him with the eyes of a drowning person.

"This is your lucky day, lady. There's probably only one person in this whole stinking city who really knows what you're going through right now, and you're looking at him." He squeezed her hands firmly and moved his face close to hers. "You did your job. You're a pro, and you did what you had to do—what had to be done, period. Now I want you to stop and think, just for a moment, what would have happened if you hadn't done your job." She wrinkled her brow and frowned. "See there, you had no choice. Now quit feeling sorry for yourself. You took care of business, no more and certainly no less. That's why you get that big government paycheck." With that, she managed a faint smile. "C'mon, Ray's going to be busy here for a while. Let's get some air."

He took her by the arm, and they headed for the unhinged, battered front door. Brandon followed and watched as they ducked under the police lines and slowly walked up the street, Garrett's arm firmly around Judy Burks' shoulders.

Brandon had just ordered coffee when Garrett walked into the coffee shop. It was shortly after eight o'clock the following morning. Both brothers looked very tired.

"I was a little worried when you didn't come back to the room," Brandon said. "How is she?"

"I think she'll be all right. She's a tough young lady. It just takes a while, that's all." The waitress brought him some coffee. They ordered eggs, hash browns, and toast. "We sat up and talked most of the night, and killed most of a fifth of brandy. Talked a lot. It's all you can do after something like that."

"All night?"

"Well, most of it," Garrett replied. "She finally passed out about four this morning. I put her to bed and caught a few winks on the couch, then took a cab here. How're you holding up?"

Brandon smiled. "I'm not sure. I didn't get much sleep last night, either."

"It's going to be a long day. You still up for this?"

"Oh, yeah. I'm up for it and then some."

"Then we better go over the plan again," Garrett said as he laid a spiral notebook on the table. "The timing is critical. We have to do this by the numbers or it's not going to work."

Brandon sat up in his chair and signaled the waitress for more coffee.

Frank Cantello stood at the head of the small conference table in his Daly City office. The tabletop was awash in construction plans and spec sheets. A group of his subcontractors was seated at the table.

"Okay, gents, that about does it. Any questions?" There were none, nor did he expect any. "Good, let's get to work. There's an early completion bonus on this job as well as a late-completion penalty. I guess you all know which side I intend to be on."

That broke up the meeting. There was a rustling of paper as plans were inserted in cardboard tubes or rubber-banded into fat rolls. The construction men filed out while Cantello returned several of his folders to the neat stacks on his credenza. He stretched with an audible groan in the empty office, then swung into his chair behind the desk. There was a picture of his wife and five kids, all dark haired, well scrubbed, and very Italian looking. Cantello deliberately turned from them and picked up the telephone. He hit a button on the autodialer.

"Hel-looo," said the musical voice on the other end of the line.

"Hi, baby. Watcha doin' for lunch?"

"Gee, I'm not sure. There's nothing on the stove, and there's nothing on me."

Cantello chuckled. "Well, put some pasta on the stove an' you stay just the way you are. I'll be there in about a half hour."

He rang off and smiled, pushing himself up from the desk. He reached over and hit the intercom to his secretary. "I'll be going out for a long lunch, honey. Tell Sally to come in here, will you?"

"Right away, Mr. C."

Cantello made his way to the small private bath that adjoined the office. He took a comb and pulled his thick hair straight back over his head. Then he splashed on some cologne and washed his hands. He carefully dried off as he walked back to his desk. Sal slipped through the door.

"You wanted to see me, boss?"

"That's right," Cantello replied as he pulled on a gray sport coat. "The car down in the garage?"

"Sure. We goin' somewhere?"

"*We* are going to th' deli and get you a sandwich. Then I'm going to Della's for some pasta."

Sal sniffed the air, catching a whiff of the cologne. "Some pasta, huh?"

"Yeah, that's right," Cantello replied as he picked an imaginary speck of lint from his lapel and tugged on his shirt cuffs. "Maybe even some pasta fazule."

They started to leave when the intercom on his desk chirped. "Mr. C., your wife's on line two."

"Tell her I'm late for an appointment. Say that I'll call her later this afternoon."

"Right, Mr. C."

He motioned to the door and Sal followed him out.

They got on the elevator and started down for the garage. Two floors later, the door opened, and Garrett Walker stepped in and moved off to one side. Cantello stiffened slightly when he saw him; he had an uncomfortable feeling that this man looked vaguely familiar. But the man made no eye contact or gave any indication of recognition. Garrett pushed the button for the ground level and then fixed his stare on the display as the elevator counted down the floors.

The offices on the fourth floor of the Cantello building were vacant except for a property management firm. Garrett had been able to wait there for close to an hour without causing any suspicion. On three occasions, he had intercepted an elevator descending from Cantello Construction. On each occasion, he had politely said, "Going up?" and let the car pass on without him. This time, when he saw Cantello aboard, he stepped into the elevator for the ride down. Garrett had no idea whether Cantello would have a car brought around to the front or proceed on down to the parking garage to depart from there. When he saw the button for the garage lit on the panel, he immediately pushed the ground floor. Garrett held his breath, praying that no one else would stop the elevator and board. Luck was with them. They dropped unimpeded to the ground level, where Brandon Walker entered the elevator.

The doors had just closed when Frank Cantello suddenly noticed that the man who had just stepped into the car was a carbon copy of the man standing next to him.

"What th' fuck is goin' on here?" he said to Brandon.

Garrett hit the stop button with his elbow, never taking his eyes off Sal. The car lurched to a stop as Sal moved to reach for his gun in the shoulder holster under his coat. Garrett drove his knee into Sal's groin. Sal gave a sharp cry and doubled over in pain. Garrett then grabbed his collar and rammed his face into the wood panel of the elevator, breaking his nose and one cheekbone. Sal slumped to the floor, unconscious. Garrett followed him down, but just as Cantello started to react, he came up quickly with a small-caliber automatic. He moved like a cat.

"Little gun," Garrett said as he shoved the muzzle under Cantello's chin, "but it makes a big enough hole."

"What th' fuck," Cantello repeated.

Brandon spun him around to the wall and jerked his buttoned sport coat down his back just below his elbows, pinning his arms to his sides. Next, he ripped Cantello's silk shirt up to reveal two long scars across the lower side of his back. Brandon held the shirt open for Garrett to see.

"Looks like kidney zippers to me."

Brandon nodded and released Cantello to Garrett. Brandon pulled the emergency stop to allow the elevator to descend. Garrett jerked the collar of Cantello's sport coat back up into place. The little automatic remained pressed against his throat.

"You speak or move, you piece of shit, and I'll turn your lights out."

Cantello remained frozen as the doors opened into the parking garage. Brandon poked his head out. "It's clear," he reported, the relief evident in his voice.

Garrett held the door-open button while holding the muzzle of the automatic under Cantello's ear. Brandon dragged the semi-conscious Sal from the elevator and deposited him in a corner, covering him with an old piece of canvas they'd stashed there earlier in the day. They then escorted Cantello between them to his car, a late-model, four-door Lexus.

"Keys," Garrett ordered.

Cantello hesitated, and Garrett delivered a short, hard blow to his solar plexus. He gasped for breath, unable to speak, but he motioned to his coat pocket. Brandon dug out the keys and unlocked the car. Together, they roughly deposited him into the backseat. Garrett joined Cantello in the back as Brandon slid in behind the wheel, started the car, and backed out from the parking space. Brandon drove slowly from the garage, taking care not to attract any attention. Within a few blocks, Brandon pulled to the curb so that Garrett could move up to the front passenger's seat. In the back, a now very terrified Frank Cantello was wedged on the floor behind the front seats, hidden from view by a blanket. His hands and feet were bound with nylon snap-ties, and his mouth was sealed with duct tape. He could only breathe through his nose.

Brandon and Garrett spoke little during the drive through the city. As they crossed the Bay Bridge, Garrett got into Cantello's CD collection and put on a selection of arias by Pavarotti. He turned up the volume, and the two brothers shared a grin. There was no attendant waiting for them at the rear entrance of the San Leandro Hospice Clinic, but the door had been left open. They cut Cantello's ankle bindings, then swathed his head with gauze, giving him the appearance of a burn victim—or a mummy. Cantello made several desperate attempts to protest and finally settled into a slumped resignation, sensing that any further struggle would do him no good. Garrett and Brandon finally pulled him from his vehicle, each taking an arm as they hauled him inside. In keeping with the arrangements Garrett had made, they delivered him to the same room where Brandon's organs had been transferred to Cantello.

Once inside, they stripped him naked and laid him on a gurney, face down. When the restraints were in place, Brandon unwound the gauze from Cantello's head. Garrett winced as Brandon then took the prostrate man by the hair, pulled his head back, and ripped the duct tape from his eyes and mouth. Cantello gave a loud, sharp cry, both from the pain of the unmasking and the bright light in the room. They gave him a few minutes to adjust to his new surroundings. If he recognized the room from his previous stay, he gave no indication. Brandon had pulled a chair next to the bed and now sat very close to Cantello, whose head was turned toward him.

"How are you feeling, Frank?" Brandon asked. He ran his hand across Cantello's chin and lips. "Sorry about the tape, but I think you're going to be all right—maybe a little rash. As a matter of fact, you actually look like you're in perfect health. Nice to see a guy who takes care of himself, don't you think so, Garrett?"

"He looks pretty buff to me. You must work out, huh, Frank?"

A cold nugget of fear had burned inside Cantello's stomach during the uncomfortable drive. It was beginning to grow and now threatened to explode into pure terror. He knew he had to try to fight it, to try to keep his wits about him, but the terrible dread churned inside him like a fast-growing cancer. He lifted his head, swiveling it to the other side, and saw the same face. Garrett Walker was sitting next to the bed and leaned over close to Cantello.

"Y'know, most guys your age are out of shape and running to fat, but I can see that you've been taking care of business. I guess, if you don't have your health, what does it all mean, right, Frank?"

"Yo, Frank." He turned slowly back to face Brandon. "It's about those scars you have on your back. How did you get them, anyway?"

"I ... I ... had an operation," Cantello managed to stutter. The fear was now boiling inside; he was doing his best to fight off the looming panic.

"No kidding. What kind of operation?"

Cantello briefly tugged at the restraints, but they held him firmly spread-eagled on the bed. "Just an operation."

"Really?" Brandon said sarcastically. "Just an operation?"

Brandon rose and Cantello watched him, his eyes riveted to his every move. Brandon slowly unbuttoned his shirt and pulled it off. He turned his back to Cantello and stood there, hands on his hips. The scars were not nearly so straight nor nearly so neat. He kept his back to Cantello for close to thirty seconds. While he retrieved his shirt and put it back on, Cantello closed his eyes in disbelief. Suddenly, he began to thrash wildly and pull at his restraints, desperate to free himself from this surreal nightmare. Soon he realized it was hopeless, and he settled onto the sheets, physically drained. He was sweating and had urinated in the bed. It was several minutes before he regained his breath and could gather his thoughts.

"W-what do you want? ... Money? ... How much?"

Brandon smiled, looking down on Cantello and slowly shaking his head. "No, Frank, I don't want your money."

"W-what is it you want?"

Brandon turned and took a white container, the size of a small Coleman ice chest, and set it on a nearby chair where Cantello could see it. He again sat down, close to Cantello. Garrett pulled his switchblade from his pocket and handed it to his brother. Brandon held it in front of Cantello's face. "What I want, Frank, is what you took from me." The stiletto blade snapped open, causing Cantello to flinch. Again, he tested the restraints, but just for a moment. He was nearly spent. "And," Brandon continued, "I'm going to take them back—right here, right now."

"Ahhh! Ahhh! Ahhh!" Garrett jammed a wad of gauze into his mouth to muffle the sound, but Cantello was now well over the edge. He continued the muffled screams of terror for close to a minute; then he passed out.

Soon after the room had gone silent, a dark-complexioned man in a white coat entered the room. He regarded the inert, restrained form on the bed with a deep frown. Then he went to the sink and began to scrub his hands and arms.

"I see that you have sufficiently terrorized him," he commented in his very precise English.

"He'll live," Brandon replied.

"I do not like this. I do not like this at all. You should not have brought him back here."

"Now you listen to me, *Doctor,*" Garrett said, his voice dripping with contempt, "you are going to do exactly what we tell you. Otherwise, I think the police and the American Medical Association are going to be very interested in some of your procedures here at this clinic." Garrett moved close to him, his voice low and threatening. "You know something else, Doc? I don't think your upper-caste background and Oxford training have, in any way, prepared you for life in an American prison. You just don't seem like the kind of guy who'd easily take to sweeping out the infirmary and emptying bedpans in the joint for the next fifteen years. My guess is that you'd have a real rough time of it in the slammer."

The little physician recoiled from Garrett and met Brandon's equally menacing stare. He dried his hands and went over to examine his patient.

Cathy and Brandon waited with Ray Stannick in the boarding area. Brandon held Cathy's hand. Stannick was comfortably dressed in polished cotton slacks, a sport shirt, and a light Windbreaker. He looked snappy, but very unofficial. It was Thursday afternoon, and the San Francisco airport wasn't terribly crowded. The flight for Little Rock didn't leave for another forty minutes. The three of them watched as Garrett approached. His hair was now short, and he was wearing the khaki uniform of a master chief petty officer in the United States Navy. He carried the same two light travel bags that he deplaned with in Las Vegas well over three months before. He walked slowly, talking with Judy Burks. They were deep in conversation, and he didn't see his brother, Cathy, and Ray until he was upon them.

"Well, hello there. Come down just to see me off?"

Stannick gave him a patient smile. "Somehow, I had to be sure that at least one of you was on a flight out of town. I'll rest a whole lot easier when I know you two aren't together and up to who knows what." Garrett and Brandon both smiled but made no comment. Then Stannick said to Garrett, "So you're back in the Navy again?"

"Never left it, Ray," Garrett replied. "Just on extended shore leave. A few days back home with the folks, then I'll return to the dreary life of a Navy SEAL. Maybe it'll give me a chance to relax a little."

Stannick pursed his lips and nodded. "Yes, I imagine you could probably do with a little R & R after your busy convalescent period here in the Bay Area." Neither Garrett nor Brandon rose to the bait.

"I don't think these ladies have met," Garrett said, taking Judy's hand. "Cathy, this is Judy Burks. Judy, this is my sister-in-law, Catherine Walker."

"I'm very glad to meet you, Judy. Garrett and Brandon have told me so much about you. Thanks for all your help."

"Hey, I was only doing my job. And they've told me a lot about you, Cathy. Happy to finally meet you."

"Really?" Cathy said, smiling easily. She and Judy's eyes met; they both smiled, and there was instant communication. "You and I are going to have to have lunch sometime. Then we can talk about the both of them."

"That would be great, Cathy. I'd love it."

"I have a quick phone call to make," Garrett said. "Give me a few minutes, and I'll meet you over by the boarding gate."

"By the way, Mrs. Walker, I wanted you—"

"Please, Ray, it's Cathy."

"Very well, Cathy it is. I wanted you to know that our helpful friend at Golden Western Insurance Company also provided us with some interesting information on a certain police detective in Las Vegas."

"Oh, really," Cathy replied, remembering a slimy man in the intensive care waiting room at Las Vegas Memorial.

"That's right. Detective Rucko has been suspended from all official duties and is in custody pending allegations of conspiracy, obstruction of justice, and attempted murder, among other felony charges."

Cathy just smiled and squeezed Brandon's hand. Nearby, at a bank of pay phones, Garrett fished a scrap of paper from his shirt pocket with a number scrawled in pencil. He dropped in a coin and dialed. The phone rang at a room extension in the San Leandro Hospice Clinic.

A man with a heavily bandaged face and two black eyes answered.

"Yeah, what is it?"

"Let me speak to the man."

"The man's sleeping and don' need to be bothered. You can tell me what you want."

"Is this you, Sal?"

"Who is this?"

"It's the guy who rearranged your face a few days ago. Now, you let me talk to your boss or I'll come over there and finish the job."

The form in the bed nearby, now awake, snapped his fingers for the phone. "Okay, wise guy, but don't ever let me lay eyes on you again. You sucker punched me. I still got a score to settle with you," Sal growled as he handed the phone to his boss.

A moment later, Cantello came on the line. "What do you want?" he said thickly. He didn't sound well.

"Just a little understanding, Mr. Cantello. I'm not the guy whose kidneys you took; I'm the twin brother. And just so you know the difference, he's the nice one. I'm the evil twin."

Cantello was about to get tough with him, but he didn't feel as tough as he once did; that much had changed. "What do you want, Walker?"

"My brother's a family man. I want it understood that neither you nor any of your people will harm them or even go near any of them, ever. They are to be off-limits. You see, I've just recently rediscovered my family, and they are more precious to me than my own life. If you bother them in any way, no power on earth will stop me from finding you. And when I find you, what you just went through will seem like a routine physical exam. This I can promise you."

"I see. And if I were to agree to this, where does that leave me?"

"You'll never see me again. You go your way; my brother and I go ours. We're quits. On balance, it's a helluva lot better than you deserve."

There was a pause on the line. Cantello quickly recalled that one of these brothers, probably this one, had done quite a job on the Russian hood out in Las Vegas. And he'd handled Sal without difficulty. "Okay, Walker, we got an understanding. But how do I know you'll keep your end of the bargain?"

"You don't. Just stay away from my family if you want to live. It's as simple as that."

Garrett hung up and found the others. They were paired up, Cathy talking with Judy, Brandon with Ray.

"Everything in order?" Brandon asked.

"I believe so," Garrett replied. "Probably as good as can be expected."

Judy Burks touched Cathy's arm, then moved quietly to Garrett's side. He looked at her, giving her a warm, genuine smile. As they waited at the gate and talked quietly among themselves, a middle-aged black couple cautiously approached them. He was dressed in a security guard's uniform; she wore a plain print dress.

"Mr. Walker?" She looked from Garrett to Brandon, unsure which person she wanted. "Mr. Brandon Walker?"

"He's the guy you want," Garrett said, pointing to his brother.

"Mr. Walker," she said shyly, "I'm so sorry to be interrupting you, but we called your office and a man by the name of Rogers, a Mr. Richard Rogers, said we would find you here. Since my husband works nearby, we took a chance of catching you."

"Uh, what can I do for you, Mrs. … ?"

"Oh, gosh, I'm sorry. I'm Fran Taylor, and this is my husband, Bill."

He reached out and eagerly shook Brandon's hand. "I'm awful glad to meet you, Mr. Walker. And God bless you, sir."

"Oh, of course. Mr. and Mrs. Taylor. Uh, how is your boy doing?"

"Thanks to you, Mr. Walker," she gushed, "the doctors say he has a good chance for a full recovery. We had almost given up finding a matching donor, given that he has such a rare tissue type and all. It was like a miracle when we heard. We were so thankful that God answered our prayers. My baby's going to be all right!" With that, she threw her arms around Brandon, holding him tight and softly crying into his chest.

"Uh, if I may interrupt, Mrs. Taylor, Mr. Taylor. My name's Ray Stannick, and I'm an old friend of Brandon's." He placed a hand on Brandon's shoulder, as if to display their close friendship. "You said something about a matching donor," he said smoothly. "Could you explain that? My old pal Brandy here, well, sometimes he's just a little too modest for his own good."

Fran Taylor composed herself while her husband put his arm around her waist to comfort her. She hesitated answering for a moment, wondering how this authoritative black man fit in. The group stood quietly, and Stannick waited patiently for their explanation—without any objection from Brandon Walker, she noticed.

"Why, this wonderful man just gave up one of his kidneys so that our son won't die. The doctors tell us that our Wally will get well now and can live a long and healthy life. Our boy's going to be all right!" She clasped her hands tightly to her breast and squeezed tears from the corners of her eyes.

"Your son?" Stannick repeated, looking puzzled.

"Yessir," Bill Taylor said. "Would you like to see a picture of him?"

"We sure would," said Garrett, a little too quickly. "Right, guys?"

Taylor dug into his wallet for a photo. The three men crowded around him. It was a color print of a fourteen-year-old in a football uniform. The shoulder pads gave the appearance of size, but he appeared tall for his age. His handsome face was fixed with an overly serious expression, more of a manufactured scowl. While they passed the picture around, Cathy approached Fran Taylor.

"Hi, I'm Cathy Walker. I'm so happy your son is going to get better."

"Thank you, Mrs. Walker. You must be very proud of your husband."

"Yes, I certainly am."

Garrett was now holding the picture of Wally Taylor. "Great-looking kid. He looks like a hitter. I'll bet he's going to be a defensive back."

Brandon took the photo. "No way. Looks like he's got some great moves, probably soft hands, too. The kid's gonna be a receiver."

"Not a chance. Look at that face, those eyes. I tell you, this guy's got a nose for the ball. Maybe a safety, but probably a cornerback. And he's got the size."

"C'mon, Garrett, he's too good-lookin', too smooth. He's going to make a great flanker. What do you think, Ray?" Brandon handed him the picture.

Stannick studied it for a moment, scowled, then shrugged. "Looks like he might have a fine arm. I think he's a quarterback."

"A quarterback?" Garrett said. "Get real, Ray. This kid's definitely a defensive back. Look at him! No way he's some pansy quarterback."

"Excuse me, gentlemen, if I may interrupt," Fran Taylor said. "I'm sorry, but we've really taken enough of your time. Bill has to get back to work, and I'm anxious to get back to the hospital and be with our boy." Stannick handed her the picture.

"Thank you all very much for your kindness," Bill Taylor said. "You can't know how grateful we are. And no disrespect, but we don't really care if Wally plays football again or not. I just thank the Lord that he'll live to go to college. He's an honor student, you know."

After profusely thanking them again, Bill and Fran Taylor made their way back down the concourse. The three Walkers, Ray Stannick, and Judy Burks all joined in waving their good-byes. Ray, standing between the two brothers, took each firmly by the elbow and guided them a few steps to one side. Neither Judy nor Cathy said anything, but turned to visit between themselves, leaving Stannick to talk with the brothers.

"All right, you two," he said with a smile—but his eyes weren't smiling, and his voice had an edge to it. "I've got just a couple questions for you, and I want some straight answers."

"Sure thing, Ray," Brandon said.

"Fire away," Garrett added.

"First of all, Brandon, is that *your* kidney, and I assume it's a single organ that was transplanted into the Taylor boy?"

"It was," said Brandon. "Wally Taylor's blood is now being processed by one of my kidneys."

"Okay, how did you know this kid needed a kidney? How did you match him to your blood type?"

"Richard helped us with that," Brandon continued. "It seems the U.S. Department of Health and Human Services has oversight for an organization called the Organ Procurement and Transplantation Network. This network is managed by a group called the United Network for Organ Sharing, or UNOS. UNOS, a private, nonprofit group, helps people who need kidneys and other organs identify proper donors. Using a program similar to the one our hacker friend Dannahey developed, Richard was able to enter the UNOS database and check the medical files of those needing organs with difficult-to-match tissue types. As luck would have it, the Taylor boy and I are an exact match."

Stannick nodded patiently. "We know all about UNOS and the national organ procurement networks. It's the *legal* way donors and recipients are matched. Now, what I really want to know is, where is your *other* kidney?"

"You might say that someone is leasing it for a while," Brandon offered. Stannick stared at him in disbelief.

"And," Garrett continued, "if the lessee were to ever violate the terms of the agreement, we'll foreclose."

"Foreclose? On a kidney?"

"Well, maybe repossession of the property is a better way to put it," Garrett replied.

Stannick stared openmouthed, looking from one brother to the other. "Now just what in the hell did you two—"

"Sorry, Ray," Brandon said, holding up his hands. "You said just a couple of questions, which we've answered as agreed."

"That's right," Garrett added, "and, besides, they're about to call my flight. Sorry, Ray, but that's all we have to say on the matter. Brandon and I were born with the standard-issue two kidneys each. Those four kidneys are now supporting four lives. Let's just leave it at that."

"I could take you both in for questioning, you know?" he said quietly. There was still a serious tone in his voice.

"Sure you could," Garrett said, "but what would that get you? And, face it, you don't really want to take us in, do you?" Stannick glared at him. "It'd be a waste of your time, Ray," Garrett continued, "because we have nothing more to say. Besides, you need to be out chasing crooks. That's your job, right? And I've got to get back to my SEAL unit. You don't really need to be fooling around with us any longer."

Stannick stared at Garrett, then Brandon. He saw the same firm, determined look on both their faces. He really would be wasting his time, he concluded, and they were right; he really didn't want to arrest them. He also knew that if he pushed this matter any further, that's what he would be forced to do. Slowly, he shook his head and sighed.

"Okay, we'll do it your way. But if I catch either one of you revisiting this business, I'll subpoena you, understood?" The two brothers exchanged a quick glance and looked back to Stannick. They were agreed. Stannick finally cracked a smile and held his hand out to Garrett. "For an old guy, you don't look too bad in a sailor suit. Glad to be back in uniform?"

Garrett grasped Ray's hand. "Yeah, I have to admit that it does feel pretty darn good. Thanks for all your help, Ray." Stannick inclined his head in acknowledgment.

Garrett walked over to Cathy.

"Thanks, Cath, for putting up with me these last few months."

"Thanks for coming to our rescue, Garrett. The kids are really going to miss their favorite uncle, now that they've found you. So am I. Come again, and come often." They hugged for a long moment. It was a spontaneous and natural embrace, one that made them both feel good.

"Judy, are you going to be okay now?" Garrett said, turning to face her. He held her by the shoulders, looking down at her.

"Absolutely. I'm feeling a lot better. Thanks again, Garrett. I'm not so sure that I could have gotten through this without you." She rose on tiptoe to kiss him. It was a strong, warm kiss on the lips. "Be sure and stop by the next time you're in port, sailor boy."

"I just may do that, Agent Burks," Garrett said, holding her gaze. "I just may do that very thing." He gave her a wide smile and a wink, then bent to retrieve his bags.

Brandon was waiting for him near the gate entrance. Neither brother spoke. Garrett set his bags on the floor and they embraced.

"Give my love to the folks."

"I'll do that."

"How long will you be able to stay?"

"Just two or three days. Long enough to let them know that the guy who looks like their favorite son is back. They're probably ready to know more about Don's life in the teams and how he died. I didn't really give them the time I should have the last time I was home."

Brandon grinned. "Maybe you and Dad can go out and bag a few ducks. They should be coming South down the flyway by now."

"Maybe," Garrett said with a shrug. "I'm not sure I want to hunt birds anymore, but we may go out and drown a worm. The largemouth should be biting about this time of year."

"Take care, little brother." The grin had grown to a broad smile.

"You, too, big brother."

They again embraced, then parted and regarded each other with an identical half smile. Garrett again picked up his bags and boarded the aircraft.

Garrett watched from his window seat as the Jetway recoiled and the plane was pushed back from the gate. For just a moment, the aircraft turned so that he could see the four of them standing in the window. They all waved, and he gave them a hand salute and a smile. The engines spooled up, and they passed from his vision.

Interesting how life can deal you a new hand when you least expect it, he mused. *In exchange for a redundant organ that I don't need and won't really miss, I have my family back. What a marvelous exchange.*

"Hey, mister."

Garrett looked at the eleven-year-old boy seated in the middle seat next to him. His mother on the aisle was absorbed in a *Cosmopolitan* magazine. The kid leaned forward to see Garrett's left breast, which held his decorations and the gold SEAL device.

"You talking to me, son?"

"Yeah, are you a Navy SEAL?"

"Yes, I am."

"Well, if you're a Navy SEAL, how come you're crying?"

"I'm not crying."

"Yes, you are. You're crying."

ABOUT THE AUTHOR

Dick Couch. Navy SEAL, Combat Veteran, CIA Case Officer, New York Times Best Selling Author–with seventeen books to his credit. During the Global War on Terror, Dick Couch alone has been allowed to embed with the component commands of the US Special Operations Command. Dick Couch alone has tracked the SEALs, Green Berets, Rangers, and Marine Special Operators as they trained for war–and written extensively about this training. Now after eight books of special-operations nonfiction, *Act of Revenge* marks his return to fiction.

CONNECT WITH DICK COUCH ONLINE

Facebook: https://www.facebook.com/DickCouch1
Twitter: https://twitter.com/dickcouch
LinkedIn: http://www.linkedin.com/pub/dick-couch/29/991/a53
Visit Dick Couch on his Website at www.dickcouch.com

ACT OF JUSTICE

A Novel By

DICK COUCH

AVAILABLE FOR PURCHASE, MAY OF 2015

ACT OF JUSTICE
AN INTRODUCTION

I've been associated with American military special operations and American intelligence operations going on forty-five years. The two–special operations and intelligence–have often worked at cross purposes or at least independently, each seeking to keep the other in the dark about what they were doing. That began to change after 9/11. The CIA Special Activities Division and Army Special Forces (the Green Berets) combined their talent and resources to mobilize the Northern Alliance and sweep the Taliban from power in Afghanistan. Or at least sent them into Pakistan and into hiding. Their respective domestic headquarter commands were not always of an accord, but the operators in the field found a way to work together. Over the course of the last decade, the special operators and the CIA field case officers have continued to build on the cooperation that began during those early days in the Hindu Kush. I've been in tactical operations centers in Iraq, embedded with SEALs and Special Forces, and had the opportunity to observe this first hand. "Those are our special friends." one special operator told me referring to a group of civilians across the room. "They're a great bunch of guys, and they're very good at finding targets for us."

There's a name for this symbiotic relationship; it's called the operations-intelligence fusion, more commonly, ops-intel, fusion. The intelligence officers in the field have become very good at generating what is known as "actionable intelligence," and the special operators have become very good at getting out the door quickly to act on this valuable and sometimes perishable intelligence product. It was this kind of cooperation that led to the successful takedown of Osama bin-Laden in 2011. On that day in May when the SEALs stormed bin-Laden's compound in Pakistan, there were eleven other special operations raids conducted on hard intelligence to capture or kill Taliban or al-Qaeda leaders. Not all of them were successful, but the hit rate was well over 50 percent–the average during recent years. Our special operations forces worldwide conduct close to 3,000 of these operations each year, most of them driven by a very defined and sophisticated intelligence collection effort.

Our special operations forces have taken their game to a new level since 9/11. SOF, as it is often referred, is a growth industry; since 9/11 their size has doubled, their budget tripled, and their deployment posture has quadrupled. Yet, their evolution and emergence as the direct-action arm of our military in the Global War on Terrorism has been more one of perfecting their existing tactical expertise. Their radios are smaller, more reliable, and more secure; their insertion platforms more refined and technically capable. Their night-vision goggles are several generations better than they were only a short time ago. Yet, their mission set has changed little; they still kick doors, and they still capture and kill bad guys. They just do it a whole lot better than they did ten years ago. Our special operators have simply grown more proficient in the business of conducting combat assault and using emerging technologies in their operations. They are courageous to a fault and highly professional, but the operations side of this ops-intel fusion pales in comparison to advances in intelligence collection–both human intelligence (HUMINT or agent-sourced information) and the vast array of technical collectors now available to our intelligence and military services.

We may never know the extent and scope of the intelligence efforts that tracked bin-Laden from 9/11, during the "first" Afghan campaign, through Tora Bora, and into Pakistan. Yet we can be sure there were some very sophisticated and perhaps even unorthodox measures employed to track him once he was granted sanctuary in Pakistan. And what was aired in the media about how we "got him" is at best the tip of the iceberg and most probably, part of a disinformation campaign to fool the press and our enemies. As someone who was both a former special operator and a CIA case officer, I've had to ask myself, why did it take so long to get bin-Laden? Why, on that particular day in the spring of 2011, did we decide to launch an operation into Pakistan to make a martyr of this man? And just how closely were we able to monitor his movements all those years when he was in hiding? Could he really have eluded us all that time unless, of course, his freedom served our purposes? Could it have been that he was intentionally allowed to live?

Aside from bin-Laden's surprising, decade-long run of freedom, there remains a number of unanswered questions about this mysterious architect of the 9/11 attacks. One of them is his health. It was widely reported that bin-Laden suffered from both Marfan syndrom and kidney disease, but the extent of his afflictions has never been documented. While he may or may not have at one time been on a dialysis regime, he did suffer from bouts of fatigue and kidney-related issues going back to the early 1990s. He was also said to have been wounded twice, once at the hands of the Russians and again as he made his escape from Tora Bora after the collapse of the Taliban in Afghanistan in 2002. He was known to be something of a hypochondriac and dependent on any number of medications. Along about 2006, during his infrequently released video clips, he began to look more vigorous and robust in his appearance. He appeared to be more fit. Bin-Laden was a vain man and took to dying his beard, and the media simply attributed the new, healthy-look to the man giving more attention to his makeup and on-screen appearance. Or he indeed may have somehow found a way to better health.

2006 also marked the beginning of the decapitation process within al-Qaeda. A great many lieutenants and key leaders began to disappear or be killed. Many others left the cause or announced their disassociation with bin-Laden on political grounds. For a great number of Islamic militants, their goal was the overthrow of monarchies like the House of Saud and constitutional monarchies like Kuwait and Bahrain–secular governments that catered to a ruling elite and spurned Sharia law. These militants felt al-Qaeda simply made these governments more entrenched and less disposed to theocratic transition. Whatever the reason, those who remained loyal to al-Qaeda and bin-Laden began to be killed off or marginalized. It was also in the 2006/2007 time frame that the inner circle of al-Qaeda began to shrink dramatically. Faced with so many senior al-Qaeda leader killings, primarily at the hands of the Americans, bin-Laden suspended the promotion of junior leaders to senior leadership positions for fear of penetration. This paranoia of outside penetrations, in effect, paralyzed the organization. As the remaining loyal lieutenants continued to be killed, al-Qaeda gradually ceased to be a functioning, top-down, coordinated organization. Leadership fell to zealots like Abu Musab al Zarqawi in Iraq, who brutalized and subjugated in the name of al-Qaeda, and made the movement unpopular with the people. The rise of regional tyrants like Zarqawi, who was killed by the Americans in 2006, marked the decline of a "centralized" al-Qaeda organization, a decline that bin-Laden seemed powerless to halt.

Finally, there was the near-absence of terrorist acts against the west. With the amateurish attempts at highjackings, the splashy-but-ineffective attacks at Heathrow, and the not-so-amateurish attacks on our embassies in Kenya and Tanzania in late 2002, al-Qaeda has had little success in spreading terror to western nations in general, and the United States in particular. The one notable exception was the attack on Mumbai in 2008, but since that time, there have been few global incidents or terror engineered by bin-Laden or al-Qaeda central. The attacks of 9/11 made bin-Laden and al-Qaeda players on the international stage. They seemed poised to bring down a reign of terror and to keep the West on the defensive. Our initial moves, first into Afghanistan and then into Iraq, were something they did not expect. From their relative safe havens in Pakistan, other pliable Southwest Asian nations, and East Africa, one would have thought that they would have been more aggressive, especially once we became bogged down in Iraq. Yet, it didn't happen and one has to ask why. After the dramatic success of the 9/11 attacks, the remarkably-secret organization built so carefully by Osama bin-Laden in the 1990s seemed to crumble during the middle and latter part of the last decade. Again, why?

I'm a fan of cowboy movies and a fan of Paul Newman. The late Mr. Newman made some great ones. There was *Hud* and *Butch Cassidy and the Sundance Kid*, but my favorite is *Judge Roy Bean*. I particularly like the disclaimer that opens the film:

"This may not be the way it was, but it's the way it should have been."

I think a variation of this phrase is appropriate for this novel: This may not have been the way it was, but it certainly *could* have been the way it happened. We'll probably never know for sure, but the unanswered questions about the life and death of Osama bin-Laden leave room for a lot of speculation. I do know from contacts in my former life that on more than one occasion we knew *exactly* where he was but elected not to take action. Some say we didn't strike for reasons of potential collateral damage. Others contend that it was an effort not to offend the tribes in the semi-autonomous Federally Administrated Tribal Areas in Pakistan where bin-Laden was at one time their guest. With the exception of the Abbottabad raid, we have gone to great lengths not to offend Pakistan whose help we needed to counter the resurgence of the Taliban. Or just perhaps, there was another very good reason why we waited for close to ten years to end his life. *Act of Justice* is but one version of what might have taken place.

Dick Couch
Ketchum, Idaho

PROLOGUE

The circumstances that brought Special Warfare Operator First Class Michael Montgomery, or M-Squared as he was known to his teammates, to this time and place was both chance and premeditation. The place: landing in front of a door to a room on the top floor of a three-story compound near Abbottabad, Pakistan. The time: Monday morning, May 2, 2011at 0311 hours–some three hours before dawn. Behind Montgomery were three other special operators, attired much like himself in ceramic body armor, Kevlar helmets, M4 assault rifles, and night-vision goggles. As they cleared the rooms of the lower two floors of the building, they followed their standard operating procedures, or SOPs. They were a four-man fire team charged with room clearance. In accordance with these SOPs, the last man in the door of one room would be one of the first to enter the next room. This rotation had its variations depending on room configuration or opposition, but it was a formatted, free-flowing progression that these SEALs had done hundreds of times. So it was this purely random, leapfrog rotation that put M-Squared at the head of the stack before this door on this particular night. The fact that Special Operator First Class Michael Montgomery was a veteran of this particular SEAL special-missions unit was wholly premeditated. He had trained for over a decade to be where he was at this very moment. And over the past decade, he had kicked many a door and killed a great many of America's enemies. SO1 Montgomery was a very experienced warrior.

Physically, he was a wiry six footer with thick red hair and a heavy smattering of freckles. His china-blue eyes were bisected by a nose that had at one time been straight, and now saved him from being pretty. When he grinned, he displayed a Terry-Thomas gap in his front teeth, and he seemed to have a perpetual grin. Montgomery grew up just outside of Albuquerque, and when he spoke it was with a soft, southwestern drawl. Aside from a face that would be well placed on a box of cornflakes, he was a prototype Navy SEAL who at this stage of the war had spent more time in combat than any soldier, sailor, airman or Marine in any previous American conflict. His body armor and Rhodesian vest, stuffed with extra magazines, grenades, radio, and assault hardware, did not entirely mask the wide shoulders and firm torso of his breed of special operators. Montgomery was on his eighth combat rotation, more than most of his teammates, but not as many as others. And like the others on this mission, he was emotionally exhausted from the flight in to the target. It was not from the anticipation of going into action, but from the anxiety that this very special mission might be aborted. This was a mission that every SEAL and special operator worthy of the name wanted to be a part of. It could be aborted for weather, a compromise in security, adverse last-minute intelligence, or most likely, for political reasons. For the last several hours, Montgomery and his mates had lived in fear of a recall. Now that they were on the ground, moving from room to room through the compound, those fears had melted away. Now it was all violence of action and professional execution.

Montgomery moved aggressively forward giving the door a particularly vicious kick, causing it to explode inward. He quickly followed the shattered door inside, moving into the center of the room–his preassigned sector. Behind him two other SEALs crisscrossed the room behind him to his left and right, digging their corners and sweeping the area with their M4s. The fourth SEAL held security on the door. The room was in shadows with only moonlight slanting in through a single window. Yet the four special operators saw the room clearly in shades of green from their night-vision goggles. Two women in burkas that were huddled against the far wall, let out a dual-pitched shriek and came at them. To M-Squared's left, a rifle cracked and one of the women went down with a gunshot to the leg. The teammate on his right took the other woman down with a barrel stroke to her temple–possibly a fatal blow. Montgomery himself was totally focused on the tall man in robes who rose from a seated position and stepped toward him. Instantly, he knew who he was and what had to be done. The green dot from his infrared LA5 targeting laser was already on the man's chest, and he had only to press the trigger. The first round was a center-of-mass shot and certain to be a kill shot unless the man was wearing some kind of body armor. He wasn't. Montgomery next lifted the laser to the man's bearded face. As the man half turned and began to fall, he pressed the trigger again–most definitely a kill shot. Special Operator First Class Michael Montgomery had just killed Osama bin-Laden. He stepped to the prostrate corpse and saw the dark cranial blood rapidly spreading from the exit wound in the back of OBL's head. Montgomery kept his weapon trained on him, as if expecting this larger-than-life figure to recover and possibly jump back to his feet. But M-Squared had shot enough men to know when he had killed one. He then toggled the encrypted tactical net of his AN/PRC 148 multi-band inter/intra team radio–MBITR for short.

"Boss, M-Squared here. We got him. Definitely Osama and a definite EKIA."

Lieutenant Commander Bill Gentry stood next to his radioman in the courtyard of the compound. Behind him and several yards down the wall of the compound lay the crumpled hulk of a crashed MH-60 stealth helicopter. Gentry's M4 rifle hung around his neck, available if needed while he manned his primary weapon, his radios. In a special-operations raid, the raid leader or ground-force commander coordinates the action and serves as a communications link. His fire teams do the assault work and as needed, the shooting and the killing. Gentry pressed the transmit button on the radio of the command tactical net.

"You sure, Mike. I mean, you gotta be sure."

"Hey, sir, he's double-tapped, down, and dead. I can shoot the fucker again if you want."

"Commander, this is Brooks here with Mike. It's the big guy all right, and he's toast– an EKIA for sure."

Gentry clicked off and took the handset from his radioman who carried the PSC-5 satellite radio. The radioman also held a portable concentric antenna array and manually held a lock on the communications satellite which linked Gentry to their base in Jalalabad and only God knew how many others up the chain of command.

"Home Plate, this is Delta Alpha One, over."

The response was immediate, "Delta Alpha One, this is Home Plate, over."

"Delta Alpha One Actual, here. Geranimo, I say again Geranimo. Primary target is a confirmed EKIA." The SATCOM link was encrypted and totally secure, but military communicators and special operators alike are conditioned to cryptic responses and code words. In military speak, a KIA is one of your own killed in action; EKIA refers to an enemy killed in action.

"We copy primary target as EKIA, is that affirm?

"That's most affirmative. We got him."

Gentry then busied himself with the mechanics of directing the intelligence collection effort at the compound and getting his force off target with the backup helo assets. He also had to be mindful of his limited time on target and potentially his worst nightmare–the arrival of a company of Pakistani infantry. Up the chain of command, to and including the White House, the news of the death of Osama bin-Laden was traveling at the speed of heat. The "For God and Country" phrasing was added somewhere along the line–along with a great deal of other unneeded, superfluous, and often inaccurate information. Gentry, a heavyset man who had waited patiently outside many an enemy compound while his teams worked the target, again wondered why he had elected to become an officer. As the SEAL chief petty officer that he used to be, he would be inside directing traffic and making decisions–take this, leave that, get this or that person ready for travel. He sighed, dropped to one knee, and waited. That his team leaders worked better and more efficiently knowing a man like Gentry was outside running the big picture and managing the support efforts, was not lost on him. Still, a part of him wanted to have been in on the compound assault and takedown, and working the site exploitation of the target. He sighed. *All of the responsibility, none of the fun.*

Up on the third floor, two more men entered the room as the two women, one subdued by her leg wound and one semiconscious, were held off to one side and treated by a member of the clearance team. One of the men who just entered the room was a special operations medic who would photograph the body of the al-Qaeda leader and prepare it for transport. The second man was a mystery. He was older, perhaps in his mid-forties, but he moved with a certain grace and purpose that said he was both ex-military and an ex-special operator. There was a calmness about him that suggested this was not his first special-operations rodeo. This stranger appeared just before they boarded the insertion helos, fitted out with body armor, helmet, night-vision equipment, a tactical radio, and an Uzi submachine gun. He stayed off to himself and out of the way. Yet the SEALs in the assault elements noted that their senior enlisted leaders, the master chief petty officer and the two senior chiefs, greeted him warmly.

Lieutenant Commander Gentry introduced himself with some deference and respect. This deference and respect did not mean that he was in fact happy to meet this man, nor that he was comfortable having to take him along on this very critical mission. In fact, he had no idea who he was or why he was on the operation. But it had been made clear to him that, subject to mission-essential tasks and responsibilities, he would accompany the raiding party. He would also be allowed all freedom of movement on target and extended all courtesies. This did not mean Gentry had to like it, but when these orders were given him by his task force commander, he had replied "aye, aye, sir," which meant he understood and he would obey.

Garrett Walker was in fact a former Navy SEAL, a medically-retired SEAL master chief, and well known to senior special operators in the tight-knit SEAL community. At one time, he held sway as one the elite SEAL special operators, like those who were conducting this very special mission. Walker was still a powerfully-built man, six-two, and with a close cap of brown hair that was cut almost within military specs. He had regular even features and a weathered complexion that stood in contrast to his deep, almost-iridescent green eyes. His mouth was a fixed, serious straight line that gave away nothing, and he spoke with great economy, as if he were a practiced ventriloquist. His load was assault-team light–only two extra magazines in his vest, flash bang grenades, cameras, a radio, and an Iridium satellite phone. His helmet was a modified combat free-fall parachutist's model that mounted the same state-of-the-art night vision goggles as the other SEALs. Under his vest he wore a safari shirt that was tucked into cargo pants and clinched to his slim hips by a nylon web belt. All special operators wear foot gear of their own choosing. Walker had low-top, olive-drab Morrell hiking shoes. He gave the impression of strength while seeming to sacrifice nothing in speed and efficiency.

The woman who was struck in the head now began crying loudly and resisting those who tried to remove her from the room. At one point she broke away from her minders and threw herself onto bin-Laden's corpse. Walker took her by the arm and spoke a few sentences to her in Arabic. She quickly quieted down and allowed herself to be taken from the room. Then he turned to the body. There was a centeredness about him and a quiet composure that said he was someone to be taken seriously. Yet when he knelt next to the body, he spoke to the SEAL medic in an affable, conversational voice.

"Help me turn him over. I need to get a look at his back." The combat medic started to protest, but there was also an unmistakable authority that accompanied Walker's soft tone. Both had turned on the IR floodlights of their night-vision goggles and worked in the near-daylight of the phosphorescent green of the floods.

He was a tall man, and it took both of them to roll him from his back where he had fallen onto his stomach. The expanding circle of blood seeped from the exit wound on the back of his head matting his hair and beard. Now on his stomach, the dark red blood bathed his face and continued to pool on the floor. Walker then drew a sharp knife from his combat vest and parted the dead man's garment from the neck to his waist. The frangible .556 round that had entered the front of his chest had not exited his back, having shatter his sternum and been deflected down into his bowel where it had come to rest. But his back was not unmarked. There on the lower portion of his abdomen were two long surgical scars that ran from the back portion of his rib cage to the tops of his buttocks. They were well-healed incisions and bore handiwork of an excellent surgeon, but scars nonetheless. The medic watched as Walker took out a small camera and photographed the scars. Then Walker took his knife and moved to the small of his back. For a long moment he manipulated the area, carefully feeling along either side of his spine. Then he looked up at the medic.

"What I'm about to do is not to be photographed nor are you to talk about it with anyone. If you have an issue with what takes place here, then take it up with your troop commander once we're off target, understood?"

The medic could only shrug. "Roger that, sir." Then he added, "And I will take it up with my troop commander."

Garrett Walker nodded. Quickly and carefully, he again felt along bin-Laden's back in the lumbar area of L4 and L5 lower vertebra. Then to one side of the spine, he made a deep, three-inch incision. Next he produced a large pair of forceps and began to probe into the fresh wound. There was very little bleeding as bin-Laden's blood volume was slowly draining onto the floor of the compound by way of his shattered cranium and chest wound. Walker bent close, too close for the medic to see much of what he was doing, and found what he was looking for. He first took a small set of side cutters and clipped two, thin nylon straps that were embedded in the incision. Then with the jaws of the forceps, he clamped onto a small metal capsule, a half inch in diameter and no more than two inches long, and he eased it from the split in the skin. A thin gold strand of wire trailed from the wound which he nipped with the side cutters. He examined the capsule only briefly, then slipped it into a small case and the case into a pocket of his combat vest. He performed a similar operation, three inches from the initial incision on the other side of the spine, producing a similar small cylinder but with only a few inches of wire. He carefully stowed the second capsule. Walker then slapped a single, specially-prepared, hemostatic battle dressing on the wounds to seal them. Once in place, the wounds were hardly visible under the plastic sheathing. Garrett nodded to the medic, and they both turned the body back over. He snapped a closeup of the al-Qaeda leader's face, and stepped away.

"Thank you," Walker said politely. "He's all yours." The medic hesitated, wondering what the hell had just occurred, and then proceeded to begin his photograph inventory of the body and the preparation for its removal from the building. Now that the compound was secure, other members of the raiding party were conducting a meticulous search of the building. Garrett Walker quietly made his way down to the courtyard and out to where Lieutenant Commander Gentry and his small command and control element had positioned themselves. Gentry was busy, giving direction to his search teams, as Walker could hear on his own tactical radio. And as Walker rightly guessed, Gentry was managing his assault element while fielding a steady stream of requests for information from multiple layers of higher headquarters. The crash of the lead insertion helo in the compound had made things complicated for him–complicated but manageable. Alternate extraction platforms were the norm, not the exception, and he had things well in hand. Like any number of competent, experienced SEAL team leaders, this was not Gentry's first compound takedown. He was busy, but in control. When Walker sensed there was a pause in the flow of radio traffic, he stepped to Gentry's side.

"My work is done here, Commander. Thank you for your patience." Gentry only glanced at him and nodded. "You and your people did a fine job here tonight. Congratulations," and he moved away, taking up a position by the courtyard wall, well out of the way. Once there he took out an Iridium satellite phone and keyed in a preprogramed number. It was answered on the first ring.

"Garrett, hello. How are you, and how are things there?"

"The insertion had its moments, but all is well. He's confirmed dead, killed in the assault, and I was on scene shortly afterward. I have the implants. We should be extracting shortly."

"That's good news. Be careful and we'll see you when you return."

"Until then, Garrett out."

Walker secured the phone and waited patiently as the raiding party completed their work and prepared to extract from the compound. As he waited, he followed the flow of tactical talk on his MBITR radio. It was precise, measured, and professional–punctuated by the time hacks of Gentry's radioman, "thirty-seven minutes, sir" then, "thirty-nine minutes." Time on target was a serious consideration on any target, but especially this one. They had just invaded a friendly foreign nation. The curious might be slow to venture out, but they would eventually move in for a closer look. And at some point, there would be an official presence on scene. It was best to be gone before that happened. Walker was not just being kind when he congratulated Gentry on the operation. These SEAL operators *were* good and so was their ground-force commander. They could be proud of this night's work. For them, it had been the result of several months of intense training and preparation. It was, after all, *the* operation–the one they would remember and savor, even if discouraged from openly talking about it, for the rest of their lives. Yet it would not be but a year before conflicting, unauthorized accounts of the killing of Osama bin-Laden began to emerge. The money offered by greedy publishers was simply too good for a few of the SEALs in the assault element. But Michael Montgomery was not one of them. While he in fact had made the shot heard round the world, he never spoke of it out of school; he never broke faith with his SEAL brothers. When asked by those close to him why he remained silent when others had not, he simply replied, "My teammates and those closest to me know what I did, and that's enough. And c'mon," he added with a boyish grin and that easy drawl, "it was a luck of the draw; I was first in the stack. How you could take money for that, let alone lie about it, is something I could never live with. Maybe others, but not me."

For Garrett Walker and his team of specialists, it was the final and closing chapter in an operation that began in late 2005. Walker couldn't help but to think back when it all began, but it was only a momentary reflection. The big MH-47 extraction helo set down just outside the compound and amidst all the noise and dust, he followed the raiding party aboard....

22973246R00215

Made in the USA
San Bernardino, CA
29 July 2015